THE LIGHTBRINGER

THROUGH THE ELDER STONE

DAEL SASSOON

authorHOUSE

AuthorHouse™ UK
1663 Liberty Drive
Bloomington, IN 47403 USA
www.authorhouse.co.uk
Phone: UK TFN: 0800 0148641 (Toll Free inside the UK)
UK Local: 02036 956322 (+44 20 3695 6322 from outside the UK)

© 2021 Dael Sassoon. All rights reserved.

No part of this book may be reproduced, stored in a retrieval system, or transmitted by any means without the written permission of the author.

Published by AuthorHouse 01/21/2021

ISBN: 978-1-6655-8478-4 (sc)
ISBN: 978-1-6655-8475-3 (e)

Print information available on the last page.

Book cover design by Dael Sassoon

This book is printed on acid-free paper.

Because of the dynamic nature of the Internet, any web addresses or links contained in this book may have changed since publication and may no longer be valid. The views expressed in this work are solely those of the author and do not necessarily reflect the views of the publisher, and the publisher hereby disclaims any responsibility for them.

CONTENTS

SON OF ODIN	1
THE CALLING	12
INTO THE WOODS	23
BLUEBERRY MEAD	30
RED CAMP	41
THE LONE WOLF	54
A NEW HOPE	60
BLACKSMITH	71
WHEN THE WIND BLOWS	77
RELEASE THE OMÜMS	88
THE INVISIBLE HOUSE	94
A LIGHTBRINGER'S DUTY	102
THE PALACE OF KINGS	116
THE STAMPEDE	122
THE NECROMANCER	131
ASH AND LIGHTNING	138
HNEFATAFL	153
THE THIRSTY GOBLIN	157
BEYOND THE LAKE	167
ALLEGIANCE	176
THE BRIDGE OF WHISPERS	190
EMERALD FIELDS	200
ATONEMENT	210
THE CAVERN	223
THE IMPERIAL BEETLE	237
ROCK AND SNOW	248
SEYNHAR!	257
WHITE HORSE	266
THE ARALAY	279
ENTER THE ÆRINDEL	284
A GHOST IN NITERIA	294
HYMN OF THE SUMMER ROSE	299
SMOKE ON THE WATER	313

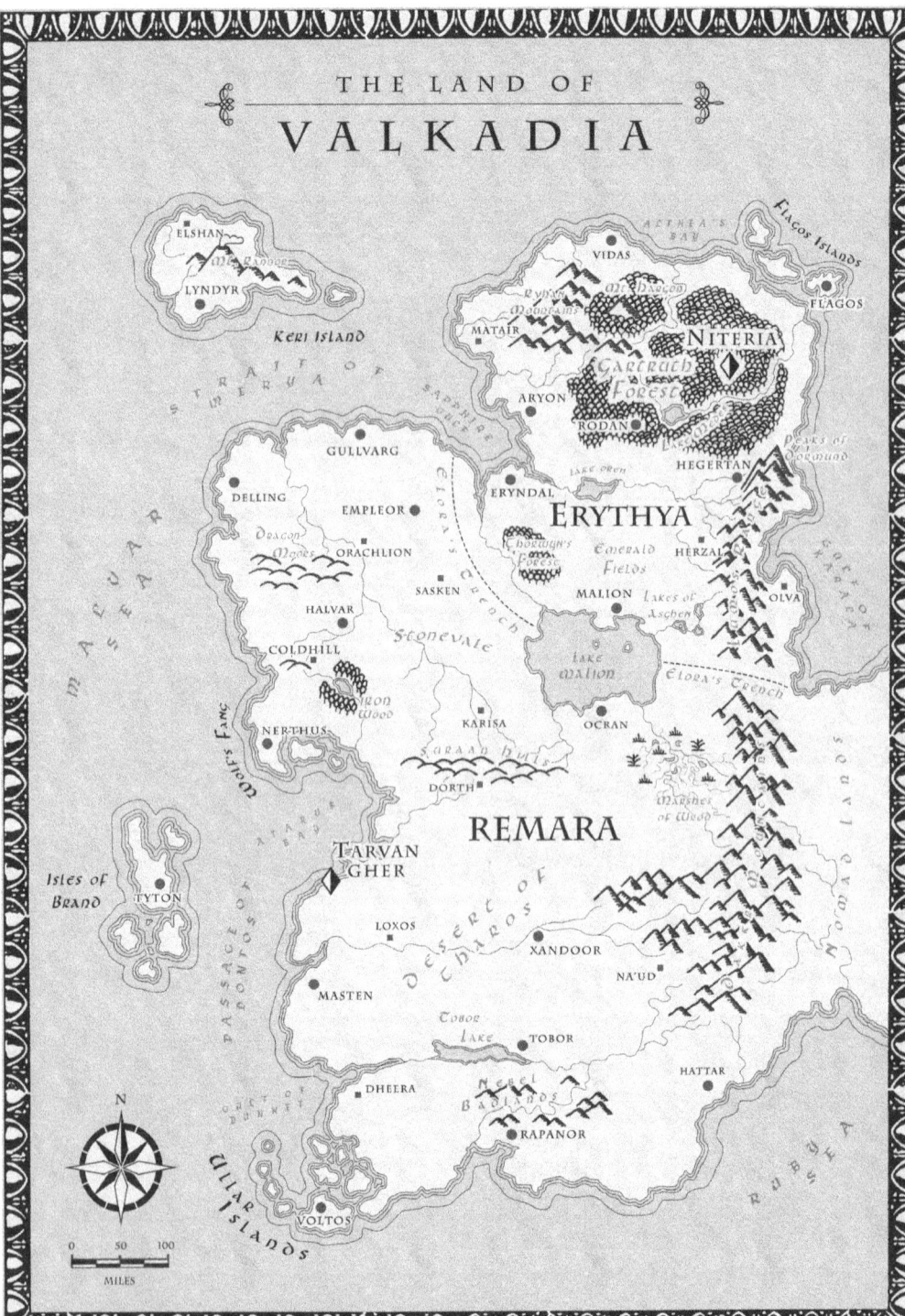

1

SON OF ODIN

Jason McAnnon had been waiting for an adventure like this. Even the exceptionally cold air that night did not stop the young photographer from venturing out onto the deck of the research vessel, where he gazed out onto the frozen landscape.

He picked up his camera, which hung from his neck, and pointed it at the white expanse. He hoped that something more exciting than icebergs and granite would fill his field of view. His eyes widened with disbelief when two narwhals emerged from the blue water, revealing their long swirly horns. Their grey skin was a leathery canvas decorated with white scratches inflicted by their rivals and the sharp ice. A sighting like this was rare. If he managed to take a good shot of them, he could go back to his boss at World Cloud satisfied, and it could lead to bigger things. He pressed his eye against the camera and regulated the zoom of his wide-angle lens. The shutter opened and closed rapidly, trapping the mythical-looking creatures in Jason's camera forever. The narwhals dipped back into the deep dark water, safe from Jason's camera, leaving behind only ripples.

The *Son of Odin* research vessel continued journeying along the frigid sea of North Greenland, steadily punching its way through the thick layer of pack ice. Dull crunches and crackles filled the white landscape with echoes, which slowly disappeared into the distant mainland where dark granite mountains stood glorious. Between the towering snow-covered peaks rested broad valleys through which glaciers flowed unbroken, forging the landscape into breath-taking fjords. The notorious white and red expedition ship, whose name recalled the powerful All-Father of the Norse gods, looked like a lonesome ghost travelling silently through the eerie Arctic scenery.

As he stared into the frozen abyss, Jason reminisced about how much his life had changed. About two months earlier, he worked at the World Cloud printing lab, taking care of photographic equipment and editing photos for the World Cloud travel magazines. Now, Jason was taking part in a world-class expedition to a very remote town in North Greenland called Qaanaaq.

After a good three years of living through other people's experiences, he was finally offered the chance of living an adventure of his own. He would go onboard of the *Son of Odin* as 'photographic assistant' with the job of helping the world-famous photographer Danny Porterman. Arthur O'Donney, director of World Cloud, convinced him by saying, "Just go there, take some good pictures, and come back with your own adventure to tell. We'll pay for your expenses." That was good enough. The thrill of the experience was all he was looking for.

Jason could not wait to spend the next two months in the blistering cold of Northern Greenland, living in close contact with the indigenous communities and learning about their customs. The team was going to carry out biodiversity surveys in the North Water Polynya—or Pikialasorsuaq, as the locals call it—an area of open water of 80,000 square kilometres between Greenland, Ellesmere Island, and Devon Island. During the day, they would monitor how Arctic animals were reacting to climate change. They planned to spend most of the time on smaller survey boats looking at walruses, seals, narwhals, and polar bears. Jason was also looking forward to the night when the midnight sun would keep shining.

"Hey, you!" called a young woman. Her hair was golden, and her cheeks were blushed from the piercing air. She was wearing a long blue coat with a hood trimmed in faux fur, and she had wrapped a thick tartan blanket around her shoulders.

Jason smiled at her softly. "Clara! What are you doing out here? Should you not be working?"

She walked towards him and stood by his side, gazing into the distance together with him. She tightened her scarf and pushed her hands deeper in her pockets. "I should, but everyone is sitting in the lounge room chatting, and it's too difficult to concentrate," Clara replied. "How am I supposed to work when they're having hot chocolate? *Hot chocolate*, I tell you!" She fell into Jason's arms, and they laughed. She looked up at him, lost in the depth of his gentle hazel eyes, keeping eye contact for a couple more seconds. A gust of biting wind forced her to turn away, and she began shivering involuntarily. "Should we go inside?" Clara suggested.

"I'd like to stay a little longer. I mean, look at this," he replied, motioning towards the frozen sea. "How can I be indoors while such beauties are waiting to be photographed? Plus, I'd rather be here taking pictures of icebergs than staying locked in a room with Mr Funny Guy."

"Oh, don't tell me you're letting a clown like Danny annoy you this much," she replied.

"It's not that I get annoyed by him," he protested. "It's just that I prefer this cold to his absurd made-up stories."

"Well, at least if you come inside you won't become a popsicle by the end of the night."

"Depends," replied Jason. "What flavour popsicle?"

Clara laughed. "Come on. It's a big day tomorrow, and I don't want you to be sick when we finally arrive," she pleaded. "You're the only one out here in the cold." She began pulling him from the hood of his thick yellow trench coat.

"All right, fine—but it's just because of the hot chocolate that I'm coming," he said, smiling. "Just so you know, if some kind of mythological beast emerges from those waters and I've not taken a photograph, it's all going to be on you!" He rapidly snapped one last picture of the frostbitten landscape and disappeared inside the ship.

The lounge room was surrounded by large windows to comfortably enjoy the beauty of the Arctic scenery as the ship navigated. Frosted decals of the famous World Cloud logo were applied to each window. Its all-caps serif font and the stylised design of a mountain topped by a cloud gave the organisation a serious and determined look.

A time-worn brass spyglass was placed carefully on one of the bookshelves, reminding the passengers of the *Son of Odin* of times gone by when ships were pompous wooden vessels, sent off to discover new remote places and uncover their treasures. Jason poured himself a cup of hot chocolate from the communal carafe sat on a large wooden table at the back of the room. Reluctantly, he walked towards the sofas where his colleagues were sitting, but all the seats were taken.

Dael Sassoon

WORLD CLOUD

He stood a couple of minutes in awkward silence while everybody else chatted away. Seeing Jason in such unease, Clara waved at him and patted on the side of the armchair she was sitting in. Jason squeezed next to her, trying to keep his shoulders as tight as possible. He was probably more comfortable standing, but Clara's warmth against his body felt nice.

Jason began listening to the conversation and immediately regretted coming back inside. The topic was, as usual, Danny's incredible adventures. Jason found him arrogant and excessively full of himself—the *official* photographer. Many other members of the team were hanging onto his every word, eager to know how he escaped the world's most treacherous mountains, the darkest swamps, the most intriguing tribes—but few realised that at least half of them were made up entirely.

"So, I was crouched behind a thorny tangle of dry shrubs in the middle of the savannah. I was stock-still, with my camera secured to a tripod and my lens stuck between the branches. Perfect position—back against an acacia tree, covered by bushes, and a great view of a herd of Thomson's gazelles. I had waited so long for that moment, hidden like a statue for hours so that nothing could sense my presence. My muscles were aching unimaginably. I even mixed some water with the soil to make mud that I put on my face to hide my scent. I pressed my eye against the eyepiece, put my finger on the shutter and—" The calm hypnotising voice paused. "*BAM!*" he shouted, clapping his hands together to make the listeners jump on their seats. "The jaws of a massive lion suddenly opened in front of my lenses, and his roar echoed throughout the whole clearing, making each and every single gazelle leap away, frightened to death."

Jason did not feel much more than a shiver along his spine, but while he did not want to admit it, he was captivated by the story as well. He had to give it to Danny—he was a good storyteller.

The young zoologist Tamali Rajan, always anxious to know how Danny managed to survive in the most questionable situations, asked, "What did you do, Mr Porterman?"

"I took a photo of him with a flash and ran away like the wind!" Danny answered, laughing loudly. Although Danny was trying to mock himself, Jason did not like him at all. His vanity and self-absorption made him nauseous.

"It's never wise to run away from the king of the jungle! You risk tripping and becoming the vultures' breakfast unless His Majesty catches you first!" joked Ray Hughes, a very unconventional ichthyologist with dreadlocks and arms covered in tribal tattoos. He was not the greatest fan of Danny either.

The ship ventured under a veil of dark clouds. Rain began pouring down, hitting the large windows with an intensifying patter.

"True, but when you have the right shoes and a good camera, you become invincible!" Jason rejoined sarcastically. "How come I've never seen the photos from this adventure? You'll have to show me when we get back, I guess."

Danny smirked. It was one of those smirks that actually mean something like, *You got me, but I'll smile just to irritate you.*

"I went five years ago when you were still getting drunk in your university dorms," Danny replied. It was clear he was trying to say that Jason was still only a beginner. "Unfortunately, the photos never made it back; my camera fell in Lake Nakuru. A rookie mistake, I know," he added, looking at his audience, who nodded back at him sympathetically.

"Oh, how unlucky!" Jason exclaimed.

"Yes, it was," Danny retorted aggrievedly.

"I just thought—given your long experience—that you would know how to handle a camera without losing it," Jason sneered.

"Since when are *you* the expert in photography?"

"The first thing they teach you at photography class: keep the strap around your neck!" Jason continued.

"You're not trying to lecture me about my work, are you?" He took a break. He was visibly frustrated and trying to hold himself back, but he couldn't. "You know what I think?" Danny said, waving his index finger at Jason. "I think you're a little jealous. If you had the determination I had, you wouldn't have rotted for three years in a basement full of rats developing film."

The ship began rocking more than usual. Flashes of electric blue shone in the distance, intermittently illuminating the lounge room. The banging of thunders came a few seconds later, but the pause between lightning and thunder became shorter and shorter as the *Son of Odin* sailed further into the storm.

"Unfortunately, I didn't have the money or daddy's fame to give me the courage I needed." Danny's father was also a famous photographer.

Danny had almost stood up to respond to this last insinuation when a hand rested on his shoulder.

"This is what you call passion!" boomed professor Hilda Jones, leader of the expedition and expert marine mammal biologist. She was around her seventies, petite but fierce. A shock of white hair reflected her a wacky sense of humour. "You know, when I was young like you two—aeons ago—I was always determined to show that I was the best, but guess what this white hair has taught me? Bickering only brings people to love each other more. You point out each other's flaws and become better people while resolving any issues. Who knows, maybe one day you'll become the perfect couple!" The team burst out laughing, while Danny sank in his armchair.

Jason looked at Clara, who couldn't hold her laughter in the slightest. Seeing everyone so joyful, Jason couldn't help but laugh as well.

A second later, his smile quickly turned into a frown when terrifying creaking noises came from below the floor.

"What was that?" Tamali asked, worried.

The LED lights on the ceiling started flickering. Then, there was a rumble. All the lamps suddenly turned off, and darkness reigned. The only sources of light were the bolts that crushed against the surface of the sea.

"I should probably go see what's happening," Professor Jones said hastily. She looked at Clara and said, pointing at Danny and Jason, "Make sure these two don't bite each other's heads off!" Hilda winked at Clara in a sign of humorous understanding and disappeared in the corridor that led to the command bridge of the ship, leaving behind a room full of glee.

The laughter was not long-lived.

Alarmed screams filled the lounge room when the *Son of Odin* was suddenly violently struck by a huge wave. Books fell from the shelves, bottles of liqueur and mugs full of hot chocolate fell from the counters. The spyglass crashed on the wooden floor, its lenses exploding into small shards. The wave's impact was so powerful that Jason and the other members of the team were jolted off their sofas and armchairs.

The ship swayed and swayed and swayed again.

Someone tried to get back up, grabbing onto the armchairs and bookshelves, but their attempt was hopeless. Another wave flung everyone against the walls with force. Ray Hughes hit his head on the side of a coffee table and dropped to the floor, unconscious.

A bright blue bolt struck the sea right next to the *Son of Odin*. It was as if the Norse gods wanted that ship gone from the sea, and it was time for Thor's unforgiving hammer, Mjollnir, to take care of it. After all, *he* was the real son of Odin. Rampant waves hit against the sides of the ship, flooding the docks and striking the windows. Lightning filled the dark lounge room with sudden flashes of electric blue, and thunders roared over the sound of the raging sea.

A sailor stormed into the lounge room, fighting against gravity to avoid being tossed against the corridor's walls. As he tried to hold onto a door frame, he shouted on the top of his voice, "Don't worry! The captain says we're just passing through a storm! They are common around here and we should—" His words were cut short when the ship halted abruptly, and the sailor was flung to the middle of the room, between water, debris and unconscious bodies.

Jason crawled towards one of the large windows and grabbed the wooden frame to look outside into the black and violent sea, where waves and lightning were fighting an epic battle.

Screeching noises began to arise from deep underneath the lounge room.

The ship had been pushed against a colossal iceberg, which stood impervious in the middle of the storming sea. The diamond-hard ice was cutting through the red metal hull of the ship. The *Son of Odin* was about to suffer the same fate of the *Titanic* more than one hundred years before.

Flammable gases began rising through the boat's ventilation system. When the lightning of Thor's hammer struck the front of the vessel once more, there was an ear-splitting explosion followed by a blinding blaze of red light. The violent burst resonated throughout the entire ship, and

Jason's hearing became muffled. As a high-pitched ringing quaked his head, he tried to get up to find Clara. The research vessel began to tilt sideways, and he found himself falling and sliding brusquely towards the opposite side of the lounge room.

Dirty water was gurgling up through the cracks in the floor and from the ceiling, flooding the entire ship. Iron beams and sparkling wires came crashing through the roof. When Jason finally spotted Clara amid all that commotion, she found her immobilised by fear. One of her legs had been cut open by floating debris, and she was struggling to get up.

"We need to get out of here," Jason told her.

Jason tried to open the glass doors that led to the deck, but the pressure from the water outside was keeping them closed. He looked around in search for something to force them opened, but the room was now inundated in water and chaos reigned. Jason had to make an impulsive decision.

When Clara realised what his plan was, she screamed. "No! You're crazy!" Clara implored. "Don't do it!"

But it was too late.

The young photographer had already begun running towards the glass doors. He threw himself against it. Nothing happened, and he fell backwards onto the flooded floor. Jason got up again and kept hitting the glass with his shoulder as hard as he could until cracks began to form. He backed up a little, and charged towards the glass once more, this time smashing it. The impact stunned him, and he felt a warm, pulsating pain on his left cheek where red blood was trickling down, but he did not stop to think about it. He went back inside, being careful not to step on any sharp shards of glass or wood, ducking his head to avoid the hanging cables. Jason lifted Clara in his arms and fled towards the bow of the ship.

"Are you ready?" he asked.

"Of course not! Just get on with it!"

Jason put his foot on the metal railing and jumped off the deck into the open, icing and angry waters.

As soon as they hit the water, they began to hyperventilate immediately. For the first few minutes, they breathed fast and deep, uncontrollably.

"It's all going to be all right! We'll be fine!" he reassured, shouting over the mighty storm. Clara began to swim frantically to keep herself from drowning. "Don't swim; you'll get exhausted! Just hold my hand and float!" he told her, remembering the emergency training they had undertaken prior to the expedition. "Float and breathe slowly! Hold my hand!" He relaxed and floated in the water and began breathing deeply to allow oxygen to flow back in his body. Clara tightened her hand around his, digging her nails into his skin.

"Don't let go," she pleaded, with terror in her voice.

"Never," he replied.

They were just in time, as a second explosion enveloped the whole ship. There was a shocking blast that tainted the dark, frigid sea with an orange hue. Pieces of metal and wood flew high in the clouded sky, and a column of thick dark smoke that smelled of burning fuel rose from the charred remains of the *Son of Odin*. The ship's flaming fragments came crashing back down in the water next to Jason and Clara, who had to dive into the frozen sea to seek protection. The research vessel was slowly engulfed by Greenland's sea, together with the whole crew. Clara followed the sinking ship with teary eyes. She looked at Jason, terrified and speechless.

After a few moments, Jason found the courage to look around the gruesome scene and spotted a large piece of orange plastic bobbing along the fire-lit waves, sailing through the ship's wreckage. Floating in the turbulent sea, the small inflatable life raft, formerly hanging off the side of the *Son of Odin*, was a ray of hope for the couple. "Clara, we need to get to that life raft! Can you swim?" he asked, conscious of the cut on her leg.

Clara shook her head and squeezed her hand even tighter around his.

The water was cold—more than cold—and Jason did not know how long they had before they would get hypothermia. "We need to get to the raft, Clara! We only have a few minutes before our muscles stop working! I love you, and I want us to survive." He could already feel his legs getting stiffer, and his breath getting fainter. Clara looked at him terrified and finally nodded. Together, they swam in the furious black water and tried to grab hold of it. Their hands and feet began to feel numb, and their thick clothes were weighing them down. When Jason finally managed to grab onto the white nylon rope wrapped around the life raft, he looked back to check where Clara had gone, but she was no longer around.

He had let go of her hand.

"No!" Jason yelled.

Jason swam frantically back to where he last saw her, but there was no trace of Clara. The waves grew enormous and indomitable like black walls rising and crashing violently against each other. Suddenly, he heard loud splashing behind him as Clara broke the surface of the water, desperately gasping for air. "Jason!" she cried. A sudden wave came again, pulling her down.

"Clara!" Jason swam above the raging waves, digging into the water with his arms and kicking as hard as he possibly could. The adrenaline-fuelled his freezing body into a superhuman spree.

Clara waved around uncontrollably as she tried to stay afloat, but the more she moved, the more she went gurgling underwater. Clara gulped down water as she tried to breathe. "J-...Jas-" she tried to call before being dragged underwater again. "Help!" she gasped, choking on the seawater. Her eyes were wide open and filled with fear every time she rose back to the surface to gulp for air.

When Jason finally got to her, he grabbed his beloved by her hand. He tried to pull her up towards him, but the waves were too strong. He held as tight as he could to her body, but her wet clothes were weighing her down, and Jason's arms were becoming far too weak to hold her and stay afloat at the same time.

The force of a wave ripped them apart. She wanted to scream, but she couldn't bring any air in her lungs. Jason fought with the water to try getting her back, but the more he swam, the farther Clara's body was dragged away into the sea.

Clara disappeared in the deep.

"No!" Jason could not give up. He tried to swim forward but found himself back at the life raft. He didn't care about saving himself at that moment; he only wanted to save Clara. He fought against the raging waves once more, but once more he had circled back to the raft.

With his mind on the verge of asphyxia, he used his last strength to pull himself up and drop onto the hard plastic surface like a bag of sand. Every breath felt like a thousand needles hitting his lungs and throat.

With numbed hands, Jason grabbed the two paddles attached to the side of the life raft and began rowing desperately, unable to give up searching for the woman he loved. "Clara?!" he shouted. "Clara!" he insisted. There was no reply. Jason felt a lump in his throat. His heart began beating fast, and he felt everything inside him drop at once. "Clara! Clara, please!"

Jason sat on the wet floor of the life raft and began desperately crying as he looked into the distance, hoping to see her golden hair once more so he could save her. He felt as if he was choking on his own breath and tears as he cried.

"Clara!" he called repeatedly. "Clara!"

He kept rowing, but there was nothing he could do.

"Clara…" he murmured.

He had met the young biologist at the team meeting in London a few months before. Since that moment, they had not been able to spend more than an hour apart. Now, he would never see her again, and that notion made him feel as if all his insides dropped heavily at once.

Every single second they had shared whizzed through his mind, and every moment he did not to spend with her filled him with guilt. Jason couldn't help thinking that it was his fault for forcing her to jump in the gelid water. He could not make the tears stop. Never would he see her smile again, never would he hear her laugh again.

A mixture of both anger and helplessness filled his heart. He promised he would not let go of her hand, and yet he did, and his heart ached.

Jason looked up to the stormy sky. Thor's mighty hammer came crashing down once more, illuminating the tumultuous sea.

II

THE CALLING

Lok was training with one of his squires in the dusty inner bailey of the *Eiriksberg* when the High Gothi, holding his hands behind his back, slowly approached him. His long red leather robe fluttered as he walked.

"Emperor Darkstrom seeks your presence, ser Lok," the High Gothi said with an elderly, feebly voice. He looked at his master—the Shadowcaster—with fear. Lok was tall, his muscular build enhanced by his black leather armour. His face was barely visible, hidden by his shoulder-length, dark and sweaty hair. The High Gothi could just about make out Lok's sharp features and a set of deep brown eyes which stared back at him sternly, glowing.

"I'll be right there," Lok replied.

"It is not wise to make His Imperial Highness wait, my lord."

"I know, which is why it won't take *you* long to go back and tell the Emperor that *I* will be there in due time," he ordered resolutely. Lok had a pair of piercing eyes that could make almost anyone bend to his will. Mostly, however, he could not stand Gothi priests.

"As you wish, my lord." The High Gothi made a quick, anxious bow, and hastily retreated into the shadows of the castle.

Lok slowly placed his longsword, *Myrkyr*, back in its scabbard. He dismissed the young squire and waved his hand in the air to call the enslaved Breegans. From the bailey's muddy sides emerged two short creatures with hunched backs and animal-looking muzzles, bald all over and covered only with dirty potato sacks. They scrambled to the area where Lok was training and hastily picked up the shields and swords lying on the floor. Just as hurriedly they left the bailey, whimpering under the weight of the armour.

Lok made his way through the dark tunnels of the castle. The Eiriksberg stronghold was the largest, most ominous building in all of the Empire of Remara. It had been standing in the Empire's capital of Tarvan Gher, on top of Mount Grohel and overlooking the sea, for over eight hundred years. The fortress had successfully done its job of protecting the capital from non-human intruders since the time it was built. He walked along the narrow passageways of the castle with confident long strides, his sword clanking against his armour. The thick smoke of oil lamps blackened the walls. Lok approached the Throne Hall's entrance—two heavy iron doors embossed with depictions of the heroic quests of Emperor Darkstrom.

Hidden in the shadows at the opposite end of the hall, the Emperor waited patiently on his imposing throne of black marble. He was alone, except for the Breegan servants crouching on either side of the throne, shackled by the neck. Their traditional long beards and hair had been completely shaven.

A rough, hammer-beaten iron crown rested on the Emperor's white hair. Thick grey eyebrows laid over serious ice blue eyes. Behind him, on either side of the throne, two enormous banners proudly hung on the wall, parading the notorious Remaran emblem—the Chained Raven. On a scarlet background, the silhouette of a black raven rested with its wings spread wide and its body in chains.

The sound of Lok's footsteps echoed against the dark stone walls as he walked through the cavernous hall. He looked up to the eight statues of the Ancestors placed all around the second-floor balcony, each double the size of an average person, each of them holding a different weapon. Erik the Red was the tallest of them all, brandishing a large battle axe with a fierce look on his face. The dark statues were like ominous sentinels, looming over Lok as he slowly approached the throne. When he was close enough, Lok kneeled before his master.

"Rise, Lok," he ordered with a stentorian voice. "Come closer, let me see you." As he gestured for Lok to join him, his long coal coloured tunic waved in the darkness like smoke. "How do you feel, my son?" he asked softly.

My son. Those two words repeated in Lok's mind like a resonant tune. He had been at the Emperor's side for as long as he could remember and never had words that formidable been directed to him. Lok felt powerful. The moment he had been preparing for all his life had finally come. He would've made all Valkadia know of what he was capable.

"I am doing well, my Lord."

"I had no doubts; the shadows are strong within you. Do you know why I summoned you here today?"

"I do, my Lord. I am ready," Lok replied.

"Are you nervous?"

"Eager to begin my mission, my Lord. I have waited my entire life for this moment. It's an honour."

"Ah, yes, so it is. A long-awaited moment has indeed arrived at last, and you are the key to it all, Lok. We shall finally put an end to our slanderer. The realm of Erythya has obstructed our progress for hundreds of years, and stubbornly continues to refute the inevitable triumph of the Remaran Empire. We will finally end our imprisonment in this god-forsaken land. Thanks to you and your powers, Lok, Humans will have access to the Otherside again, as our ancestors did six-hundred years ago.

"I was so close last time, my son. I broke through the Erythian defences. I destroyed Malion and reached the Lakes of Asghen. I defeated the Lightbringers and took their stupid dagger. I would've conquered all of Erythya if we hadn't lost so many lives in the process. Yet, this time will be different. The army is stronger than it has ever been, and this time I have you, a Shadowcaster, on my side. You think like me, Lok. You want the same future for Remara as I do.

"Now all the pieces are in place and thanks to you, Lok, the Empire will rise again! We will finally live in peace. After this, you and I will be treated like gods both in the Empire *and* in the Otherside!" Darkstrom declared pompously. "Bring me the *Steinndyrr,* my son, so we can finally open the Elder Stones and free our people." Darkstrom walked back and forth in front of the black marble throne, clasping his hands behind his back. "I do trust you'll maintain secrecy. We don't want any one of those scheming Erythian spies to find out about our plans. Not even the Remaran soldiers or my closest allies know about this mission, so be careful. This is the only way we can win, and this time we can't afford any mistakes." The Emperor rested both his hands on Lok's shoulders and looked at him in the eyes intensely. "Make me proud, my son. Bring honour to me, to the Empire and most of all, to yourself."

"I won't let you down, your Greatness," Lok replied solemnly. He extracted Myrkyr from its sheath and placed its flat blade on the palms of his hands. He kneeled in a sign of devotion to his master, offering his sword to the Emperor.

Darkstrom grinned. "One last thing." The Emperor pulled out from the pocket of his tunic a small, golden gadget. It was spherical and about the size of a marble. A fluorescent blue core floated inside its shiny exoskeleton. "Use this *Jaul* to communicate with me at all times. Any problems you encounter, any creature that may compromise your mission, let me know, and I will see to arrange the best possible solution." He placed the Jaul carefully in Lok's hands, and then announced, "Now it's time to celebrate, Lok! You deserve a good meal before your journey." He clapped his hands authoritatively. "Let's feast!"

The hall's door burst open, and a man with a mandolin entered the throne room playing cheerful music. He was followed by three maids dressed in silken emerald tunic entered the hall carrying large silver platters crowded with food. A wild boar surrounded by roast potatoes and other vegetables was the first to be placed on the stone table in the centre of the hall. Its crispy skin trickled with butter. Then came a large platter filled with cured meats from Voltos, followed by another silver dish packed with hard cheeses from the Dragon Moors. Two Breegans wearing their usual brown rags entered the room, carrying jugs of fresh wine from Tyton and fruit bowls overflowing with apples, plums and grapes.

"My Lord, this is too much. Thank you," Lok said humbly.

The Emperor stepped down the stairs of the pedestal resolutely.

"Nonsense. It's my pleasure, dear Lok. This is an occasion that will happen only once in our lives."

"You are too kind, my Lord."

As they proceeded to sit down at the table and enjoy the feast, a loud crash coming from behind startled them. The mandolin stopped. One of the Breegans carrying the wine had tripped, dropping a jug which had now shattered onto the floor, creating a puddle that looked like blood against the dark basalt floor of the throne hall.

"I- I am so s-sorry, my Lord. I will clean that up right away, if it pleases you, my Lord," the Breegan muttered with a choked voice. The small, mole-like slave looked down ashamed, and held his stocky hands tight together, rubbing his thumb against the back of his other hand anxiously.

The Emperor's face hardened. "If it pleases me?!" he howled as he stood up from his chair, making it fall on its side. Blue veins began throbbing in the middle of his forehead. With a swift wave of his hand, he propelled the fallen chair against the wall, reducing it into a pile of wooden splinters. The Breegan shrieked in fear. Lok seemed unaffected by his terror; this was a common occurrence. "Of course it would please me, you fool!" The Breegan dropped to the floor and frantically began to dry the wine off the floor with his sleeve. The Emperor looked at Lok in disbelief. "What is he doing—what are you doing, you little monster?!"

"I- I- I am cleaning, sir, like you said—"

"*Sir*?! Do I look like a mere *sir* to you? I am your *Emperor*, you ungrateful little beast!" The Breegan nodded his head nervously, looking at his hands and knees, deep in the puddle of wine. "Look at me when I speak to you!" The Breegan raised his head and looked in Darkstrom's bloodshot eyes. As the Emperor raised his hands menacingly, so did the shards of glass from the jug and wooden splinters of the chair. With a swift gesture, the fatal fragments shot towards the servant's abdomen. In an instant, the motionless body of the Breegan fell heavily to the floor with a thud.

Darkstrom walked up to the corpse and hovered his hands over him. With a whooshing sound, a luminescent, translucent essence swirled out of the body of the Breegan. It was his soul, extracted by the dark sorcery of the Emperor and being stored directly inside him. Darkstrom's power grew further.

"Does anyone else feel the need to waste precious Tytonese wine? No? Good. Now, for the love of Odin, could somebody clean that mess up," Darkstrom ordered, indicating towards the Breegan lying on the floor.

Lok had already begun carving into the side of one of the boar's legs. Darkstrom looked at him seriously and added, "That wine came from my private reserve. It was aged in willow barrels."

Lok seemed used to it all. Without batting an eyelid, he helped himself to another serving of roast potatoes and mushrooms.

Before leaving for his mission, Lok went back to his chambers to pack his belongings in a tight bundle. As Darkstrom's elite disciple, he had been specially treated with a balcony looking out onto the capital city of Tarvan Gher. The large window shutters with intricate floral carvings were wide open, and Lok looked out to the extensive city from above. The capital spread wide over the walls and towers of the stronghold. Stone houses with slate-tiled roofs were packed tightly, with cobbled streets that ran between them like a spider's web. Lok could see the Temple of Odin in the centre of the city, with its tall dome shining in the distance. His eyes wandered down to the streets, where the city's inhabitants looked like ants taking care of their menial tasks. The Shadowcaster thought how meaningless their lives were compared to his. Such frighteningly mundane lives they led—such exceedingly futile lives, plagued continuously by a plenitude of foul smells and tedious jobs.

He was the Emperor's best warrior, handpicked among the masses when he was just an infant, and trained with special care by the Empire's best swordsmen, Gothis, scribes and alchemists. Lok had learnt how to read and write; he had read everything he possibly could get his hands on about religion, war tactics, great warriors of the past and the Ancestors.

Most importantly, Lok was a Shadowcaster, and thus Remara's most precious asset in winning the war against Erythya. The Emperor himself had trained him night and day since Lok had found out about his abilities when he was four years old. Even though Darkstrom's dark sorcery was powerful, Lok's Flare was the only chance to get the Steinndyrr.

Throughout the years, Lok had fulfilled the Emperor's orders with pride, and he had brought honour to his name. He had led many raids over Elora's Trench, and his Flare had grown greater each year. The war against the 'Enchanted Realm' of Erythya had been going on and off for decades, but peace was not on the table until Darkstrom would pose an end to his enemies and open the Elder Stones.

Lok gazed far ahead towards the impervious city walls, which were kept under watch by eight-pointed towers that surrounded Tarvan Gher like the fangs of a giant beast. Far ahead was his destination, past the slums of the capital, across the plains of the Stonevale and over Elora's Trench. Erythya would only have a limited amount of time before facing its imminent annihilation.

He sat on the side of his bed and stared at the floral decorations of his walls and waited until it was night. The Emperor had made it clear that no one could know about his mission, not even in the confines of the Eiriksberg. Remara was crawling with Erythian spies, just like Erythya was crawling with Remaran spies.

Once the stars had rose high, and the melancholy glimmer of the moonlight spilt through the streets of Tarvan Gher, Lok decided it was time to go. He picked up his bundle, which contained all the clothes, food and bribery items he would need during his journey and flung it onto his shoulder. All the weapons he needed were concealed beneath his black armour and ready to be utilised. As he walked out of his quarters, the oil lamps hanging on the walls magically extinguished themselves behind him, leaving trails of dense smoke.

Lok slipped through the castle's gates, which he opened with the wave of a hand. Quietly standing outside the Eiriksberg's walls was a black stallion, waiting patiently for its rider. Lok placed the bundle on the horse's back and proceeded to mount on the leather saddle. Like a ghost, he swiftly rode down Mount Grohel and through the narrow alleys lined with tightly packed stone brick houses. The horse's hooves clapped against the cobbled streets of the city as it galloped.

Lok paid no mind to the shops and taverns that he rode past. He rarely went outside the castle unless he had to take care of business; he didn't enjoy mixing with the ordinary people. The proles would always engage in frivolous conversations, they begged him for money, and they loved to sing and whistle in the street. If they were butchers, they would be covered in pig's bloodstains. If they were fishmongers, they would smell of fish guts. If they were merchants, they'd always be yelling. He found the capital chaotic, dirty. Lok liked order.

As quickly as he could, he led his steed through the thick stone walls of Tarvan Gher, over the moat bridge and across the overpopulated slums where people lived in huts and tents made of scrap material. If the inner city was dirty and disordered, the slums were chaos incarnate. The rancid smell of rotting food and open-air sewers permeated the streets of the city's slums, better known as the Rat Den. People were always on the brink of survival there, with routine murders, deadly diseases and starvation continuously threatening the inhabitants. The laments of adults and children alike ripped the night's sky. Though disturbed, Lok finally arrived at the end of Rat Den and headed towards the Suraan hills, the quickest and best way to get to Erythya unseen by prying eyes.

After a few hours travelling through the murky night, Lok found himself riding past the time-worn ruins of Dorth. He slowed his horse's pace. The fallen columns and remains of buildings sprinkled along the Suraan hills were all that remained of what was once the largest city of all Valkadia. One thousand years before, Dorth used to be grander than any city in Remara or Erythya, home to glorious Elven kings that ruled unanimously over the vast lands of Valkadia. The famed Golden City on top of the Suraan hills was like a majestic lighthouse illuminating Valkadia with harmony and hope. Imposing white buildings made of the finest marble and plated in gold, carved by the best stonemasons, used to stand on either side of the broad cobbled roads, through which beautiful carriages led by horses would glide up and down. Dorth was a place of wealth and culture, where *innovation* was always on the mind of its people. Now, the city was just a pile of rubble. Lok, however, was pleased. The perishing of the Elven kind was just what had made it possible for Humans to take over.

Learning about the Elven times was frowned upon in Remara, but Lok's education was an exception. Lok had learnt all about the arrival of the Ancestors led by the legendary Erik the Red, a formidable warrior king from the faraway lands of the Otherside. Lok had read about how one thousand years earlier, King Rennhall—the ruler of Dorth—had welcomed humans into Valkadia and promised them land and wealth. But oaths were broken, and King Rennhall closed the portal to the Otherside by using the Steinndyrr, the key to the portal between worlds, thus cutting Humans off from their homeland in the Otherside and trapping them in Valkadia forever. Humans rebelled and defeated the Elves, destroying Dorth and proclaiming Remara theirs forever. Lok looked at the moon peeking through the clouded sky, shining a dim light beam onto the rubble of that forsaken city. Darkstrom had already tried once before to steal the Steinndyrr from the Erythian capital of Niteria. However, the magic of the Enchanted Realm was too powerful, and the Remaran army was defeated before the Emperor could fulfil his goal. This time would have been different. This time, Lok was there. He would not let the monsters of Erythya defeat the Empire again.

As he was about to dismount and take a break from riding, he noticed a shadow lurking behind a pile of eroded columns. It might have been a fox, he thought, but he was always taught not to assume anything—especially the nature of what could kill you. He slowly guided his black steed towards the unknown peril.

There was just enough time for Lok to pull on the reins and move his stallion to the side before another man riding a white mare jumped over the rubble and galloped fiercely towards him. The mysterious rider's face was hidden by the shadow of a large hood. Lok placed his hand on Myrkyr's hilt and prepared to unsheathe it when the rider spoke.

"Lok," he called. The sound of the rider's voice was familiar; Lok had already fought this person before. The Shadowcaster drew his longsword, conscious of the identity of his adversary. "There's no need for that, Lok," the hooded man said calmly, pacing his horse to a slow walk. His name was Alamor. He was a Veheer, and he was a Lightbringer—an all-round despicable creature, in Lok's eyes.

"Leave me alone, *Lightbringer*," Lok grumbled.

"What has Darkstrom instructed you to do now? Whatever it is, it's a mistake!" Alamor exclaimed.

Lok's fist closed tightly around his sword's handle. "What do you want from me, old man? What compels you to come looking for me each time I leave Tarvan Gher?" he confronted.

"You are not who you think you are, Lok. You are not an assassin. You are so much more, and I can show you that if you come with me."

Lok must have fought the Veheer twenty times already, but the old bastard would not die. If that wasn't enough, Alamor always said the same things: that Lok wasn't who he thought he was, and that he could show him the right way—the Lightbringer's way. Lok's anger began to rise, and he felt a rush of adrenaline crawl up his spine.

Lok pulled on the reins and his horse dashed towards the hooded rider, digging its hooves in the dirt. With a grunt, the Shadowcaster swung his sword at the Lightbringer's head. Myrkyr clanked as it collided with the steel edge of his opponent's longsword. His adversary's weapon was unlike any other sword he had ever seen, and Lok feared its blade as much as the warrior that wielded it. *Isidir.* It was an Elven sword, one of a kind, decorated with a leaf-shaped emerald placed elegantly in the middle of the crossguard.

Lok hit the older man on the side of his head with Myrkyr's pommel, making the Veheer lose control of his precious sword. With a spur to the backside of his horse, Alamor rode backwards and took precautionary distance. Lok grinned eagerly.

"You don't have to fight me again, Lok. You remember what happened the other time we fought…" the man said. "Come with me. I will show you where you came from. Stop serving the Emperor; you're just another piece in his chess set. Join me and become who you were always meant to be."

"Leave me alone," Lok barked, his sword held low ready to inflict an uppercut.

"Stop being daft, Lok. You are not who you think you are. You can be so much more than Darkstrom's puppet. Wouldn't you want to use your powers for a better cause than doing Darkstrom's dirty deeds?"

"Go back to where you came from, Lightbringer."

"You say it as if it's an insult, but that's what you are too, deep down. There are neither *Lightbringers* nor *Shadowcasters* without the Flare."

"My powers are nothing like yours," Lok growled.

The Shadowcaster rode fast towards the Lightbringer, but his attack fell short when Myrkyr was readily deflected by Isidir's blade.

While holding his longsword with his right hand, Lok reached out with his left. As his fist closed, a wall of rock suddenly appeared in front of his opponent. Alamor's white horse whinnied loudly and halted abruptly, and the Veheer went crashing to the ground. As Alamor fell, he lost hold of Isidir and his hood came off, revealing his white hair and pointed ears. Lok wanted the Lightbringer to die. He had interfered with his missions too many times.

Lok jumped down from his horse and passed his sword from one hand to the other, walking confidently towards the Lightbringer, who was struggling to get back up. "You shouldn't be here," Lok said.

As Lok raised Myrkyr to finish the job, Alamor turned around and blasted an intense stream of cold air from his hands. Lok could not move his sword anymore; it was as if it was trapped in a rock. Ice began to crystallise on the blade, and the handle felt colder and colder until, with a loud crash, Myrkyr shattered and turned into frozen dust, leaving Lok unarmed.

Before he could even stop to think how furious he was, Lok was hit by a blaze of fire, which made him stumble and fall on his back. The Lightbringer grabbed him and pinned him down to the ground. Lok's ears rang as he received a decisive blow to the face, splitting his bottom lip. Angry, the Shadowcaster summoned a violent gust of wind which lifted Alamor off him, freeing himself from the older man's weight. They both stood up and faced each other. Lok ran towards the Lightbringer and simultaneously produced a beam of red glowing shadows that hit Alamor in the stomach, propelling him against one of the hard limestone columns. The Veheer laid motionless on the ground, his face resting on the dust of the ruins.

Hastily, the Shadowcaster stood up and mounted on his horse, leaving his enemy behind in the dirt. Lok's ribs ached as the horse's gallop shook him up and down. He rode away without thinking of where he was going, travelling for hours in the dark shadows of the Remaran lands until his horse was too tired. Suddenly, the stallion's front legs gave way, and Lok was thrust off his saddle and landed hard on his back. He heard a loud crunch—the Jaul had broken, cutting his communication with Darkstrom. All around him were birch trees, their banded silver trunks poking through the dark earth covered in fallen leaves. When Lok stood up, he suddenly realised where he was, and wished he had thought of where he was riding. Lok had stumbled into the Iron Wood.

III

INTO THE WOODS

It had been two hours since the *Son of Odin* had sunk in the middle of the raging sea of Baffin Bay—since Jason had lost Clara. To avoid hypothermia, Jason had taken his soaked clothes off and put them aside to dry, but they had instead turned into stiff pieces of frozen cloth. Luckily, the life raft came equipped with a first aid kit, water, emergency food bars, and a heat blanket—which he immediately wrapped around his freezing body.

The storm had now passed, and the small orange life raft slowly carried the sole survivor away from the disaster zone. So far, with only blocks of pack ice as a reference, it seemed to Jason as if he had barely moved. The only way he could tell that he had travelled was that the ship and its debris were no longer around him.

For the following two days, Jason laid on the hard surface of the orange life raft, staring at the endless arctic sea. He had stopped fighting with the waves, and he just let the water take him wherever it wanted. All he could do was to stay wrapped up in his yellow trench coat and heat blanket and nibble on the sweet and crunchy emergency bars as he gazed at the empty sea. Jason couldn't believe Clara was gone. The image of her face disappearing into the ocean kept playing over and over in his mind, and he couldn't shake the feeling of utter helplessness. He had been weak; he felt like he didn't do everything he could. He was trying to save his own life when he should have died with her, or instead of her. Her screams haunted him every time he closed his eyes and re-lived the moment.

On the dawn of the third day, when he almost couldn't keep his eyes open for the exhaustion, Jason saw something appear in the distance. At first, he thought it was a mirage, just some sick game of his sleep-deprived mind. Yet, the more he looked, and the more the life raft sailed forward, the bigger and closer the object got.

Slowly, a dark silhouette emerged from behind a cloud of mist.

Land.

Jason sprung up in disbelief and almost fell off the raft. After those three agonising days spent drifting in the frosty sea, he had nearly given up and accepted his fate, but this changed everything. Jason forced himself up and placed his numb hands onto the handles of the paddles. With great pain and fatigue, Jason pushed and pulled the paddles in and out of the water. His heart began pounding against his chest, and his tired lungs struggled to breathe in. As he gasped for air, all Jason could taste was metal and blood. He forced his dizzied mind to focus. The dark silhouette of the land got closer and more defined. Before he knew it, Jason felt the paddles' plastic hit the hard pebbles beneath the raft. He jumped into the bitter sea, shambling eagerly towards the shore. His knees gave way, and he tumbled onto the dark sand. Jason turned around to rest on his back and looked at the life raft, which was slowly being carried away by the frigid waters. A crushing sense of remorse soon met his gladness of being safe. Clara should have been with him.

He had grown so used to her company that he still felt as if she was with him, but each time he would come to the horrible realisation that she was not there anymore. Jason kept thinking about the gurgling sound of Clara trying to reach out the waves for air, and the terrifying silence every time she was dragged back underneath. He could not get the cold unresponsiveness of her eyes, usually so curious and full of life, out of his mind.

Exhausted and shaken, Jason wrapped himself in his yellow trench coat and sat in the ash-coloured sand for a few minutes, just enough for his body to revive. A slight breeze blew on the side of Jason's face, almost as if someone—or something—had breathed on him. Jason sat up, looking around to see if there was anyone in his vicinity.

Nobody.

Another breeze caressed the back of his neck. With his legs still shaking,

Jason stood up and probed the landscape, confused. The draft got more intense, and it sounded as if it was carrying whispers. Entranced, Jason ventured into the unknown land.

It wasn't long after he began walking that his path took an unexpected turn. At first, he thought it was a mountain in the distance, with its summit reaching higher than any other. As the misty air cleared, the peak became more defined, and Jason realised this wasn't a mountain at all. Rather, it was an immense boulder standing alone in the middle of the barren land. Jason dragged himself towards the massive monolith, and as he got closer, he noticed intricate designs engraved in the stone.

The carvings seemed to depict a door, with columns at either side, wrapped in spiralling vines. In the middle, a winged stag with peculiarly curved horns was surrounded by whirling and winding snake-looking embellishments. Above the stag was a seven-rayed sun, dominating the monolith like the eye of a cyclops, staring back at him with intense power. Jason felt compelled to drop to his knees. After everything that he had endured, the sea had decided to lead him to that specific spot, and the wind had called him to the monolith. This could not have been a merely fortuitous encounter; the immense rock and its carvings had to mean something. Jason kept looking further up the monolith. Above the sun, engraved in an archway, beautiful runes topped the ancient piece of art. Jason had learnt about Norse runes before his expedition, in a book entitled *The Handbook of Nordic Inscriptions*, but these were not the runes he knew.

With a sudden flash of intense blue, the monolith's runes and engravings lit up, basking Jason in a blinding brightness. Averting his eyes, he felt a force pulling him magnetically towards the rock. A second later, the runestone was gone, and Jason found himself surrounded by shadows. He examined his surroundings. The mountains, the dark sand, the sea—it had all disappeared. Instead, they had been replaced by an eerie grey forest, densely covered by tall birch and ash trees and a mat of fallen leaves.

The Iron Wood was feared by many. Legends told of the horrible things that happened to the unfortunate adventurers who dared to enter. Formidable warriors had wandered in without ever leaving, confused by the dark magic that permeated the forest and overwhelmed by the chilling creatures that inhabited it. The Iron Wood was cold and reigned by a vast silence. It was a place of loneliness and sadness, yet it hid a hint of deceitful mockery. The few people that made it out had spiralled into madness, unable to tell illusions from reality. There were tales of murderous gnomes, skinless horses and club-wielding trolls roaming this tenebrous woodland.

Most of all, though, Lok was concerned about one particular creature, the *Ulkar*. This giant lone wolf was said to have taken more lives than any other creature in Valkadia, lurking in the overgrown bushes, ready to ambush any unwary traveller. According to the legends that bards sang at the taverns of Tarvan Gher, the Ulkar used to be an honourable Elven soldier who betrayed his king and was sent to the woods to live his life in shame. Slowly, he was stripped of his essence and cursed with fangs, dark bristly fur and long claws, trapped in this beastly form as a punishment for his betrayal.

Lok knew that these were all just stories that parents told their children so they would behave and not wander off to the woods. Yet, out of caution, he kept his pace slow to avoid falling prey to anything hiding in the shadows. He'd already had enough surprises for the time being, but hopefully, the energy of his Flare would keep unwanted creatures away.

As he walked through the dark forest, Lok heard a rustle coming from behind a stand of bushes. He looked around. His heart began to beat faster. He motioned towards his belt where his sword should have been, but he realised that it was gone, shattered by Alamor's magic. He grabbed a dagger from beneath his cloak and slowly advanced between the trees. From the foliage, an owl flew up and perched on a branch high in the canopy. Its plumage was a mottled grey-brown, and it almost perfectly camouflaged amongst the backdrop of birches. In the middle of its tawny facial disc, two large yellow eyes stared back at Lok with an inspective demeanour.

"Stupid bird," Lok muttered.

He proceeded carefully, trying not to make too much sound as he walked on the crispy ground covered in papery leaves. The Iron Wood was ancient. Old, contorted birches, slumbering timelessly, alternated with younger trees that grew thin and straight. The birches looked down on Lok like watchful guardians. The composting, organic smell of decomposing wood permeated the forest.

Suddenly, a light breeze caressed the back of Lok's head. On impulse, the Shadowcaster emanated a stream of fire from his hands, hitting a tree trunk. As the birch went ablaze, Lok summoned water from the ground, which slowly went creeping up the torching tree, extinguishing the flames as it enveloped it before the fire would engulf the rest of the forest. Lok analysed his surroundings. He was alone.

Then, the breeze came back, now slightly stronger. It carried a whisper that made Lok's skin chill. The Shadowcaster kept treading along, following the murmuring wind. In the distance, he noticed a yellow dot advancing towards him. A bright light shined brightly in the mist behind it, tinging the forest with a blue hue. As it got closer, he realised it was a man, wrapped in what looked like a yellow cloak.

"Stay where you are!" Lok urged, brandishing his dagger.

The stranger did not reply and kept lurching towards him, lifting the leaves from the ground as he dragged his tired feet.

"I said don't move!" Lok yelled across the wood.

The man tripped on a lumpy root that suddenly poked out of the ground, summoned by Lok's magic. He fell clumsily on his knees. The stranger tried to stand up again, but another root wrapped around his foot, making him fall backwards in the musty ground. He got up once more and stood on his wobbling legs with a vapid look in his eyes.

Lok felt a sense of admiration for the will of this peculiar man, and he marched towards the stranger to examine him more closely.

"What's your name?" Lok inquired, grunting.

The man did not speak. He was dressed very oddly with strange materials Lok had never seen before. The yellow cloak he wore was shiny, like metal, but looked as flexible and soft as linen. Lok looked at the man inquisitively. "Do you have a name?" Still no answer. The man was young and had short brown hair and a thin, uncultivated beard. A deep infected cut ran on the side of his left cheek. His eyes were bloodshot, and the livid bags around them suggested he hadn't slept for quite a while. The man wasn't even trying to maintain eye contact—he was exhausted.

The man's knees buckled, so Lok grabbed him before he could hit the floor. As he did so, something strange happened in the middle of the Iron Wood.

Leaves began spiralling around them as if a cyclone had just hit that part of the forest. The whispers grew louder and louder, and Lok felt as if his heart swelled up to double its size.

He began panting heavily, and his vision got blurred. He could feel his energy depleting; it was as if his Flare was being drained from his body. Lok tried to let go of the man, but his body was as still as stone.

They looked at each other. The stranger looked panicked, but he also seemed more aware, less on the brink of death. The cut on his cheek appeared to be healing before Lok's eyes.

"My name is Jas…Jason…"

A moment later Lok and Jason fell together onto the litter of the forest floor, unconscious.

IV

BLUEBERRY MEAD

The faint light of Remara's clouded sky glazed across Jason's eyelids as they sluggishly began to open. A gentle breeze tingled his face as it blew, bending the stems of dry grass and the trees' foliage under its will. Jason awoke to find himself lying on a woollen blanket with his head resting on the hard leather of a horse saddle. His left cheek was itchy, and when he tried to scratch it, he felt an oily film stuck to it. As he peeled it off, he found it was a large leaf covered in an orange, acrid smelling ointment that had been applied to his wound. Jason wrinkled his nose as he felt the scent of the lotion seeping into his throat and nostrils. He stroked his cheek, but the cut was gone.

Jason realised he was still wearing his yellow trench coat, with just a pair of boxers underneath. He raised his head and looked at his surroundings. He was in a clearing enclosed by birch and ash trees. A metallic, tingling sound came from the small stream which flowed nearby. The air was cold and pungent and carried the smell of burning wood that rose from a campfire a few feet away from him. A small pan was sitting on the flames, and Jason could hear the bubbling of something cooking inside it.

"Top of the morning, son! Slept well?" a cheerful voice asked. It was coming from behind.

Jason sat up and turned around. An elderly man, with a thin white beard and long wizard-like hair, was standing at the edge of the clearing, brushing the mane of a sturdy white horse. He was slender and tall, of coltish build. He wore a long, emerald green tunic, and a dark green cloak draped gently down his back. His fawn leather trousers were held together at his waist by a thick black belt. Jason thought he was dreaming. Was it an elf? A leprechaun?

"Where... where am I?" Jason asked. He looked around and furrowed his eyebrows as he tried to make sense of it all. It seemed so real; it couldn't have been a dream. "Who are you?" he inquired.

"My apologies, how rude of me!" the old man apologised. "My name is Alamor Eklund, son of Sehr the Bold." He made a small bow, which Jason found surprising. "How would you prefer me to call you, son?"

Jason looked at Alamor, dazed. His mind was going through a rollercoaster of thoughts and emotions.

"What's your name, son?" the old man insisted.

"Oh, sorry... I'm Jason. Jason McAnnon. Nice to meet you." Jason stuck out his hand, and Alamor reciprocated with a firm shake.

"Pleasure to make your acquaintance, Jason McAnnon," he said. "Say, how did you manage to get lost in here? This place is perilous, you know?"

Jason followed Alamor with his eyes as he got closer and sat next to him. He noticed the old man had abnormally pointed ears, tanned skin and eyes the colour of golden amber.

"I... I don't really know. It's all so hazy. What is this place? Where am I?"

"You're in the Iron Wood, and you're lucky that I found you! The creatures inhabiting this forest are not known to like Human folk all that much." Alamor reached towards the pan that was sitting on the fire and stirred it with a ladle. "Are you hungry, son? I've made a rabbit stew."

"N- no, thank you... Did you say the *Iron Wood*?"

"Are you sure you don't want any soup? It's really quite delicious. You must be hungry after sleeping for so long! Or would you prefer some blueberry mead instead?" Alamor offered.

Jason looked at Alamor, astounded. "How long was I asleep for?"

"Just about a day, son. I found you in the middle of the forest. You were unconscious."

"The forest..." Jason muttered.

Alamor picked up a wooden bowl and served him a ladle-full of stew. As the old man offered him the bowl, Jason realised his left hand was scarred, as if it had been burnt by scorching fire a long time before. "Eat, it'll help you remember," he said.

Jason picked up the bowl hesitantly and stared at it for a few seconds. Pieces of meat, carrot and what looked like lavender were floating in a yellow broth. It looked weirdly inviting, especially the sweet aroma that reminded him of cinnamon, though he was hesitant to eat rabbit that a wacky stranger prepared for him. Then again, he didn't want to appear rude to the old man who saved his life.

"Oh! Pardon me," Alamor suddenly apologised. "I just realised I haven't given you any cutlery! I can be so forgetful sometimes. I'm getting old, you know!" Alamor reached into a leather satchel and pulled out a battered, slightly tainted silver spoon.

Jason took the shiny utensil and looked at his bowl for another moment, but his hunger finally compelled him to try it. He plonked the spoon in the stew and brought it to his lips. An explosion of flavours made the back of his throat tingle, and the saltiness of the vegetables made it all so much more indulgent. Jason quickly proceeded for a second taste.

"Do you remember anything about how you got here, son?"

Jason slurped a third spoonful of stew.

"I... I was in the sea. It was frozen." Jason struggled to remember what happened, his mind still hazy. "There was a storm, and there were lightning bolts everywhere." Jason racked his brain. He knew he was forgetting something, something tragic. "Our ship... it sank," he remembered, and then it hit him, "Clara..." A wave of sadness overtook him as he remembered, his heart sinking into his stomach. What had happened as they swam to the safety of the raft was harrowing. "Clara..." he sighed. It all came back to him, as the guilt from what had transpired welled up in his soul.

"Who's Clara?" Alamor asked.

"Someone very dear to me..." Jason could hardly get the words out; he felt a choking sensation as he tried to hold the tears back. "I can't believe she's..." He buried his face in his hands and attempted to breathe, but all he could see now was his beloved Clara disappearing in the raging sea.

"My deepest condolences, son," Alamor said, shaking his head. "Tell me more."

Jason took a silent pause, reminiscing about the events that brought him to that place. "There... there was a rock—a large rock," he finally recalled. "It was engraved with runes and symbols."

"What symbols?" probed Alamor.

"There was a great stag with wings, and above it there was a symbol—a sun with seven rays." Jason frantically traced it on the ground with his finger.

"Ah, yes. Rotar's Sun," he commented with nonchalance.

"Wait. You know about this?" Jason said inquisitively.

"It is a symbol known across all Valkadia and revered in the realm of Erythya. It's the symbol of our Lord Rotar, the god of the sun, king of the Eredom," he exclaimed.

"I have never heard of... *Roat*?" Jason attempted to repeat.

"Rotar," Alamor enunciated. "What else do you remember?"

"At the top of the large rock were carved three words, but I could not read the runes."

"*Ʒo'or alegsiar eith*—light protects you. It's written in Hæmir, the ancient language of the Elves," Alamor explained. "You must have come in through an Elder Stone... This should not be possible..." There was a certain sense of concern in Alamor's voice.

"An Elder Stone?" Jason asked, curious yet perplexed. "Elves?" What kind of place had he just stepped into? In fact, what even was that language the old man was speaking? He could tell it was different to English, but he could understand it perfectly as if he had always known it. "How... how can I understand you? Where are we?" as he said those words, he realised he too was using the same tongue without any effort. "Why... what language am *I* speaking?"

"You're in Valkadia, son! You're speaking Valkadian!"

"*Valkadia*?" He had never heard of this country. Was it a local way of calling one of the regions of Greenland? To his knowledge, Greenland was divided into five municipalities: Avannaata, Kujalleq, Qeqertalik, Qeqqata, and Sermersooq—and Valkadia wasn't one of them. Perhaps he ended up in an even more remote island of the Arctic circle, but still, that did not explain his sudden, uncannily accurate fluency in a foreign language.

"It is curious that you managed to get in Valkadia. Humans should not be able to cross over... But hey, here you are!"

"You keep referring to humans as if you're not one—what's that about?"

"That's because I'm *not* Human," Alamor replied bluntly. He quickly gestured towards his pointed ears. "See these? I'm a Veheer."

"So… you're not human…" said Jason, rolling his eyes.

"Are you insinuating that I'm lying?" Alamor confronted. His tone suddenly became stentorian. "I am proud of being a Veheer, you'll be glad to know!" Alamor's golden eyes looked like blazing embers, and his ears perked up just like a cat's.

"I- I'm sorry," Jason muttered. "I didn't mean to offend—"

"For centuries Humans have persecuted us, and I wouldn't have saved you if I knew you were like all the others!"

"I didn't mean to disrespect you," Jason apologised awkwardly.

The old man's face relaxed. "It's all right; I always forget Humans aren't as openminded as other beings. Always afraid of what's different…"

Jason sat quietly until he was sure Alamor had calmed down. "So, there are more beings like you… Veheers?"

"Indeed. There isn't many of us remaining, but whoever is left lives mostly in the kingdom of Erythya. We are distant relatives of the Elves, who are now sadly gone."

Otherside, Elder Stones, Elves, Veheers. Jason couldn't believe what he was hearing. He thought he just entered the Lord of the Rings and that he had stepped into Middle Earth. Or, maybe, this was all just a lucid dream, and he was still really aboard the *Son of Odin*. Worse yet, he was afraid he was dead after the shipwreck, and this was where he ended up.

"You have to forgive me, Alamor. Nowadays in the… *Otherside*… people talk about beings like Elves and things like magic as if they are only stories. This all sounds very strange to me."

"I'm not surprised. It has been many centuries since our realms have come into contact. Even six-hundred years ago, the Otherside was always trying to disprove the existence of magical creatures—too afraid of their power. So, you don't believe magic exists?"

"Not really, I'm afraid," Jason admitted. "I like to read stories about it, but there is no such thing as magic where I come from."

"Well then—let's see if I can change your mind." Jason sat up. His eyes were full of wonder. Alamor looked around the glade, rubbing his hands together. "Ah, yes!"

Alamor swiftly waved his hand, and a bottle full of blueish liquid inside a satchel beside Jason lifted in mid-air and flew quietly across the camp as if an invisible waiter was carrying it.

"Would you like some blueberry mead?" Alamor asked.

Jason was speechless. He looked at the bottle levitating in front of his face. Nothing was holding it, but the air beneath it looked as if it was swirling, just like when a tarmac road has been baking under the sun and refracts the trembling sunlight. As Alamor motioned with his hands, a glass joined the bottle of blueberry mead in mid-air. Alamor, from a distance, tilted the bottle and filled the glass. The old Veheer calmly waved again, and the bottle placed itself back in the satchel. The cup of mead landed smoothly on the ground beside the young Londoner.

Jason stared at his drink, speechless. He didn't dare to take a sip from the enchanted grail, though the sweet and alcoholic smell of the beverage was genuinely inviting.

"So, you're a... wizard?" he asked, marvelled.

"I'm a Lightbringer," Alamor replied, adding to Jason's astonishment.

"A *Lightbringer*?"

"That's right, and I'm the only one left of our Order."

Jason took a moment to let everything in. How did he end up in such a world? Why did *he* manage to get in, when it was apparently so difficult to enter? Was Valkadia where humans found the magical creatures that inhabited all the myths and legends? Jason's head spun, filled with questions, curiosity, fear, excitement. All he wanted was to go back to England and mourn Clara's death in peace together with his family. He thought of his parents and how distraught they must have been when they got the news of the shipwreck. Did they even know he was alive?

Jason put his bowl and cup to one side and got up. His legs were weak, and as he stretched his vertebrae popped and crackled. The thin, dry grass pricked his feet and the soil stuck between his toes as he walked around the clearing. The white mare approached him and nudged him gently with its nose. Jason was startled at first, but he soon began to pet its bristly yet soft coat. He had never seen a horse that white.

"She's called Silvyr," Alamor said.

"She's beautiful."

Jason thought of a time he travelled to Wales for a hike with Clara, and he remembered a horse coming up to them as they passed by a farm. Clara had brought carrot sticks in her packed lunch. Jason pictured her happy smile as she fed them to the horse one by one. He recalled her giggling as she felt the horse's lips trying to grasp carrots out of her hand.

"How do you think I got here?" Jason finally asked the old man.

"I'm not entirely sure, to be perfectly honest. A long time ago, King Rennhall used the *Steinndyrr* to close all the Elder Stones and stop Humans from entering Valkadia. Nobody has come to Valkadia from the Otherside ever since. Did you say there was a storm when your ship sank?"

"That's right, with lightning and everything."

"Maybe that caused a disturbance in the portal's magic and opened it for a moment. That would be some coincidence!"

"There was a strange breeze too; it was as if it was whispering something."

"Whispers? Of what sort?"

"I didn't understand what they were saying. They sounded like another language, but when I found myself in the forest, the whispers grew louder." Jason remembered only at that moment about the other man. "There was someone else—another man," he said. "He kept calling me 'stranger' and wanted me to stop walking. I remember tripping over the roots of trees a lot, but I can't remember much about what happened after that. I think I must have passed out."

"That's odd," Alamor commented. "What did he look like, this man?"

"Erm… he had armour on, I think," Jason recalled. "I dunno… I was exhausted; everything is a little hazy. He was definitely dressed in black. He had long dark hair down to his shoulder. I fell, and he grabbed me, and I felt really weird. It was as if my energy was replenishing."

"I'm not sure who that could have been…" said Alamor. "I have a dear friend who lives in Malion. His name is Baldor—he's the Curator of Rennhall's Library. I do not know what those whispers were or how you got into Valkadia, but if we want answers, then Rennhall's Library is where we will find them."

Jason was reluctant to go anywhere. He was tired, cold, and wanted to be back in his tiny London flat with Clara. "I'd just like to go back…" he muttered.

"I know you're feeling confused and tired, Jason, but we cannot do anything until we have some answers. We must get to Malion, and only then we will know what to do."

The Londoner glanced at the whimsical wizard with a sense of gloom on his face. "Can't we just go back to the Elder Stone and take me back? It can't be that far…"

"It's not that easy, son. The Elder Stones are closed for a reason," Alamor responded.

Jason knew he had to put his fate in the hands of this eccentric stranger. After all, he had taken care of him so far, and perhaps following somebody who had magical powers could be the best chance for survival. "How far is this Malion, then?"

"At the moment we are in the Empire of Remara, but we want to get to the kingdom of Erythya. We will have to be extremely careful. Darkstrom has spies everywhere in Remara, and he doesn't really like me all that much."

Everything the Lightbringer told him came with more information, and Jason's mind began to overload. Frustrated, his head aching, he asked, "Who is Darkstrom?"

"The Emperor of Remara. His real name is Ingvar Maddock, but you'll hear him referred to as *Darkstrom*, or the Red Raven. He is a psychopath tyrant who rules over Remara," Alamor quickly dismissed. "Don't worry; you'll be safe with me. Nobody will look for us here in the Iron Wood—even the Remaran soldiers are too afraid of the creatures lurking in its shadows. If we follow the river for a few miles, there is a town called Coldhill where we can stop to eat and rest. If not, we can head straight to Malion. Keep in mind that Erythya is at least three hundred miles from where we are now, but Coldhill could be a risky place for us both. Do you feel good enough to walk, or do you need more rest?"

"I… I think I'm OK to walk… Did you just say there are *creatures* in the Iron Wood? What creatures? Are they bad?" Jason's mind raced as he became increasingly frightened to begin his journey. They were safe in the clearing, and he wished they could just stay there.

"Very bad, but they won't bother us as long as I'm here. They respect Lightbringers," Alamor reassured.

Jason gulped. He looked at his yellow trench coat. If they were about to leave, he needed to be slightly more clothed. "Do you have anything that I could wear under this? It's a bit chilly."

"Have a look inside the satchel where I keep my blueberry mead; there might be some spare clothes in there."

When Jason opened up the small leather bag, which was carefully decorated with embossed floral patterns, he found himself suddenly flabbergasted. The satchel looked normal at first, carefully lined with purple velvet, but as Jason kept looking, he realised it had no end, and objects were floating in a weightless void. This physics-bending space was full of tools, books, food, flasks, even cooking items.

Seeing Jason's astonished expression, Alamor began to laugh aloud. "I forgot you have never seen a Bag of Plenty before," he observed between one laugh and another.

"How... how do I get something out of here?"

"It's easy, son! Just reach in and what you are seeking will come to you." Alamor explained.

Jason opened the Bag of Plenty and stuck his hand in, but nothing came his way. He kept reaching further inside, but he couldn't feel anything clothe-like. He kept going. The void felt cold and tingly, and objects collided softly with his arm just to float away again. He thought of a pair of trousers and a shirt, and as he did so, he felt a gust of air coming towards him.

In an instant, all the clothes inside the Bag of Plenty came gushing out forcefully, and Jason was propelled backwards. Garments and outfits and various objects flowed out like a leak in a barrel, and before he knew it, Jason was covered in a mountain of shirts, trousers and capes. Surely enough, however, he was holding a white linen shirt and a pair of brown trousers.

"You'll get the hang of it," Alamor said, giggling.

Jason got dressed and put his trench coat back on—the only thing he had left from his life before the shipwreck. They packed up their belongings in the Bag of Plenty and Alamor strapped a saddle on Silvyr's back, ready to leave the clearing. Jason noticed that on Alamor's belt hung a longsword. From the leather scabbard poked a wooden hilt with silver floral decorations and shiny emerald shaped like a leaf embedded in the middle of smooth golden guards. Jason wondered if that sword had a name like in many of the fantasy books he had read growing up.

"Stay close to me," Alamor told Jason and began walking towards the interior of the Iron Wood pulling Silvyr behind him by her reins. Jason followed.

They walked along the riverbank for about three hours, taking regular intervals to rest and drink. The Iron Wood was an eerie place, Jason thought. Not only it was dark and damp, but Jason felt watched as if there were eyes constantly observing him from behind the thick stands of bushes. Old trees full of knots and crooked trunks stood ominous between decomposing leaves and grey stones, monitoring the two intruders. Every so often, Jason heard a rustle from deep inside the forest or from above in the canopy. A web of branches concealed the sky overhead, and the light rarely touched the bramble-covered ground. Moss grew everywhere, on the bark of trees and even hanging off their branches. Jason felt cold. A gentle breeze occasionally brushed his hair.

As Jason walked by Alamor's side, he wondered what was in store for him. What would he see on his journey to Malion, and what would he find when he got there? Would he ever go back to his tiny flat outside London? Probably not.

For another couple of hours, they proceeded slowly through the forest. It was a remarkably lifeless forest compared to what Jason was used to. No insects seemed to crawl near them, no birds were singing. An owl hooted once, glancing at them with large yellow eyes. Maybe even the animals were too afraid of going near the Iron Wood. Jason wanted to ask Alamor so many questions, but he was too scared of making noise in that obscure place. Each step resonated in the grave silence of the Wood. Every branch that broke, each leaf stepped upon, each rustle in the bushes—it all spread like an atomic shockwave through the forest of grey twisted trees. Not for one moment did Jason dare to leave Alamor's reach.

Suddenly, the old Veheer halted. His pointed ears tensed backwards, flickering. "Someone's here," he said.

Then, there was a ruffle in the bushes. Jason's mind raced. This time, it wasn't just an owl fluttering its wings in the canopy. There was someone, or something, lurking behind the wall of dark trees.

"What is it?" Jason asked anxiously.

A branch snapped.

"No time to find out. Run," Alamor urged.

Jason's heart began pounding as the adrenaline rushed through his body, and he sprinted, following the old Veheer. The white horse galloped in front of them, leading the way. Jason's calves were aching. All he wanted to do was to rest after such an intense trek through the absolute scariest place he'd ever stepped foot in. Now, however, he had to run for his life.

Whatever was hiding in the thicket was following them, and he could hear steps rushing through the leaf litter behind him.

As they ran out of the dark forest, all sorts of frightening thoughts rushed through Jason's mind. Who was running after them? Why were they being followed? Jason did not want to die.

The light coming from the edge of the forest became brighter and brighter, and before he knew it, they were beyond the line of trees. All around them was a flat expanse of yellow dirt, devoid of any life or distinct geographical features. Jason looked behind; the Iron Wood stared back at them like a dark void. He looked at Alamor gladly, and the old man smiled back at him. Then, the ground suddenly collapsed under them. Two large wooden planks concealed with gravel opened beneath their feet, and they tumbled inside a deep and dark ditch.

✺

V

RED CAMP

Jason stood up and dusted himself off. Alamor was still lying in the dirt, motionless, with his eyelids shut, his snow-white hair stained with red. Jason ran towards the old Veheer and checked if he was still breathing. He was relieved when he felt the vein on his throat pulsating—Alamor was alive, but they were still trapped.

The photographer looked around; there was no way to get out. Even if he managed to climb up the high walls, there would have been no way to pull Alamor up. He jumped repeatedly, desperately scratching at the crumbling walls of the ditch and trying to grab the dry, flimsy roots sticking out of the soil. Silvyr was nowhere to be seen, or perhaps she could have helped them somehow. As he tried to find a way to escape, Jason heard the sound of footsteps approaching, accompanied by an unsettling sound of clanging metal. Jason rushed to Alamor's unconscious body and pulled Isidir out of its sheath. Anxiously, he turned around to face the direction of the incoming footsteps and prepared himself for the worst, with Alamor's sword held tightly in his hands. His muscles trembled as he raised it. Jason looked at the shiny blade, and a sense of uselessness suddenly pervaded him. He had never held a sword before. The closer the footsteps got, the faster his heartbeat became. Jason tightened his hands around the wooden hilt and waited.

"We caught something!" a nasal voice proudly declared. A thin, scraggy man in black armour appeared over the edge of the ditch. Two large scars ran on the left side of his head, from his scalp to his chin. He looked at Jason with a disturbing grin.

"What did we catch, Etrel?" barked another man with a lower, more guttural voice.

"A lad with a strange yellow cloak and a sword, and a passed out old chap!" the skinny one replied.

"Move out of the way! I want to see!" Another figure leaned over the edge of the hole in the ground. He too was dressed in black armour, but he was of a much stockier build and had a wooden peg for his left leg. A thick pair of bushy sideburns framed his round face.

"What are you two morons doing?" shouted a third voice, resolute and severe. "Glod! Etrel! Get a move on and go down there!" Jason didn't see the third man, but his braying voice made his stomach curl.

With a single synchronised leap, Glod and Etrel jumped off the ledge and transformed in two crows. They croaked loudly as they grew wings and became covered in charcoal black feathers. They beat their wings and flew down the pit, spiralling until they landed, raising a cloud of dirt. The dust made Jason's eyes water. As the two crows touched the ground, they grew legs and arms and became human again, and looked at their prey inquisitively.

"Nice cloak, boy," squealed Etrel, the scraggy one. "That's not something you see every day." Close-up, his grin revealed a set of blackened, corroded teeth. His scars looked even more gruesome. He was much taller than Jason.

"What are you?" Jason asked between heavy breaths, terrified. *What the hell is happening?* He was convinced he was in a dream at that moment. *People can't turn into crows.*

"We are the Omüms," they answered in unison.

Their armour was black, but the chainmail red. In the middle of the chest, the armour was embossed with a peculiar symbol—a bird spreading its wings with its body wrapped in two thick chains. Jason wondered what psychopath would choose that image as a coat of arms. Then he remembered Alamor's fleeting comment. *Emperor Darkstrom.*

"Leave us be," Jason confronted, fearing for his life. The two creatures looked maniacal and deadly, and he didn't want them to get any closer. As they advanced towards him, Jason swung the sword awkwardly, making them take a step back.

"He's got quite the temper!" Glod snickered. He was shorter than Jason but still looked just as dangerous and crazy as his partner. As he walked around Jason, his peg-leg knocked on the ground. "We won't harm you... if you don't fight back, of course." They both chuckled.

Jason swung the sword again at the Omüms as they circled him slowly, prowling like a pair of hyenas.

"Woah! Easy, boy!" Etrel screeched. Jason attempted another clumsy attack, but Glod grabbed Isidir's blade with his hand and pulled it out of Jason's grip. He chucked it to the other side of the ditch. They began closing in on him.

Jason couldn't understand why they were attacking them. What had they done wrong? Apparently "What do you want from us?" Jason asked.

"You are not welcome here," Etrel and Glod grunted in unison.

"Let us free, and we'll go our own way," Jason replied—he only wanted to get out of that ditch and run away, through the Elder Stone, and back onto the *Son of Odin*. He did not want to be killed by these horrible creatures. He just wanted to be back home. The sooner they left the ditch, the sooner that would happen.

"Oh yeah? And where are you going, exactly?" Glod asked. Etrel began walking around the unconscious body of Alamor. Jason was not sure what to answer to Glod's question. He only knew the name of two places— Malion and Coldhill. If these were Remaran soldiers, they probably wouldn't have appreciated if he told them they were heading towards Erythya.

"Coldhill," he finally replied.

"Coldhill, huh? You are going in the wrong direction then, *boy*." Glod licked his lips compulsively as he grinned.

When Etrel saw Alamor's pointed ears, he gasped and burst into a maniacal screech. "A Veheer!" The soldiers glared at Jason with furrowed brows and wrinkled noses.

"You are lying to us!" Glod screamed.

"Liar!" they both shrieked.

Etrel's armoured fists hit Jason in the stomach violently. He dropped to his knees and felt like he wanted to throw up. To try and protect himself from any more incoming hits, he curled into a ball and wrapped his arms around his stomach. He had only been beaten up once before by some bully in school when he was twelve, but that particular aggressor didn't have iron boots. Jason wanted to get up and fight back, but he was in too much pain.

"Liar!" they kept shouting. "What are you doing here?" they yelled. "Scum!" They hit him again.

There was no time to catch a breath between one wallop and the other. One of the two psychotic soldiers swung his foot violently at Jason's face. His head snapped back, and he felt the skin on the ridge of his nose split. The iron-rich taste of blood was surreal. Fear assailed the photographer as his vision became blurred. Alamor was now an uneven blob of white and green, laying on the ground beside him. As he rested with his back on the bottom of that dusty pit, he saw the silhouette of the third man appearing at the edge of the ditch. He couldn't make out what he looked like, but he was taller than any man Jason had ever seen. This man's armour was crimson red.

"Enough," their leader ordered.

Before Jason knew it, Etrel pulled him up and put a canvas bag on his head. The blood dripping from his nose soaked the fabric, which stuck to his face. Jason felt his head dropping, and he lost control of all senses, and he didn't remember much else after that.

A gentle voice woke Jason up. At first, he thought Clara had awakened him from a bad dream, but when he opened his eyes, no Clara was lying beside him in bed. The cold air bit his fingertips and toes, and he realised that everything had indeed been real.

He tried to get up, but something held him back, digging into his wrists. He realised he was bound to a large wooden plank with rusty iron shackles. Alamor was restrained to a second plank a little further away. The old Veheer was still unconscious, and the whole left side of his head was now covered in blood. Jason struggled, pulling on the chains as hard as he could in the hopes of destroying the manacles, but the more he moved, the deeper they cut.

"Hey! Easy!" said a woman sat beside him. It was the same voice that had woke him up. When he glanced up, away from the awful surroundings, he realised a young woman was kneeling beside him, holding a jug of water. "Here, drink," she said as she handed him a cup to drink from. Her turquoise eyes were glimmering in the twilight, and the woman's corvine hair was as dark as night.

Jason calmed himself down, breathing slowly, and accepted a drink from the dark-haired woman. He realised his nose had stopped bleeding, but he could feel the dry blood stuck on his upper lip and nostrils. Curiously, however, his nose wasn't as sore as the young Londoner had expected, and neither was his stomach. Jason opened his yellow trench coat and saw there was no sign of any bruises. He ran his fingers along the ridge of his nose, and there was no cut or break. Back home, even just hitting his shin against the corner of the coffee table would leave a mark. *What's going on*, Jason thought.

Dizzied, Jason looked examined his surroundings, but all he saw were scarlet tents arranged around a circular, unpaved yard. In the middle of it stood a lonesome pole. The disturbing coat of arms with the chained bird was paraded on banners everywhere he looked, and men in black armour marched around with swords hanging off the side of their belts and carrying their helmets under their arms. Little people with shaven heads and dressed in filthy canvas sacks trailed miserably behind the soldiers. They were carrying heavy boxes, pots and pans and buckets of water. Alternatively, they were simply being dragged along by their shackled necks and ordered about by the men in armour.

"You and your friend must have really pissed Tortugal off to have ended up here," said the woman.

"Who are you?" Jason asked as he took the cup.

"I'm Anyir. I'm the healer," she replied. "You don't look like you need much healing, though. Who are you?"

"Jason," he replied. "What is this place?"

"I'm afraid to tell you that you've landed in one of the roughest pits of swine in the whole of Remara. You are in the Red Camp."

Jason took another sip of water, clearing his throat from the dust of the Stonevale. "Red Camp?" he asked.

"It's Darkstrom's largest military base," she explained. "Are you a knight?"

Jason didn't know how to respond, so he just deflected the question. "What are they going to do to us?" he asked Anyir.

She gave him an apprehensive glare. "I'm not sure. They usually torture anyone who they think is against the Emperor."

"What makes you think we are against the Emperor?" Jason asked, defensively. After being beaten and shackled by the soldiers, he didn't know what the right thing to say was in this new, strange world. What if this woman was evil too?

"For starters, you are chained up. Secondly, your friend has pointy ears—he's a Veheer, isn't he?"

"He... he is," Jason admitted. There wasn't much point hiding that fact.

"Well, if you and the Veheer manage to get out of here, promise you'll take me with you. I must get away from here," she implored.

"How do I know you're not one of them?" Jason asked, unsure whether he could trust her. He was afraid of being deceived by her kind eyes.

"Believe me; I would kill them all if I could after what they did to my husband and me..."

"What... what did they do to you?"

"Bad things," she replied, without elaborating. "Anyways, I must get back to my village, back to my husband. I've been kept here for far too long."

"I'll see what I can do," Jason whispered. He sincerely hoped they'd manage to leave that godforsaken place.

"You put up quite the fight, dirt rat," an eerily familiar voice suddenly boomed, deep and croaky. A colossal soldier appeared before him, covering the little light that still illuminated the sky. From atop the pit, Jason hadn't realised quite how huge this man actually was. Anyir scattered away, clearly terrified. She gave her new friend a last look of understanding as she disappeared between the red tents.

Jason squinted his eyes and looked closely at the behemoth. He was wearing red armour and black chainmail—the opposite of the other soldiers, which automatically gave him an authoritative appearance. Around the waist, he wore a heavy leather belt to which was attached a large broadsword, with a leather-lined grip and snake heads adorning each end of his metal guard. The large square skull of the soldier rested on an almost non-existent neck. Thick black moustaches descended along the corners of the mouth, and his scaly skin made him look like a troll from videogames that Jason used to play as a teenager.

"I'm General Tortugal," he said. "Welcome to the Red Camp—the largest military camp of Remara. You will have the honour of serving the Red Raven in the guise of my servants, and if you only try to do anything that differs to any of my commands, or you attempt disobeying me, or even worse you try to escape, then you *will* be punished. As you can see, there is a pillar in the middle of the camp's yard. Disobey once, and you shall be acquainted with the Pole of Justice," he said resolutely. "Disobey again, and you shall respond to the wrath of my soldiers—you already met the Omüms Glod and Etrel—or you could have the honour of meeting my beloved sword, *Rhazien*." He wrapped his fingers around the black leather of his sword's grip. "Speaking of which, thank you for the wonderful sword you gave us back in the pit. It will be a splendid addition to our collection. Say, where did you and your Veheer friend find it?"

Jason looked directly into the general's black, shark-like eyes. He really wanted Alamor to wake up and help him face this monstrous soldier, towering over him and ready to stick a three-foot-long broadsword in his stomach. Jason could feel his heart lodged in his throat, beating at twice the pace. Although it was cold, he began to sweat.

"We didn't find it, general. It belonged to the Veheer to begin with."

"Oh, the Omüms were right for once! They don't tell the truth about many things, but they were definitely right when they said you were a liar!" he roared. "That sword is not one for commoners, and certainly not for a Veheer to wield! Tell me the truth, dirt rat, or your life here could become very difficult and very short."

Jason began shaking. Tortugal was a level of terrifying the likes of which he had ever experienced.

"I… I am telling the truth. I would not lie. I hate liars. There was this other guy, Danny—he used to make up the most ridiculous stories—"

Tortugal responded with a very precise blow to Jason's jaw, sending him swaying to the side. The metal plates on Tortugal's knuckles had bashed hard on Jason's nose and broke it—again. Jason spat blood on the ground.

"Let's see if your friend decides to help more than you. Lieutenant Modùn!" he called. Jason squinted his tired, contused eyes and looked up. Another man in red armour arrived, carrying a wooden bucket with both hands. He was considerably shorter than Tortugal and many of the soldiers around, but he looked just as deadly.

The eerie Remaran sky became clouded. The night was approaching.

"General," he greeted. Without waiting for any commands, he proceeded to launch a bucket-full of grimy water at Alamor's face, who woke up gasping for air. "Wake up, filthy Veheer," Modùn ordered ghoulishly.

Alamor looked up at the two soldiers with his face dripping with dirty water. His expression turned from confused to scared as if he had just seen a ghost. He immediately realised where he was.

"Who are you, old man? What are you doing here?" the lieutenant asked.

Alamor didn't answer. He looked apprehensively at Jason's

blood-covered face and then looked back at Tortugal. He spat on the general's shiny metal shoe. Tortugal looked at him with stern eyes and then turned to Modùn and nodded. There was a silent agreement between the two. It seemed as if they had done this routine many times before. Rather than hitting Alamor, Modùn turned again to Jason. Another armoured fist pummelled Jason's face, this time hitting him on his temple. As his head swung violently to the side, he lost his sight for a brief moment, and all sounds became muffled.

"Leave him alone," Alamor confronted. "He has done nothing wrong to you."

Tortugal crouched down and looked straight into the old man's eyes. Even then, he looked massive. "I'll let the boy live if you tell me who you are. You better not try any kind of trickery, or the next thing that hits him is my sword—on his neck." Modùn laughed perversely as the general said that.

"All right," Alamor said. "I am ser Frey Ofson. I am a knight from Orachlion, and the boy is my squire. We are on our way to Coldhill to deliver a message of very urgent matter to Lord Dorson. Unfortunately, I cannot release any information about the message as it is confidential—otherwise, I would tell you. However, I guarantee you shall be fairly compensated if you let us go without any further harm. I do not think that Lord Dorson will be pleased when he finds out how you treated one of his best knights and his squire." Jason was amazed at Alamor's ability to improvise. Yet, he didn't understand why he hadn't already unleashed his powers onto the evil soldiers.

"I have been to Orachlion many times, and I have never heard of a ser Ofson. To think of it, I have never met a Veheer knight either," Tortugal contentiously observed as he tightened his hand around the grip of Rhazien. His small, black eyes became narrow, and his square jaw tensed. "Where did you get that sword? It's an Elven sword, and if I'm not mistaken those are difficult to come by."

"I assure you I am telling every bit of the truth, general," Alamor stated. "I am a knight, and that sword belongs to me, and it belonged to my family for generations. It was passed down by the Elves of Dorth to my ancestors a long time ago."

"You are wasting your time on us," Jason intervened. As he confronted the general, he examined his peculiar face. Large teeth protruded from his bottom lip, his eyes were small, and his nose was short and flat. Tortugal reminded Jason of the orcs from Warcraft—still a behemoth, though less exaggeratedly muscular.

"See, I think of it differently," Tortugal said. "There is a fine line between lying to save yourself and using the truth to be convincing enough to make your lies sound real. If I allowed anyone to walk through Red Camp unharmed when they arrived carrying an Elven sword, blabbering about knighthood and Elves, I'd be a very questionable leader."

"We didn't decide to be here. You took us," Jason retorted.

Tortugal pulled his sword, Rhazien, out of its scabbard. The blade was as black as coal and almost invisible in the evening's twilight. He slowly laid the edge of the sword close to Alamor's throat. "Tell me why I shouldn't kill the Veheer. If I didn't know any better, I'd say he's an Erythian. What do you think, lieutenant Modùn? Are they lying to us?"

"As you say, general. The sword certainly doesn't look Remaran," the lieutenant replied.

Alamor seemed indifferent to the whole situation. Jason thought he must have gone through this before.

"I think what my associate is trying to say, general, is that it was very unfortunate of us to fall in your trap. We didn't mean to cause any disturbance in your beautiful military camp," Alamor said from behind the sharp razor of Tortugal's six-foot longsword.

Why is Alamor being so nice to them? Jason thought. *They're literally threatening to kill us.* He felt an uneasy sense of anxiety and found himself overwhelmed by rage. "Stop sugar-coating this." Jason snapped at Alamor. "Why did you imprison us?!" he yelled.

"I've got to say, old man—your *squire* has a fire within him!" Tortugal said to Alamor. "Maybe you'd like us to take care of his sharp tongue? Or, maybe, would your squire enjoy watching while we teach his master a lesson?"

"Will we be requiring the whip, general?" Modùn asked.

"Indeed, lieutenant," the general replied.

Modùn whistled, and a young boy less than ten years old appeared from within the sea of scarlet tents and handed him a black leather whip.

The lieutenant grabbed the whip and snapped it in the air. Its end was split into seven strands, each terminating with a small wooden bead. A loud pop followed a high pitch hiss.

"You're a coward," Jason growled.

"What did you just say to me, dirt rat?"

"You're a coward," Jason repeated.

Tortugal smirked.

Jason wriggled in his manacles and chains, pulling so hard that his skin ripped.

Modùn snapped the whip in the air again, eagerly waiting for the general's order to unleash its power on Alamor's back.

Fearing the worse, Jason felt an unprecedented need to fight back. He didn't want to see his friend hurt in such a violent way. He had only seen violence on TV, but if torture was half as bad as in movies, he wasn't ready to see anything like that happen in real life. A surge of energy flowed through his veins, and he found himself yelling, "You should be glad I'm chained up!" He regretted lashing out as soon as the words left his lips, but something was fuelling him uncontrollably.

"Oh yeah? And why is that? Would you hurt me? Would you fight me?" Tortugal teased.

"Jason, please, you won't stand a chance," Alamor tried to warn, but Jason was too quick.

"I would love to," the young Londoner replied sternly.

"Just let them get on with whatever they want to do," Alamor pleaded to Jason. "It'll be quicker this way."

"And let these scumbags torture you?" Jason looked directly into Tortugal's eyes. His fury had taken over his judgement and sense of self-preservation. "I will kick your ass to the dirt."

Tortugal slowly nodded and looked at Jason as if he had just signed an agreement for his own execution. He seemed perversely pleased. "Get him out of his chains."

The old Veheer looked at Jason apprehensively, but he also seemed to be secretly smirking. Jason's heart was pounding against his chest, and his stomach felt tighter than ever. Was he really about to duel that colossus? Modùn unlocked the manacles around Jason's wrists with a large iron key and lifted him brusquely from under his armpit. The lieutenant pushed him in the centre of Red Camp's square.

"You are dead meat," Modùn whispered.

Tortugal looked as if he had just laid his eyes upon a prey, just like a tiger would.

"Modùn! Give the boy your sword."

The lieutenant's jaws clenched and, reluctantly, he drew his longsword and handed it to Jason. The weapon was heavy, made of hardened steel, and Jason's weak arms fought to keep it raised.

"That sword is called *Draukar*, the Undead. I think you will be *very* dead soon, though!" Tortugal teased, and a burst of hysterical laughter arose from the audience of soldiers.

Tortugal took his armour off and dropped it to the ground with a thud, raising a cloud of dust that lit up against the lantern fire. He was now bare-chested, and only wore only a pair of leather trousers. His bulging muscles were covered in scars. He jammed his sword in the ground and said, "There—we're even now. No shield. No armour. Just me, you and two blades. Let's see what you are made of."

The Remaran soldiers gathered to observe the duel that was about to take place. Jason recognised Glod and Etrel standing close to each other in the first row. Even the Breegan slaves joined the crowd, though they were pushed away brusquely by the soldiers. They all hoped for a show ending in death, and the odds were in favour of their general. A drum began booming rhythmically, resounding in Jason's chest.

Jason was anxious, frightened, worried. Yet somehow, even though he had never fought with a sword—never mind face a colossus whose job was to kill people with swords—he was weirdly enlivened. Something inside was fuelling him.

Neither of the two men spoke as they circled each other, eyes locked onto the opponent. The lanterns and cooking fires laid an orange light on the camp, making the scarlet banners even more gruesome, and Tortugal's face even more fierce. The smell of burning wood permeated the air. Against Tortugal, Jason looked like a child, half the size of the general. Sweat began running down Jason's forehead, dripping off his nose and chin.

Tortugal attacked first, grunting as he plunged towards Jason with a vicious overhead strike. The sound of steel against steel was loud as Jason lifted his sword and the two blades collided.

The force of Tortugal's blow was much more than Jason could handle, causing him to lose his footing as his sword recoiled. Tortugal took advantage of Jason's poor balance and attempted another blow. Luckily, Jason stepped to the side just in time to avoid the general's attack, aimed right at his shoulder. Jason quickly got back into position, holding Draukar low.

Jason accepted this might have been the end. Still, he did not back off.

"Give up, dirt rat," Tortugal said. "You stand no chance against me." Tortugal began swinging his sword, advancing heavily towards Jason and launching a series of slashes in his direction. With the surprise of everyone that was witnessing the scene, the photographer managed to parry each pummel. Jason attempted a desperate attack, but Tortugal's blade readily deflected it. The soldiers watching the fight laughed derisively.

"I want to know the truth, boy. Where did you get that Elven sword? Where are you really from?"

"We've already told you."

"You expect me to believe any of the words that come out of your mouth? You're a liar, dirt rat."

Tortugal circled Jason and charged against him once more. Under each wallop, the young Londoner became weaker and weaker. "Tell the truth, boy! Who are you?!" he roared.

The swords clashed again, but this time, Jason held his stance and pushed with both hands against Tortugal's mastodontic weight. Shards of steel broke off as the edges of the blades collided. The titanic general roared with frustration and his muscles tensed, veins bulging on his biceps and neck.

The general began throwing feints at the photographer, who soon lost his concentration and failed to parry a sly hit. Jason felt his leg quiver as Rhazien's blade slashed his calf. The long gash began throbbing with blood.

With one ferocious kick in the stomach, Tortugal shoved Jason into the dirt, making him lose grip of Draukar. He rolled away just in time because the general plunged his sword in the ground right by Jason's ear. A high pitch tinkling reverberated in his head. Instinctively, Jason took a handful of dust and threw it in the air, directly in the face of his gigantic adversary.

"I'll tear you to shreds!" Tortugal barked, trying to wipe the dust out of his eyes. Jason took the chance to retrieve his weapon, which was lying a couple of feet away. Jason lifted the sword to protect himself from an incoming blow, but this was so powerful it broke the blade in half. He found himself completely disarmed.

The soldiers cheered on as Tortugal loomed over the boy, who laid helplessly in the dirt of Red Camp's yard. Even Modùn, whose sword had just been shattered, cheered Tortugal on—seeing Jason die was more important to him. The grey dust of the Stonevale formed a thin layer of haze in the air, making the soldiers look like silhouettes against the Camp's lanterns.

Jason watched Tortugal's blade as it plunged towards his face. He was sure at that moment that his life would come to an end. He took one last breath and closed his eyes.

All of a sudden, a flash of blinding light exploded from Jason's body, enveloping the whole camp. Everything went white in an instant, and Tortugal's blade never came.

VI

THE LONE WOLF

Lok was back at the Eiriksberg, in the cavernous Throne Hall. It had been completely emptied, and only Darkstrom's imposing throne and the Ancestor's statues were still in their original place. Lok was standing at one end, and the Emperor at the other.

"I can't do it, my Lord," Lok said, panting. "It's impossible."

"It's only impossible until you try, dear Lok."

"I don't have enough power, my Lord."

"Nonsense!" he roared. A gust of wind suddenly entered the hall, conjured by the Emperor. Slowly the Remaran ruler began levitating, his long cape dragging on the floor. Darkstrom soared up in the air until he was about halfway to the ceiling. Lok saw droplets of moisture condensing in front of the Emperor. After a few seconds, they turned to ice. Before he knew it, the frozen bullets shot towards the Shadowcaster, but he jumped high enough to dodge them. "Use your powers, Lok. Odin gave you the Flare, and you must learn how to master it, even when it's dark. That's the power of a true Shadowcaster," said the Red Raven.

Lok kept trying to conjure the elements, but there just wasn't enough light. He had been able to use the Flare in the dark before, but something was stopping him that evening. More ice blasted towards Lok, and he used his sword to deflect it with one rapid move. His frustration grew.

"What are you doing?! Use the Flare!" A stream of flaming lava erupted from the ground, inundating the hall. Lok ran from the incandescent molten rock and didn't know where to go. He did all he could to control the scorching flood, but it just wouldn't stop flowing towards him. He jumped and grabbed onto one of the Ancestors' statues. As Lok hung there, Darkstrom shouted, "You are a pathetic excuse for a Shadowcaster! You will never be my best warrior."

Lok looked at the Emperor, floating mid-air above a pool of glowing lava. He swore he saw Darkstrom's face change for a brief moment into that of a woman. Her hair was long and auburn, and a pair of bright green eyes stared back at him.

Lok lost his grip and began falling towards the lava.

Wake up, Lok.

The Shadowcaster jolted and opened his eyes. It was a dream.

He was lying on a layer of puckered leaves, and the smell of decomposing litter infused the Iron Wood. It was morning, though he didn't know of which day it was, and the meagre foliage shook in the canopy under the soft wind. Dank pillars of bark protruded from the humid ground, where mushrooms had just spawn. Thin saplings grew beneath the older trees and ferns. Beside him, a slug slowly advanced, leaving behind a shiny trail.

The man with the yellow coat wasn't there any longer. Had he dreamt that too?

Lok, said a voice, carried by the wind.

Lok turned his head abruptly in the direction of the voice. No one was there. Was this one of the tricks of the Iron Wood that the bards sang about? Instinctively, he went to grab Myrkyr, but his hand tightened onto empty air. His treasured sword was gone, broken by the fury of the Veheer. Luckily, he had come prepared. From under the plates of the leather armour on his forearm, he pulled out a foot-long dagger. Its blade shined in the shadows of the ash trees.

Your Flare is gone, the voice echoed.

It sounded like a woman, though she had a second, braying undertone. Lok's breathing grew heavier. Where was that voice coming from? He put one hand forward and tried to conjure the wind and lift the brown leaves that covered the forest floor. Nothing.

"No," he muttered. "This... this is not possible..."

He tried again, and this time he summoned water. Nothing, again. Not even a measly droplet of moisture rose from the ground or fell from the sky. All his insides drop at once; he felt as if he had just lost part of his soul. Lok looked around; someone must have been pulling a sick joke on him. His Flare was everything. It was the essence of who Lok was—a warrior, a Shadowcaster. Without his Flare, he was nothing.

Desperately, he called the fire and the earth, but nothing answered his will. He had learnt how to use his Flare in the dark—he was a true Shadowcaster. Though the forest was dark, he should have still been able to use his powers. There was only one explanation: he had lost the Flare. He had truly lost it. Just like in his dream, just like the voice told him.

"Who are you?" Lok asked, shouting into the depths of the forest.

Come to me, Lok. I will help you retrieve your powers.

"Who are you? Show yourself!" he cried desperately, his voice to the point of breaking.

Your Flare has been taken. You must seek the person who stole it.

"What do you mean? Someone '*took*' my powers?!"

The voice didn't answer back.

"Hello?! Show yourself, for Odin's might!"

He was alone in the Iron Wood. No sword, no Flare. Then, he realised. The man with the yellow trench coat had taken his powers. He was sure of it. "Jason…" he grumbled.

He analysed his surroundings anxiously, looking in every direction. The Iron Wood was quiet, though Lok knew creatures hid in its shadows.

From somewhere behind the bushes a few feet away, a growl answered back. For a moment, Lok saw a pair of glowing eyes move fast behind the trees, but when he glanced again, they were gone. He tried to breathe slowly to calm his racing heart. He focused and observed the forest, listening carefully. The Iron Wood was silent, and it was playing with his mind. It was evident that the stories he heard as a child were making him see things that weren't actually there.

Then, a branch snapped, but he couldn't see anything.

The creature must have been fast, as the noises kept coming from different directions. Lok could hear the sound of its breathing becoming louder, getting closer. Before he could move away, something huge crashed into him from the side. He found himself in a tangle of earth, leaves and fur, as the beast dragged him down with its momentum. The dagger flew out of his hand and landed on the leaf litter, away from his reach.

A wolf of abnormal dimensions pinned him to the ground with sturdy, muscular legs. The smell of its thick bristly fur was so foul Lok could taste it.

It was the Ulkar.

The gigantic beast looked down on him with red eyes like jewels from the underworld. Its muzzle curled back to expose its yellow fangs, each canine the size of a human hand. Filthy saliva drooled from the sides of its mouth. Its ears were shoved back, tense. It growled, and its fetid breath froze in the air as it left its mouth, spewing in a cloud of vapour.

Lok stared at the beast, and the longer he stared into its ruby eyes, the calmer it seemed to get. In the past, he had been capable to communicate with animals, but the Ulkar was no ordinary creature and he wasn't sure his ability would work this time. Eventually, he felt the pressure of its huge paws lay off him, and he managed to sit up in front of the Ulkar. The beast lowered its head, relaxed its ears and hid its sharp teeth, and Lok slowly put his hand closer to its nose. The large wolf jerked briefly, unsure whether to trust him or not, but then it moved closer to Lok's hand until the two made contact. Maybe it was because the beast used to be a warrior like him once, or perhaps because the Ulkar was tired of living in solitude in the darkness of the Iron Wood.

Nevertheless, warrior and beast connected. Lok didn't understand why everyone was so afraid of this creature. It was majestic, powerful.

Come, Lok, said the woman's voice.

The Ulkar hunched its back and snarled, its fangs appeared again. It seemed to hear the voice too.

"It's all right," Lok reassured as he stroked its muzzle, ignoring the twenty-inch-long fangs. He got up and stood next to the wolf, which stood taller than a horse beside him. Lok grabbed hold of the Ulkar's fur and pulled himself upon its back.

Your path has been chosen, said the voice. *You must join me in Orachlion. Answers await.*

Lok didn't know whether to trust this woman, but he needed his powers, and if he had to delay his mission to get his powers back, then that's what he had to do. Darkstrom would understand. After all, Lok's Flare was the Emperor's greatest weapon against the Erythian army. Lok pulled on the tufts of long rough hair of the Ulkar's back, and they rode on, out of the Iron Wood.

As they approached the bare land of the Stonevale, the creature halted and whimpered, refusing to advance. This would be the first time the lone wolf left the dark forest. Its red eyes were adapted to the wood's gloominess, protected by the thick canopy of the trees and the dense, murky bushes.

Still, it didn't want to disappoint its new master. After a moment of doubt, the wolf stepped out of the shadows.

They rode for days through the dusty Stonevale, stopping regularly to hide under the shade of a boulder whenever it got too bright and hot for the beast. They travelled along the cultivated lands of the Stonevale, where miserable farmers did their best to grow crops in the very infertile grey land. At the sight of the Ulkar and its rider, scared farmers would gasp and screech and run back inside their wooden houses, dropping their tools on the ground and leaving their chores unfinished. Nobody wanted to risk being left outside on their own while the colossal wolf roamed their fields.

They stopped after a few hours of travelling as the pale light of the Remaran day faded and made camp for the night so that the Ulkar could go hunting undisturbed. Lok gathered twigs and branches for his campfire and placed them neatly in a stack over a hole he had dug in the ground. He tried to start the fire by spinning a stick between his hands and drilling down onto the other piece of wood to create friction. After rubbing two sticks together for the better part of an hour, he had barely made smoke appear. Never in his life had fire disobeyed him. He felt humiliated and angry. Eventually, he gave up and laid on his back and gazed at the stars peeking behind the passing clouds, wondering how he ended up in that situation. If it weren't for Alamor, he would have never entered the Iron Wood, and he would have never lost his powers. He swore he would take his revenge on the Veheer. First, however, he had to find Jason. Hopefully, the woman in Orachlion would be able to help.

That night Lok didn't sleep. Thoughts were rushing through his mind, and the frustration kept him awake. Occasionally, he would hear loud grunts and growls in the distance, followed by the wail of a sheep or a goat. Howls broke the silence of the night, soaring upwards in the air as they reached their highest note and slowly died off. For one thing, Lok was both shocked and amazed at his success at taming the Ulkar and thought of how proud the Emperor would be of him—if only he hadn't lost his powers.

The following morning, Lok and the Ulkar left at the break of dawn, eager to begin the journey to Orachlion.

One hour passed, and a second hour went by until they came to a stone bridge passing over a broad and fast running river. Lok thought he had been on that bridge before on his way to Lake Malion, and it was with a grunt that he suddenly realised that they had gone the wrong way. He had been following the Eastern Road, while the road to Orachlion from the

Iron Wood was the Scarlet Way, due north. If he was correct, that bridge wasn't too far from a town called Karisa, so Lok decided to keep travelling until they got there to rest and get food. They would then start their journey again the next day going in the correct direction.

Lok led the Ulkar to the edge of the bridge, but the Ulkar didn't budge. "What's wrong, beastie?" A snarl came from between the beast's teeth. "The bridge is large enough; it won't collapse. Come on, move it." But the Ulkar didn't move. "All right, let's try wading the river then." Lok led it to the riverbank, but when they were closer to the water, the wolf tensed its front legs and dug its claws into the ground. "What now? Do you not like water?"

The wolf grumbled.

"We have to cross the river somehow. There's a town not far from here where we can get some food. Hopefully, they'll know something about this *Jason*. Come on, get in the water." The Ulkar turned its head to the side and looked back at Lok with one red eye. "You might have eaten, beastie, but I haven't. You're big; the water will do you no harm."

The wolf tentatively advanced towards the water, but as soon as its first paw got wet, it whimpered and stopped again.

"It's just water! We need to get across, beastie!"

The Ulkar tentatively put its paw in the water again, and then a second paw, until all its four legs were in the river. As it waded along the flowing water, which barely seemed to budge the wolf, it looked like an enormous boulder rolling across the river. Its paws ploughed deep in the riverbed, regardless of the large rocks scattered among it. Eventually, the wolf reached the other end.

"Well, that wasn't that bad, was it?"

As a response, the Ulkar shook the water off its rough fur, sending his rider flying on the ground.

"You're not making this easy, my friend," Lok groaned, lying with his back in the dirt.

VII

A NEW HOPE

With a blast, the Red Camp was engulfed by light. When the white blaze disappeared, Jason found that Tortugal had backed up a couple of feet, and stood dazed as he looked into empty space, his eyes open wide like an owl's.

"You bastard! My eyes!" he barked as he rubbed them vigorously.

All around him soldiers were stumbling about the camp like zombies, blinded.

Jason got up and moved back, safe from the general's sharp longsword. His right leg felt weak as he stood, and he looked down at the damage Tortugal had inflicted him. Blood was trickling down his calf and was dripping on the yellow dirt. The wound felt as if a scorching knife was being pressed on his bare flesh, but it could have been worse given who he had just faced. At least he was still alive.

Jason looked around to see if Alamor was all right, but he found that the old Veheer wasn't tied to the wooden plank anymore. The iron manacles were lying on the floor, molten.

He felt a tap on his shoulder and jolted, his adrenaline rushing to his head. It was Alamor, brandishing his sword. He had gotten rid of the manacles as if they were butter and had retrieved his sword. His eyebrows were raised, and he had the widest grin on his face. The emerald leaf shined in the dim orange twilight of the night.

"Was that you?" Jason asked.

"Nay, son… that was you," he revealed. "You have the Flare. I knew it!" he exclaimed.

Jason looked at the wrinkled face of the Veheer with confusion and excitement. His hands were sweaty and shaking, both for the fight and for the surreal incident that had just happened.

"You mean I'm a…"

"You're a Lightbringer, son," he declared. He looked down at the wound on his calf. "That doesn't look too good. Don't worry; you'll heal fast. Now quick, we've got to move before they gain their sight again!"

"Don't I need a bandage or something?"

"Not really—those are the perks of having the Flare! It'll heal in a matter of minutes."

Jason limped as he tried to follow Alamor into the depths of the Red Camp. Soldiers were meandering between the large military tents, their arms raised forward to attempt finding their way around the camp. Alamor walked in front of Jason, with his sword raised. The runes engraved on Isidir's blade shimmered in the darkness.

"How did I get these powers?" Jason asked, still perplexed by what had happened.

"We must not worry about that now! For the moment, we need to go," Alamor said.

"Wait," Jason said. "We need to find Anyir."

"Who's that?"

"The healer. She gave me water earlier. She asked me to help her escape," Jason explained.

"We have no time to save everyone who gives you a drink," Alamor retorted. "We need to leave—now."

Jason found himself stuck, unable to decide. It didn't feel right to leave without Anyir after promising to help her get out of Red Camp. All she wanted was to go back home and be reunited with her husband, and if Jason couldn't have that, then he would help Anyir get it instead. He knew how she must have felt. "I promised I'd help her."

"Why would you do that?" Alamor complained.

"She only wants to get back home…" Jason responded.

Alamor stared at Jason comprehensively. He nodded, and reluctantly said, "All right. Where is she?"

"I have no idea…" Jason admitted.

The old man passed by one of the blinded soldiers, pulled the Remaran sword out of his belt and handed it to Jason. "Use this one, for now, son. I think you can handle it after the show you put on back there. Don't worry— we'll find the girl."

They ran through the camp, jumping over and under the tense cables that supported the tents, but the soldiers began regaining their vision. Some of the stronger warriors were already staggering towards them, brandishing their swords.

"What's the girl's name, again?" Alamor asked.

"Anyir."

Fear assailed Jason as Alamor began to shout the woman's name. "Hey! Anyir!" the Veheer called. "Anyir!"

"What are you doing?!" muttered Jason, panicked. "They'll hear where we are!"

"If you don't know where she is, there's one way we can find it out for sure. Anyir!" he shouted again.

As Alamor predicted, a nearby soldier yelled, "They're looking for the healer! Go to the infirmary!"

Alamor turned around and looked at Jason with a proud smirk. "Told you."

They followed the soldiers to the infirmary, where two guards were waiting for them, their hands wrapped tightly around a pair of axes. Anyir was on her knees, her wrists tied one to the other with iron shackles. She looked at Jason with hope in her eyes.

"You came," she said.

Alamor swung his sword at the guards, knocking both axes out of their hands with a single blow. He grabbed the head of one of the two Remaran soldiers and pulled it fiercely towards his knee, breaking his nose. The other soldier tried to strike the old man in the jaw, but Alamor instinctively grabbed his hand and used his momentum to propel him out of the tent. Jason was amazed by the strength and ability of the old man.

"Come with us, Anyir," Alamor said. "We'll get you out of this hellish place." With a slash of his Elven sword, the manacles around her wrists crumbled like biscuits. Anyir wrapped her arm around Jason's neck, and together they walked outside the infirmary.

In the darkness, surrounded by the intimidating Remaran banners, a wall of men in black armour was waiting for them. Alamor walked in front of Jason and Anyir, and calmly adjusted his guard position, holding his shiny longsword with both hands.

Tortugal emerged from the crowd, standing at least two feet taller than his soldiers. The black blade of Rhazien was like a shadow in the night, and only the dim lanterns made it visible.

"So, what are you… Sorcerers?" he questioned, looking down at Jason. Whispers and mutters arose from the soldiers.

The two Omüms joined Tortugal's side. The lanterns' lights set a low-lying shadow on their terrifying faces, causing their maniacal grins to look even more disturbing. Modùn elbowed his way through the soldiers so he could gain a spot in the first row as well.

"Nay, general. We are Lightbringers," said Alamor, proudly.

The face of the soldiers dropped. Tortugal and Modùn were speechless for a moment. "How is this possible, general? Lightbringers have been gone for centuries…" asked Modùn. "Wasn't Lok supposed to be the last one with the Flare?"

"Evidently they have returned, lieutenant," Tortugal uttered, incredulous.

Tortugal grunted and swung Rhazien above his head, but his attack was cut short. Alamor waved his hands, and fire drawn from the lanterns hanging all over the camp came spiralling in the air, merging into one huge flaming tornado. With a roar, the swirling stream of fire struck Tortugal and his warriors. They all plummeted to the ground and desperately rolled in the dirt, trying to smother the flames that had enveloped them.

The other soldiers attacked at once, but from afar Jason heard the rhythmical sound of hooves beating the ground. Like a beacon of brightness, a white mare appeared from behind the dusty haze that lingered in the air.

"Silvyr!" Jason cheered. Perfect timing.

Alamor grabbed the saddle and jumped swiftly up onto the horse's back. "Quick, get on!" he said, extending his arms towards Anyir, who wobbled towards the horse and let the Veheer drag her up. She wrapped her arms around the Veheer's waist. Alamor extended his arm out towards Jason as well, but he was frozen.

Witnessing the power of Alamor's magic was incomprehensible, and Jason watched as the army advanced towards them. The rumble of the soldiers charging in their direction was overwhelming, and the sight of armoured men wielding their weapons was utterly horrifying. Suddenly, a massive wall of rocks emerged from the ground in front of Jason, separating them from the soldiers. Alamor had his back.

The photographer finally snapped out of his trance and grabbed Alamor's hand, jumping behind Anyir on Silvyr's saddle. Before the armoured men could climb the wall of rocks or get on their horses, the three companions galloped out of Red Camp.

As they left the sea of scarlet tents behind, they heard the rumble of soldiers shouting grow quieter and quieter until even the Camp's lights became dimmer. They found themselves riding in the darkness of the desolate Stonevale.

Jason expected an army to appear behind them amidst the darkness, but nothing appeared. The soldiers of Red Camp seemed to have given up. "Why aren't they following us?" he asked, puzzled.

"I cut the reins of their horses and set them free while they were all busy watching you fight that Orc. I also managed to destroy all their Jauls, so they won't be able to communicate with the Emperor. You did a good job distracting them, I've got to say!" Alamor giggled. Jason didn't know what a Jaul was, but he was glad Alamor had stopped the soldiers from following them.

"Thank you," Jason replied as he tried to balance himself on the back of the saddle. He thought back at the duel with Tortugal, still baffled by the fact he survived. Then Jason thought more closely about what Alamor had just said. "Did you just say he was an Orc?" he asked worriedly.

"Indeed, they are allies of the Humans," Alamor replied, leaving Jason disconcerted. "Pretty nasty creatures."

"Nasty? You wouldn't just call them nasty if you had lived with them…" Anyir interjected. "Thank you for getting me out of there."

"It's our pleasure," Alamor responded. Jason smiled, glad to have been able to help someone.

For the next two days, they rode along the lifeless plain of the Stonevale. Often, the wind would blow fiercely, sending fine particles at the travellers' uncovered faces. For hours they would not see another human being, or indeed any live being at all.

The Stonevale was a monotonous, unforgiving place, where dusty patches alternated with hard volcanic rock, making it difficult for Silvyr to tread along. Most of the time, they had to walk along the rough terrain to avoid injuring the white mare, though stepping on the jagged rocks was painful.

"Alamor, does your sword have a name?" Jason asked as they strolled along the big lumps of hard rock. Anyir was walking ahead, leading Silvyr by the reins and enjoying her freedom.

"Isidir—it means 'hope'. It's an exceptional sword. It was forged by the ancient Elves of Dorth using an alloy derived from the depths of the Lumos mountains. It will never lose its edge and never break. There is nothing quite like this sword anymore. Only very few Elven swords are left now—one is Isidir," he said, tapping on the hilt of the sword hanging from his side. "One is *Zarak*—Darkstrom's two-handed sword; another is *Dolear*—the longsword of king Kavanagh, passed down to him by king Arganthal and king Rennhall before him. All the others have either been lost to the ages or during the war against Darkstrom."

"How long have you been fighting this Emperor guy?"

"Well, there was peace in Valkadia before the Humans arrived from the Otherside. The problems began when Erik the Red, around a thousand years ago, entered Valkadia thanks to the help of an Elf called Hod—"

"Wait, did you say Erik the Red? You mean the great Viking explorer?" Jason remembered his school history teacher telling his class all about Erik Thorvaldsson, a Norse trailblazer who founded the first settlement in Greenland. The nickname 'the Red' was due to the colour of his hair and beard.

"*Great explorer?* Is that what you call him in the Otherside?" asked Alamor.

"Well, we know him for exploring Iceland and Greenland, certainly not for discovering Valkadia."

"Humans forget so easily..."

"I can't argue with that—we do tend to have a very short-term memory, especially nowadays with TV and all that."

"What's a... *teevee?*"

Jason realised Alamor would have never heard of anything like a TV, or any other technology from the ordinary world. "I forgot you might not have them here. TV is short for television. It's like a box that people keep at home to watch shows, kind of like a small theatre," Jason tried to explain. "We definitely watch it too much, but we just can't stop. The shows get better and better every year."

"So, it's like a puppet show that people keep in their houses?"

"I guess you could say that, yes, except that the puppets are real people and appear in everyone's TVs by broadcasting the show."

"*Broadcasting?*"

"Sharing it with electronic signals."

"*Elec... tronic?*"

Jason was beginning to get frustrated. He never thought explaining what a television was could be this hard. "Yes, electronic... electricity—it's like an energy, the same energy that lightning bolts are made of. We use it to power our machines."

"So—you use lightning to power your show-boxes so you can watch them inside your house? Isn't there a better way of spending time?"

"What can I say, we love it."

"Humans are odd..."

"Indeed, we are. Tell me more about Erik the Red," insisted Jason.

"All right, where was I... Oh, yes. Erik the Red and his party forced Hod to let them enter Valkadia through the Elder Stones—the same stones you came in from—and once they were in, chaos began. The Human ancestors started raiding Valkadia, and King Rennhall, one of our most formidable Elven rulers, decided to send an army against the new enemies. However, Erik brought back more troops from the Otherside. Tired of losing lives, King Rennhall decided to grant the Humans a portion of land in the East and created the kingdom of Remara."

"I really wish they taught us this in school," commented Jason, marvelled by the fact that the ancient Vikings had discovered Valkadia, yet distraught by the fact they had also started a war against its inhabitants. "What happened next?" Jason asked, eager to learn more.

"When king Rennhall gave Remara to the Humans, he made Erik swear an oath: if Humans hurt even one more Valkadian, then they would have to pack their bags and leave our land, and the Elder Stones would be closed forever using the Steinndyrr—the key which controls the passage between worlds."

"I guess they didn't respect the oath." Jason had watched enough Game of Thrones to know how often agreements between rulers were broken.

"No, they didn't. Though there was peace for a long time, a new king called Aeinar Trogar decided that Remara wasn't enough for Humans. Humans took to raiding once more, and king Rennhall used the Steinndyrr to close the portal. Chaos ensued, ending with the total obliteration of the

Elven kind and the destruction of Dorth. With the Elder Stones closed, the Humans' connection to their colonies in the Otherside was blocked. Humans grew weak, and for a while, there was peace again."

From his history classes, Jason recalled that at one point the Norse settlements in Greenland had succumbed to illness, malnutrition, and warfare. There was a lot of speculation about the specific reason why the Vikings perished in Greenland, but Jason thought he had the answer now. He could have never imagined that the truth would be anything quite like what Alamor had just told him. Was there more to ancient historical figures that humanity didn't know of? Was there more to Earth that humans didn't know about? Valkadia was probably the place from where all the myths and legends of monsters, dragons, fairies and elves originated. What if there were actually dragons there? "Back home, we learn that the Vikings couldn't survive the harsh climate of the new territories they conquered. I had no idea this would have been the true end to their colonies," Jason told Alamor.

"That's fascinating. Do you have no record of Valkadia? Are there no stories sung by the bards?" Alamor enquired.

Jason laughed, thinking of a medieval bard singing folk songs about elves and orcs in the middle of a trendy pub in London. "Not at all," he replied. As he tried to piece all the information together, Jason wanted to know more about someone that gave him the chills. "What about Darkstrom?"

"Darkstrom…" Alamor sighed. Speaking about the Emperor clearly disturbed the old Veheer. "The son of Jahrto Maddock… where to start…" He paused to think. "He was troubled since the beginning and displayed special abilities from a very young age—abilities to control various elements; to take and manipulate people's souls. His mind has always been tortured and dark.

"He believed—and still believes—that the Elder Stones should be opened, and that Humans should be freed. He wants to bring Humans from the Otherside to Valkadia to help him conquer Erythya. He is so focused on achieving his goal that he even killed his own father so that he could become the ruler of Remara," Alamor told, distraught. "Darkstrom's power is fuelled by the souls of his citizens, which he absorbs and uses to become ever stronger. By forfeiting their soul to him, thousands upon thousands of people in Valkadia are subjugated by his spell, and he can transform them into invincible beasts, the ones we call *Fímegir*. With the right command, these soulless soldiers can be ordered to transform and attack."

Jason's skin crawled. He listened carefully, entranced by Alamor's storytelling. Darkstrom's name gave him goosebumps, and he really hoped they would never have to meet. He was glad they had escaped the grasp of Tortugal and his goons and that they were now on their way out of Remara. "What stops Darkstrom from invading Erythya?" he asked, worried that a war would suddenly erupt, and he would find himself in the middle of a battlefield between two formidable armies.

"The magic of the Enchanted Realm has held up against Darkstrom and his army for a long time. Mostly, Erythya has been protected for thousands of years by the Order of the Lightbringers, a timeless group of warriors that could conjure light, sworn to protect the innocent from the dark powers of evil sorcerers who threatened the balance of Valkadia. I was part of the Order when Darkstrom rose to power. My fellow Lightbringers and I, led by Elgan Lannvard, forged a dagger of insurmountable power known as the Eluir to destroy the Emperor. Alas, I was the only Lightbringer to survive. After Darkstrom took the Eluir, he hid it in a place that only he knows, and no one has ever been able to find it since."

Jason looked at Alamor's scarred hand and wondered if he got it while fighting as a Lightbringer. He was fretful about his newfound abilities, and reluctant to end up with a huge burn-scar on his body. If he was a Lightbringer now, did that mean he had to face Darkstrom? He really didn't want that to be his fate. Before he could ask anything else, Alamor said, "You are a Lightbringer too now, Jason. You could help us defeat Darkstrom."

A sudden sense of panic assailed Jason. The young Londoner turned abruptly and looked at the old Veheer in his severe but gentle wrinkled eyes. "Me? Defeat Darkstrom? I don't know the first thing about fighting Emperors. How am *I* supposed to defeat him?" Jason babbled.

"Erythya has long needed a new Lightbringer. I'm too old now, and my powers are not as strong as they used to be. Darkstrom would have never expected you to arrive in the picture. We could really catch him by surprise."

"But... I'm not a knight—a warrior—a Lightbringer—whatever you want me to be..." Jason replied. His jaws clenched involuntarily. He grabbed the sword Alamor had stolen for him from a soldier at Red Camp, which was now hanging off his belt, and shook it angrily. "What am I even doing with a sword?!" he barked.

"Jason, you *are* a Lightbringer," said Alamor. "We'll head to Malion, and we'll find all the answers you seek. I will train you on our way there. I'll teach you everything you need to know about controlling your Flare."

"You've made a mistake... I- I'm just a photographer," Jason muttered.

"A what?"

"A photographer!" Jason cried. "I'm only a common photographer from London! How do you expect me to defeat what sounds like the deadliest, craziest and most terrifying person basically ever?!"

"Jason, I know it's a lot to take in—"

"A lot to take in?!" he exploded. "I just want to go back! I've left everything in the '*Otherside*', and Clara is dead! I haven't even had time to mourn her death properly because I've been stuck in this weird world that doesn't make any sense!" Jason stopped and looked at the grey expanse of never-ending rock. "I let her die, and now I'm stuck here..." Tears built up in his eyes, and his stomach dropped. Jason didn't have the energy to cry, but he also didn't have the energy to keep walking. He sat down and buried his head beneath his arms.

Alamor sat down next to him. "Jason," he said softly. "The truth is... You will not be able to go back home through an Elder Stone without attracting the Emperor's attention. He seeks to open the portals to the Otherside too. You must defeat him before you try going back."

Jason looked at Alamor with desperation. "What do you mean I can't go back home?" he asked as he felt a surge of anxiety inside his chest.

"You can, Jason. But we must use the Steinndyrr to open an Elder Stone first, and there is no chance we can do that with Darkstrom still around. It would be far too dangerous for everyone."

"I can't do it, Alamor," Jason said, his voice muffled by his arms covering his face. "How can I do it? I'm not from here; I'm not used to this."

"If you trust me, I'll teach you."

"And why would I trust you? I don't even know you." Jason kicked a pebble, which went flying in the distance. Alamor remained silent, watching him sternly. "Let me get this straight. You are one of the greatest Lightbringers ever, right? And you want me, a newbie, to defeat Darkstrom when not even you and your friends managed?"

"We were betrayed. This time it'll be different."

"And why is that? There is no chance I can do this on my own."

"You' won't do it on your own. You have me, and we'll need assistance, of course. You'll need your own companions." Alamor looked at Jason intensely, his golden eyes shimmering. "We need you, Jason. Valkadia needs you. If you don't defeat Darkstrom, you'll never be able to go back to the Otherside. While he is still around, we cannot open the Elder Stones to let you out," the Veheer reiterated.

Jason stood up and stared at Alamor. He was shaking, his pulse echoing in his ears, blocking all the other sounds. Nothing felt real anymore. He turned around and began walking aimlessly, thought spinning in his mind like a Merry-Go-Round. He was angry; he was scared. He was worried he'd die in this world and never see his family again. He was frustrated at the world for tasking him with such a feat and wished the road back home would be easier.

"Don't you dare turn your back on me, boy!" Alamor cried.

Jason knew that following the Veheer was his only way back, but he still found the whole thing unfair. He hadn't asked for any of this, and Alamor reprimanding him was not what he needed. "Why? Why should I follow you? What have you done for me?!"

"For one thing, I've kept you alive and safe!"

The new Lightbringer stopped and turned around to look at his white-haired mentor. It was true—without Alamor, he would have probably died in the Iron Wood. However, Alamor had also let Jason fight that colossal beast without knowing about his powers. The boy found himself snapping, though he knew he wasn't being reasonable. "And how did that go? I almost died back there! How could you let me fight that monster?"

"Jason, you must stick with me. It's a matter of time before Darkstrom himself comes to know about you. If you let me train you, you stand a chance in surviving. You will be a hero, Jason—how many people get this chance?"

"I don't want to be a hero. I just want my life back."

"You will get it back if we do things right."

"It sounds like an impossible feat…"

"Nothing's impossible until it's done, son."

✹

VIII

BLACKSMITH

Karisa looked deserted and lifeless. Lok and the Ulkar rode along the main road that divided the town in two, with wooden houses tightly packed on either side. Here were forged many of the weapons for the Remaran army, as proven by the many blacksmith shops. Karisa had its own blacksmith guild, even though it was a very small town. The windows' shutters on each house were closed, and no shop, bakery or blacksmith had its doors open. Carts with heaps of hay had been left outside, the pitchforks still lying beside them. It seemed as if nobody was there, but Lok knew there *were* people. Columns of smoke rose from the chimneys of many houses.

I forgot how filthy this little place was, he thought. "Is anybody here?" Lok yelled.

Nobody answered.

Lok kept leading the Ulkar along the road, beaten by horses and wagons earlier in the day. He felt like he was being watched. They stopped in a square at the centre of the town, where a large wooden building decorated with sculptures and a long set of stairs dominated. It was a temple for the goddess Freya. From its multiple layered roofs sprouted the heads of dragons, meticulously carved by skilled ancient craftsmen.

Lok dismounted, and the Ulkar laid down to rest. The wolf's front legs curled comfortably under its body, and its head rested on the gravel-covered ground. The gigantic wolf watched as Lok walked around the square, moving quickly from one side to the other and carefully observing each store. The town was quiet; nobody dared to let out even a cough. An eerie sense of solitude prevailed.

Suddenly, a door creaked, startling the Ulkar. A tall, muscular man with long and fair hair, appeared from one of the shops. The wolf's baritone growl rumbled.

"Halt there, peasant!" Lok ordered.

There was no need to ask because the man stood stock-still under the porch of the store, petrified at the sight of the man in armour and his immense, fierce companion. Lok marched towards him, his muscular build imposing over the town dweller.

"Please, do not harm us, ser. We will provide you with anything you request," the man said anxiously.

Lok looked down at the man, his grimy fair hair covered a rough and bronzed face. He wore ragged clothes, full of holes, smeared with dirt from working in the fields. Beneath them, a pair of sturdy arms and broad shoulders.

"Food… and beer," Lok ordered resolutely, his face impassable.

"Certainly, m'lord. Please, do follow me in," the man said.

Lok was hesitant at first, walking in the shop of ordinary men. Above the entrance door, a sign read: 'The Hammer and Anvil'. A metal fire pit sat in the middle of the beer house, and long tables with wobbly wooden stools were spread around it unevenly. A couple of lonesome drinkers kept their heads down as Lok walked by. At the far end of the beerhouse was a counter where large barrels of beer were stored. Behind it stood a short old man, unsure of what to do or where to go. The smell of beer was strong and sweet, and it stuck to the walls together with the odour of meat and sausages. The burly man walked briskly to the counter. "Fitsuk, please serve this man your largest horn of beer and ask Erika to prepare a bowl of her finest fish soup."

Lok grabbed a stool and pulled it towards him from under a table, dragging along the wooden floors, and sat down heavily. The older man picked up a large bovid's horn and held it under the tap of a barrel, filling it with liquid the colour of golden amber.

The burly man grabbed the horn and offered it to Lok.

"What's your name?" Lok asked as he took the drink. The sweet smell of honey combined with the bready flavour of the yeast rose like a plume. A burning yet relieving sensation struck him as he took a large gulp.

"Gregor Svenn, son of Bron. I'm the chief of Karisa, ser. It's a pleasure to make your acquaintance, ser…"

"Lok," he answered, trying to cut the conversation short.

"Lok?" Gregor gasped. "Ser Lok of the Eiriksberg?"

Lok nodded and drank the whole horn in one gulp.

"Ser, it's a pleasure to meet you. Please allow me to get you some more." Lok nodded. Gregor's hands shook as he refilled Lok's drinking horn. "Are you here on behalf of the Emperor?"

Lok didn't answer.

"Forgive me, that was a stupid question," Gregor apologised, flustered. "You might have seen my parents, ser? Brun and Marcelle? They were taken to the Eiriksberg about a month ago."

Lok ignored the question. "I'm looking for a man that goes by the name of Jason. Have you seen him or heard of this person?"

"No, ser," Gregor answered. "That is a very unusual name, but if I ever come across him, I will be sure to remember and let you know. Why do you ask?"

"He took something from me," Lok stated.

"Here is your soup, ser," announced an old woman—Erika—as she carried the hot bowl of fish soup with skinny arms like twigs. She hobbled towards the Lok's table, but one foot caught the other, and she fell face first. The bowl of soup went flying in the air, and yet it did not drop. Lok looked stupefied as the bowl hovered mid-air, then he looked at Gregor. His arms were extended forward, his hands open, his eyes glued to the fish soup. Steadily he lowered the bowl and landed it on the table. He was a Sorcerer.

"I'm really sorry about this, ser," Fitsuk said as he helped Erika up. She was weeping, covering her face in shame. She looked down and limped to the back of the beer house.

Lok remained silent for a moment and looked into the bowl, where a fish's head bobbed in the yellowish broth, its gelatinous eye staring back at the warrior.

"A spoon, please."

"Certainly, m'lord," Fitsuk responded, who rapidly began rummaging through the cutlery behind the counter.

"No," erupted Lok. "Her," he said, pointing to the old lady.

"But ser, she's —" Fitsuk tried to counter, but was readily interrupted by his town's chief.

"Fitsuk, do what ser Lok says," Gregor suggested.

The old man helped Erika stand up and handed her a spoon to give to Lok.

"I didn't say you could help her," Lok admonished.

Fitsuk let go of the woman, who staggered once more towards their guest. She dragged along her left leg, which she had hit in the fall, but eventually made it to the table. "Here, *ser*," she said with a tight grin and irreverently dropped the spoon on the table. The metal clinked as it bounced on the wood.

At the sight of her small attempt of rebellion, Lok grabbed her hand and pulled her towards him. He looked at her wrinkled face, skin thin like paper, eyes vapid as if her soul was gone before it was time. "I will *not* be disrespected," he said, addressing everyone present in the beer house but keeping eye contact with the elderly woman. Consider that a warning for everyone in this town." He let go of the elderly woman and watched as she limped back to the far end of the room.

"Ser," Gregor interjected. He cleared his throat. "I hope you enjoy your soup. Is there anything else we can do for you?"

"You make good swords here, don't you?" Lok asked.

"Some of the best in Remara," Gregor replied.

"Who's your best blacksmith?"

"Uh, that would be Oblivan Sköld, ser."

"Bring him here," Lok ordered.

Without waiting any further, Gregor walked out of the beer house. Lok slurped a spoonful of soup. The pungent smell of fish was masked by the taste of white wine and cloves. Lok had another spoonful. After five minutes or so, Gregor entered the room again accompanied by another man. This one was almost as tall as Lok and did not look like a blacksmith at all. He was much thinner than Gregor, not at all muscular. He wore baggy, dull clothes, and a leather apron stained with black coal. He kept his hands clasped behind his back.

"Good day, ser. My name is Oblivan Sköld, son of Vidar. I heard you are looking to purchase a longsword?"

"Not *purchase*, though I'm looking for one—yes," Lok corrected.

Oblivan paused and looked at Gregor, who nodded anxiously. "Of course, ser. Anything for you, m'lord. And what were you looking for in this sword?"

"Three feet long. Light, resistant, deadly. Big enough to chop a king's head off." Silence reigned in the beerhouse. "I don't suppose you have any Elven swords lying around, do you?"

Oblivan chuckled in astonishment. "Elven swords? I don't actually think I have ever seen one in my life, ser."

"It's just something from the legends..." Gregor added tentatively.

"I can't offer you an Elven sword, m'lord, but I *can* offer you an iron sword that meets your other requirements if you are interested." Lok was not pleased about Oblivan's response, but now that his thirst and hunger had been satisfied, he desperately needed a sword and didn't want to cause any trouble that would attract attention to him. "Please, follow me, m'lord."

Lok followed Oblivan and Gregor out of the beerhouse and walked along the main road of the town. Nobody had ventured out of their houses yet, although Lok could feel the eyes of strangers observing him from behind the safety of windows and doors. He looked back to the square in the middle of the town where the Ulkar was resting. As it slept, its ribcage expanded and contracted, and every time the beast exhaled a small puff of dust rose from the ground in front of its snout. Lok kept walking.

Though the Gothis had taught him all about the dwellings of peasants, he had never been among them. He had always lived in the confines of the Eiriksberg and only ventured outside the walls of the castle to raid and pillage Erythian villages, only for war. Living with soldiers as a nobleman and a respected warrior was a lot different than travelling alone. Now, he had been dunked into a new reality—a much darker, colder and more miserable existence. The walls of most houses were covered in moss, the windows cracked or smashed, rusty metal signs hung off the side of shops and broken wagon wheels lying on the ground everywhere.

Eventually, Oblivan and Gregor stopped in front of one of the few stone houses. Its thick metal doors were open, and Lok could feel a gush of heat emerging from inside where orange light glowed. "After you, m'lord," Oblivan announced.

Lok walked in and was immediately hit with the scorching warmth of the furnace made with large stone bricks. The fire was alive, a mixture of white, red and orange coal sweltering underneath. In front of it, a large sledgehammer leaned against an iron anvil and next to it, a turning wheel. Lined against the wall to the right were multiple working tables, filled with moulds for making everyday items such as nails, hammers, tongs and other tools that Lok didn't know. To the left, a rack full of swords and parts of Remaran armour shined in the light of the furnace. Shields and lances hung from the walls. Oblivan walked to a door right beside the entrance and disappeared for a minute. When he re-emerged, he was holding a three-foot-long bundle wrapped in rags.

"Here it is, m'lord." As Oblivan offered him the bundle, Lok realised all the fingers from his left hand were missing.

"Your hand," Lok grunted.

"Ah, it's a long story. Not worth wasting your time, m'lord," the blacksmith replied. He tapped his stubby hand on the bundle. "This sword was one the best I have ever forged myself. I have kept it all these years for an occasion such as this. It's called *Viggr*. It will never lose its edge. It's the closest thing you'll ever get to an Elven sword in the real world."

"I assure you Oblivan is the best blacksmith in town, ser," Gregor intervened.

Lok peeled apart the various layers of cloth and revealed a polished steel blade. Lok inspected the sword, running his fingers gently along the runes engraves in the blade's fuller. The grip was made of black iron, with grooves spiralling down to help to hold it tightly. The shiny cross guard spread out like a leaf, ornated with intersecting knotted patterns. The pommel was round and decorated with more knotwork. Lok grabbed the sword by the hilt and let the rags drop on the stone floor. Viggr was light, and the weapon's balance was impeccable, better than his previous sword forged by the blacksmiths of the Eiriksberg.

There was a long break. Oblivan felt his heart sink in his stomach as Lok inspected the sword. "What do you think?" he asked.

Lok didn't make eye contact. "It'll do."

"I'm glad you like it, m'lord," Oblivan sighed in relief.

Lok couldn't stop thinking about Oblivan's mutilated hand. He was aware that missing fingers from the left hand were a Remaran army punishment for Erythian sympathisers. "So…" Lok's eyes met Oblivan's, then wandered to the furnace. "You sold your weapons to the Erythians, didn't you?"

IX

WHEN THE WIND BLOWS

After a couple more days of riding swiftly from the Red Camp's soldiers, only taking breaks when necessary, Jason, Alamor and Anyir took shelter in an old enclave surrounded by large boulders. It was an ancient settlement of the early inhabitants of Valkadia, Alamor explained, and possibly later used by Giants to practice their ritualistic religion.

The sharp rocks of the Stonevale had cut the soles of Anyir's bare feet, and she had been forced to ride Silvyr for most of the way. Jason helped Anyir lay on the ground with her back against a large rock. She was tired from the journey and exhausted by the enslavement at the Red Camp.

Alamor's stew was boiling in a pot over the campfire, the smoke rising in the cold air of that murky evening.

"Anyir, I'll get you some buckleberry oil to treat your wounds," Alamor said.

She groaned as she got more comfortable against the rock. The long, deep cuts were badly infected from the black dirt of the Stonevale, and the irritated skin around the wounds was sore and purple.

"How do they look?" Anyir asked as her jaw clenched. "It really burns."

"Not going to lie—it's pretty bad," Jason responded.

"Amazing, thanks… Ever heard of a white lie?" she grunted.

"Well, you'd rather know the truth, right? Otherwise, you'll keep wondering when they'll heal," Jason retorted.

"He does have a point, I'm afraid," Alamor commented as he came over with a bowl full of sweet-smelling ointment. Jason realised it was the same mixture the Veheer had used to treat the cut on his cheek days earlier. "Let's have a look at how bad this actually is." Alamor refrained from commenting on the state of Anyir's feet. "We need to disinfect them first. Give me some alcohol or something from the Bag of Plenty."

Jason ran over to Silvyr, who had the Bag strapped onto the saddle. He put his hand in, and after a few seconds, a glass bottle full of mead approached him. No surprises this time. Jason ran and handed the bottle to Alamor, who poured the alcohol onto Anyir's feet. She screamed as she arched her back. Her teeth tightened, and she squeezed her eyes shut as the alcohol burnt through her wounds. "Stay still, my dear, or you'll get them dirty again!" Quickly, Alamor washed his hands with the alcohol and rubbed the ointment on her cuts, ensuring he covered them all. Alamor wrapped her feet with clean bandages, soaked in buckleberry oil. Anyir felt a sudden sensation of numbness, followed by an overwhelming feeling of coolness. She couldn't feel her wounds anymore.

"How did you do that?" Anyir asked.

"Neat, huh?" Alamor replied.

"In all my years as a healer I never heard of buckleberry oil..." she observed.

"The perks of old Veheer medicine," Alamor replied. "Now, please keep in mind that you are not yet healed. It'll take about a week before you can walk properly again."

"One week? Are you serious?"

"Can't heal any faster, I'm afraid—unless you're a Lightbringer."

"Are you kidding? That's incredible!" she replied. "It would take me a lot longer to heal something like this with the medicines available to us in Remara!" Her turquoise eyes were glowing with life. Her voice sounded energetic and cheerful. "By the way, I really owe you for saving me. I couldn't spend another day in that horrible place."

"Don't mention it, my dear," the old Veheer replied. His pointed ears relaxed as he smiled endearingly at Anyir. "Say, where are you from?"

"I was born and raised in a town called Karisa. It's actually not that far from here—about another day's worth of walking towards the Suraan hills."

"Sure, I know Karisa," Alamor said. "It has the best blacksmith guild of Remara, surrounded by the rivers Tot and Fahal. How did you end up in that cursed camp?"

"Nothing goes unseen here in Remara. See, my husband was a blacksmith, and he had a particular distaste for the Empire. He had grown up in Remara in a family of blacksmiths, but he felt it was wrong to contribute to the war against Erythya. So, he decided to forge weapons and armour for the Enchanted Kingdom secretly and smuggle them over Elora's Trench. Of course, he knew the consequences of what he was doing, but neither of us thought anyone would ever find out. We forgot how vicious and pervasive the Remaran spies are.

"One evening, my husband left Karisa to meet a buyer, but he came home feeling very worried and paranoid. Someone must have seen him leaving our village at night and got suspicious. The next day Modùn and four other soldiers rushed into the village claiming they had heard that somebody was smuggling weapons to Erythya. They went door to door, asking everyone what they knew. They barged inside my husband's workshop, chained us up and separated us. That night they took me to the Red Camp, and I have been there ever since—until you came along."

Jason thought of how easy his life was back in London. Of course, his life wasn't ideal, but his below-average income, poor diet and a small apartment in one of the greatest economic hubs of the world suddenly didn't sound that bad. He wondered if all of Valkadia had remained stuck in a Viking-like era, or if what he had seen so far was only the tip of a far greater iceberg of magical innovation and societal constructs distant from his understanding of what is 'modern'. Then again, people still seemed to fight mainly with swords and armour, and slavery still existed as well as kings and emperors.

"How long were you there for?" Jason asked.

"Long enough," she replied.

"I'm so sorry, Anyir," Alamor murmured, shaking his head.

"I tried to escape a few times, but there would always be someone to find me and punish me…" Though she spoke with distraught voice, her face suddenly lit up. "I did get them back a few times, though! One time I put some 'special' herbs in the slob they ate, let's just say that I enjoyed watching them run into the forest holding their bellies." Jason laughed imagining Tortugal kneeling next to a tree as he cursed at the world.

"Admittedly, that was a pretty intense prank that I pulled on them, but they did punish me for more trivial things."

"Were you the only Human slave at the Camp? I didn't see any other slaves other than the Breegans," Alamor observed.

"There were other Humans until a month or two ago, but their services took the better of them—not many could deal with life at the Camp. It's mostly Breegans as usual now. The soldiers are a bunch of pigs," said Anyir, staring at the sky. She ran her fingers through her corvine hair. Her turquoise eyes were full of sorrow.

"Well said," Alamor replied. He took her hand and looked at her intensely. "That's all over now, my dear."

Anyir glanced at the old Veheer, then at Jason. "I can't believe I'm with two Lightbringers now."

"You sure are! Times are changing, Anyir. You can join us if you wish to," Alamor invited, smiling kindly.

"Thank you so much; I'd be honoured—although I would like to get back to my husband," she replied.

"That's understandable," the Veheer said. "However, I don't think it's a good idea for you to go back just yet. Darkstrom may have already sent someone to look for us after he found we were Lightbringers. You'll be safer with us. Come to Malion; we'll be safe in Erythya."

"I appreciate your invitation, Alamor—but I really do wish to go home as soon as I heal," she replied. Anyir looked down to the ground, her eyes slowly filling with tears. She looked at Jason, who was lost in his thoughts, reminiscing about home. He was thinking of his parents, Robert and Denise McAnnon, wondering when he'd see them again.

Suddenly, Alamor bounced up in excitement. "Get up, Jason! Let's give this lady a nice show!"

Jason snapped out of his memories and was thrust back into reality. "What do you mean?" Jason replied, confused.

Alamor danced around as he loosened his joints. "We've got a while until the stew is ready. Might as well kill some time by beginning your training early."

The photographer looked at the Veheer with furrowed brows. He wasn't ready to do anything that involved magic. He still struggled to believe any of it was true and that a legendary power was stored within him. "Really? Now?" Jason replied. "I'm... I'm really not sure—"

"Yes, now!" interjected Alamor, stretching his back and his arms. "Let's start with something easy. See that rock a few feet away?"

"Which one? There's a million of them," Jason said with the same tone as a grumpy teenager who had been asked to take the bins out.

"This one." Alamor raised his hand in front of himself and looked intensely at the rock he was referring to. He quickly lifted his finger a couple of times, and the stone began floating in the air, flying in circles around the enclave.

"How... how am *I* meant to do this? I didn't decide to use my powers back at the Camp. They sort of... came out," Jason said.

"Start by lifting a small pebble. Just raise your hands and direct them to the object you want to cast your magic upon. Then, concentrate on the core of the element you wish to summon and bend it to obey your will. A good Lightbringer must be able to imagine an end result and use the elements to achieve what they created in their mind. For this reason, a Lightbringer's mind must always be clear, particularly when controlling multiple elements at once, and especially when controlling light. Go ahead, focus on the rock, and summon the air to lift it."

Alamor then raised his hand, his palm facing upwards. When he closed his fist, the stones and boulders around them quivered, then lifted off the ground, leaving behind large dents where they had been resting for so long. Alamor extended his arms to the sky, and the rocks followed his motions. Chunks of stone floated in mid-air above the three companions and spun all around them with speed. Jason and Anyir covered their heads with their hands and ducked instinctively as boulders the size of horses brushed their hair. The two Humans gazed at the flying rocks in disbelief and awe, with their mouths gaping yet curved into an amused smile.

Alamor lowered his arms, and the boulders landed back onto the ground, back in their ancient spots. "Now you try, son!"

"I could never do that..."

"Why don't you give it a try?" Alamor insisted. "The Flare is inside you. Just concentrate on the rock, and your powers will come out on their own."

"All right..." Jason replied sceptically. He stood with his legs apart and his back straight. His eyes fixed onto the smallest out of a myriad of pebbles and raised his right hand towards it. Jason furrowed his eyebrows; his lips pressed tightly together as he focused all his thoughts onto the small piece of stone. He barely blinked, he barely breathed. The pebble didn't budge.

He tried to clear his mind, but so many thoughts were stirring. The more time passed, the more sceptical and stupid he felt as he stood there, trying to lift a piece of soil. He had always wanted to have powers, ever since he was a kid reading comic books with a torch under his covers so that his parents wouldn't know he wasn't sleeping. Now that he had them, he wasn't sure if he wanted them anymore. If he was indeed a Lightbringer, then his responsibility was huge, and the road back to London would be a very difficult one. Jason grew afraid. If he couldn't even lift a pebble, how was he supposed to defeat the Emperor?

"This is pointless!" he said, waving his arms at the sky.

"Watch out!" Anyir suddenly screamed. The pebble had shot across the enclave, hitting the boulder which Anyir's head was resting on. Jason was bewildered. His powers had actually worked. The boy looked at his hands incredulous—he had just moved something with his mind. He felt like a Jedi.

"Control your thoughts, son! You need a clear mind—control your breathing. Try again," Alamor encouraged.

Jason focused. This time his aim was a larger rock about the size of his hand. If he was going to use his powers, it wouldn't be on an insignificant pebble. He breathed, inhaling and exhaling, calmly and slowly. He looked intensely at the rock, its rough black surface reflecting the light of dusk. A soft breeze gently blew, moving a few small grains of sand and dust, making Jason's trench coat flutter. His mind was clear. He was only thinking about the wind and the rock. He felt a strange energy surge in his body, flowing through his veins almost as if his blood had turned into liquid fire. The tingling sensation ran up his spine, then in his arms, his hands and finally his fingers.

All of a sudden, he could hear everything—from the crackling of the wood in the campfire to the grains of sand rolling on the ground, to the ants working away deep in the soil. He could smell everything; the scent of dirt, the mosses and grasses, the stew cooking, the buckleberry oil.

Then, the wind listened.

A violent gust of wind suddenly blew into the enclave, smothering the campfire and tipping the pot over. The stew spilt on the ground, but Anyir and Alamor didn't even notice as they were too busy covering their faces with their hands from the sudden dust storm that attacked them. Still, the rock didn't budge.

"Oops," Jason uttered.

When Alamor realised what fate had befallen the soup, he brought his hands to his head and held his long white hair in desperation. "My soup!"

"I'm so sorry," Jason murmured. "I can't control my powers."

"Your powers are strong, Jason. You'll learn in no time, but you'll need diligence and perseverance."

"I hope so. Sorry about the stew," he said, looking at the food spilt all over the ground.

"That's ok; there's more food in the Bag of Plenty. Now, try again."

Relieved he hadn't doomed them to death by starvation, Jason felt a strange excitement to try out his powers once more. "Again?" he asked gladly.

"Yes, or else spilling the soup wasn't worth it," Alamor responded.

Jason focused on the rock once more, which seemed to look back at him derisively. He stood up straight, his legs in a confident stance. He breathed slowly, clearing his mind, and put his hand forward to conjure the wind. This time the wind really listened, and the rock quivered, then shook, then lifted a few inches off the ground. It stayed there for just a couple seconds, hovering in mid-air. Jason was ecstatic. The elements had listened to his powers. He couldn't believe it. Coming from the Otherside, he thought magic was only something from fairy tales, myths and movies. The tingling sensation flowed out of his arms and escaped his body, enveloping everything in his surroundings. Then, the rock dropped, and Jason wobbled. The energy in his body was depleting.

"Woah! Watch it, son," Alamor exclaimed, rushing to Jason's support. "It's getting dark. A Lightbringer's Flare is never as powerful in the dark."

The following morning Jason was awakened by a melodic singing coming from the distance. The rhythmic beating of hooves and the repetitive squeak of a wagon wheel accompanied the music. The sound of it was cheerful and folky, and it almost reminded Jason of the songs by Jethro Tull:

From the ashes a tree will spring radiant.
Barren lands shall bear sweet fruit and wine.
And although the sun looks yet so distant,
Life and strength will it bring with its shine.

When the summer rose shall bloom in the fields
Of a land that is emerald green,
The power of light and a sword shall he wield
To defeat the shadowed regime.

Jason moved his covers and stood up to get a peek of the mysterious singing man from behind the large boulders. The wagon left behind a trail of dust that faded into the morning sky. The man was of stocky build, with a big bushy black beard that shook as he sang. He wore a leather waistcoat and a green flat cap, and he danced along with his song as he pulled on the reins of his horse. A thick cigar stuck out of his mouth, and as he puffed smoke rose in the air.

"Alamor, wake up!" Jason called as he nudged him with his foot. "Can you hear that?"

"Yeah, it's called 'Hymn of the Summer Rose'. That man could get killed if the wrong people heard this song," Alamor commented as he woke up and stretched.

"Who is he? A merchant? He's riding a wagon full of barrels and hay."

"He's certainly not Remaran if you ask me, or he'd be too afraid to even whisper this song."

Jason gave another look at the large, bearded man. "He's coming this way. Come have a look!"

Alamor joined Jason behind the boulder and observed the wagon rider. "Wait a minute," the Veheer suddenly said. "I know this voice. This man is no merchant!" Alamor ran out of the safety of the enclave and began waving his arms. "Grando! Grando!" he called.

The man was startled at first, but then a large smile appeared beneath his beard. He pulled his cigar out of his mouth and muttered in surprise, "Alamor? Is that really you?"

"Grando, my old friend! It's been too long!"

Grando jumped down his wagon and lumbered towards Alamor with open arms, holding his cigar with one hand and embraced him, lifting him off the ground. "Alamor! It *is* you! I thought you were living on Mount Hargon with the Brotherhood!"

"I was, but I had matters to attend to here in Remara. I will explain everything in due time. We've got quite a surprise! Anyhow, what are you doing, singing the Hymn of the Summer Rose so blatantly in the middle of the Stonevale?"

"I've got to listen to what my heart wants me to sing! If anyone heard, I have my own ways to defend myself, as you know…"

"Of course! I sure miss your pyrotechnic displays; you could really put on quite a show back then." Alamor looked back at the enclave. "I've got great news, Grando, which I can't wait to share with you. However, I also have a sick young lady that needs attending to. Say, would you like a cup of tea while I treat her wounds?"

"I'd be delighted to offer *you* a cup at my house instead, and a place for you to stay while she gets better if you'd like" he invited, drawing the cigar back to his lips.

"That would be greatly appreciated! Let me just go and call the others."

After they cleared the camp, Jason and Anyir followed Alamor to meet his old friend. When they emerged from behind the rocks, Grando's face lit up with a glowing smile of enthusiasm.

"Pleasure to meet you both, I am Grando Bergfalk, son of Tod."

"Anyir Sköld, daughter of Rongvald Soward."

Jason had never presented himself to anyone this way. "Jason McAnnon… son of Robert…" he awkwardly stated.

"That's an odd name!" Grando commented. "You two must be exhausted from walking so much; you'll feel better with a cup of tea! Please, jump on the back of the wagon. Just be careful about those barrels—they're full of gunpowder."

Jason and Anyir jumped on the wagon, and Alamor joined Grando on the front. Silvyr trotted along next to them as they travelled, occasionally running ahead and running back, and nudging Grando's horse with her head.

"So, what brought you two to the gracious company of this decrepit fella, huh?" Grando asked, puffing out a cloud of smoke.

Jason looked at Alamor, unsure what story to tell, but the Veheer reassured him, "You can trust him, we've been friends for quite a while."

"Two-hundred-and-four years, to be exact!" Grando added.

"You've seriously lived this long?" Jason asked Alamor astonished.

"Oh, my dear Jason, people here in Valkadia live long lives," Alamor replied. "The Elves could live thousands of years. As a Veheer, I've lived two-hundred-and-eighty-seven years, but I could go on living for another fifty if the circumstances are favourable!"

"People only live about eighty years in England."

"What's that—*England*?" Grando asked.

Jason glanced at Alamor with apprehension, realising his slip of the tongue. He wasn't sure whether he could divulge the truth about his origin. Alamor nodded back at him smiling. Reassured he could trust Grando and Anyir, Jason finally responded, "It's a country in the Otherside."

Grando and Anyir looked at Jason with incredulous expressions, their mouths gaping, and their eyebrows raised over wide eyes.

"The *Otherside*?" Grando repeated, briefly taking his eyes off the road to turn around and look at Jason with astonishment.

"This can't be…" Anyir muttered.

"The portal has been closed for centuries. How did you get here?"

"Through an Elder Stone," Alamor replied. "We have no idea how. We're going to Malion to seek answers at Rennhall's Library. Someone there should have some explanation."

"Are you sure they'll have an answer? This seems rather irregular to me."

"It's worth a try."

"The *Otherside*…" Grando pondered, brushing his beard. The end of his large cigar slowly turned to glowing orange, and a smile replaced his bewildered look. "What's it like there? How are Humans getting along?"

"We have lots of technology that dictates most aspects of our lives. We have machines that allow us to communicate with people really far away, to travel really fast along great distances and even to fly."

"What do you mean *fly*?" Anyir asked, flabbergasted.

Jason chuckled. He found it crazy that magic was seen as totally normal in Valkadia, but flying machines weren't. "They're called *aeroplanes*. Big metal vehicles with wings—they're our fastest way to travel."

"Flying without magic… are you sure?" Alamor asked, in awe.

"That's right. We use a different source of energy called 'fuel'," Jason explained, without getting caught up in the ramifications of the fuel industry on nature and society. "Our cities are huge and full of light. We don't have swords anymore. Yet, it's a chaotic and volatile world, the *Otherside*. Many people act selfishly and think their actions won't have consequences. Money is what most people think of," said Jason, inevitably going on a bit of a tangent.

"I guess Human nature will never change… innovation and money are always the priority," Alamor commented.

"It doesn't sound very different than what the Ancestors did to Remara, does it?" Anyir contemplated as she looked at the vast, dull land of the Stonevale.

"That's true," Alamor replied. "When Erik the Red arrived, Remara was as lush and fertile as Erythya is now, full of forests and grasslands where animals roamed freely, and creatures lived in harmony. As Humans started settling in, they began cutting down trees and building their grey cities and pastures. The more Humans arrived from the Otherside, the more forests they destroyed and the more resources they wanted. Eventually, as the Remaran kings succeeded each other, the land started to die. Now, The Stonevale is bare, Xandoor is surrounded by the Desert of Tharos, and the Suraan Hills are treeless. The Iron Wood is the only large forest left because people are too afraid of what's in it to cut it down," told Alamor. Then, a large grin grew on his face. "But fear not, because this is all going to change very soon."

"Why is that, old lizard?" Grando sighed.

"Jason here is a Lightbringer!" Alamor declared exuberantly.

Grando's jaw dropped like in a 90s cartoon, and his cigar almost fell on his lap. He was stunned. "Are you serious? I hope you're not pulling a sick prank on me!"

"I am serious, Grando. As serious as this land is dry," Alamor replied.

"This means…" Grando muttered under his bushy beard.

"That we might actually have another chance against Darkstrom."

Grando turned around and let go of the reins of the wagon temporarily, patted Jason on his shoulder, and bellowed, "You are full of surprises, Jason McAnnon!"

✷

X

RELEASE THE OMÜMS

Glod and Etrel, the two vicious Omüms, arrived in Tarvan Gher when the sun was setting. They had been riding non-stop for a day to get to the capital as quickly as possible, conscious of the fact that Darkstrom would not appreciate their visit. The news was bad—terrible, in fact—and the two soldiers had been arguing the whole way about who would deliver the message to the Emperor. They hadn't decided yet. They rode swiftly through the Rat Den, and down the narrow, cobbled streets of the interior city. It had taken them a while to retrieve their black steeds after the old Veheer had set them free into the Stonevale, but that had also given the soldiers of the Red Camp time to assess the situation. The Lightbringers were back, and they had failed to stop them. Not only that, but they had let the old man take the Elven sword. Darkstrom would not like that, and even though it was Tortugal that had the ultimate responsibility of Red Camp, Glod and Etrel still feared for their lives. The Emperor was not known to be merciful.

The inhabitants of Tarvan Gher looked nervous as they rode past them, swords clanking against their black metal armours, horse hooves clapping on the cobbles. The people bowed in awe, respect and fear of the powerful soldiers, yet unaware of their hidden powers. The Omüms rode up Mount Grohel until they reached the gates of the Eiriksberg, which stood before them like an impervious mountain of stone, scraping the sky with its massive towers and turrets. Small windows were scattered sporadically on the walls of the fortress, along with small holes for archers and artillery. Above the tall, fortified stone walls surrounding the castle, soldiers in black armour marched back and forth. They knew very well that the sentinels would have no problem shooting them down with poisoned arrows if they were ordered to do so, even if they were part of the Remaran army.

The hefty front gate was raised, and the two soldiers looked at each other apprehensively before entering. Neither of them was sure of what to say. They still hadn't decided who would deliver the message to the Emperor. They held tight to the reins and rode through the inner bailey of the castle. After leaving their horses to one of the young squires, who rapidly proceeded to take their horses to the stables, a Gothi approached the soldiers, pulling behind him a Breegan slave who whimpered as he tried to keep up. "His Majesty is waiting for you. Please follow me," he told the Omüms.

The Gothi guided the two soldiers through the tight, blackened corridors of the Eiriksberg, and stopped outside the embossed double doors of the Emperor's throne room. He opened the heavy gate and stepped in first, followed by the two Omüms. Darkstrom was waiting silently on his throne, stroking his bearded chin. The statues of the Ancestors looked down on them as they approached the Emperor.

The Omüms walked side by side along the long crimson carpet. The clangour of the iron boots was the only sound, and the rate of the soldiers' heart sped up quickly. They stopped a couple of feet away from the steps that led to the throne. Solemnly, they bent the knee to their Emperor.

"Your Highness," Glod began. "It's an honour to be in your presence."

"It's an honour, my Lord," Etrel said.

Darkstrom did not answer.

"We would prefer to be here in other circumstances, Your Highness. We hate to have to bring you bad news, but it is our duty." Darkstrom remained silent and kept stroking his chin. His ice-blue eyes pierced deep into Etrel's as he spoke. "We caught two intruders trying to enter Red Camp a couple of days ago, and we imprisoned them as we usually do with anyone who interferes. One of them was a Veheer and said he was called Frey Ofson, and that he was a knight from the house of Lord Dodson in Orachlion. The other lad was apparently his squire—he wore a strange yellow cloak of a material I had never seen. They told us he was on his way to Coldhill to deliver a message to Lord Dorson, but I was sure they were lying. General Tortugal tried to teach a lesson to his squire—a true bigmouth—so we got him out of his chains to get him to talk. All ordinary until this point, but then the squire attacked us with magic—but not any kind of magic," said Etrel.

Glod continued, "Your Highness, he attacked us using the Flare. He blinded us by using light," he paused, building the courage to deliver the message. "He is a Lightbringer, and so is the old Veheer. They managed to escape and take one of our healers with them. They even destroyed all our Jauls and took our horses, which is why we had to come here to deliver the message and why it's taken us so long." Etrel and Glod watched the Emperor's face harden as he told the events. The more he explained, the whiter the Emperor's knuckles became as he grabbed the throne's arm-rest tighter and tighter. The usually grinning faces of the two soldiers were stuck in a terrified frown. "We tried to stop them, my Lord. We did everything we could, but their Flare was strong, really strong, and the Veheer had an Elven sword—"

Darkstrom remained silent for a moment, moving his eyes from Glod to Etrel. He stopped stroking his chin and stood up very, very slowly. He walked down the steps and walked past the two soldiers.

"Come with me," he ordered in a monotonous tone. He looked at the Breegans chained beside his throne and ordered as if they were dogs, "Stay."

The Omüms looked at each other once more, this time their apprehension turned into absolute terror. They stood up and walked behind the Emperor, following him out of the Throne Hall, and through the passageways of the fortress. They went left, then right, then along a straight corridor with open archways that faced the inner bailey. Darkstrom led them down a spiralling set of stairs and into the Eiriksberg's dungeons. Darkness prevailed, and the soldier's breathing became fast and heavy. Their heart was beating so fast that their bodies became warm even in the cold and humid underground of the castle, and they began sweating profusely.

When they reached a large wooden door, Darkstrom stopped. He put a hand forward, and without touching it, the door opened. On the other side of the door was a large dark room, so murky and so big that the walls seemed not to exist. A wooden table laid in the centre of the room, on top of which something glistened in the shadows, reflecting the faint light coming from the open door.

"Tell me, how many Elven swords are left in Valkadia?"

Glod hesitated, wobbling on his peg-leg.

"Not sure, my Lord," Etrel intervened.

"Three," the Emperor replied. He stepped deeper into his private cellar, and the soldiers followed. Their footsteps echoed in the empty dungeon. Darkstrom reached in the darkness, and from the shadows, he unsheathed a two-handed sword. The blade was red; the grip was made with white ivory and polished golden guards that extended curved like the horns of a bull. "*Zarak*," he introduced. He held it straight in front of him, turning is in his hand, observing the rippled quality of the metal the blade was made of. "King Kavanagh has *Dolear*. Do you know what the third one is called?"

"I dunno, my Lord," Glod answered shamefully.

"It's called *Isidir*, and do you know who owns it?"

"The Veheer...?"

"Correct answer, finally. And do you know who the Veheer is?" Darkstrom asked ferociously.

"Frey... Frey Ofson," Etrel replied.

"No, you imbecile!" he erupted, swinging *Zarak* towards Glod's neck, stopping the blade just about an inch from his throat. "His name is Alamor Eklund! Do you remember nothing of our history?! How can you claim to be some of the strongest soldiers of the Red Camp when you can't even remember the name of one of the Lightbringers?! If you knew that there were only three swords left and that two belonged to the rulers of Valkadia, then you would have done the maths pretty quickly! You would have realised it was Alamor's and that he was a Lightbringer, and you would have taken the appropriate measures! But no, you didn't do the right maths, and now he is on the loose—again! Do you know for how long I have been trying to catch that traitor? And you... you had him, and you let him go! *And* you have lost his apprentice as well. I can only hope that Lok arrives in Niteria fast enough to complete his mission before Alamor and his new pet screw us over."

Darkstrom slowly pressed the red blade against Glod's stocky neck until a small amount of blood trickled down. "If my plan fails, it will be because of you. The fate of Remara rests on your two stupid heads." The blade vibrated sharply as he pulled it away from Glod's neck, who had just seen his entire life flash before his eyes. Darkstrom turned around and put *Zarak* back in its sheath and rested it back on the table. Beside it was a small wooden box, and when he opened it bright blue light enveloped the dark underground room. He grabbed one of the small marbles inside the box and held it on his palm.

"I will give one of these Jauls to you, and you will bring another one to Tortugal, so that you can keep in contact with me. I don't have many of these anymore. I'm only giving this to you because the situation is of extreme urgency. Do *not* lose them or break them, or I shall have you hung."

Glod looked at the Emperor petrified, his hands shaking. "What would you like us to do, sire?"

"Find Alamor and his apprentice and kill them both. They cannot get to Niteria."

Glod gulped. "But my Lord, what if we don't find them?"

"You *will* find them. There is no scenario of reality in which I will allow you *not* to find them. Two Lightbringers loose in Valkadia is not a joke, and you will certainly not treat it that way."

"Excuse me, Your Highness, but what can two Lightbringers do? Sure, they are powerful beings, but not even the best ones managed to defeat you."

"Lightbringers are like the plague, Glod. There was only Alamor a week ago, and I had let him slide mercifully back and forth over Elora's Trench. But now there's two, and how long will it be until there's more? Two Lightbringers are as much of a threat as a hundred. I went through a lot of trouble to kill any descendants of the Lightbringers, and there's no way I'm letting a new one threaten the success of the Empire."

"But how can *we* defeat them if they are so powerful? Surely Lok is more qualified than us to deal with a threat like this…"

"Lok is busy."

There was absolute quiet for a moment as the Emperor handed the Jauls to them, but merely giving them an order was not enough for the Emperor. His power was derived from terror. There was no guarantee the soldiers would follow his orders if they weren't scared of their master. *Beat them down, and they will listen. Like a god, the Emperor must be feared.*

Darkstrom reached his hands towards the Omüms, and a swirling black haze flowed out of his fingers. Before they knew it, the two soldiers found themselves on the ground, transformed into fish. They floundered about on the floor, their gills desperately gasping for oxygen.

"I gave you two morons these powers, and I can take them away. You *will* do what I asked and do it right. You *will* find them, and you *will* kill them. I'm sure you understand what the stakes are if you don't deliver."

Darkstrom pulled water out of the ground, but as the fish flapped around in it with their tails slapping the floor, the water began turning frosty white. The two fish found themselves surrounded by ice, and soon the water in their gills would become ice as well. The Emperor stopped the ice spreading just before that would happen, and as quickly as the Omüms had transformed into fish, they turned back to their natural form.

"Everything is clear, I hope."

"Yes, my Lord," they replied in unison, submissively.

"Now go. Do *not* disappoint me."

After the Omüms left the dungeons, Darkstrom ambled back to the throne hall. He thought back at what the two shapeshifters had just told him. What happened at the Red Camp with Alamor was inconvenient, sure, but nothing would come between him and his plan, not even a new Lightbringer. The Empire would thrive, no matter what.

✸

XI

THE INVISIBLE HOUSE

Grando stopped the wagon in front of a sizeable rusty gate with thick iron bars, which stood lonesome in the middle of the desolate nowhere. A couple of patches of dry yellow grass poked through the ground sporadically. "Here we are!" he announced.

"Here? Really?" Anyir asked, uncertain.

"It just looks like an old gate to me," Jason commented.

"Don't let your eyes deceive you, my dear friends." Grando jumped off the wagon and unlocked the gate, its heavy iron doors creaking as he opened them. When they saw what was on the other side, the three companions were stunned. The sound of birds chirping filled the traveller's heart with joy. Grando drove the wagon along a lush tree-lined avenue surrounded by dozens of hectares of green fields where horses and cows grazed serenely. The sun was high in the sky, and the light was warm and welcoming. At the end of the road, there was a two-storey wooden house with a large sloping turf roof and a very welcoming porch overlooking the fields.

"Welcome to the *Leynahüs*, my invisible home," Grando cheered.

"How… how does this work? Is it some kind of spell?" Anyir asked.

"My son Yron helped me, he's good with this sort of stuff," the large man replied.

"Is he a Sorcerer?" Anyir inquired.

"Yes, the only one of the family. He can make things disappear though they're still there. He built this invisible house and this land for me," Grando explained. "I'm so proud of him," he added, his voice choking up.

When the wagon stopped in front of Grando's house, Jason jumped off and stepped onto the lush grass, still wet with droplets of cold dew. Jason and Alamor helped Anyir down—the effect of the buckleberry oil was slowly fading, and Anyir started feeling a slight itch on her feet. Jason wrapped her arm around his shoulders, and together they walked up the steps of Grando's house and onto the porch. Jason looked back at the gate, over which he could see how desolate and monotonous the Stonevale really was. The Leynahüs was a green jewel in the middle of the gloomy, grey Empire.

"Come in, come in," Grando invited. "Welcome to my humble abode. Make yourselves at home! Does anyone want a cigar? No? Ah, more for me then."

Jason's first impression of Grando's house could be summarised in two words: welcoming and cluttered. The wooden walls were crowded with strange objects ranging from the paddles of a small boat to framed paintings depicting woodland animals; from plants hanging on the walls to strange musical instruments made of brass and wood. Even the spare wheel of an old wagon was displayed on the wall. Hanging from the beams on the ceiling were pots, pans, mugs of all shapes and sizes. Shelves lined with glass vials and jars full of brightly coloured ingredients adorned one of the walls on the side of the room. Next to it, a large oak table filled with flasks, beakers and tubes connected to each other, sitting on top of candles dripping with wax as if ready for some wacky experiments to begin. On the opposite side, wood crackled in the fireplace, and in front of it a large green sofa that looked a hundred years old.

"Who wants a cup of tea?" Grando asked his guests.

"I don't suppose you still have some Oreka tea?" Alamor enquired, rubbing his hands together in anticipation.

"Of course!" Grando announced. "Coming right up!"

Grando rummaged through the shelves and drawers hidden around his living room and took a glass jar filled with blue herbs. He grabbed a pot and put it over the fire with some water and stirred in a couple of heaped teaspoons of blue leaves.

"What is that?" Jason asked.

"Do you not know what tea is, in the Otherside?" Grando replied.

"Yes, we drink lots of it too, but none of it is blue!" Jason answered.

"Ah! You don't know what you're missing out! This is called *Oreka*.

It's a herb that grows on the foothills of Mount Hargon, grown by the Brotherhood of Thytelis," Grando explained.

"The brotherhood of what?"

"Monks," Anyir answered. "They vow for a life of silence and devotion to the gods of the Eredom. Many of the monks are past soldiers or criminals who seek repentance for their sins."

"I joined them for a little while after the war," Alamor said, as he sunk in the old green sofa.

"I bet you had a lot of Oreka tea back then!" Grando exclaimed.

"I did, and I can't get enough! I used to collect it and dry the leaves myself," the Veheer replied, staring at the various objects hanging on the ceiling. His mind was travelling back through his memories, and a smile mixed with delight and regret suddenly appeared on his face.

"What did you do when you were a monk?" Jason asked, detecting a certain sense of sorrow on Alamor's part.

"Mostly meditated, thought about what it meant to be Alamor Eklund, about what my purpose in Valkadia was. I thought about the gods a fair deal. Oreka is great for that; it's so relaxing. Great for meditation, too."

"Have you ever met them in your meditation—the gods?" Grando enquired.

Alamor's face brightened upon hearing that question. "Not yet, though if I meditated for long enough and really cleared my mind, I could sense their presence, governing the elements. In a certain way, as a Lightbringer, I have always felt them—especially their power. It's as if you are a vector of their magic. That's what the Flare is," Alamor elucidated excitedly. His amber eyes were glowing.

"The Flare—it tingles," Jason observed. "It's as if a scorching yet somehow soothing river of lava is flowing through you," he said as he stroked his arms to indicate the movement of magic.

"That's right! You've felt it too! That's the gods' power being channelled through your veins. Humans think it's the blood of the Æsir, but that's nonsense. Those new gods, as powerful as they sound, have no place in Valkadia," said Alamor.

Jason believed in science too much to consider the possibility that the world was governed by gods and their capricious needs. He loved to study about the ancient gods of polytheistic religions, who explained the natural phenomena by assigning each god a specific position in heaven. For the Old Norse, it was the Æsir, ruled by Odin, while the Ancient Greeks believed in the gods of Mount Olympus, ruled by Zeus. Though he found ancient religions fascinating, he struggled to live by the rules of modern religions. In a fast-changing world where science could answer the most complicated questions about life on Earth and beyond, Jason didn't like his life being obstructed by antiquated rules laid out by intangible beings. Yet, now that a magical power was running through his veins, he didn't know what to believe anymore. "But if you've never met the gods, how can you be sure they're real, and that the Æsir are not?" Jason retorted.

"I can feel them inside me, Jason," Alamor replied, caught off-guard by the question. It dawned on Jason that in a world where everybody believed in gods, not many people had questioned their existence. "Their energy flows within me, as well as you. How else can you explain the powers we have? Every creature in Valkadia is connected by this energy, which is why there is so much magic around us. There must be forces beyond our own at play, or else none of this would be possible. Look around. Take these trees, for example. What makes a plant grow so strong and tall? There must be some greater force, stronger, more intelligent, that makes our world turn," the Veheer replied passionately.

"It's strange how people in different parts of the world all believe in a higher power, but everyone believes in something different. Where I come from—in the Otherside—people believe in many things," Jason said. "My parents believe there is only one god."

"One? How does it control all the aspects of the world on its own?" Grando answered sarcastically.

"He's meant to be omnipotent," Jason responded.

"*He*? Why *he*?" Grando asked.

"That's the way it is written," Jason answered.

"So, you're saying he rules over the seasons, over time and space, over the moon and the sun?" Grando inquired, astonished.

"Over the warriors, over the dead?" Alamor probed.

"That sounds like a lot of work... next thing you'll say is that he's immortal..." Grando commented.

"Actually... he *is* meant to be eternal."

"So, he was here before the Earth was created?" Anyir asked.

"That's right. He's the one that created it. Why, how do you explain the beginning of it all here in Valkadia?" Jason's curiosity was buzzing. Though he struggled to believe in any god, he was fascinated to learn more about what his friends believed. It seemed they had a fresh view of nature—or at least an alternate idea of what existed beyond their plane of reality to what he had heard all his life in the Otherside.

"It all began with the Primordial Orchid," Alamor explained, "which bloomed from a speck of dust floating in the heavens. From its petals were born the gods of the *Eredom*, who to this day take care of the Orchid and ensure the elements of Valkadia are in balance. From its pollen were created the stars, the sun and the moon. From its roots was created the earth, and its nectar made the rivers and the oceans. The Orchid's stem connects our world to the Eredom."

Alamor paused and looked at Jason, who was hanging on his mentor's every word, eager to know more.

"Rotar was the first to arrive," Alamor continued. "He controls the sun and is all-knowing. Then, Fradin arrived, the goddess of the moon, beauty and wisdom. Together they had Tresha, the goddess of fertility who gave birth to all animals and plants, including all the creatures. After her arrived Grimmon, the god of thunder and rain, he who makes everything live. Then we have Sagham, the goddess of death, and Mhorjen, the god of peace and war.

"But the gods are not eternal, like yours. They bloomed with the Orchid, and they will die when the Orchid dies. Then, another Orchid will grow from the heavenly dust. New gods will arise; a new world will be created," said Alamor, satisfied by his recounting of the Valkadian creation story. He looked outside the window at the sky with a graceful smile, almost like a salutation to his gods.

"That's beautiful," Jason commented.

The water started bubbling, and Grando poured the blue drink in a small cup made out of bone. "Try it," he told Jason, offering it to him with both hands.

Jason brought the cup to his nose and smelled the Oreka tea. He was startled. Never had he smelled quite such a fragrance. It was sweet, yet bitter and zesty. It was as if Grando had mixed raspberries with cinnamon and added ginger to it. When he took a sip of it, the flavours mixed and changed as he swirled it in his mouth. A sudden feeling of extreme relaxation and awareness enveloped him. Jason wished he could take a bag full of Oreka tea back to England so he could drink it for the rest of his life.

"I knew you'd like it," said Grando as he saw Jason's smile grow wider and wider as he drank.

Grando poured some tea for Anyir too. "I've been looking forward to having Oreka tea since I was a kid!" she said. Yet, when she leaned over to grab the cup, she jerked and screeched, her face suddenly contorting. The pain from the wounds on her feet was too much as the buckleberry oil's effect weaned off. The bowl fell to the ground, spilling blue tea all over one of Grando's carpets. Anyir gasped. "I'm so sorry," she said in a hushed tone.

"Don't worry, let me pour you another cup," Grando offered.

"We need to change those bandages. Help me take Anyir to the sofa," Alamor said to Jason.

Gently, they laid her down onto the old beaten sofa, and Alamor proceeded to change the medication. When Grando saw the horrible wounds on her feet, he gasped. "What happened?!"

"Tortugal never gave us shoes…" Anyir muttered as she held back her tears. Grando was shocked upon hearing that name.

"Anyir was a slave at Red Camp," explained Alamor.

"Red Camp?!" Grando gasped. "How are you alive?"

"Alamor and Jason—they saved me," Anyir said, her face grimacing as Alamor changed her bandages.

"I'm so sorry to hear that," the bearded man said with sorrow in his voice. "Why were you there?" Grando inquired.

"My husband and I are Erythian sympathisers," she replied.

"That's good to hear!" Grando exclaimed, trying to tone down his excitement. "Still, nobody should endure the horrors of that place. Where are you from, Anyir?" he asked, attempting to change the subject.

"Karisa," she replied.

"Ah, the Forge of Remara," Grando pointed out.

Anyir shook her shoulders. "I know—it's not a great place, but home is where home is. I miss it. I want to go back as soon as possible."

"We must wait for your feet to heal," Alamor interjected. "Besides, after the fuss we caused at the Red Camp, I'm sure Darkstrom is looking for us."

"Stay here as much as you need, my friends! I love the company!" Grando offered "I've been alone in this place for too long."

"Thank you, Grando," Anyir said softly.

"What is it that you do, exactly?" Jason asked. "Why live here instead of Erythya?"

"I'm an alchemist, first and foremost," he replied. "I also work as an informant for king Kavanagh, which is why I live in an invisible house, in the middle of the Stonevale," he replied.

"Grando used to fight along with me and the Lightbringers," Alamor explained. "He used to make the most wonderful explosives. Thanks to him, we managed to make our way through the most impenetrable Remaran strongholds. We would have never managed to reach the Eiriksberg if it wasn't for Grando."

To Jason, alchemists were wacky scientists of the past that made potions and elixirs to live forever or speak to the dead—not experts in bombs.

"Can you still do any of your... demonstrations?" Alamor asked Grando.

"Sure!" he replied nodding, making his black beard shake. "Come with me." The trio followed Grando to the large wooden desk cluttered with flasks and beakers full of liquids and coloured powders. "Put these on," Grando said, offering his guests three pairs of brass glasses with thick lenses. "I am working with very reactive elements, and the solutions are hazardous. It won't be a huge reaction, since we're at home, but it will be strong enough to blind you if you don't protect your eyes."

Grando took a jar that contained a strange silvery substance which Jason realised was mercury. When Grando poured it into a flask, it rolled inside like it was made of heavy metal balls, but it became liquid again as soon as it settled on the bottom. He placed the flask on a small gas burner. Then, he took another jar containing a yellow substance, and when he opened it, the room was filled with a smell of rotten eggs. *Sulphur*, Jason thought. He combined the two substances and put the mixture back on the fire. The chemicals began to evaporate inside the flask, and when there was nothing left but a silvery powder, Grando removed the flask from the fire. Then, he poured the powder onto the table and with a matchstick, he ignited it.

Boom!

A ripping roar and a burst of wind enveloped the room, causing the curtains on the windows and Grando's bushy beard to flutter. The roar was accompanied by a green flash and a shower of sparks. Jason and Anyir remained immobilized, watching the sparks change colour as they floated in the air. Alamor began to laugh uncontrollably, remembering the old days and the adrenaline rush that all those explosions used to give him. Eventually, all four of them laughed happily, forgetting their duties and demons for a moment.

While Jason and Anyir slept soundly, Alamor and Grando sat outside on the porch, enjoying a couple of cigars, blowing smoke into the distance. The night was cool, and the wind was still.

"Do you have any news about Lok?" Alamor asked Grando.

"I'm afraid not, my friend. Why?"

"Make sure to let me know if you find out anything. I have a feeling that the boy's powers might be linked to Lok."

"How can you be sure?"

"When I last faced Lok at the ruins of Dorth, he escaped to the Iron Wood to seek shelter. I followed him, and I found Lok and Jason passed out on the ground when I arrived. Dressed oddly as he was, I had no idea where Jason had come from, but I understood he was special. I decided to save him, taking him away from Lok."

"What's your point?" Grando enquired.

"My point is… something happened before I arrived. The fact that Jason has powers and is not from Valkadia, and the fact that there hasn't been any news about Lok lately… I think Jason has Lok's Flare."

"I see," Grando murmured, inhaling on his cigar intensely. He blew a cloud of smoke slowly, pondering. "Is… is that a bad thing?" he asked.

"Not entirely," answered Alamor. His eyebrows were furrowed, thinking hard. "This way we have a Lightbringer on our side, but I'm afraid Lok will come looking for his powers as soon as he realises who's taken them."

"What should we tell Jason?"

"You mustn't tell him where his Flare comes from," said Alamor. "He will have to know at some point, but now is not the time. He just came to terms with his powers, and he must feel like they're his if we want him to learn how to control them."

"And you're sure nobody else will tell him?" Grando asked.

"Nobody else knows," Alamor replied.

"Very well, I'll keep the secret. But you must be aware of the position you are putting me in."

"I realise that, and I am sorry, dear friend. Erythya will be forever grateful."

XII

A LIGHTBRINGER'S DUTY

That night, Jason had a strange nightmare.

He was in a vast room with marble walls the colour of cream. Tall blue columns made of stone rose so high that Jason couldn't see where they ended. There were large lancet windows all around, yet when he glanced beyond them, all he could see was a black void. Green carpets weaved with golden patterns stretched across the white floors, extending far out of Jason's sight.

In the middle of the room, behind a marble table, a woman crouched as if she was protecting something. Her hair was red. She was thin, her skin pale and her limbs long and graceful. Jason walked over towards the woman, and when she lifted her head to look back at him with emerald eyes, she revealed two new-borns cradled in her arms. Around her neck, she wore a silver necklace and, hanging from it, a metal pendant shaped like a droplet of water.

Jason heard loud, crashing noises coming from the outside, rumbles echoing throughout. All of a sudden, the room began shaking as if a giant had punched it, and the beautiful marble walls began cracking. The columns came crumbling down, and the stone bricks tumbled off the walls. The infants cried aloud, and the mother held them tight.

As the room disintegrated, a hooded man in a dark cloak barged in, ignoring the cracks on the floor and the falling chunks of marble. He looked at the woman, and without speaking to her, he took the two newborns from her arms. Like a shadow, he swiftly left the room, carrying the babies with him and leaving the woman behind in the crumbling building. Jason ran after the hooded man, but it was too late. The Child Snatcher had left no trace. Jason looked behind him where the woman was sitting, but she was gone too.

Abruptly, Jason awoke and found himself in a puddle of sweat, breathing heavily and exhausted. Who was that woman? Who were the two infants? Who was the Child Snatcher that hid beneath that cloak?

"Are you ok, son?" Alamor asked.

Jason looked out the window of the room Grando had given him and Alamor for their stay. The bright sun shined onto the green fields, and the cows and sheep were already out grazing on the fresh grass.

"Yeah," Jason replied, somewhat still confused. "It was just a strange dream. I'm not even sure it was a nightmare."

"What was it about?" Alamor prodded.

Jason told the dream to the old Veheer, who listened carefully with his pointed ears perked back.

"What do you think it means?" Jason asked.

"It's hard to say… you said it felt like a memory, but it might just be your mind playing jokes. The mother, the infants, the 'Child Snatcher'… it all just seems like a standard nightmare to me," Alamor dismissed. "It must just be the recent stress getting the better of you."

"I guess so," Jason replied. "But it was so real; it was as if I knew this woman. And I could swear that room looked familiar…"

"An infinite room made of marble and blue stones? Not even the most powerful magic can create such an illusion."

"But it must mean something…" Jason continued, unsatisfied by Alamor's answers. "And you say you've never met any woman that fits that description: auburn hair, pale skin, emerald eyes?"

"I can't say I've ever met this woman. From your description, it sounds like it could be anybody," Alamor said. "Now then, let's not dwell on our dreams, son. Let's focus on what's our duty instead! Get ready, for today your training begins!"

The two Lightbringers stood in the middle of a green field in front of Grando's house. The Remaran sword Alamor had given Jason at the Red Camp was safely stowed in its scabbard. The focus of the first lesson was on the use of the Flare. Anyir and Grando watched from the porch, comfortably sat on lounging chairs and relaxing under the warm sun. The large, bearded man enjoyed smoking his cigars while observing Jason and his old friend Alamor duel, and most of all appreciated having some company at the Leynahüs.

"There are four main elements that you must learn how to control. These are *heyra*—air, *fhyr*—fire, *ekka*—water, and *jard*—earth. With these, you can effectively dominate each aspect of your surroundings. You can make things fly by manipulating air; you can create rivers of fire; you can control plants and rocks by summoning the ground."

Alamor adjusted his stance. He moved his hands in spiralling waves, gently rising and falling. Deep gurgling noises emerged from beneath the ground as if the earth had become a living creature for a moment. Droplets of water materialised in front of the old Lightbringer and merged to create a swirling column of water. With a snap of his fingers, the liquid pillar turned into a blazing fountain of scorching fire, its heat suddenly hitting Jason in the face. Alamor kept his eyes focused, his long white hair undulating in the fiery storm. When the Veheer finally put his arms down, and the blazing hot tornado disappeared, a majestic oak tree appeared before them, and there was no sign of burning on the grass surrounding it. The oak's leaves were green, and its acorns adorned the crown of the tree like precious gems. Alamor looked at Jason with a pleased smirk.

"How did you…" Jason muttered, pointing at the tree, looking around himself with an eyebrow raised. He glanced at Anyir, whom too was speechless. Grando stood up and clapped his hands, bellowing with excited laughter.

Alamor continued, "As you know, a Lightbringer can control all elements, including light, which in Hæmir is called *zo'or*. You'll remember the inscription on the Elder Stone: *zo'or alegsiar eith*, light protects you. The Flare is what distinguishes Lightbringers from Sorcerers. A *Sorcerer* can only harness energy from the elements around them, depleting their environment in order to use their powers. For example, wind sorcerers move the air by creating vacuums within it, while those who command the earth will deplete its minerals. Meanwhile, the Flare of a *Lightbringer* can turn light into the elements, and into light itself, without draining their surroundings." As he spoke, Alamor opened his hand with his palm facing up, and a small sphere of light the size of a marble appeared and hovered silently in front of him. The light was white and intense, glowing like a miniature star taken from the night sky.

"The Flare heals you faster, gives you heightened senses and greater agility. When you tried to lift that rock yesterday, you might have felt a strange increase in awareness—better hearing and better vision. With light as your source of power, your magic is stronger and replenishes fast. However…" Alamor clapped his hands, and the small orb of light disappeared, "…darkness is our greatest enemy. At night, a Lightbringer's powers diminish. In a completely dark room, consider your powers useless.

"As I mentioned before, king Arganthal asked the Lightbringers to create an amulet that could defeat the Emperor—a magical dagger called *Eluir*. Because of Darkstrom's meddling with arcane sorcery and his ability to harness the souls of other beings, he is essentially immortal. Thus, the Eluir represents the only way to defeat the Emperor—and defeat him we must. All that is needed is to drive the Eluir through Darkstrom's heart." Alamor walked closer to Jason and put a hand on his shoulder. "This is where you come in, boy. Only a strong Lightbringer can face the Emperor and harness the power of the Eluir to defeat him."

Jason was overwhelmed by the amount of information he was being fed and by the quest he had been assigned. Would he really need to drive a dagger through an immortal Emperor's heart? He struggled to make sense of what to say, words getting stuck right behind his lips and not coming out of his mouth. "H- How am I supposed to find this Eluir?" he finally managed to mutter, though all he wanted to ask was: *Do I really need to do this?*

"When Darkstrom defeated the Lightbringers, he took the Eluir from them and hid it. The great Usnaar Bearol—a Breegan Lightbringer—created a device to track the Eluir if it were ever lost, but that too has been left to the ages. We might be able to find something about its location at Rennhall's Library. It has been the headquarters for the Order of the Lightbringers for centuries. They'll have at least some answers there." Alamor paused and nodded encouragingly at his student. "Now, you try."

"Try what?"

"Anything. Use your Flare, Jason."

Jason was nervous. The stakes of him managing to control his powers were high, and he didn't want to let Alamor down. He now understood how important it was to stop the Emperor. If Darkstrom managed to open the portal again, Erythya and Valkadia would be exposed to the whole world.

Jason's heart began palpitating fast when he thought of all the consequences of the eventuality. If the Humans of the Empire hadn't already done enough damage, the Humans of Earth would annihilate it. They would raid it with tanks, choppers and submarines. The magic of Erythya would stand no chance against the atomic bomb if a gigantic war between the two worlds broke out. Scientists would find no better to do than study the poor enchanted creatures, and governments would try to exploit their magic and resources. Nothing good would come out of opening the Elder Stones.

Jason took a deep breath and closed his eyes. He extended his arms forwards, his fingers facing the ground. As he felt the energy grow stronger, running through his veins fast, Jason began hearing the myriad of noises that surrounded him. Even though his eyes were closed, he could almost see what was happening all around: the squeaking of Grando's lounge chair as he rocked back and forth, the flickering of leaves and acorns high in the canopy of the oak, beetles nibbling on the bark of the beeches, cows grazing on the green grass fields. Jason could hear the rumbling of water flowing deep underground, which was listening. He could feel the strength of the water pushing through the pores in the soil, flushing the roots of trees and fungi.

Alas, the strength of the water was too much, bursting through the ground beneath Jason's feet like a geyser. As it ripped the earth, the jet propelled the new Lightbringer in the air and slumped him a couple of yards away, his face covered in mud.

"You won't be able to control your Flare until you've learned to control your mind, Jason. You must calm yourself down, breathe deeply. Be one in one with the Flare, be in control of your thoughts. Only then you will be able to channel the Flare correctly."

Jason looked back at Alamor as he wiped the mud off his face and arms. "How do I do that—*control my mind?*" he asked.

"It's all in the way you breathe, son. Four deep breaths usually do the trick. Once you've mastered this, and you can clear your mind, the Flare will be much easier to control."

The training went on every day for the following two weeks. When Jason wasn't practising his sword-fighting skills or how to use his Flare, Alamor was teaching him how to read Hæmir. It was a language spoken by the Elves, the ancient rulers of Valkadia and the first people to study and understand magic. Jason learnt that it was written and read from right to left, much like Hebrew or Arabic. Somehow, the new Lightbringer picked the old language relatively quickly. Seeing his inexplicably fast progress, Alamor gave him books upon books to read so he could get accustomed to the land he got thrown into just a couple days back. Grando kept all the Erythian books, forbidden in Remara of course, in a locked trunk just for precaution.

Jason soon managed to read the *Tales of the Ancestors* by Knut Oklear, where he learned about the first arrival of Humans in Valkadia; he read the *Book of Day*, the sacred text of Lightbringers. Jason also delighted himself with *The Harmony of Creatures: Life in the Olde Forests and the New* by Rogor Dreymos, where he enjoyed reading about the zany creatures that lived in Erythya such as the Ulkar, an immense wolf that is said to be a cursed warrior that was exiled in the Iron Wood; or the Unahms, small cats that can glow in the dark, with fox-like tails and sabre-long teeth. Jason's stomach churned when reading about the Omüms, terrible shapeshifting creatures who can transform into any animal. He was terrified to learn that Glod and Etrel, the two Omüms he had met at Red Camp, had been artificially created by Darkstrom. Above all, Jason was intrigued by reading about a creature he saw engraved in the Elder Stone—the winged stag, known as the Aralay. The beautifully detailed illustrations in the book depicted its tawny fur, its long antlers that twisted and branched out widely, its long wiry tail and wings covered in majestic golden plumage.

"Ah, you like Aralays, do you?" Alamor said, peeking over the page of the book. "King Kavanagh loves them too, so much he chose them as his house emblem."

"They're fascinating. I've heard about winged horses but never about winged stags," Jason replied.

"They are one of the rarest and most sacred creatures in Erythya, dare I say of all Valkadia! You know, my ancestors used to say that stroking their antlers can grant wishes and that their tears can bring people back to life. They say their feathers turn to silver when they shed," Alamor explained.

"Have you ever seen one?"

"Only once, and it was from very far away. The other Lightbringers and I were passing through Thorwyn's Forest, and we heard a rustle in the bushes. Then something big jumped onto the crowns of the trees. I manage to get a glance of it between the leaves, but it flew away almost immediately."

"And what about these? The... Goplen?" Jason asked, pointing at the picture of what looked like a massive turtle with a tree on its back.

"The Goplen are ancient and colossal animals made of plants that migrate from one water resource to another. To defend themselves, they curl up on the ground and hide from predators by camouflaging into hills, blending perfectly in the landscape," Alamor explained.

"Big walking vegetables, in a nutshell," Jason responded with sarcasm. "How big are they?" he probed.

"Huge. Just one of their legs is more than twice your size. In all, they are about twenty feet tall and weigh twenty tons," replied Alamor. "They are heavy, but they are also fast and powerful," he added.

"They look spectacular," the Londoner mused.

"Well... they *were* spectacular," Alamor sighed. "Ever since Darkstrom's mining campaigns for iron and other minerals, much of the water in Remara has been polluted. The Goplen can't get enough nutrients from the ground, and whatever they drink is contaminated. Now, their plants grow deformed, and their minds are poisoned; they rampage across Remara trying to find clean water sources. It's really heartbreaking."

"And if that wasn't everything, the Remaran army cuts off all the trees and shrubs growing on their back to turn them into towing pachyderms, and take them to war," Anyir said in a melancholy tone.

"Why would Darkstrom do such a thing?" Jason asked, shaking his head.

"He doesn't care for nature. He only wants to expand the Empire, and he'll use all the resources available to do so. He's caused so much poverty and anguish among his people, and now Remara is almost devoid of life," Alamor told, his voice sombre.

Jason found himself increasingly irritated the more he learned about the Emperor. Humanity had already done enough damage to nature in the Otherside, and it angered him to think that even in Valkadia the story was the same. *Will we ever learn?* he pondered.

Eventually, Jason was dragged away from the books and into the fields of the Leynahüs to continue his training. Eventually, too, Anyir's feet got better, and she asked to join in with the fun.

"Anyir, this is yours," said Alamor as he handed her a bow. It was light and balanced and beautifully manufactured, with flexible olive wood for the limbs, which curved and recurved gently, and an ivory handle that fitted ergonomically in Anyir's hand. The staves at either tip of the bow were dipped in gold. The string felt tense, ready to shoot at any moment.

"This? For me?" she asked incredulously. The weapon was a thing of marvel.

"Grando made it for you," Alamor specified. "He used some of the finest materials he kept in his house."

"I... I don't know what to say... How did you know I'm an archer?"

"It just seemed right," Alamor said nonchalantly. "Come on. Let's have a look what you've got."

"All right," Anyir replied with a firm and determined tone. "Bear with me, I haven't done this in a while." She walked up to one of the straw mannequins that were being using for training. Anyir took an arrow and placed the nock on the bowstring. She was excited about shooting an arrow after so long—years before, she occasionally hunted with her father, and she had developed an innate aptitude to archery. With a deep breath, she straightened her back and pulled the string resolutely towards her ear. She aimed straight at the torso of the hay mannequin and let the arrow fly. To her disappointment, the dart disobeyed and stuck itself in the fertile soil of the field.

"Don't worry, Anyir. Try again."

Frustrated, she grunted and drew another arrow from the quiver. She focused, imagining the trajectory in her head. Anyir nocked the arrow back onto the string. As she pulled it back, she felt the tension building in the bow. Flakes of straw burst in the air when Anyir's arrow pierced the mannequin's sternum, causing it a fatal wound. Without waiting, Anyir shot another arrow, which whistled through the air and cut in half the arrow already lodged in the straw dummy.

Her companions cheered and applauded. "By Rotar's beard! Good shot, Anyir!" Grando shouted.

"All right then, I don't think Anyir needs much more training! I think you are both ready for some more advanced exercises," Alamor said.

"Are you sure? Already?" Anyir asked anxiously.

"You doubt my judgement?' he said humorously. "Go to the opposite ends of this field. It will be your battleground."

"What do you mean? You want us to fight?" Jason asked.

"That's right! Let's start having some real fun around here!" their mentor exclaimed jumping from foot to foot. With his green tunic, Alamor looked like an excited leprechaun, impatient to see what his two apprentices were capable of. "I won't allow anything to happen, don't worry. Jason, I expect you to use both your sword fighting skills and your powers. Just go easy on Anyir—it's her first day!"

"Yeah, try not to blow me up with any unexpected geyser, please," Anyir mocked.

Jason smirked as he unsheathed the Remaran sword. "I'll try my best."

Without any notice, it was Anyir who dared to make the first move. Her arrow shot a few inches past his head, hissing as it cut the air by his ear. He held his sword with both hands, and began circling his adversary, ready to deflect her arrows and dodge them. Before he knew it, another arrow flew towards him and scraped his arm.

Alamor dug his face in his hands. "Jason! What's the matter with you?" he said as he gesticulated passionately. "Learn to see what's happening around you, predict your opponent's moves. Come on! We discussed all this already!"

Jason breathed slowly and let the tingling energy of his Flare flow through his body. After a few moments, he could hear the string tensing, and he could see the arrows coming towards him at half the speed. He felt like Neo in The Matrix, dodging arrows in slow motion instead of bullets. Alamor was magically putting the arrows back into the quiver so that Anyir would never run out of ammunition. Jason sliced the arrows in half with smooth movements of his sword as they got close enough, and he jumped and twisted to dodge the endless stream of arrows that Anyir released on him.

Anyir was impressed by her partner's cunning tactics. She hadn't realised how much progress Jason had made in only a couple of weeks. She began to move, roll and jump in the air, giving Jason less time to observe her and predict her moves. Anyir's heart was beating fast with excitement. She couldn't remember the last time she had this much energy and fun.

All of a sudden, the arrows burst in flames and turned to ashes before they even reached Jason. Anyir began getting frustrated and confused, so she shot another three arrows, but they too lit ablaze, falling onto the ground like black powder.

Jason stopped moving; he too was confused. The air surrounding them became cold, making their skin chill. It was as if they had been suddenly dumped into a walk-in freezer.

Anyir looked back at the photographer, the colour quickly draining from her face. She couldn't breathe for a moment, and a feeling of dread crept up from the pit of her stomach. Mortified, she dropped the bow and ran back inside the house.

"Anyir! What happened?" Jason asked, knitting his eyebrows.

Grando walked over, into the field where they had been training. "What's going on?" he asked.

"Don't worry," Alamor said. "She's just scared. It's always a strange experience when someone uses magic against you."

"Alamor. That wasn't me…" Jason pointed out.

The Veheer looked at his apprentice with wide eyes. "I knew it," he muttered.

Jason was more and more confused. "You knew what?"

Alamor took a moment to compose himself. "Anyir is the daughter of a famous Remaran Sorcerer, Rongvald Soward," he revealed. "It only makes sense that she inherited his powers. She just needed a safe place to find it out."

After a couple of hours, Anyir still hadn't walked out of her room. Jason decided to take it upon himself to check out if she was doing all right. When he knocked on her door, she didn't answer.

"Hey, are you ok?" he asked.

"Go away," she huffed.

"Anyir, you can't keep it all in. Can I come in?"

Anyir huffed again. "All right…"

When he entered the room, he found Anyir lying on her bed, wrapped up in a blanket and staring at the wooden beams on the ceiling.

"Hey," he greeted endearingly. "So, you're a Sorceress, what's wrong with that?" asked Jason.

"What's wrong with that?!" she snapped. Jason almost jumped, not realising the question he asked would be so impactful. "Do you know what they do to witches in Remara? If I'm lucky, they would throw me in a well with stones tied to my feet and watch me drown, or they would burn me alive in front of everyone, even children. For the Empire, women who can control magic are just demonic beings who bring disease and famine," she babbled as the tears came rushing.

"You're not a witch, Anyir. You're a Sorceress. If you come to Erythya with us, you'll be safe," said Jason, hoping that pointing out the difference would help his friend.

"It doesn't make a difference what I am… In Remara, they'll kill me for my powers. In Erythya, they'll kill me because I'm Remaran," Anyir elucidated, sitting up on the bed, grasping tight onto the blanket.

Jason couldn't understand why she was so paranoid. Surely, growing up in Valkadia meant that people were used to magic. Jason certainly sympathised with her, but if he could somehow come to terms with his supernatural powers, why couldn't she? "If you learned how to use your powers, they wouldn't be able to touch you," he said.

"Sure," Anyir rejoined. "Alamor can teach me how to control my magic in two days and I'll become invincible..."

Jason took a moment to formulate his thoughts. "Look, I felt strange too when I found out I had powers. I mean, I didn't even know magic existed until I got here. There's no magic in the Otherside; it was so weird for me. Alamor found me and helped me, and he can do the same for you."

Anyir laughed nervously. "But it's different for you! You're a Lightbringer. Even if I could get away with hiding the fact that I'm a Sorceress from the Empire, how would I lie to my family? I could never keep that from my husband..."

"But... I thought you decided you'd be staying with us?" Jason said, frowning.

"I want to go back, Jason. I'm sure you understand that," she replied as she played with the blanket between her fingers.

The image of Clara's face flashed in Jason's mind. "I know how you feel, Anyir, but we must stick together. It's not safe out there."

Anyir's tone became soft as she spoke. "I don't know where I would be if it weren't for you and Alamor." The corvine-haired woman smiled kindly and her turquoise eyes glimmered with delight as she remembered something. She suddenly got up, still wrapped up in her blanket. She walked to her chest of drawers and pulled out a knitted piece of clothing. "Here, I made this to you while I was healing. As soon as we leave this warm, sunny invisible land, you'll need it."

It was a dark blue sweater, made of thickly woven wool. It wasn't much, but Jason's insides burned with joy. "Thank you," he said. Nobody had done anything like that for him before.

"Try it on!" she voiced with anticipation.

Jason felt awkward, but he didn't want to upset Anyir, who had already gone through so much. When he put the sweater over his head, the wool immediately began itching his neck and back. To distract himself from the discomfort, as well as trying to change the topic of conversation and help his friend, Jason suggested, "Tell me a story."

"A story?" Anyir replied, confused by the question. "Why?"

"I dunno," he said. "I've always found stories calming."

She smiled. "I do remember one story," she said, her face brightening up. "Have you ever heard the one about the Aralay's antlers?"

Jason shook his head, chuckling. "Never."

"Very well." Anyir sat up and cleared her throat, and she began to tell. "Long, long ago, before the arrival of the Ancestors, in the Lands of the Nomads, there once was a boy called Nabee. He was the son of a powerful tribe leader. His mother had died while giving birth to him, and his father hated him for it.

"One day, Nabee's father kicked him out of the village, and he was forced to venture into the lands of Valkadia in search of a new home. The gods were saddened and decided to send a wonderful Aralay to help him. When the Aralay appeared near a spring where the boy was drinking, it said, "I will protect you wherever we'll go. Stroke on my antlers and I will grant your wishes." Thus, a deep friendship was born. They walked far. They crossed the great Desert of Tharos, the heights of the Suraan Hills and the great woods of Valkadia. When Nabee was tired, he rode on the Aralay's back and stroked its majestic antlers to wish for food and water.

"One day, while crossing the plains, Nabee and the Aralay met a big angry ox. "I will fight against that ox and defeat it," the Aralay declared. A terrifying struggle took place, and the ox was defeated, as the Aralay predicted. The boy was able to ride again, and together they continued the journey.

"A few days later, they met a ferocious wolf. "I'll fight that wolf but die," the Aralay declared. "You must take my antlers with you. When you're hungry, stroke on them and they'll help you. When you're thirsty, stroke on them and they'll help you. However, you mustn't stroke them so much that they become smooth, or else their magic will be lost forever." A terrifying struggle took place, and the Aralay died, as it had predicted. When the wolf was gone, Nabee took the antlers of the Aralay and began his long journey again.

"After many days, the boy arrived in a village where a severe drought had destroyed all crops, and the inhabitants were hungry. The village chief invited the boy to his house and offered him a small bowl of soup. Seeing how little food they had, Nabee stroked on the antlers and asked for food for each villager.

"A jealous man from the village saw the miracle and wanted the antlers all for himself. One night he snuck inside the boy's tent and swapped the magical antlers with the horns of a ram.

"When the boy left to continue his journey and needed to drink, he looked for the Aralay's antlers to wish for water but realised they had been swapped. Because of this terrible event, Nabee was forced to return to the village. As soon as he saw the thief with the antlers of the Aralay, he told everything to the head of the village. The thief was punished, and the boy thanked the whole village, supplying it with enough food until winter would arrive.

"The next day, Nabee resumed his journey in search of a new home. He found a new village but was refused because he was dirty and indecent. He travelled for many years in the lands of Valkadia, and he grew into a young man. Finally, he was welcomed in a beautiful village. The chieftain had a beautiful daughter and Nabee stroked on the antlers to supply the girl with gifts. After a few weeks, the young man got married to the chief's daughter and had a big party, always with the antlers' help. When the chief of the village died, Nabee became the new chieftain, and he used the antlers to build a new house for his family. He then wished for a boat, and for more land. The antlers granted him every wish.

"A few years later, Nabee decided to return to visit his father, who welcomed him and his family with great joy and honour. His father was proud of what he had become. To impress his father, Nabee used the antlers to give his father a new house and better tents for the other inhabitants. However, the antlers had become smooth after all the times Nabee had used them for himself, and he was only able to give his father a loaf of bread. Just like the Aralay had warned him, the antlers had exhausted their magical ability. His father kicked Nabee out of the village once more. This time, however, he decided to rebel. There was a big battle between the two villages, but Nabee lost, and his father took everything from him—his house, his boat, his land, his family—and he was forced to roam the lands of Valkadia once more.

"Nabee grew old, and he eventually died. He went to the Eredom where all the souls of the dead rest. There, he met the Aralay, who asked him: "What have you done with my antlers?" and Nabee responded, "They have gone smooth. I lost everything, and now I am dead." The

Aralay shook its head, "When the earth gives, you mustn't take too much." Nabee spent the rest of his time in the magnificent Eredom above the sky, although he always wished he could go back to Valkadia to see his family. This time, however, there was nothing the Aralay could do."

Anyir took a deep breath, her eyes swelling with tears.

"Wow," murmured Jason, blown away by the fable. "That is quite a bedtime story."

"This was my favourite bedtime story that my mum used to tell me when I was a kid… I wonder if I'll ever get back to my mother in Ocran. I wonder what she'd say if I told her I was a Sorceress…"

"I wonder what *my* mum would say if I told her I was a Lightbringer in a magical realm full of fantastical creatures where people don't know what a television is," Jason replied.

"She'd probably say you were crazy!" Anyir said.

"I think I'd say the same," Jason chortled.

XIII

THE PALACE OF KINGS

A little girl named Vicken ran through the corridors of the *Ærindel*, her bare feet tapping rhythmically onto the intricately jointed wooden floors, her shadow rushing along the candid sandstone walls. She was holding tightly onto a small paper scroll, bound by a thin red ribbon and marked with the Golden Army's wax stamp. The dovetail of her red coat flapped behind her like a flag in the wind. The Aralay, the regal emblem of king Kavanagh, was embroidered on her chest with golden thread.

Vicken ran past the Royal Gallery, where majestic paintings of the best Erythian artists had been displayed for centuries. She then entered the Great Banquet Room, where feasts were held to celebrate valiant warriors, royal weddings and gala dinners. Vicken rushed through the Armory Room. Swords of kings and knights were displayed in breathtaking elaborate patterns that filled the high ceilings.

Suddenly, a tall Minotaur dressed in shiny brown boots and a long sapphire blue cloak lined with golden silk, appeared in front of little Vicken. "Where might you be going, girl?" he asked, snorting through his bovine nostrils. His large horns and thick dark fur made him look intimidating, but the little girl didn't seem to be exceedingly bothered by his menacing appearance.

"Ser Dorean," she said as she humbly curtsied. "I have a message for king Kavanagh."

"I see. What is your name—is it Vickar?"

"*Vicken*, ser."

"Ah, Vicken, of course. You can give *me* the message, girl, and I can take it to the king," he suggested, his voice deep and resounding. "He's resting in his private chambers at the moment."

Little Vicken looked at ser Dorean Amble, the king's chamberlain, with inquisitive eyes and a crinkled nose. "But ser, *I* have been instructed to give the message to the king... ser."

The Minotaur knelt to look into the kid's eyes. "Do you know what the message says?" he asked. Vicken shook her head. "What if it's bad news? The king can get angry if it's bad news, and you don't want him to be angry at you, right?" The girl shook her head again, the corners of her mouth turned down. "Well then, give me the message and *I* will take it to the king, so he'll be angry with *me* instead."

Vicken raised the scroll towards ser Dorean, but then her frown turned to a mischievous smirk, and she pulled her hand back. Before the chamberlain could even attempt to grab her, Vicken's bare feet were already pattering away along the corridor. "Vicken!" Dorean boomed. "Come back here, you little rascal! The king will not be happy about this!" he yelled as he ran after the child. Even with his Minotaur speed, Vicken outran him. As the kid swiftly squeezed between the guards and entered the king's chambers, she smelled the aroma of Oreka tea that infused the entire salon.

Vicken found herself in a large room with wooden floors and wooden walls, with large oval windows of irregular shapes and sizes. Sculpted sandstone pillars supported the ceiling, which was adorned with golden mosaics arranged in swirls and spirals. Outside, Vicken could see the glorious city of Niteria spreading before her, growing in harmony with the magical forest of Gartruth. On one side of the room was a large bookshelf and a heavy maple desk, surrounded by armchairs; at the opposite end was a long table, set with a beautiful white lace tablecloth and porcelain cups. Sat at the head was no other than the king of Erythya himself, King Noes Kavanagh, having his morning meal.

The king was a pompous man, dressed in large furs that covered his shoulders. Atop his head was a large golden crown that reflected the warm light shining through the room's irregular oval windows. The king's round face was adorned with a well-groomed beard and amber-coloured eyes. Pointed ears poked through his long wavy brown hair. To the king's right sat beautiful queen Emiliya, her golden locks gently cascading down her shoulders. She too had pointed ears and eyes the colour of the sunset. A sparkly tiara embellished with opals rested on her head. To the left of king Kavanagh was princess Thurin, a scrawny dark-haired girl happily indulging on a decadent apple pie.

They all turned when Vicken barged inside the Royal Hall, followed by an out-of-breath Dorean Amble. "Sire, I'm terribly sorry to interrupt your morning meal. I tried to stop her…" he panted, grunting heavily. The Minotaur was growing old. "She was too quick. Apparently, he has a message for you."

Vicken extended his tiny arm to the king, presenting the scroll. Her smile was wide, and her eyes glimmered as the king stood up and walked towards her to take the scroll.

"Well done, my dear girl," he said. "It is very honourable of you to deliver the message yourself. You'll make a fine knight one day." Vicken squirmed, and she shyly ran out of the Hall, the pitter-patter of her feet echoing in the distance. "Now, let's see what this fuss is all about." Kavanagh untied the red ribbon and broke the wax seal. He slowly unfurled the piece of paper. As he read, his face became hard and cold. For a few moments, he remained silent, his eyes narrowed, and his lips pressed tight. He looked at his wife, then at his chamberlain. "Ser Dorean, call a meeting with the Royal Council immediately. This is a matter of extreme urgency."

The most ominous silence reigned in the Royal Hall. The morning meal had been cleared, and queen Emiliya and princess Thurin had gone to their private chambers. The members of the Royal Council were sat around the table, each of them eagerly waiting for the king to speak.

"Dear friends," Kavanagh began. "This morning, I received disturbing news from our allies over the Trench. It appears that Lok has been reported attacking Karisa, one of the towns with the highest number of Erythian sympathisers in Remara," he announced. "Not just this, but he was apparently seen riding the Ulkar, which of course has caused terror and concern. Most of Karisa has been burnt down, and it seems he is heading towards us, riding the beastly wolf." Gasps and worried grunts arose from the members of the Royal Council. "Lok has done enough damage in Erythya, and we cannot allow him to come back again. The fact that he's alone and not accompanied by his usual band of mercenaries means that Darkstrom has planned something more than just a routine attack over Elora's Trench. We must be ready for anything. Lok is a Shadowcaster, and the Steinndyrr is always in danger, so we must be ready. I ask you, as my Royal Council, to advise me about the best course of action. As the war continues, Erythya becomes weaker, and the Emperor grows stronger. We have already lost too many souls since Darkstrom ascended to the throne."

"We have to stop Lok at once, Your Highness, before he enters Erythya. He's a Shadowcaster! Even without an army, he is too dangerous!" Dorean erupted.

"I disagree, ser Dorean," replied Syrio Froy, waving his thin and lanky arms. He was a Dryad—a Forest Nymph—and the Master of Treasury of Erythya. His disproportionately large and purple eyes glowed intensely as he spoke with a nasal voice. "We don't want the Remarans to know that we are aware of his whereabouts. Darkstrom will just take him back to the Eiriksberg before we can get to him. We should allow him into Erythya where we have an advantage, and then capture him here."

"I'm sure we can get to him before Darkstrom's soldiers do," Dorean replied in a confident yet stern tone. "What do you think, commander?"

Commander Sigrid Gudmund, a Veheer, was a well-respected woman. She had a stern, sharp face, and long blonde hair the colour of hay. Her eyes were the colour of deep, orange amber. "I think Syrio might be right. It could be too soon to seize him—it would just irate the Red Raven. We should wait until he's in Erythya to take him; maybe send a group of handpicked soldiers and keep it between a small number of trusted people."

"I understand your point, commander," Kavanagh said, "But isn't it too much of a risk to wait until he's past Elora's Trench?"

"Indeed, Sire," interjected Rollo Waldyr, Chief of Justice in the kingdom. He too was a Veheer, all dressed in red. "If he weren't a Shadowcaster, I'd be all up for the commander's plan, but given he *is*, I don't think it is wise to take any chances and let him inside Erythya."

"I actually believe the commander's plan is good," said Lady Lera, stroking her bristly blue hair. She was small and her face amphibian, with peculiar membranes protruding from the sides of her face. She belonged to the clan of the Azur, water-dwelling people from the Lakes of Asghen. Lady Lera was the Head Priestess of the Eredomyhms, appointed to managing the many temples of Erythya—each of them ran by women devoted to serving the gods of the Eredom. "Stopping him in Remara would only mean sending our soldiers in the enemy's territory. Let him in, and let the soldiers deal with him in our land."

"Lady Lera is right, Your Highness. It will be enough of a challenge to attack him and capture him when he's in Erythya with the support of the Golden Army. Capturing him in Remara where support is unreliable and Lok has allies is just asking for more trouble," commander Sigrid added.

"It's far too dangerous. The soldiers don't have much experience dealing with a Shadowcaster," ser Dorean pointed out with severity, shaking his large head and horns. "Once he's in Erythya, he *will* make his way to Niteria and we *will* have to start a war with Remara in order to stop him."

"The war has never stopped, ser Dorean," Syrio stated. "The simple act of sending Lok towards Erythya must be seen as an attack on us. Regardless of him being a Shadowcaster or not, and whether or not we can stop him, we must be ready for retaliation by the Remaran army. We will have to do our best to fight the Shadowcaster with what we have."

"There might be some hope," chimed in Estrid Øllnir, Head of Secrecy, charged with managing the Erythian spies in Remara and unmasking the Remaran spies in Erythya. She was the only Human in the Royal Council. She had come from Remara, seeking refuge for her family from the atrocities of the Empire. Her bald, tattooed scalp reflected the rays of sunlight shining through the stained windows. "Some of our sources closest to the Eiriksberg have reported strange stories amongst the soldiers of the Red Camp. They speak of two Lightbringers attacking them, an old man and a young lad. The old man is no doubt Alamor Eklund, although I don't know about the other boy."

"I thought Alamor was... dead," commander Sigrid replied, her eyebrows raised.

"He's been repenting on Mount Hargon," Lady Lera responded, the membranes on her face folding and unfolding as she breathed.

"We can't ask for his help, Your Highness," Dorean the Minotaur contested. His large, furry fingers were pressed hard on the wooden table. "If it weren't for him, we would have defeated Darkstrom a long time ago, and we wouldn't be in this situation today."

"He is a changed soul," Lady Lera argued. "What good would sending people to the Brotherhood be if we can't forgive them?"

"Thank you, Lady Lera. I agree," Kavanagh voiced. "We must take all the help we can get, and if asking Alamor for help is the only way to defeat Lok, then we must do so. We will send a message to our informers— Estrid, let them know we need Alamor to come to the Ærindel as soon as possible and to take with him this young boy. We must meet them and ask for their help to fight Lok and Darkstrom. They might be our only chance."

"Of course, Sire," Estrid replied, nodding respectfully at her monarch.

The king then turned to Sigrid. "Commander, I disagree with your plan. I don't think it would be wise to wait until Lok is in Erythya. The situation seems dire in any case, and we must do everything we can to stop it from getting worse as quickly as possible. I believe sending an elite troop to capture Lok is the right course of action, and you shall lead the expedition. Select a number of your best soldiers to fight by your side."

"You can count on me, Your Highness," the general responded. Although she clearly had doubts about the plan, her eyes were filled with determination. She lived to protect Erythya.

"Very well," the king resounded. "We have to be ready for anything the Emperor decides to throw at us. Our armies must be prepared. General, I trust you will see to that as well. Lady Lera, please pray for Erythya. We will need the help of the gods if we want to win this war. Pray for our families, and for the endurance of our magic."

"I shall, Your Highness, and I will spread the message to all our temples to do the same," the Head Priestess replied.

"Very well," said Kavanagh in a stentorian tone. "Ser Dorean, send a message to all the clans. This war is about to turn in our favour once more, though we must all be ready for the worse."

XIV

THE STAMPEDE

On the last day of the second week, Jason was the first to wake up, and he enjoyed the sun slowly rising in the distance, laying an orange veil on the magical lush fields of Grando's land. Over the gates, the miserable rocky Stonevale still sat in the darkness.

That morning everything was peaceful, and the only melodic sound came from the wind charms hanging outside the windows dangling and jingling as a gentle breeze blew. Jason put the kettle on the fireplace so everyone could enjoy some Oreka tea when they woke up. In the safety of the Leynahüs, Jason made the most of those lonely moments in the living room. He hadn't been on his own since he had left London to meet the rest of his team in Reykjavik and get onboard of the *Son of Odin*.

Alone with his mind, Jason could finally think about Clara, whose delicate face and deep blue eyes he kept seeing every time he was asleep. The roar of the waves crashing and the image of Clara disappearing into the ocean had haunted him every night. There was no god, he thought, that could be so heartless to take away such a perfect being from Earth. It should've been him to die, not her. If only he got to the life raft quicker… He thought he did everything right at the moment, but if he really had, Clara would have still been alive.

Jason walked around Grando's alchemy workstation, observing the beautifully coloured solutions, powders and rocks. On one of the shelves, a leather-bound notebook caught Jason's eye. Embossed on the cover were minute floral designs, similar to those on Alamor's Bag of Plenty. The pages were empty, and the paper was thick and rough as if it was handmade. Next to the book was a thin charcoal pencil, which Jason picked up and used to scribble a smoky black line on the notebook's first page.

The kettle began hissing. Jason pulled it out of the fire and made himself a cup of Oreka tea. He cleared away some of Grando's jars and flasks and sat on the large oak dining table. As the tea cooled down and the steam swirled up, Jason began drawing. He couldn't take pictures anymore without his camera, but he hoped his art lessons in school would aid him. Clara's face was still fresh in his mind; her long fair hair, her blue eyes always curious, her plump lips always smiling, a freckle under her left eye. The pencil flowed along the paper and, stroke after stroke, Jason found himself with an image of the woman he loved, as close to his memory as possible.

A gentle knock on the wooden wall startled Jason, making him slam the notebook shut. It was Anyir, who had finally woken up. She was still in her night robe, and her hair was ruffled.

"Who is that for?"

Jason looked at her as if he had just been caught red-handed committing a cardinal crime as he held onto the charcoal pencil. "I... I..." he muttered, not sure what to say. He began sweating awkwardly.

"The tea, who is it for?"

"Oh! Of course!" he said, relieved. "That's for... everyone... would you like a cup?"

"I would love that, thank you, Jason," said Anyir as she sat down next to him. "She is beautiful, you know," Anyir said, pointing to the notebook. Jason reluctantly opened it up again. "Who is it?" she asked.

Jason took the kettle, poured the Oreka tea for Anyir in a cup and brought it to the table. "Her name was Clara. She died the day I got here when our ship sank."

Anyir looked at him with surprise at first, but then with compassion. "That's... really terrible. I'm so sorry," she sighed. "What was she like?"

"She was always so kind and altruistic. All she cared for was the wellbeing of our planet and the animals and people living on it. We made such a mess back there, in the Otherside—destroying and exploiting everything we could to satisfy our greed. All Clara wanted was to bring some balance back between nature and humans. She was so driven, that's what I loved most about her. She had a fire in her, and you could see that in her eyes whenever she looked at you. I miss that the most, how she used to look at me."

"It's never easy, losing a loved one," Anyir said. "All we can do is remember them the best way we can, bring them back to life in our mind. They never truly leave us if they stay in our memory."

Jason thought about that for a moment. "I remember one time—it was our first trip together, and I had surprised Clara with tickets to go to Florence. She always went on about how much she wanted to go to the Uffizi Gallery. We strolled along corridors full of huge classical paintings by Leonardo, Raffaello, Michelangelo, and sculptures by Donatello. When we finally got out, after five hours of non-stop walking around, I asked her what she thought. She looked at me real serious and replied, "It was better than I expected! I would've never thought that mutant turtles could be such great artists!" We laughed, and we walked along the Ponte Vecchio holding hands. That was the best day of my life, all thanks to her."

"I didn't understand much of what you just said," Anyir commented frankly, "Yet, judging by the way you speak of her, she sounded great."

"She really was—more than great."

Suddenly, the front door burst open and Grando ran in flustered. He flung his leather coat onto the green sofa, and between heavy breaths, he urged, "Where's Alamor? I need to speak to him immediately. Alamor!" He seemed so stressed out he wasn't even smoking his usual cigar. Grando rumbled through the house and knocked heavily on Alamor's door. "Alamor! Wake up, you old git! I have news about Lok!"

A rustle came from the other side of the door, followed by some incomprehensible mutters and curses, as Alamor got ready to answer. "You said Lok?" he inquired when he finally opened the door.

"That's right. He seems to have stirred up chaos in Karisa and is heading towards Orachlion for some reason."

"Who is Lok?" Jason asked nonchalantly.

"Did you say Karisa?" asked Anyir, her eyebrows raised.

Grando took a deep breath. "We should all sit down and have a cup of Oreka first; this might be disconcerting."

Alamor cleared the oak table completely while Jason filled up another two bowls. They laid a large, time-worn map onto the table, and weighed it down with books and jars.

Grando looked at Alamor, who nodded back at him, so he began to explain, "Lok is a Shadowcaster and Darkstrom's best warrior. He has been raiding villages in Erythya and causing an uproar on the Emperor's behalf for years.

"What's a Shadowcaster?" Jason probed.

"Erm… Shadowcaster—a Lightbringer gone rogue… a Lightbringer who has lost control of his true identity," quickly explained Alamor, caught off guard.

"That can happen?" Jason asked as he felt his forehead starting to sweat.

Alamor put a hand on his shoulder to reassure him. "Don't worry, that won't happen to you. Lok was taken by Darkstrom as a child. The Emperor corrupted his mind, and trained him to use his Flare for evil, turning him into the Shadowcaster he is today."

Jason felt a great unease learning this fact. He didn't want to lose control of his powers and get turned into an evil warrior by the Emperor. Another fearful thought formed in his mind—would he have to fight Lok too, now? "What… what can he do?" he inquired.

Alamor seemed very reluctant to answer this last question. "Don't let Lok's nature bother you, son. The shadows cannot defeat the brightness of a Lightbringer."

"Yes, but… what are his powers, exactly?"

Once again, Alamor was dismissive. "He can control shadows, and darkness doesn't bother him."

Grando cleared his throat impatiently, eager to deliver the message. "Lok was seen travelling out of Tarvan Gher about three weeks ago, before he disappeared into the Iron Wood," Grando announced. "I hadn't heard of any news about him until today when I met with my informer. Just over two weeks ago, a man in black armour rode into Karisa on top of the Ulkar and confronted some men in the village. Apparently, some of these men were Erythian sympathisers. Lok found out and burned down their house. The fire spread and burned down half of the town, killing a few people."

Jason thought about the description Grando just gave of Lok. Was he the man that he met when he arrived? *Two weeks ago.*

"I need to go back," Anyir said. "Today."

"Anyir, we need to be careful not to make any rash decisions," Alamor intervened.

"I've waited here long enough now, and I want to go back home. My feet are healed, and I want to leave. I have waited almost a year to see my husband, and now… he might… he might be…" Anyir faltered, her eyes tearing up. "I need to go see if he's ok."

"I understand how you feel, Anyir, but I don't think it's wise to go to Karisa just yet. Darkstrom will have sent someone after us, and the first place they'll go to look is Karisa."

"I don't care. I have two Lightbringers with me, and I can burn the Emperor's soldiers to a crisp now."

"It's not safe, Anyir, especially with Lok on the loose," Alamor replied. He then turned to Jason, "What Lok's plan is, I don't know, but if Darkstrom has unleashed his best warrior on his own, it means he's planned something more than a simple raid. I fear Valkadia might be in danger…"

"It's not all," added Grando, handing a small paper roll tied with a red ribbon. "The king has requested your presence at the court in Niteria."

"The king? King Kavanagh?" Anyir asked, astounded.

Jason was bewildered by the speed at which information spread in Valkadia. They didn't even have telephones. Then, he remembered that Grando was an Erythian spy. His network of intelligence was impressive, and Jason wondered how the bushy-bearded man managed to get in and out of the Leynahüs unseen to carry out his surveillance job.

Alamor took the scroll and read silently. "I see…." He muttered as he stroked his beard. "We must leave today. If Kavanagh knows we're here, Darkstrom will find out in no time. We must head straight to Elora's Trench and cross over to Erythya as soon as possible. We'll have to use the secret passages that the Erythian spies use. There's one in Sasken, a long staircase down one side and up the other, and it's the fastest way to get to Erythya from Grando's house. Once we have crossed, we'll go to Malion. I need to speak to Baldor, and then we must go to Niteria to meet the king." He then looked at Anyir. "sorry, Anyir, but Karisa must wait."

A deep sadness slowly appeared on Anyir's turquoise eyes. "I must go home, Alamor. I cannot come with you," she replied. "I will get a horse and travel with you for a while, but then I'll head to Karisa."

"It's not safe," Alamor protested.

"If my husband is dead, then I don't care about being safe."

Alamor looked at Anyir with apprehension, but then realised he had to give up. "Very well, if you've made your decision, then I won't stand in your way. That said, we should leave now without further ado. Let's get our bags ready and the horses saddled."

The three companions packed their bags, and Grando supplied the trio with sausages, bread, cheese, some vegetables and fruit, two bottles of mead, blankets, clothes, and two healthy horses for Jason and Anyir. They loaded all their belongings onto the horses and led them to the gates of the Leynahüs. They stopped briefly at the rusty gate to say their goodbyes to Grando. Jason took a moment to snap a mental image of the magical invisible house before the dark Stonevale would drag them back in.

"Goodbye, my dear friend. It was such a pleasure to see you again," said Alamor. "However, I have a feeling we shall see you soon, so this is not a goodbye after all."

"I have the same feeling," Grando replied, smiling beneath his big black beard. The two old friends embraced warmly, roughly patting each other on the back in a brotherly manner.

"Thank you for everything, Grando," Jason exclaimed.

"Yes, thank you, Grando," Anyir repeated. "I don't know what I would've done without your hospitality."

"No, thank you, my dear friends. You have reminded me how exciting my life used to be, and you have given me hope for the future. Have a safe journey. Good luck with whatever you may encounter. Oh! I almost forgot! I have something for you two—a parting gift, as it were." He put his hand in the pocket of his leather waistcoat and took out three small and round bottles sealed with cork and wax, containing a bright green liquid. "If you ever need to clear the way, these will come handy. Try not to sit on them though!"

"Thank you, Grando," said Alamor. "We've been fortunate to have found you. May light protect you."

"And may light protect *you*."

The three companions jumped on their horses and rode out of the sunny Leynahüs. Once more, they found themselves in the desolate Empire of Remara. The cold penetrated Jason's bones, so he promptly grabbed the knitted sweater Anyir had made him and slipped it on beneath his yellow trench coat.

They mad many hours of riding ahead of them, following a faint path through the Stonevale that would lead them to a secret passage in Sasken.

However, shortly after they had left Grando's land, Alamor urged them to halt. "We're being followed."

"Are you serious?" Anyir yelped.

Jason closed his eyes and let the Flare take over. As the fire flowed through his veins, he heard the sound of horse hooves hitting the hard ground getting louder. "Alamor's right. I hear two horses."

"Do you hear that rattling noise? That's armour. Two soldiers on horseback are coming this way. I thought we'd be followed at some point, but not this soon. Darkstrom must be really worried. Quick, let's keep riding."

"Wait," Jason exhorted. "I hear something else. It's like a storm—thunders."

Alamor focused, but then he replied with increasing concern, "That's not a storm. That's a herd of Goplen."

"Goplen? You mean those huge walking vegetables?" asked Jason, thinking back to his books.

"That's right. They're heading for Lake Malion, and they're fast beasts. We have to keep moving if we don't want to be caught between them and the soldiers."

As they galloped along the expanse of grey dirt, Jason looked to his left where hundreds of green dots advanced quickly towards them. They looked like simple trees, some taller than others, shaken by the wind. Yet, they kept getting larger, and the rumble of their pachyderm feet beating the ground grew louder as they approached. Soon, their green, scaly skin covered with moss reflected the icy light of the Empire. Their eyes looked deranged, and they drooled out of their turtle-like orange beaks. Enormous, contorted trees and shrubs grew in the middle of their back and enveloped the animals' bodies with a network of rotting roots. It was clear they were sick, just like Alamor had told him. It was as if an enormous, poisoned forest was flooding the Stonevale, rushing towards the three travellers. Fir trees grew on some Goplen, while others had elms or oaks, all surrounded by thick, leafless bushes and dying flowers.

The whistling noise of an arrow cutting through the air startled Jason. He turned around, and behind them, he saw two figures in black armour riding black horses.

"It's the Omüms!" Jason exclaimed.

"Quick! We can lose them if we get to the other side before the herd of Goplen crosses!" Alamor replied.

The earth shook, and another arrow planted itself in the hard ground next to Anyir's horse. Seeing the Goplen approaching faster and faster, the three spurred their horses to a mad gallop.

Feeling between a rock and a hard place, Jason started panicking. Without Alamor or Anyir, it would have been the end for him. He would no longer have anyone to guide him or to teach him the most basic parts of everyday life in the mysterious land of Valkadia. Where would he go?

Who could he trust? There was no way for him to go back to England or save Valkadia without their help.

A third arrow whizzed past Jason's ear, snapping him back into reality. The Omüms were getting close now, so close Jason could see Etrel's gruesome face scars.

Then, the herd of Goplen arrived, lifting thick clouds of dust with their enormous flat feet. Jason couldn't see anything except for the massive green legs passing by him, crashing into the ground like stone columns. All the sounds got muffled by the roar of the stomping herd. In the background, he heard the faint yells of the two Omüms, accompanied by the neighing of horses, and the occasional whistle of an arrow.

Jason tried to call Alamor, but no voice replied. The feet of the Goplen landed so near to him that the earth shook. Jason's horse whinnied and reared on its hind legs, it's eyes widened with fear. Another foot hit the ground next to him. There seemed to be thousands of Goplen all around him, hammering the ground with their mastodontic feet. Jason tried to move from there, but there was nowhere to go. His horse had lost all sense of direction. Jason tried to locate his friends under the thick layer of dust, but the Goplen's thumps and grunts were too loud and confusing. He tried to call Alamor and Anyir again. No one answered. He had no idea where the Omüms had gone either.

Jason closed his eyes, concentrating on his Flare, and held tight onto the reins of his horse. Time slowed down, and even the dust seemed to puff up in clouds less violently. He called for the air, and the air listened. Jason flung his arms open, and suddenly the dust cleared away for at least a moment before another gigantic foot hit the dirt. This gave Jason enough time to see Anyir, who was sat on her horse stock-still, petrified, looking ahead into the empty space. "Anyir!" he called. "Anyir, snap out of it!" She just couldn't hear him.

He looked around before the dust could rise again like a storm, but there was no sign of Alamor and the Omüms. Had Alamor just sacrificed himself for them? Had he gone and left him and Anyir behind to save himself? "Alamor! Alamor!" he shouted, but nobody replied. He was alone in the dust, amongst pachyderms. He prayed Alamor hadn't left him. There was so much he still had to learn, so much he wanted to know. How would he get to Niteria and meet king Kavanagh, who could help him go back home, without Alamor's mentoring? Jason felt lost.

When the last Goplen trampled the earth and the dust settled, and Jason still couldn't find the Veheer, he rode up to Anyir and grabbed her by her arm to shake her out of her shocked state. "Anyir! Come on! I can't find Alamor! We'll be screwed without him!" he shouted.

At last, he caught her attention, and she looked back at him with a confused expression. Distraught, her eyes teared up. "I'm so sorry, Jason. I don't know what happened to me…"

"Are you all right?" Jason asked.

"Yes… I… It was just the noise, the ground shaking… I just didn't know where to go," she replied.

"Can you see Alamor anywhere?"

Anyir looked around. The Stonevale was dustier than ever, and there was no sign of Alamor. She shook her head and looked at Jason apprehensively.

There was no sign of his mentor, and no sign of the Omüms either. "He must have led them away," Jason observed. His heart tightened at the thought of being left alone, without any guidance.

"I'm sure he'll come back. He wouldn't leave us alone for too long," Anyir tried to reassure him. As her gaze travelled into the distance, her eyes widened with disbelief. "What's that?" Anyir suddenly asked, squinting ahead.

"What's what?" Jason responded, unsure what his friend was looking at.

"There, can you see it?" Anyir said, pointing her finger towards a seemingly devoid landscape.

Jason looked ahead in the desolate plain. "I can only see rocks and dirt. What are you looking at?"

"Something is glimmering under all the dust." She got up and ran to what Jason thought was an empty spot. As she began removing some soil with her hands, she revealed a long, shiny sword. Anyir looked at Jason with a combination of excitement and grief. "Isidir," she murmured.

Not only Alamor had driven the *Omüms* away, but he had also left them a great weapon. However, the Veheer was now without its trusted companion.

Jason lifted Isidir carefully and blew on its shiny blade. The leaf-shaped emerald shimmered even in the gloom of the Stonevale. He unsheathed the Remaran sword he had been using since the Red Camp and dropped it in the dust, and slid Isidir in its place. Without his mentor, he felt hopeless, but at least that way, he felt like Alamor was still by his side.

XV

THE NECROMANCER

A plume of smoke rose high in the sky behind them as Lok and the Ulkar left Karisa and made their way to Orachlion. He had packed his bags with plenty of food that he had taken from the beer house, and he had his new sword, Viggr, strapped to his belt. Lok and the Ulkar continued their journey along the Scarlet Way.

The journey was long but easy. Nobody dared stop or question them. People knew who Lok was, and they wouldn't have disturbed him even if he was riding a horse. However, the Ulkar was a more effective deterrent. Lok felt a perverse satisfaction flowing within him whenever people fled at the sight of the Shadowcaster and the Wolf.

Lok was aware of the risk he had put himself into, exposing himself and potentially Darkstrom's plan to the Erythians. The Emperor's orders were clear: maintain the secrecy, get the Steinndyrr. He was sure that the news of him attacking Karisa had already reached both the Ærindel and the Eiriksberg, and that he had put Darkstrom in a sticky situation. More than anything, he knew the Erythians would soon be on his back, and this would complicate his attempt to cross Elora's Trench.

His stomach churned when he thought of Darkstrom's reaction to his loss of powers. The Emperor had trained him as the best warrior in Valkadia and had taught him how to use his Flare to be the best Shadowcaster that ever existed. Without his powers, he would not be able to complete his mission. Without the Flare, how could he get to the Steinndyrr? He had to go to Orachlion. He had to find out how to get his powers back.

After four days of travelling, the monotonous expanse of the Stonevale made Lok realise how boring the Remaran landscape was. Finally at Orachlion, the grey, stone-built town spread out in front of them. Low lying stone houses with wooden roofs were placed neatly against each other, with River Oriya flowing through the city, cutting it in half. Orachlion was renowned as one of the Empire's most significant provider of granite, derived from quarries in the hills of the Dragon Moors. Most of the people in Orachlion were stonemasons, cutting and processing stone into building blocks to be loaded on flat riverboats and transported all over Remara.

Suddenly, the woman's voice echoed in his mind, taking over every thought and memory. Lok staggered as the woman spoke inside his head, almost falling to the ground. The voice was loud. She was near, yet the voice sounded like it was coming from far away. The words were so clear, so punctuated. Her voice penetrated his head like a nail. Lok kept advancing, attracted by the sound of the woman's voice.

Lok, she called. *Come to me, Lok.*

The sky became covered with dark clouds, and thick fog permeated the village, rising from the ground. From behind the mist appeared a figure dressed in a long white tunic. Her hair was grey except one candid white lock, and her face was marked with arcane symbols that not even Lok knew. One particular detail, perhaps the most disconcerting and impactful, struck Lok's attention. Her eyes were completely white, and yet they stared right into Lok's soul.

Follow me, Lok. You seek answers. I shall help you find them. Though he could see the woman, her voice was still in Lok's head.

In a state of daze, Lok left the *Ulkar* behind and followed the woman in white. She walked in front of him, barefooted, though she left no prints on the muddy ground. Lok didn't know the reason why, but he trusted her blindly. He walked through the haze, following the white spectre until she led him to a large tent in the middle of the city's poorer quarters. Nobody was around, and the city was silent, except for a few faint whispers, and the cries of hungry toddlers. Occasionally, a cat's meow disturbed the quiet. Everyone and everything knew something beyond their understanding was going on that evening, and nobody and nothing wanted to be part of it.

The tent was dark, made up mostly of thick blankets and old rugs, supported by flimsy sticks that could fall with the slightest breeze. Inside were more blankets, some pillows, and the bones of birds and other animals hanging off the ceiling and lying around on the floor.

"Welcome, Lok," she said, with her real voice. The voice shattered Lok's mind like a hammer on a frozen sword.

"Who... who are you?" asked Lok, jolting out of his clouded state.

"They call me the Necromancer," she announced. "I realise I asked a lot of you coming here. Thank you for trusting me."

"You said you have answers," Lok spouted. "Where is this man named Jason who holds my powers?"

"Yes, of course... many questions you have, and answers I shall give."

Finally someone who can tell me what the hell is going on, he thought. "How did he take my powers? How do I get them back?" he uttered, not waiting for a second longer. He needed to know, and he wanted to get back on the road as soon as possible.

"One thing at a time, dear Lok. I have waited a long time to see you again," the Necromancer replied.

Lok huffed. "What do you mean 'see you again'? I've never seen you before." He raised the tone of his voice, "Listen, I have travelled a long way to find out something about the loss of my powers. Tell me what I need to know."

"Do you know what a Necromancer is?" she asked, completely ignoring Lok's questions and rising anger. Her tone remained calm and composed.

Lok clenched his fists, his knuckles turning white. He felt the veins on his neck bulging as he grew impatient. "I have no time for meaningless chats, woman. I must go complete my mission. The fate of Remara depends on me."

"A Necromancer is someone capable of talking to the dead," she stated. "You see—the dead know everything that has occurred in the past. They are the true wisdom of the world. Lives lived; lessons learned. People met; people lost. Mistakes made; right turns taken. The dead have knowledge that earthlings have no access to. Necromancers are the bridge in between."

"How does this have anything to do with Jason or my powers?" Lok growled.

"You seek answers, correct? I do not know all the answers to your queries, but the dead might. The dead have seen things that we have forgotten, and often have answers to our deepest concerns. Ask yourself something, Lok. Have you never wondered about who you are—who you really are? Why did the Emperor decide to choose *you* as one of the last people with the Flare? Have you never wondered about where you came from?"

"I was born and raised in Tarvan Gher, at the Eiriksberg."

"Were you? Remember, Lok... remember."

"Why is this relevant? I want to know where my powers have gone. What does this have anything to do with it?"

"What is your first memory of the Flare? Can you remember, Lok?"

"I... I was..." Lok could not remember. He felt his mind tightening as if it was being crushed from the inside. "Stop playing tricks with me, woman!"

"You can't remember, can you? You think you were the *chosen one*. But the Emperor did not choose you. You were handed to him, and he saw an opportunity."

"Of course he saw an opportunity. I am the only one Shadowcaster in Remara. That's why I'm so precious to Darkstrom—that's why I need my powers back; that's why I need to find Jason."

The Necromancer lit up two candles on a wobbly, wax-covered stool at one end of the tent and set fire to a bundle of mixed dried leaves. A thick smoke swirled up as she began waving the herbs in the air. "Go to Niteria to find him. It is written in both his and your destiny that you shall meet each other. It shall all be clear soon, my boy. You will get your powers back, but first of all, you *must* remember."

With a feline leap, the Necromancer jumped next to Lok and waved the smoking leaves under his nose, making him breathe in the fumes. As he inhaled the thick smoke of the herbs, Lok's consciousness began fading. He tried to hold onto reality, grasping on the hilt of his sword Viggr. The face of the Necromancer staring back at him became blurry.

"No..." he murmured as his head slumped. He felt cold all of a sudden, and he started to sweat. "I... need answers..." he whispered.

Then, Lok's body dropped on the tent's floor like a bag of sand as he went into a deep sleep.

Lok found himself in a white marble palace, with large lancet windows and green carpets. The room was large, much like one of the chambers in the Eiriksberg. The ceilings were decorated with intricate plasterwork. Dark wooden tables and cabinets were placed thoughtfully around the room, and everything was clean as if it had been attended to earlier that day. Lok walked around inspecting the room, intrigued by the place he had just landed in.

He looked outside one of the large windows. The room was high up in the building, and a large city spread before his eyes. In the distance, the sun shining on a large body of water glimmered into Lok's eyes. Far ahead was a large harbour with a monumental entrance. He realised with utter disgust that he was standing on Erythian ground. Lok was in Malion, and according to his studies, only one building stood so tall you could see the rest of the city: Rennhall's Library.

Had he made it into Erythya? How? When? He had no recollection of crossing Elora's Trench and certainly didn't remember entering the Library. The last thing he saw was the Necromancer's white eyes gazing into his own, followed by sudden darkness. *This must be a dream*, he thought. He wanted out of it.

All of a sudden, a ball of fire crossed the sky like a comet, crashing into the city and destroying a whole block of buildings. After a couple of seconds, more fire came rushing through the air, landing violently onto the ground and laying more waste to the city. Terrified screams rose from beneath the Library, and among the cobbled streets. Lok watched in horror as a fireball hit a crowded square, killing everyone present. He had seen death, but this was so much and all at once. During his raids in Erythya, Lok had only fought warriors and soldiers. Sometimes he had battled with villagers, but they were still brandishing weapons, making them a threat. The people down in the streets of Malion were not a threat—they were hiding from the menace of Remara. Did the fact that they were Erythians make them dangerous? Lok thought so, but his heart sank either way.

The sky turned dark. Columns of smoke appeared all around. Lake Malion was in flames, and Lok realised that the smoke and fire were from Remaran and Erythian ships floating like cadavers in the black water. Swords were clanking and steel was banging, and the eerie bellowing sound of war horns echoed throughout the city.

Lok looked around the room for an escape. His fists closed so tight his knuckles became white. A door appeared in front of him. From the other side, he could hear the cries of babies and the calming sound of a feminine voice trying to reassure them. Lok opened the door. In the middle of the room, a woman was hiding behind a large marble table carved with the map of Valkadia. Lok realised he knew her. She was the same person from his previous dream—the woman who took over Darkstrom's face for a moment. He recognised her auburn hair; her skin was pale. She looked elegant and graceful in her long white nightgown. Two new-borns were cradled in her arms, their cries piercing Lok's ears. Between the heads of the two new-borns, Lok noticed a silver necklace with a metal pendant hanging around the woman's neck. "Shh," she murmured to her children. "Don't cry, my darlings. Everything will be all right. I love you both so much."

The auburn-haired mother looked up at Lok and said, with tears in her eyes, "Help them, I beg you." It was only at that moment that Lok saw the bloodstains on her nightgown, running all the way onto the floor. "Take them, save them."

Lok rushed to the woman's help, but before he could even get close enough to her, Lok felt himself being dragged away. The woman and her two sons zoomed out of his vision and disappeared into a black void.

He abruptly found himself riding a white horse in the night. Strapped to his chest were the two babies, wrapped up tightly and cosily in thick blankets. Behind him, he could hear men shouting. They wanted the two new-borns. Lok kept riding and riding until he got to a hill littered with ruins.

Dorth.

He crossed the Elven ruins, wary of the men who were following him. An engraved monolith stood before him. He dismounted, and placed his left hand on the stone, cradling the two babies with his right arm. There was a sudden blast of light. It was as if all the lightning in the sky converged into his hand and flowed through the rock. He screamed as his hand burned with the scorching heat of the light. Soldiers appeared behind Lok, but a breach opened in the monolith and he tried to jump in before the soldiers could get to him.

Alas, it was too late. One of the soldiers grabbed hold of his shoulder, ripping the sling that was strapped around Lok's back, carrying the two babies. Lok managed to catch the boys before they fell to the ground, but the soldiers pinned him down and took them from him.

Lok fought with his life, adamant about getting the new-borns back. The runes on his Elven sword shined in the night, and the soldiers fell before Lok's might. He struggled and battled, but in the end, he could only retrieve one infant, and he watched as the soldiers rode away with the other.

Lok snapped back into reality, sweating and panting heavily and almost choking on his own breath.

"What was that? What did you do to me?" he yelled, but the Necromancer was gone. He was alone in the tent, confused and full of yet more questions. His mind was rushing. He looked at his left hand—to his relief, there was no sign of any burn.

Lok ripped the tent open and rushed out into the silent city of Orachlion, looking around himself like a feral animal that had just been ambushed, in search for his attacker. He screamed, banging his feet onto the wet floor. He had been deceived, lured by the old woman with a promise of answers, yet his questions and doubts had only grown. He walked along the shadowy streets, looking behind every corner for the Necromancer, but nobody was around. Eventually, he saw the *Ulkar* calmly sleeping where Lok had left him, like a mountain inflating and deflating as it breathed and snorted. Lok stroked the thick, rough fur of the beast, which woke up with a snarl. "This was such a waste of time, beastie. Let's get out of here, and let's go to Niteria. I need to find the bastard who took my powers."

As they left Orachlion and began making their way towards Erythya, Lok's mind spun with thoughts. Who was the woman with auburn hair that kept appearing in his dreams? Who were the two babies? Why was he trying to open an Elder Stone? Why had the Necromancer shown him that vision—was it a memory?

Lok didn't know. Maybe going to Erythya would help.

XVI

ASH AND LIGHTNING

Jason and Anyir ate little that night, absorbed in thoughts and concerns about the future. They had decided not to light a fire for their camp to avoid attracting soldiers or spies. The thundering sound of the Goplen marching over them resounded in Jason's mind. They felt lost without Alamor.

"Have you ever been to Erythya?" asked Jason, trying to break the silence.

"Never," Anyir replied. "But my husband went there once or twice to deliver weapons over the Trench, and he was astounded by the beauty of it—nothing to do with the depressing grey place that Remara is. The Erythians have managed to turn their kingdom into a true paradise. Apparently, Malion is an amazing city, with white marble buildings and large domed roofs. There are trees and plants everywhere, and the people dress in the most colourful tunics."

Jason mused over the idea of meeting these fancy inhabitants dressed in Erythian clothes. He imagined everybody strolling around the white city of Malion like actors attending the Academy Awards, elegantly clothed and celebrating their extravagant lives. As he envisioned what his life would be once he arrived in Erythya, a daunting thought struck him. "How do you suppose we cross Elora's Trench?" he asked. "Do you have any idea where this secret staircase might be? Alamor didn't tell us much other than it's near Sasken."

"He said there were multiple ones along the Trench. I'm not sure how we'll find it—he never said exactly where it was either, but I'm sure we'll know what to look for once we're closer. We'll keep heading towards Sasken, and we'll see what we can do from there."

"All right," replied Jason, not totally convinced of their plan. He really wished Alamor were there to help them. "It'll be like finding a needle in a haystack."

"A what?"

"A needle in a haystack—you've never heard this expression?"

"Never," Anyir replied giggling. "You speak funny sometimes, Jason. Does everybody in the Otherside talk like you?"

Jason snickered. "I guess," he replied. "It's strange, being here. I miss it back home, in the Otherside. Everybody knows what I mean, and I understand how everything works. As a kid, I dreamt of finding myself in a world like this. Having powers and magical abilities was all I wished for growing up—what every kid wished for, really. I never thought this stuff actually existed. I'm not really sure how much I want this anymore. So far, this has only brought trouble and death."

Anyir looked in the distance, her mind spiralling with thoughts. "You'll get back home, of that I'm sure. However—and I hate to say this—but considering what Alamor has set out for you, there will only be more trouble. Darkstrom won't stand by if there's a Lightbringer on the loose, and I only believe this is the beginning of a much bigger storm. I know you've already lost a lot, and I can't imagine how hard it must be for you to deal with all of this after Clara's death, but you're the only one that can really make a difference."

"I just wish it didn't have to be me," he sighed. "I couldn't save Clara *or* Alamor. How am I supposed to save Valkadia?"

"You don't know if Alamor is dead," Anyir replied.

"Still, I'm not strong enough for any of this."

"You're the only one that can save us."

During that night, Jason dreamt about the Child Snatcher again. The hood once again veiled his face, and the auburn-haired woman was just as beautiful as he remembered. Like the last time, the palace crumbled, and the Child Snatcher took the two new-borns away. Yet, this time he took a closer look at the hooded man. As he kneeled over to take the two infants, his hood moved slightly—just enough for Jason to notice pointed ears like those of a Veheer, and long fair hair. *An Elf?* Jason woke up with cold sweats on the hard and cold ground of the Stonevale, heavily breathing as if he had just been choked.

The following day, Jason and Anyir kept riding, driving their horses to near exhaustion. Eventually, they got to a large river. Jason had studied the map of Valkadia, and he was confident that the path to Sasken from Grando's Leynahüs didn't involve crossing any more rivers. If he remembered correctly, they had to go north for about ninety miles, across the flat land of the Stonevale.

"Are you sure we're going the right way?" Jason asked his travel companion.

"Yes, I've gone to Sasken many times," Anyir was quick to dismiss.

"You're positive about that? I don't think we're supposed to cross a river. I have a feeling we might be going the wrong way."

"Trust me, will you?" Anyir snapped, leaving Jason no choice.

They crossed the river, and their horses neighed as they waded through the freezing water.

Surely enough, they got to a village, but when they saw what had happened, they both halted and jumped off their horses. Anyir froze with her eyes wide and full of tears, her lip quivering.

The village was in smoke. It was a pile of rubble and ash, and bricks and wooden beams were piled up on the sides of the streets where the houses should have been. The wooden roofs and walls were now dust, and only a few buildings still stood, waiting only for a breath of wind to tip them over. The few stone walls and columns that supported the houses were the only parts that had survived the fire. Everything else, ash. Grey dust fluttered in the air, shrouding the village.

"Please, son! Wake up!" cried a woman as she dug her face in her hands and wailed. Her child was resting in her lap, motionless. Jason looked towards another side of the village. "My home!" screamed a man with clothes covered in ash, standing in front of what once was his house. The loud creaks of the charred wood made the man jolt, and he retreated just in time before the rest of the building collapsed heavily around him. Orphaned children wandered in search of something to eat, holding hands with their brothers and sisters. Stray dogs were lurking around for something to eat.

Jason looked at Anyir, who had fallen to her knees and was digging her fingers in the ash-covered ground as she breathed heavily. She couldn't stop her tears. Her face was that of utter horror and disbelief. As terrible as it was to see Sasken burnt down and its inhabitants in distress, Jason couldn't understand why Anyir was so distraught. Then, it daunted on him. He had been right—they *had* gone the wrong way. This wasn't Sasken at all. A deep feeling of mistrust assailed Jason's consciousness. "You took me to Karisa, didn't you, Anyir?" Jason questioned. They were supposed to be in Sasken by then, looking for the hidden staircase and busy getting across Elora's Trench. Now, they were stuck in a pile of rubble.

Anyir looked up at him, struggling to breathe between her sobs. Her gaze was glued on the smoke plumes rising from the ashes of the village. "I- I... had to... I'm sorry. I... I had to see..." she stuttered. "My home..."

The feeling of betrayal hit him in the gut. "Why did you trick me, Anyir?!" he boomed. He felt his body heating up uncontrollably. "We were supposed to go to Sasken! How are we going to make it to Malion now?! We agreed we wouldn't come here; it's too dangerous!"

"I- I had to try..."

"How can I trust you if you can't even take me to the right place, huh? You were meant to help me!"

"I'm sorry, all right?!" she yelled, her voice breaking, her fingers digging deeper into the soil. "I haven't seen my husband for months; I have to see him! I'm sorry I ruined your plans!"

"It's not safe here for us, Anyir! What if there are soldiers here?! Do you think we could fight them all by ourselves?!" Jason howled, waving his hands maniacally.

"We have powers!" she screamed back. "We can protect ourselves!"

Jason brought his hands to his head. "Can we?! We don't have enough control over our powers to defeat the soldiers yet!"

"You trained! You're ready! Of course you can!"

Jason breathed, realising he was starting to lose control. They did have powers, but he still doubted himself too much to face somebody like Tortugal again. The idea of finding the Orc standing in front of him scared the living hell out of the young Londoner. He looked at his friend, her hands covered in ash, her cheeks streaked by her tears. Why was he getting so angry, when it was Anyir that had lost everything? She was the one that should have been angry. "What I've learnt is still all too new to me. I can barely protect myself. How do you think I'll be able to protect us both?"

"I can—"

"You can what? Burn them to a crisp? We can't just assume that because we have powers, we can do everything we want. Without Alamor, we are in constant danger until we get to Malion."

"I'm sorry," muttered Anyir, looking at the ruins of the homes scattered all around. She remembered every misplaced brick of the buildings, every patch of paint flaking off the doors of the houses. Now, the village no longer existed. Returning to Karisa had been her dream since she was taken to Red Camp, and that's what kept her going. Now, it was gone.

Jason was silent for a moment. He had to be there for his friend. If he had the same opportunity to go back home, he would have taken it too. He would have given everything to see Clara again. "I'm sorry too." The Lightbringer smiled at Anyir and offered his hand to pull her back up. "Come on, let's go find your husband."

Together they walked towards the main square in the centre of the village, where a collection of makeshift tents had been set up in order to give shelter to the survivors of Karisa.

A man in his thirties with long fair hair, and a sturdy build, appeared from behind the crowd of villagers. "Anyir?" he called. A sudden silence fell among the people, followed by tentative whispers. "Is that really you?"

A shimmer of hope appeared in Anyir's eyes when she saw her old friend. "Gregor!" she cried, running towards the man. They embraced tightly, and Anyir struggled to let go.

"We all thought you were dead," said Gregor. "It's so nice to see you again."

"This is Jason McAnnon… a dear friend," she introduced.

"Pleasure to meet you," the fair-haired man greeted. "Gregor Svenn, son of Bron."

Jason leaned forward for a handshake, which remained awkwardly unshaken. "How long have you known Anyir?" Jason asked.

"Long enough," he replied bluntly. "Where have you come from?"

Even if Gregor was a long-time friend of Anyir's, Jason had a bizarre feeling about him. He didn't really know how to answer that question, as he feared he would give too much away with anything he'd say. "I was a prisoner at Red Camp, just like Anyir. That's how we met."

Gregor's jaw dropped. "Is that where you have been all this time?" he asked his friend.

"If it weren't for Jason, I would never have left the Red Camp," interjected Anyir.

"You two escaped?! How?!"

"We had to," she replied. "It wasn't easy... but I had to escape. I had to return." After waiting for months, Anyir looked up at her old friend and finally mustered the courage to ask, "Gregor, where is Oblivan?"

Gregor looked down, struggling to make eye contact with Anyir. He shook his head slowly. "We can't find him anywhere," he said in a tone full of grief.

Anyir didn't seem to understand what Gregor was really saying. "Have you looked properly? Karisa may look small, but there are plenty of places one can hide," she asked, naïvely.

"He's not hiding, Anyir," Gregor said slowly.

"Are you sure? Maybe he's still hiding from the person that did this to our town."

"He's not hiding," Gregor repeated firmly. "I was there when ser Lok set fire to his workshop. I tried to get him out, but the flames were too hot. I couldn't risk leaving my kids without a father... I'm so sorry. This is all we found," he explained, pulling a brass bracelet out of his pocket.

Anyir took it, her hands shaking like leaves. "It's... it's his bracelet," she said in a croaked voice. "This can't be. He's alive," she contested. "He's somewhere—maybe not in Karisa. Maybe he's escaped. I'm sure he's alive. I'll give him this back when I see him," she said as she stroked the bracelet.

"Anyir... Oblivan is dead," said Gregor.

"No... he's alive. He's here," Anyir babbled, confused. "He's..." she asked, looking at Gregor, dazed.

"Oblivan is dead, Anyir. I'm so sorry..." Gregor reiterated in a hushed tone.

"That's not true," she protested. All of a sudden, Anyir let out a loud, maniacal laugh. It was a laughter Jason had never heard before—a mixture of a crazy cackle and a desperate wail. "You're lying!" she said between her giggles. Her eyes were wide, filled with disbelief. "Where is Oblivan?" she repeated.

Gregor and Jason looked at each other, concerned for their friend. Gregor intervened, awkwardly approaching Anyir. Though he had dealt with the death and despair that had assailed the village, Anyir's reaction seemed to worry him the most. He looked around with concern—Anyir was attracting the unwanted attention of the villagers. "No one could have survived that fire, Anyir. So many people died in the village because of it," said the burly man.

"No. He's alive," she argued, her laughter slowly turning into a lament. "He's here, and he's alive." She walked back and forth for a minute or two, embracing herself tightly, staring at the burnt buildings. "No!" she cried, falling to the ground, grabbing onto her long hair in desperation. Jason had never heard anybody cry like that. Anyir's anguish made Jason's heart ache—he knew exactly what she was going through. "This can't be…" she murmured. Her tears dropped on the ash-covered ground.

Jason walked over to his friend and crouched beside her. He hugged her, and she hugged him back, grabbing onto his yellow coat tightly. "I'm so sorry, Anyir."

Anyir glanced up at Jason with teary eyes, and they stared at each other deeply, sharing each other's sorrow for a moment. No words were needed. They had both lost so much.

"Sorry for taking you here," Anyir said.

Jason smiled kindly. "Stop being daft. If I were you, I would have dragged anybody to my village to find my partner," he said.

Suddenly, Gregor's deep voice bellowed behind them, "Anyir, I'm so glad you're alive, but I cannot allow you to stay," he urged. He looked around impatiently, torn between his friendship with Anyir and the protection of his fellow villagers. "Soldiers have been coming here every day for the past week. If they find out that you are here… well… they'll kill you and destroy what's left of the village. I am just trying to protect who's left."

"But… this is my home," Anyir replied, her eyebrows furrowed.

"It's not safe here, Anyir," Gregor stated, hiding his regretful tone with a stern face.

"Where do you suppose I go?" Her eyes began tearing up again. This was not how she had expected her return home to go.

Gregor folded his arms and stood with his legs wide. "Anyir, I'm sorry, but this is how it must be," he said decisively.

"How can you be sorry? You have no idea what I've been through! All I wanted was to be back here…" Anyir looked at her husband's bracelet, turning it in her hands, and gazed upon the ruins of her old home. She wiped her nose and tears and asked Gregor, "What's the safest way to Ocran?"

Why is she asking about Ocran? Jason thought. He tried to place Ocran on his mental map of Valkadia, and realised it was the Remaran outpost on Lake Malion, and therefore on the way to Erythya. He turned to Anyir, surprised by her change of heart. "Wait, you're coming?" he asked her. A mixture of gladness and sadness whirled in his consciousness. She had just lost so much, and because of it, Jason had gained a travel companion to Erythya. He felt slightly guilty about that.

"This is my home, but apparently I'm not welcome here any longer. Without Oblivan, there's nothing left for me here…" Anyir replied in a cold tone. It was as if she had pushed every emotion down. She looked at her old friend from the village. "Gregor, at least help us find our way."

The burly man inspected them for a moment. "You could take the East Road, but I'm worried that will make you too much of an easy target for the soldiers. You could go along the side of the Suraan Hills, though that might add a day or two to your trip." Gregor rummaged through his pockets again, and Anyir hoped to the gods it wasn't another of her husband's relics. He pulled out a small bag of coins and offered it to his friend. "Take it," he said. "I can't allow you to stay here, but you are still my good friend, Anyir. Take it; it'll help you find another place to stay."

"Gregor… I can't…"

"You can, and you must," he replied. "It's the least I can do…"

"Thank you, Gregor," Anyir finally said, taking the money.

"I'm sorry I couldn't help more. I hope you can understand one day," he said.

Anyir watched her old friend walk back into the burnt down village. Her eyes watered once more, her emotions resurfacing involuntarily. She did her best to force the tears away, and then they headed towards the Suraan Hills.

With Anyir so distraught, Jason decided to ride just long enough to find somewhere to hide and make a point of the situation before continuing to Ocran. They climbed up the nearby low-lying foothills, from which they could see Karisa and the surrounding area so that if any soldiers showed up, they would have enough time to escape without being seen or put anybody else in danger. They camped behind the tall grass and had some stale bread and dried meat to eat. Anyir, who hadn't spoken since they had left the village, decided to get up and go and look for something she could forage in the thin stand of birches that grew atop the hill.

Oblivan couldn't be dead. He had been her rock and only source of hope in the dreadfulness of her life. Her father, the famous sorcerer Rongvald Soward, worked for the Remaran army. She had grown up seeing him only rarely, sometimes with intervals of months, sometimes of years. The only occasions they had spent quality time together was when they hunted quietly in the woods of Remara. Her mother, Galeena, was always very ill, and Anyir had taken care of her for as long as she could remember until she finally passed when she was seventeen. Ever since, she had been alone, searching for jobs at inns all over Remara, until one day she found Oblivan.

She could remember that day vividly. She had travelled for weeks, but her horse had stopped at the edge of Karisa, refusing to advance. Oblivan walked up to her, carrying large bags of coal on his back. Anyir could still remember his white linen shirt, his leather vest, and the red handkerchief that he had tied around his neck. Oblivan was tall and handsome, his big green eyes glistening as he looked at her. "Is something wrong with your horse, milady?" he said. She had never been called that—the term was usually used for noblewomen. "I think that horse needs a new set of shoes. I'm a blacksmith; I have some new ones at my workshop. Just wait here, I'll bring them and change them for you." Oblivan's voice reverberated in Anyir's mind—it was deep and cultured, and exuded a slight sense of mischief. Anyir had accepted the offer, and she had waited beside her horse for at least half an hour. She remembered it being the longest half an hour of her life. When Anyir began thinking he'd never return, Oblivan appeared in the distance waving two new pairs of horseshoes. Once Oblivan was done fitting them, they walked to Karisa together, and they talked. He was kind, knowledgeable, and he had a solid set of morals that Anyir had never seen on any other person. From that moment, he had been by her side, and she had never left Karisa.

"Anyir!" Jason called, breaking her reminiscence. "Come here! Quick!" Anyir ran back as fast as she could, trying not to drop the berries and flowers she had picked. From below in the village, she could hear the rattling noise of iron armour and the yelling of men. She found Jason lying flat on his stomach, hiding behind the bushes. "Stay down!" he urged. "Look who just arrived."

Tortugal and Modùn and other Red Camp soldiers gave orders left and right, ripping down the tents and taking the little food left in Karisa. If anyone dared get in their way, voluntarily or not, they would only be met with the hardened steel of a baton or an iron fist.

"Why didn't you kill Tortugal when you had the chance?" Anyir asked. Her voice was bitter and cold.

Jason's thoughts were momentarily catapulted back to that terrifying moment at Red Camp. "I had no idea what I was doing back then," he admitted sheepishly.

"They must be stopped," whispered Anyir decisively. Jason noticed a change in her eyes. It was as if a fire had just lit inside her.

The soldiers were laying waste to the burnt village. Whatever and whoever was still left was treated as if it were worthless. A group of kids ran away and hid behind a derelict house, only to be grabbed by the collar by two soldiers. Defenceless elders were being thrown to the floor abusively.

Jason's gaze fell on the fair-haired muscular man that he had met not long before, who stood beside Tortugal and spoke to him very intensely. Gregor appeared to be waving his hands around and indicating in the direction of the derelict buildings, the beaten villagers and the looted houses. Were they arguing? Jason suddenly felt sorry for Gregor, who looked like he was only trying to protect his people.

A brief moment later, though, Jason saw Gregor pointing towards his and Anyir's way, arising great interest on the general's part. Tortugal placed his hand on the burly man's shoulder and smiled arrogantly. He then pulled out a purse of coins from under his cloak and dropped it in Gregor's hands.

"Did he just…" Anyir muttered, her eyebrows pushed together, her lips pressed tightly. She looked at Jason puzzled.

"Tortugal just gave him money. He definitely ratted us out; I knew we couldn't trust him," Jason said, clenching his fists. He had a funny feeling from the first moment he had met the guy, and now that his suspicions had been confirmed he felt stupid for not zapping Gregor before. If he had actually given Tortugal information about their whereabouts, then they were in real danger. A feeling of anxiety suddenly overtook Jason's anger.

"This can't be," murmured Anyir. "I would never have expected it from Gregor. He was always on our side; he knew we were helping the Erythians. Perhaps, he was truly on the Remaran side all along. He's probably the one who ratted out Oblivan and me," said Anyir, a deep sense of disappointment and resentment emanating from her words.

Tortugal unsheathed his sword *Rhazien* and pointed its shiny blade towards the direction to take. He yelled something, and the soldiers jumped back on their horses, and they all galloped to the west.

"Wait," said Anyir. "It looks like the soldiers are heading in the opposite direction."

"We shouldn't wait to see if they come our way. Let's go."

"I think Gregor might have misled them. He's helping us."

"You saw him take the money, Anyir. That's a bribe; he's definitely told them where we are."

"I don't think so. I think we should go back down there."

"What?! Are you mad?!"

Without answering, she stood up and packed the blankets she had laid on the ground and jumped on her horse.

"Anyir, wait. We can't just waltz back in there willy-nilly. Besides, there might be other soldiers around."

"Gregor helped us. With the soldiers gone, perhaps he can help us more. Even if we get to Ocran, we need help to cross Lake Malion, and I know for a fact that Gregor has a boat docked at the harbour."

"Even if Gregor helped us, what makes you think Tortugal and Modùn are not coming back?" Jason asked. He had to admit it—Anyir was driven. With everything that had just transpired, her will to keep going was admirable. Yet again, maybe this was just a way for her to cope.

Jason huffed. He didn't want to be caught and have to fight Tortugal the Orc again. Once was enough for him. He vividly remembered the searing anguish that he felt when Tortugal's blade sliced his calf open. Even though he could heal fast, he could still feel pain. His heart began beating at the mere thought of standing in front of the colossal general. Yet maybe Anyir was right, and Gregor was only trying to help them. If Anyir trusted him, perhaps he should have listened to her given she had known Gregor for so long.

"I really hope we don't get caught," Jason said as he jumped on his steed's back and followed Anyir down the hill, making sure they stayed away from the soldier's eyes. Luckily, they seemed to have actually left. Nobody saw them, and nobody stopped them. Gregor seemed to have genuinely helped. However, when they got to the village, the people were eerily quiet and watched them ride in with disgust.

"Leave!" one woman shouted. "Nobody wants you here, Anyir! You brought them here; you did this to us!" Anyir looked at Jason dazed. He was unsure what to say or do to comfort her. The villagers were blaming them for the soldiers' arrival, but they both felt like something worse had happened. "Go away!" they kept repeating, as Jason and Anyir led their horses slowly through the ruins.

Anyir jumped off her horse and ran to the main square to find Gregor. Jason followed, reluctantly. When they got to the large tent, their hearts dropped. A woman held a lifeless old man in her arms, crying desperately, surrounded by a crowd of villagers sharing her pain. The man had been fatally wounded by one of the soldiers. He laid on the ground with a large cut on the side of his abdomen.

As soon as he saw them, Gregor marched towards Jason and Anyir, "Why are you two back? Can't you see what your presence has done? You have to leave. Now." His voice was loud and full of anger.

"We saw you speaking to the soldiers," said Jason.

"What of it?" Gregor erupted, puffing his chest to make himself look bigger. "I told them you went West. I owed that to Oblivan, but I don't owe you anything else now. Please leave."

The sky grew cloudy, and the rumbles of an impending storm echoed in the distance.

Anyir looked at her old friend. "We didn't mean for any of this to happen, Gregor. I know you helped us, but we must ask more help from you," she said endearingly, hoping her calm tone would make Gregor come to his senses.

"I helped you enough, Anyir," he huffed. "I paid my dues to you and Oblivan, and somebody else got hurt in the process. I must protect my village, and you two are endangering us every second you stay here." Gregor looked around. Most of the villagers were looking at them at this point. "Go away now, or I will have to send you away by force," he threatened, advancing menacingly.

Anyir backed up, startled by the intimidating figure that loomed over her and Jason and confused by the change of heart of her old friend. Seeing his companion in such distress after everything she had already gone through, Jason stepped forward, placing himself between Anyir and Gregor.

Thunder rumbled in the background.

"Move aside, you scrawny twig," spouted Gregor as he walked up to Jason with his chest out and muscles tense until he was a few inches away from him. He stared at him with ice blue eyes, bloodshot and deranged.

"You're scaring her. Anyir is your friend—act like one," Jason scolded. Gregor reminded him of the bully from school.

"By Odin's beard!" Gregor groaned. "Haven't I helped enough?! Leave us be!" he spewed. Gregor signalled to a group of four malicious looking thugs sat far back in the tent, who nodded back at him and uncovered hammers and knives from under the table. They marched intimidatingly towards Jason and surrounded him, and Gregor looked at him with flaming eyes.

The sight of the burly man and his four goons made his heart speed up. Although Alamor had trained him, he didn't want to test his sword-fighting skills so soon. Jason could feel his Flare rushing through his veins and became worried that Gregor's confrontational behaviour would make him explode like he did at the Red Camp. "Look, we can talk this out, mate," he offered.

"Mate? I am not your mate in the slightest."

As the eventuality of a five on two fight became more and more impending, Jason put his hand slowly on the hilt of Isidir, hoping that drawing attention to the Elven sword would deter Gregor and his thugs.

"Should I be scared of that piece of tinfoil?" he said, closing in on Jason and Anyir more and more. "What do you ever think you'll do to me, anyway, *mate*? You look like you haven't worked in a field your entire life." he continued. "You should have saved yourself some trouble and left."

Gregor raised his arms to the sky. He closed his eyes, and the clouds above turned from white to dark grey, swirling in the air and covering the faint light from the sun. Jason felt the air grow dry and parched around them as if all the moisture had been absorbed by Gregor's sorcery. The Karisan chief was conjuring a storm, unlike any storm Jason had ever experienced. Blue flashes of light followed by banging roars made the villagers jump back. Suddenly, lightning rushed down from the sky, and Gregor caught it with his hands. As he pulled his hands apart, the electric bolts sizzled and glowed, manipulated by his sorcery. When he let go of the lightning, it shot right next to Jason and hit a wall behind him, tearing it down.

Jason looked at Anyir, who was standing stock-still next to him. She clearly had no idea her old friend was a Sorcerer.

The Lightbringer channelled his Flare to his closed fist. He hoped he could control the power of light this time. Slowly and carefully, he created a ball of glowing light that grew brighter and brighter until people had to cover their eyes and turn away. Cracks began to open in the ground beneath their feet; the bellowing sound of the earth splitting was loud.

Gregor took a step back as soon as he realised who he was dealing with, and his goons retreated as well. The storm suddenly disappeared, and the sky cleared.

"It's… it's not possible," Gregor babbled and looked at Jason as if he had just seen a ghost.

"He's… he's a Sorcerer too?" muttered one of the thugs. His bulging eyes widened, incredulous.

"No. He's a Lightbringer," corrected Gregor slowly, sweat dripping from his forehead in fear.

"How can this be? Lightbringers have been gone for years…" observed the biggest of the goons with a deep guttural voice.

"He's a danger to all of us," said another of Gregor's companions, raising his voice so all the village could hear him and waving his thick fingers at Jason.

"Quiet, everyone!" Gregor urged, motioning to his goons to back up. "He may be dangerous, but he is not a danger to any of you. We have a legend in front of us."

A villager barged through the crowd. She had a ripped blouse with blood streaks all over it. "You saw what their presence did to our village, Gregor. Haldor is dead because of them two!" The fear in her trembling voice was palpable.

"You can't let them go!" another man said, his face drained and skinny, with purple circles under his eyes.

"They didn't do this to us," Gregor replied commandingly, attempting to calm the heated mob. "The soldiers did," he pointed out firmly.

"They would have never come if it wasn't for them!" shouted an elderly man from the back of the crowd.

The villagers grew louder, people shouting curses and threats over the top of their voice, overcome by fear and concern. "Go away, freak!" "Leave us be!" "Go back to where you came from!"

Their words became muddled as the mob became rowdier.

Jason and Anyir huddled together anxiously. Jason had never been in the presence of an angry crowd, and his breathing grew faster, panicked. The only time he had experienced people shouting like that was on television, protesting for their rights or rioting during civil unrest—but on TV, everything felt distant. He feared his Flare would catch him by surprise and that the villagers would get hurt because of him. A rotten potato flew across the crow and hit Jason on his chest, its rancid smell covering his white linen shirt.

"Hey! Everyone!" boomed Gregor. "Calm down!" As the crowd closed in, Gregor approached Jason and Anyir nervously. "We need to leave—now. I have a boat at the docks in Ocran which you can use. It would be an honour to serve you, Lightbringer," he said hurriedly.

Jason and Anyir rushed away from the mob, following Gregor out of the central square of Karisa. They jumped on their horses and swiftly escaped the angry villagers, who had begun to follow them brandishing broken pieces of burnt wood and throwing more rotten vegetables at them.

Gregor and Anyir didn't even look back at their old village as they rode to safety. The expression on Anyir's face was more distressed than before. Not only she had lost her husband; not only her village had burnt down. Her fellow villagers had also forced her out ferociously. She bit her lip firmly as she spurred her horse forward, riding away from her home and into the unknown.

XVII

HNEFATAFL

Darkstrom had the High Gothi's king piece almost surrounded. He always enjoyed being the attacker when playing *Hnefatafl*. The board game cleared his mind and helped him think strategically.

The High Gothi picked one of the beryl stone game pieces that was still positioned in the centre of the board and moved it two squares up to defend his king piece, which was backed against the edge of the board and flanked by two of Darkstrom's black marble pieces. The High Gothi's drew his eyebrows together as he realised another of Darkstrom's pieces was lurking on the left, ready to block the king's escape to the corner of the board.

"What are you going to do?" asked Darkstrom, his voice reverberating in the throne hall. He sat comfortably on his chair and put both his hands on the large stone table where he had shared his last meal with Lok not long before. He got irritated whenever he thought of the boy and what he had done to Karisa. That was not the plan. The plan was to get to Erythya silently and unseen by anyone. His best warrior had failed his orders, and his plan had been compromised.

Darkstrom had high hopes for Lok. He had trained the boy since he was a child to be a Shadowcaster. He thought Lok was ready, but he had been wrong. Darkstrom tried to shake the negative thoughts by focusing on the game, which was almost won.

The High Gothi suddenly realised the Emperor had left one blank square unguarded, enough for his king piece to briefly escape the attackers and buy himself time to get out of his enemy's grasp. It was a risky move, not only because there were more of Darkstrom's pieces around that particular square, but because he wasn't sure how the Emperor would react. The High Gothi believed Darkstrom would admire his bravery, and that not taking the chance would expose his vulnerability to the Emperor. He picked the green chess piece, with a carefully carved face and crown, and moved it through the opening.

"Nice move," Darkstrom commented. "I did not expect that."

"Thank you, my Lord," replied the High Gothi, who sat crouched forward, holding his hands between his knees, replaying the move he had just made in his mind.

Darkstrom observed the board, cut and carved out of the mastodontic skull of a Goplen. He had let his doubts obscure his vision, and one small oversight had cost him a sure win. He took one of his marble pieces and moved it down next to the Gothi's king, attempting to flank him again on both sides. His adversary, however, had been clever and had kept plenty of space to play around with. He moved the king away from Darkstrom's attacker piece, getting closer and closer to the corner.

Darkstrom was not going to lose a silly Hnefatafl game.

The High Gothi wished he hadn't tried to be brave when he saw the Emperor's eyes grow severe and dark. The table began tremoring ever so slightly, and yet Darkstrom was immovable, his hands solidly placed on the stone. Slowly, the king piece lifted off the board and in the air, levitating upwards until it was at the same height as the High Gothi's head. Darkstrom looked at him fiercely, the veins on his forehead pulsating. Like a bullet, the king piece shot through the Gothi's forehead, landing onto the basalt floor behind him, bouncing several times before it hit the opposite wall. The High Gothi's head flung backwards and hung over the backrest of the wooden chair, motionless.

"Checkmate," the Emperor declared.

Just as he was about to go rest in his private chambers, Darkstrom felt something vibrating in the pocket of his cloak. He looked down and saw the same object glowing intermittently with blue light. The Jaul. He pulled the golden marble out of his pocket and turned the small toggle on the side so he could hear the transmission out loud. He hoped no more bad news would come his way.

"Your Highness?" It was Glod, his voice crackling. "Can you hear us?"

"Speak," Darkstrom ordered.

"My Lord, we have a message for you, but we doubt you'll like it."

"When have you ever brought me satisfying news, Omüms?"

"It's about Alamor," said Glod. "We... erm... we lost him."

"What do you mean 'you lost him'?" the Emperor inquired in a monotone voice.

"Well, we were chasing Alamor and his comrades in the Stonevale when a herd of Goplen arrived. It was so confusing, and we couldn't see anything because of all the dust. We lost them all for a while. After a few minutes we saw Alamor and his white horse whizz past us, so we decided to follow him, but his horse was so fast that we couldn't catch up to him. We chased him for an hour or so, but then he disappeared completely. We didn't know what to do or where he took us, and he was just gone. *Poof!*"

"What about the other Lightbringer—the boy?"

"We don't know, Your Highness, we thought Alamor would be a greater threat, so we followed him."

"Glod," the Emperor called.

"Yes, my Lord?"

"Does Etrel back your story?" he asked.

"Of course—he was there with me the whole time," he replied. His voice got slightly muffled as he asked his companion, "It's all true, isn't it, Etrel?"

Etrel's voice sounded far away as he replied, "Absolutely, it was just like Glod said."

"So... there were two of you, am I right?"

"Yes, my Lord," replied Glod.

Darkstrom stood up from his seat, making the chair fall backwards. His iron crown almost fell off his head. The Emperor's thundering voice broke loudly through the Jaul transmission as he barked, "Then why didn't you two split?! Why didn't you two transform into something useful?! Now both Alamor and the boy have escaped, you morons! I should have never given you this responsibility! How could I trust two idiotic Omüms like you?"

"We're extremely sorry—" Glod tried to apologize.

"*I* am sorry for you two. I told you I would torture your soul if you failed, but I am a merciful ruler. Consider this your last warning." Darkstrom could hear Glod gulping through the Jaul. "Get on your horses and find the boy, I will deal with Alamor myself. Try every city, town and village along the Trench. You must find him, and kill him, and don't let his companions get away either. The Lightbringer must not reach Erythya. It will spiral into something that we cannot afford to deal with."

"We'll find him, my Lord," Glod assured.

"You better do," the Emperor retorted. "Your lives are hanging on a very thin thread."

The communication disconnected, and Darkstrom pocketed the Jaul before he could throw it across the room in a fit of anger. He breathed deeply and walked up to the High Gothi he had killed moments before.

"I'm very sorry, my friend," he whispered in his ear. Darkstrom looked at the Breegans under his service and ordered, "Clean this up. I don't want to see dead vermin on my table when I return."

Calmly, the Emperor walked away, leaving the Gothi's corpse sat in the wooden chair he had died in, in front of the Hnefatafl game he had almost won. Just as Darkstrom was about to exit the throne hall, he saw the king piece covered in blood lying on the floor. He kneeled and picked it up, staining his fingers in red. As if it was made of porcelain, the Emperor closed his fist and crushed the chess piece into fine particles of sand. He opened his hand and looked at the remains of the king. Slowly, Darkstrom strolled back to the long stone table in the middle of the hall, and he poured the powder of the crushed king piece on top of the Hnefatafl board with indifference, like the ashes of a burnt body on a battlefield.

XVIII

THE THIRSTY GOBLIN

It took the new trio about three days to ride to Ocran. Not many words were shared during the day, other than brief discussions about the direction to take. Every night, they took turns on the lookout while the other two slept, watching over the hills and the vales for any potential threat. Every two hours or so, they would rotate, making sure everyone got enough sleep. Alas, their rest was never quiet, their minds haunted by the recent events.

As they approached the lake, the greenness of the vegetation grew, and even small tufts of fresh grass sprouted occasionally from the ground. "The water from Lake Malion is known to benefit life, which is why Goplen come here every year to water their plants, so to speak," said Gregor, breaking the monotonous silence.

"Please, Gregor, don't speak about those creatures," Anyir begged, shutting her friend down immediately.

"I… thought it was interesting," he replied.

"Sorry. We had a bit of a bad encounter with the Goplen," Jason intervened.

"I see… those creatures have gone kind of crazy…" Gregor muttered. "Why don't we go to a nice little tavern I know to rest for a while before we embark? We need to get some food for the journey as well."

"That's a good idea. How long more will it take to get to Ocran?" Jason asked.

"It'll be about another four hours, but the view from the lake will be worth it," Gregor replied. "And this inn, the Thirsty Goblin, has the best stew you'll ever have."

They rode the last stretch of the way, and as they approached the town in the late afternoon, Lake Malion became visible. It was immense, the largest lake in all of Valkadia. Anyir said it measured about 100 miles between Ocran and the city of Malion—nearly half the size of Lake Victoria in Africa. It was so large that the opposite shore laid over the horizon—closer to a sea, with waves crashing onto the sandy beaches blown by a light breeze. The bright sun shone through the dull white sky, reflecting and flickering on the lake's surface. Yet, the water looked unforgiving and dark, just like that fateful day when Jason lost Clara. A sudden looming sensation took over, and he felt like his lungs were crushing his heart. He realised only then he would have to go back on a boat. Jason kept riding, not saying anything about his sudden state of fear, which grew the closer they got to the lake. He had to look strong. He was a Lightbringer.

All around, the low-lying hills surrounding Lake Malion were dotted with the small huts of fishmongers. A small fishing town, Ocran was entirely made up of wooden buildings, some of which protruded onto the lake supported by stilts. It was also Remara's outpost on the lake, and the harbour was larger than the town itself. A myriad of boats of various shapes and sizes were scattered on the water, bopping along with the waves. From far away, Jason could see the masts of two large Remaran vessels, with the Chained Raven proudly displayed on the open sails.

"That's odd," said Gregor. "Those ships have never been here. It's been a long while that since I've seen Remaran ships in the docks."

"Are you sure this is safe and that nobody will see us?" Anyir asked.

"Just lay low. Put your hoods up," Gregor replied.

As they led their horses through the town, they passed by many small taverns and emporiums, each with names that recalled fish or fishmongers, such as 'The Sturgeon's Tavern', 'The Giddy Trout' or 'The Black Eel'. Each of them had brightly decorated signs hanging over the doors with drawings of whatever fish they had decided to use for their shop's name, the first bright colours that Jason had seen in Remara since he had arrived.

Many people were hanging about on the streets, and Jason finally got to see the reality of Remaran life.

People outside the shops were busy gutting and descaling fish, announcing prices of the daily catch, selling fresh clams in trays and buckets. Others were fixing the houses, cleaning the windows, setting up the sign of a new shop. Kids ran around barefoot, dirty with mud, chasing each other or running away after stealing bread from an oblivious shop owner. The conditions of most people, however, were questionable. Many of them had few teeth, others just thin strands of hair poking through otherwise bald heads, bag under their eyes, skinny limbs. Nonetheless, the citizens of Ocran were a busy bunch, who were too occupied surviving the day to be concerned about Jason, Anyir and Gregor riding into the town.

Eventually, when they arrived in front of a battered old house on the front of the lake, Gregor told them to stop. "Here it is, the Thirsty Goblin tavern," he announced. It looked more like a glorified shed, with a collapsed roof that leaned on one side and a door that hung on its hinges as if it was clinging for its life. Yet, laughter and music came from inside, accompanied by the sound of glasses clinking against each other, and Jason could see people having fun through the skewed windows.

Gregor jumped off his horse and tied the reins on the wooden fence that surrounded the tavern, and then invited, "Follow me, keep your hoods up and don't look people in the eye."

Jason breathed fast, his heart pounding, as he jumped off the horse's back and followed Gregor through the door along with Anyir. There were only a dozen people in the tavern, but they were too busy guzzling beer to mind the strangers' presence. In the back, a young boy in orange tights played a mandolin and sang happily to an indifferent audience, who mostly ignored him or were too busy drinking to listen to his tune. He sang of a woman named Loreta, and her star-crossed lover called Sunnir.

"I'll find us somewhere to sit," Gregor whispered.

They headed to the back of the tavern, not too far from the mandolin player, where Gregor had found an available table made out of a beer barrel. The only person who acknowledged them was the innkeeper, a short, stocky man with a bald spot and a stained apron. He signalled to come over to the counter, so Gregor went over to the innkeeper while Jason and Anyir waited at the table, sat on wobbly stools.

After a couple of minutes, Gregor came strolling back to the table holding three large pints of beer, overflowing with foam, and a smile on his face. "The stews are coming, and I've asked him to pack us some cheese, bread and a large piece of ham."

"Can we afford all this?" Jason asked.

"What I gave you before should do, and I've still got all of what Tortugal gave me as well."

"Shh! Don't say that name! What if someone hears you?" Anyir reprimanded Gregor.

"Everyone's too drunk in here to understand a single word, don't worry," he replied.

Jason looked at the innkeeper, who was wiping glasses with a filthy cloth. He turned to Jason and stared at him with deep, dark eyes, and a slight eerie grin. "Why is he staring at me like that?" he whispered.

"Because *you're* staring! Seriously, you two, stop being so paranoid," Gregor pressed.

Anyir looked up at a beady-eyed painting of a duck hung on the wall, staring down at her eerily. The patrons were suspiciously quiet, chugging down beer at oddly timed intervals. The pleasant music resonated through the tavern, yet people seemed strangely focused, shrugging off the rhythm in favour of their drinks. "There's just something not right with this place," said Anyir as she scanned the room.

"You're overthinking, and quite frankly ruining our nice meal. Stop panicking and enjoy your beers. Come on, let's cheers—to change!" insisted Gregor, raising his glass.

Jason and Anyir looked at each other, awkwardly trying to loosen up. They raised their glasses and clinked, cheering to change.

The innkeeper came limping on his left leg towards their table, carrying a large cast-iron pot full of stew. "Bear with me," he said, "My leg's not good anymore. I'll go and get you some bowls."

Jason watched as the stubby man staggered to the counter to pick up the plates. It was only then that Jason noticed a cat sitting on the side of the counter, busy licking his paws and cleaning his ears. When the cat looked back at him, it revealed the two large scars running across its face. The feline appeared to be smirking ever so slightly, giving Jason a strange gut feeling. Those scars; the odd anthropomorphic expressions on the cat's face. Perhaps Jason was overthinking, but he didn't want to take the risk.

Jason leaned over to his companions. "We've got to get out of here," he urged, whispering.

The Lightbringer – Through the Elder Stone

"For Odin's beard! What is it with you two? There's nothing wrong here, just enjoy the meal! If anything goes wrong, there's three of us with insane powers, why are you so scared?"

"Because we've already lost enough," Anyir snapped.

"It's not safe here; we need to leave. Anyir, look," he nudged his head towards the two suspects. "Doesn't it look very familiar, his limping and the scars on the cat's face?"

"What? Are you joking? You want us to leave because of someone limping and a cat with some scars? Do you have any idea how lunatic that sounds?" Gregor complained.

"If they are what I think they are, you'll be sorry you doubted me," Jason retorted.

The innkeeper came back with plates and cutlery and placed them on the table next to the pot of stew. "Here you go," he said. "If you don't mind me asking, where are you people heading?" Jason was sure he recognised that voice—the voice of a man that beat him to the point where he couldn't breathe. He could feel his Flare rushing through his veins, beneath his skin. Like a hound, Jason recognised the essence of the man, and he could smell the cat's true form as well.

"Just going for a stroll," said Anyir.

"A stroll, aye? How nice!" the innkeeper replied cheerfully. "You've got to be careful out there, with those Erythian spies from Malion, you know. I hope you peeps have something to protect yourself with?"

"Something like that," Gregor replied haughtily.

"Good," the innkeeper said. "Because Ocran—I love it don't get me wrong—but it is a cove of Erythian rats," he jeered, emphasising the last two words. *Erythian. Rats.*

"Are Erythians really that bad? Surely not," Jason asked rhetorically, rolling his eyes. "I've never met one, should I be scared?" Anyir and Gregor looked at him like he was crazy.

"Ah, yes, mate. And if you're not scared, you're either a fool, or an Erythian, and I would rather be the fool," the innkeeper replied.

"Jeez, what if I meet one? Will I even know in time that it's a spy?" he kept taunting.

The innkeeper began looking frustrated, breathing heavily through his nose. "Stick 'em," he said. "Stick 'em like any other Erythian. Power to Remara!" he cheered, slamming his fist into his open hand. He glanced at his cat, which came moseying around the innkeeper's legs for a few seconds before he bounced on the windowsill beside their table.

In an instinctive act of desperation, like a decision between fight or flight, Jason picked up a bowl of piping hot stew and threw it at the innkeeper. He shrieked loudly, desperately trying to wipe the stew off his clothes, the chunks of vegetables and meat hot like burning coal.

"What have you done to my soup!" complained Gregor. But his annoyance soon turned into fear, when the innkeeper's skin began bubbling and morphing into a completely different man, still stocky but with a wooden peg for a left leg.

"Etrel! Get them!" shouted Glod, now reverted to his original appearance.

The cat dawdling on the windowsill suddenly pounced at them claws first, and as he jumped, he lost his fur, and he grew until he was a man again—a tall, lanky man with two scars on his face. Etrel landed onto Jason, throwing him off his chair and onto the ground. The Omüm pinned the Lightbringer down and raised his fist, ready to pummel it down onto Jason's face. The young Londoner's Flare instinctively fired up, and without thinking, Jason conjured a gush of air, which blasted Etrel off him, propelling him to the other side of the tavern.

Seeing the commotion, the rest of the people busy drinking at the Thirsty Goblin suddenly noticed the trio. Unhappy he had disturbed the quiet, somebody threw a glass at Jason but instead hit another patron. It was then that chaos ensued in the tavern. Plates and pints of beer went smashing into people's heads. Punches went flying into faces and ribs, sending people onto the ground and ending in drunk wrestles on the sticky floor. This was the best opportunity to escape and mix in with the disarray. "Quick!" incited Jason, dashing to the door with his companions before the Omüms could get up again.

They ran out of the tavern and into the streets of Ocran, and quickly jumped on their horses. They could hear the Omüms' shrieks rising from inside the tavern. Luckily, the town was small, and Gregor knew his way to the harbour, so it didn't take them long to get there. The gloomy docks smelled like fish guts, and by that time all the fishermen had gone home, ready for an early wake the next day. Only a few Remaran soldiers patrolled the docks close to their ships, but they were mostly busy talking and sharing bottles of wine.

They rode to the far end of the dock, where Gregor kept his boat

The Lightbringer – Through the Elder Stone

away from wary eyes. From a couple of streets behind, the sound of two dogs howling and barking came rushing, quickly becoming louder. Soon, two greyhounds with blood-red eyes and drooling mouths were shooting towards them, ready to dig their teeth into their legs.

Anyir turned her horse around swiftly and flaming balls of fire went blasting on the ground in front of the two dogs, but this didn't stop them. The dogs snarled and dug their claws into the dirt as they sprinted towards Jason and his companions.

Jason tried conjuring the earth to raise a wall and block the dogs in a dead-end, but his Flare wasn't responding. He realised only then that the moon was high in the evening sky, and the light from the sun was fading away, along with his Flare.

"Guys, we have a problem!" he yelled as he ran. "It's too dark to summon my powers; I can't stop them!"

"Don't worry; I'll take care of it," Anyir replied. She turned around and put both her hands in front of herself. A stream of fire whirled ragefully against the greyhounds, forming a wall between them and the three companions. The heat was so much that even Jason and Gregor could feel it a few meters away. The hounds whimpered as they found themselves blocked by the scorching fire.

Just as the trio thought they were safe, one of the Omüm-dogs—the strongest and most agile, with two scars on its snout—jumped on top of a low-laying roof to escape the blazing flames. Before they knew it, the hound pounced on Anyir, throwing her off the horse and flooring her. It snapped its teeth and drooled in the attempt to maul her throat. She tried to hold the hound away, but the monstrous canine was strong and whipped his head back and forth. Gregor reacted readily. He jumped off his horse and rammed against the dog, tackling it. With his mighty strength, he picked the dog up and threw it over his shoulders and into the deep waters of Lake Malion. Etrel the Omüm-dog whined and splashed around, trying to swim back to the shore to save itself. But the hound was too tired, and though the companions were safe, they looked in horror as the dog sank into the dark water.

There was no time to dwell. "Follow me!" shouted Gregor, running a few meters further where his sailboat was bopping along with the waves, tied up to a pole on the side of the boardwalk. It was modest, made of old wood and with paint flaking off the exterior. The vessel was long and thin, with a large triangular sail, and a pulpit which curled upwards as if to slice the air.

"What about the horses?" Jason asked.

"They won't fit; it's a fishing boat. We'll have to leave them here," Gregor replied.

They unbuckled the saddles from their horses and hastily filled the small boat with luggage. As they jumped onto the tiny vessel, Gregor untied the rope from the pole and gave a push, setting into the waters of Lake Malion.

Jason couldn't believe it. They were going to be in Erythya soon, the famed land of magical creatures and lush gardens, where he could finally stop being on the run from killers and soldiers. Jason sat down and let Gregor play with the various chords and ropes of the sailboat. He looked out to Ocran as it became smaller and smaller, until the lights of the houses were the size of fireflies, fading in the distance.

Before Jason could take a sigh of relief, something hit the hull, making the boat rock violently sideways. "What was that?" Jason gasped. For a moment Jason was back on the *Son of Odin*, struck by the iceberg. He began breathing heavily.

"I don't know, but it was big," said Gregor.

"What lives in this lake?" Anyir asked.

"It could have been a Bolear; it's like a large fish that sometimes comes up to eat flies and insects. They're almost blind, so it probably didn't see the boat," Gregor answered.

"Are they big enough to rock the boat this much?"

"Hmm... Not really..."

The creature bashed into the hull again, flinging the three companions to the other side of the sailboat. Jason looked out to the water and saw something white and long, double the size of the vessel, moving beneath the surface in an almost serpentine fashion.

"Look!" Jason cried.

What looked like a creature from the Jurassic, with a thin snout armed with hundreds of sharp teeth and long flippers, emerged briefly from the water to breathe. Its yellow eye looked right into Jason's, and only then he noticed the two long scars on its face.

"It's one of the Omüms!" Jason exclaimed as he realised the true identity of the monster.

Diving back into the water, Etrel sped up, aiming for the boat's hull once more. This time, he achieved what he had set out, and Jason was flung into the cold water of Lake Malion. He began swimming frantically, unable to think straight. Being thrown in the water like that reminded him too much of the *Son of Odin*'s shipwreck. He could see Clara in the waves with him, being dragged further and further away from him. The frigid lake quickened his heartbeat; his legs got stiffer and his breath became faint. The monster swam towards him at an unbelievable speed, its jaws wide open, but Jason was too panicked, trying to stay afloat.

Gregor threw over a rope. "Grab it! Jason, grab the rope!"

The photographer broke out of his terror and clutched onto the line. Gregor pulled him away just in time as the monster's jaws snapped shut with a bang right where Jason was swimming.

Etrel turned around and went for another attack. Jason swam as fast as he could, and Gregor pulled him with the rope with all his strength.

"He's not going to make it!" Anyir shouted with angst.

Gregor suddenly had an idea, and he turned to Anyir as he kept pulling the rope. "Lightbringers can heal fast, right?"

"Yes, why?"

"I have a crazy idea," he announced. "Jason, hold tight! You won't like this!" he yelled.

The sky became clouded, and thunders roared. A storm formed and lightning began to illuminate the night sky.

"Are you sure this is a good idea?" Anyir asked apprehensively.

"It's the only chance we have."

With a bang that ripped the sky, a bolt struck the water of the lake and spread along its surface, hitting anything that swam in it—including Etrel, including Jason.

Both the monster and Jason wriggled and contorted in pain, splashing in the water and gasping for air. Anyir watched terrified as the electrical current fried her friend. "Stop! Make it stop!" she pleaded. "Jason!"

The Omüm had reverted into a man once more and had sunk in the water for good. Gregor cleared the sky and jumped in the water to retrieve his companion, who was now floating on the surface, still clinging onto the rope. He brought him back onto the sailboat with Anyir's help, who was on the verge of tears. She knew his body could take such a hit, but she was still just as affected. His skin was red and full of lightning scars that spread along his body in the shape of fern leaves.

After a few seconds, Jason woke up and spat out the water he had swallowed. He squeezed his eyes and tightened his teeth in pain. With the few ounces of energy he still had, he whispered, "Thank you, Gregor," then he fell into a deep slumber, utterly exhausted. His two companions laid him against the side of the boat gently.

The peace and quiet of the lake took over, and the only sound was that of the sailboat gliding along the water, slicing through the waves, headed finally towards Erythya.

XIX

BEYOND THE LAKE

The sound of people yelling woke Jason up from his deep sleep. When he opened his eyes, he found himself in a boat. He suddenly remembered what had happened the previous night and was sure he had been killed by the scorching current of Gregor's lightning bolt. Jason looked around, but all he could see was water, still and dark; a thin layer of mist covered the surface. Was his soul being taken through to the Underworld, transported by Charon, the mythical ferryman of Hades?

When Jason realised the person shouting was Gregor and not the souls of the dead, he felt utterly relieved and took a deep breath. He examined his hands and arms and was astounded to find that the lightning scars entirely disappeared. Adrenaline rushed through his veins, and he felt a peculiar, itchy warmth.

Gregor was yelling at someone, and the voice that replied back seemed to come from very far away. "Let us through!" he shouted.

"We cannot allow Remarans through," replied the faint voice.

Jason turned to see what direction Gregor was speaking towards. To his surprise, a massive wooden watchtower was breaking through the water and soaring hundreds of meters high, and a vast wall was running along its sides, connected to other towers in the distance. This was the border between Erythya and Remara in the middle of Lake Malion, protecting the magical realm from Human invaders.

"We have a Lightbringer with us. We bring news for king Kavanagh," Anyir explained.

"How do we know you're telling the truth?" the guard asked from atop the tower.

"I understand you may not believe us, but please, we must come through? Please. It is of the utmost importance that we enter Erythya and meet with king Kavanagh!" Anyir begged.

"I cannot satisfy your request. You must have the appropriate documents signed by the king himself to enter and exit Erythya."

With all the shouting, Jason sat up and tried to look at what was going on. When Gregor realised the Lightbringer was awake and healthy, his eyes widened, and he sighed in relief. "I can't believe you survived that," Gregor told him. "I'm glad you did, my friend. Sorry again."

"It's all right," he replied.

"Jason!" cried Anyir, who walked towards him as fast as she could, trying not to fall from the boat, and hugged him tightly.

"What's happening?" Jason asked.

"We are on the border, Erythya is just a few meters from here. But we need the guards to grant us access. They don't believe our story," Anyir explained.

"Let me try," said Jason. He didn't know where the guard was, so he tried to yell upwards to the top of the tower. "My name is Jason McAnnon. I am a Lightbringer. Let us through; we must go to Malion to speak with Baldor Haral and proceed to Niteria to meet with the king. King Kavanagh himself has personally invited us."

"Where is your invitation? We can't let you in without proof that what you're saying is true."

It suddenly dawned on Jason that Alamor had taken the invitation on the sealed scroll with him. Aside from not having any proof for the Erythian guard, a negative spiral of thought took over Jason's mind. What if this whole adventure was a trap? What if he was going from a horrible situation to an even more gruesome one? He had put trust in people he barely knew, and although they had helped him survive, he didn't know what their aims were.

The only thing he knew was that Alamor believed so much in the cause he was fighting for that he was ready to sacrifice himself. Jason did not take that lightly. That single thought cleared his mind, and he knew exactly what he had to do.

A golden light with blue hues burst from Jason's hands, enveloping his body and swirling around the rest of the ship and his companions, shimmering with sparks. With a surge, the light stream shot upwards, beaming into the sky in front of the guard tower. He imagined the soldier's incredulous expressions as they watched the light being conjured. Jason kept the light up for a few more seconds, before releasing it into the distance, rippling out to the shores of Lake Malion.

"Is that enough proof?" Jason shouted.

The soldiers didn't speak for a moment and then began discussing between themselves. Their feeble murmurs filled the eerie quiet of the lake. Jason, Gregor and Anyir looked at each other in uncertainty, waiting for a verdict. The boat floated calmly on the surface of the lake, the gentle waves chuckling as they hit the hull.

After a good twenty minutes, a guard shouted, "Open the gates!" The loud clunking noise of iron chains being pulled over gears ripped through the silence, stunning the three companions. Slowly, a large gate opened up, sliding horizontally within the large wooden wall. The mechanism stopped abruptly with a bang.

"So... can we go through?" Jason asked sheepishly.

"All good! We only needed a while to communicate with the Ærindel!" the guard replied.

Communication is almost faster here than in London, Jason mused.

"I look forward to seeing more of you, Lightbringer!" the guard then added.

"Ah, I hope never to come this way again! No more Remara for me, thank you!" Jason replied, laughing.

"Erythya is a place of wonders and hope, my friend. Please, go forth and enjoy," the guard stated.

As soon as the ship went through the immense wooden gate and crossed the border, Jason's eyes were filled with the turquoise colour of the Lake's water. In the distance, bright green rolling hills covered in lush shrubs and trees surrounded the lake. Myriads of small boats were dotted along the shore, each with their own brightly coloured and decorated sail. Some were navigating across the lake as well. Others were anchored where the water was deeper, and people were busy throwing nets overboard to fish.

Gregor and Anyir looked behind as the large wooden gates closed shut, locking the Empire away in its greyness, but Jason kept looking ahead. The vibrant colours filled Jason with joy, and the smell of the air was so clean and pure.

Anyir almost fell into the lake when a long fish jumped out of the water, taking her by surprise. It had large orange fins, almost like wings, and glided over the lake's surface after each jump. Its long and thin body was decorated with black and blue stripes, and a large dorsal fin, orange as well, that looked like a ship's sail. Jason and his companions watched with delight as dozens of other flying fish suddenly emerged, leaping out of the water and gliding for a few meters before diving back in.

"I saw these in the book Grando gave me—*The Harmony of Creatures*. They're called *Molters*," said Jason, excited to spout out the information he had learnt. He rummaged through his bags, pulled out his notebook and quickly sketched the fish with his charcoal pencil. He turned the page around and immediately outlined the unbelievable landscape he was witnessing.

Hours went by, and the trio enjoyed the warm air of Erythya and its blue skies, sat on the edge of the boat, allowing the water to wet their feet slightly. A sense of relief took over their hearts.

"So, Anyir tells me you're from the Otherside," Gregor said to Jason.

"That's right," the photographer replied, "From a place called England."

"*England*, what a strange-sounding place," he commented. "What's it like there, in *England*?"

"It's cold, it rains a lot, but it's still quite a lively place. After a day of work, people like to have a couple of pints, relax with friends—you know, usual stuff really. Oh, and we definitely love our tea."

"What kind of tea? Do you have Oreka tea as well?"

"No, but we have many, many kinds of tea. Though I've got to admit that nothing compares to Oreka tea."

"I can't wait to get a nice cup of Oreka tea in Niteria. I've heard so much about it, but never had any," Gregor said.

"It's unbelievable," Anyir said. "I can't believe I spilt it all over Grando's carpet!" she giggled.

Jason laughed with her. "He was too nice to say anything, but he must have been so annoyed!"

"Who's Grando?" asked Gregor.

"A friend who helped us after we escaped from Red Camp," explained Anyir.

"Have I told you how sorry I am about what happened to you, Anyir? I can't believe you made it out alive," commented Gregor.

"It doesn't matter now," she replied with a conciliatory tone, her face relaxed and her eyes away into the distance. "What's happened is in the past. Anything before the moment we crossed that gate, I want to forget—everything except Oblivan. This is a new start for all of us."

"A chance to make things right," added Jason. Anyir smiled.

"Speaking of a new start," said Gregor, "we're here."

They could finally see Malion's docks and their breath-taking monumental entrance. It reminded Jason of St. Peter's Square in Rome, but it was larger. Immense sets of sandstone colonnades ran along either side of the docks forming a sizeable elliptical area, where ships of all shapes, sizes and colours were anchored. Behind the entrance, the skyline of Malion stood glorious, full of gothic looking buildings topped with large domes and dotted with beautifully decorated windows. Wide avenues cut through the city like rivers in a valley, and the streets were swarmed with people. Vehicles that looked like carriages zoomed past, but these weren't drawn by horses—they were *steam-powered*. Lush trees poked through the buildings like needles, creating a mosaic of white and green. Jason was sure he recognised that place from his dream about the Child Snatcher, and his skin suddenly chilled for a moment.

It was only when they finally tied their boat to one of the piers and stepped off onto the cobbled street that Jason really understood what land he had stepped in. Malion's waterfront—unlike Ocran's where Jason had mostly perceived poverty, miserableness and a strong smell of rotten fish—was a vibrant meeting place for creatures of every kind. Some of the inhabitants were Veheers, with pointed ears and golden eyes, just like Alamor. Others had horns and animal legs but still resembled the general anthropomorphic body shape. Some creatures were tall and with only one eye; others were short and minute, and they were wandering the streets fast as they tried to keep up with the tallest inhabitants. Everyone wore sumptuous clothes in gaudy colours and expensive silks. Around him were Fauns, Cyclops, Gnomes, Minotaurs, Centaurs—every creature that all the most famous legends from the ancient world that Jason had heard or read about as a kid was there in front of him, strolling around the wondrous city of Malion. Jason looked around himself lost in the wonders of the city, almost forgetting what he was there for and what they had to do.

"Jason," called Anyir, snapping her fingers in front of him. "Jason!"

"Sorry, this is... it's too much. It's beautiful," he said.

"It really is," she replied.

"Come on," Gregor incited. "Help me get these bags off the boat."

As they unloaded their luggage, a tall man with tanned skin, pointy ears and purple eyes approached them. He was a Dryad, dressed in an aquamarine damask shirt and fawn silken trousers. His skin was a light hue of green, and his hair was bristly, almost as if made of plant material.

"Greetings, my friends," he said in a poised tone. "It would be a pleasure to assist you. My name is Freydar Ivor, son of Pytar. I trust you had a good trip to Malion?"

"Nice to meet you, Freydar. I am Jason McAnnon, son of Robert. It has definitely become a good trip since we got here."

"That's good to hear," Freydar replied. "What are you here for?" he inquired.

"We are here to meet with a Half-Giant called Baldor Haral, in Rennhall's Library," replied Jason.

"Does he know you're visiting?" asked Freydar.

"I'm not sure... I assume so. He was a dear friend of my mentor, Alamor Eklund."

Freydar remained silent for a moment, then smiled eagerly as something in his mind clicked. "*You're* the Lightbringer?!" he murmured, trying to contain his enthusiasm. "You've made it! I passed on the message for you and Alamor to come here directly to Grando," he said. "Speaking of which, where's Alamor?"

Jason looked back at Freydar with sorrowful eyes. "We got caught between a herd of Goplen and a couple of Omüms. We lost him, I don't even know if he's alive," he said in a hushed tone.

Freydar remained silent for a few seconds, looking out towards the lake. "I am very sorry to hear that," he replied. "Well, I am glad you made it here alive, and that you have found trusted travel companions. Here, let me help you with those," he offered, grabbing one of the saddles.

Once they had unloaded the boat, Freydar whistled loudly, and one of the automatic carriages drove up to them, rocking about on the cobbled street. Sitting on the front of the carriage was a Gnome—a small, stocky creature the size of a ten-year-old child with blueish skin, and a great white beard that trailed behind him. From beneath the mass of thick hair stuck out two pointed ears, much longer than a Veheer's. He was wearing a tailored blue vest, which made him look reliable and trustworthy, and he pulled levers and steered the wheels of the carriage with a bicycle-like handlebar.

The carriage appeared to be powered by steam—Jason had assumed technology was confined to the ordinary world, but that was not the case. Anyir and Gregor watched the mechanical carriage as if it were a monster; they were more surprised about that than the strange creatures roaming the streets of Malion.

"G'day, Freydar!" the Gnome greeted. "What can I do for you today?" Jason was astounded hearing the creature's confusing accent.

"Good day to you, Olag. Help me load the luggage and take my friends wherever they need to go," Freydar affirmed.

"Nice to meet ya all! Please, jump in while Freydar and I load your bags on the carriage."

Dazed by the reality of Erythya, the three companions stepped inside the steam-powered carriage. Jason watched Freydar wave his hands and summon the air to lift their bags and place them gently on the roof of the carriage.

"So, where to?" asked Olag.

"Erm… Rennhall's Library, please," muttered Jason to the driver of the whimsical taxi.

The gears and pipes popped and sputtered as the carriage's steam engine fired up, and with the stridulous sound of a whistle, the vehicle began plodding forward. "Rennhall's Library coming right up! See ya later, Freydar!" exclaimed the Gnome.

"Hope to see you all again very soon!" said Freydar, waving goodbye.

"Nice to meet you, thank you!" replied Jason.

As the carriage travelled along the streets of Malion, Jason observed the buildings, the shops and the people flashing past him. Huge buildings soared luxurious on either side, each with sumptuous huge windows and terraces overlooking the city. Green reigned everywhere. The meticulously gardened flowers of every colour flowed like waterfalls on the balconies and poured onto the road. People from every Clan in Erythya strolled on the sidewalks meeting merchants, buying fresh food from sale stands, haggling with the shop owners. Others worked to maintain the city fixing drains and roads, cleaning litter, tending the flowers. Everyone seemed at peace, content with their lives. It was the epitome of a well-oiled society, going through what seemed a Renaissance-type age.

"What's that?" Jason asked Olag as they drove into a large round square, pointing to the large obelisk that stuck out of the paved floor.

"That's the Obelisk of Ergaard. It's been standing there since the time of the Elves, well before the Human invasion. It has witnessed more change than any Valkadian king or emperor have ever seen in their lives. Nobody knows where it came from. The inscriptions on the stone are nothing like Hæmir or the common tongue. Although many scholars have attempted to understand their meaning, nobody has ever been able to decipher any of them."

Like a fantastical, enormous Rosetta Stone, Jason thought, remembering the famous stele that archaeologists used to translate Egyptian hieroglyphs from Ancient Greek. His mind momentarily travelled back to his trip to the British Museum with Clara. They had mused over the Rosetta Stone for at least half an hour, admiring the knowledge and wisdom of ancient civilisations.

Olag drove the steam carriage for another five minutes or so, passing through a maze of streets and alleys before arriving in a large square. "We're here!" the Gnome finally announced.

When Jason looked outside the carriage and glanced upwards, he found himself speechless. They had made it. They were actually out of Remara and had made it into Erythya. *Alamor would be proud*, he thought.

The architecture of Rennhall's Library was unique and pompous. The central dome rose more than three hundred meters and was wide at least two hundred. Smaller domes followed all the way down. It was a mix between Roman and gothic styles, made with white marble stone. Meticulously decorated lancet windows were scattered on the facades and their stained glass reflected the bright light of the Erythian sun. Supporting buttresses stuck out of the structure on either side, like the ribs of a whale.

Olag jumped off of the carriage and began unloading the saddles and bags, while Jason and his companions admired the library, turning and spinning to see each feature.

The Library's entrance was portentous, with a large stone staircase leading up to a wooden doorway four times the height of a grown person, held up by beautiful floral iron hinges.

They each grabbed a bag and, after thanking Olag and paying him a fair wage, Anyir and Gregor followed Jason up the staircase and to the bottom of the wooden front gate. A man-sized door was cut into the larger gate and attached to the front was a cast iron door knocker. Jason looked at his friends, not sure what to do next, but was only repaid with shrugs and confused faces. Jason grabbed the door knocker and banged it against the door. He could feel the sound echoing within the Library.

There was no reply, but Jason swore he could hear the sound of hooves beating on the ground getting louder. He signalled to his companions to stay beside him until they heard the sound of locks being opened.

A creature with the torso of a human, goat's legs and ram's horns on his head greeted them at the door—a *Faun*.

"Good day. My name is Kiro Hustad, son of Tov. I am one of the Treasurers here at the Library. How may I help you?"

"Nice to meet you, Kiro. I am Jason McAnnon, son of Robert, and these are my two friends and travel companions Anyir Sköld and Gregor Svenn."

At the sight of Jason, the Faun's jaw dropped. It was evident that the news of the new Lightbringer arriving in Malion had travelled exceptionally fast. "*You* are Jason?!" cried the Faun, jumping on his goat-like legs as if he was standing on a pogo stick. Jason thought Fauns were a lot smaller than Kiro was, but he guessed that was only a misrepresentation by ancient populations from the Otherside. Kiro was just as tall as Jason. "You're here! You're actually here! Baldor will be so delighted to meet you!" he cheered. "It's great to meet you all!" Kiro replied, but then his cheerful face, framed with a fuzzy goatee and thick sideburns, suddenly turned anxious, "Where is Alamor?"

Jason struggled to get the words out one more time. "We lost him. We got attacked by two Omüms, and he disappeared."

"That's such a… shame," he commented, though he seemed to struggle saying those words. "Baldor was looking forward to seeing his old friend," Kiro answered. "So, you managed to get here all on your own?" he asked, stupefied.

"I had some help, but it wasn't easy," Jason replied, motioning towards his new friends.

"I'm very glad you made it. You must be tired, and you must have lots of questions. Please, come in! There's much to discuss," Kiro invited, motioning towards the entrance of the Library.

The three companions followed the Faun through the doors of the monumental library and into the glorious main hall where many Lightbringers before Jason had walked.

XX

ALLEGIANCE

The sound of their steps echoed as the companions walked through the grand atrium of Rennhall's Library. It reminded Jason of the Natural History Museum in London, where he had been countless times as a child with his parents. Similarly to the museum, the Library evoked a certain feeling of grandness and wisdom. The red marble of the imposing Erythian building, with all its black and white veins, gave it a certain sensation of brilliance and timelessness. On either side of the central nave, double aisles were denoted by the many stone columns that poked through the floor and spread across the ceiling like leaves to form meticulously sculpted fan vaults. Between the aisles stood rows and rows of towering mahogany bookshelves, full to the brim with ancient manuscripts, rolls and leather-bound volumes. At the other end of the central nave, a large sweeping staircase flowed down from the first floor. The amount of knowledge stored in this building was unlike anything Jason had seen in the Otherside, and he knew the Library was much bigger than what he could see at that moment. Occasionally, between the rows of bookshelves were displayed old swords, helmets and ancient relics from past warriors and honourable figures. The sanctity of Rennhall's Library was palpable.

"I can't believe I'm here," Anyir said. "My mum used to tell me stories about this place and how beautiful it was meant to be. I can only imagine what she'd say if I told her how marvellous it actually is."

"Oh, you haven't seen anything yet!" Kiro exclaimed. "There are five-hundred-and-forty rooms in the Library, and not all of them have books! Some have ancient artefacts, some are the old living quarters of our trainees, and of course, there is a whole wing dedicated to the Lightbringers. Rennhall's Library was once considered the 'headquarters' for the Order of the Lightbringers. It was a place where those who could summon the energy of the Flare lived, studied and learnt how to master their powers, for over four thousand years. Before the great Elf Coràl Owan built the Library, Lightbringers were just creatures without an aim, roaming Valkadia in search for a purpose. Rennhall's Library has allowed many Lightbringers to find their cause, their vocation, and has given them a safe space to survive hard times through history. Alas, there are no Lightbringers left here any longer, and so the halls remain empty."

"We've been waiting forward to a new arrival," declared a bellowing and cultured voice coming from atop the sweeping staircase. "Come forth, my friends, and welcome to Rennhall's Library. We've been expecting you, Jason. Grando told us all about you."

The three travellers felt disoriented, immersed in the grandness of the place and the power it exuded. They stepped forward, following the figure of an extremely tall, heavily built man who was making his way down the staircase. He was almost double the size of an average person and carried a long staff with a clear crystal lodged in the top end. He had white hair kept in a ponytail behind his head, but the sides were shaven off, giving him a severe yet wise appearance. His long white beard was bound in the middle with a golden ring.

A slender woman followed the man just a couple of steps behind. She moved in a feline manner, quiet and graceful, and she kept her dark hair in a long braid that draped over her left shoulder. She was a Dryad, a Forest Nymph. Just like Freydar, the woman's skin was green and her hair liana-like. Her eyes were deep and bright purple, and her nose and cheeks were sprinkled with freckles. She carried a menacing-looking glaive—a pole with a long, sharp sword attached on one end.

"I am Baldor Haral, Curator of Rennhall's Library," the Half-Giant announced. Then he motioned to the woman. "This is Rhulani Trygve. She and Kiro have worked alongside me for many years, and we are honoured to be of assistance to the new Lightbringer."

"Thank you, Baldor," said Jason, slightly intimidated by the Half-Giant who loomed over him. "It's my pleasure. I'm sorry Alamor is not here, I know you two were very close," he added.

"It is not your fault he disappeared, Jason," Baldor replied. "Knowing him, he's doing all right. He always has something up his sleeve."

"Alamor is one good with plans," Rhulani rejoined. "Especially those that benefit him."

Baldor scolded the Dryad with a warning gaze. "Let's pray for our dear friend Alamor to join us safely soon." He turned to Jason. "In the meantime, let me take you to the Lightbringer's chambers, given that you are now the new arrival as well as the last member of the Order. Word has already travelled about your arrival at Niteria, so we'll have to decide quickly. Will your friends be joining us?"

"Absolutely," Jason affirmed. "We have gone through so much together already, and I couldn't have made it here without their help. They'll be coming with us the rest of the way—they are both Sorcerers and good fighters."

Baldor scrutinised Anyir and Gregor, who until now had been silently immersed in the mysticism of the Library, overwhelmed by how not even the legends they had heard as children could compare. The Half-Giant looked at the two Humans with analytic eyes from head to toe, his face immovable like that of a totem gazing down. "If the Lightbringer trusts them, then I shall too," he accepted. "Now, if you'll please follow me," he invited, presenting the way up the staircase with a courteous open hand gesture.

As they walked up to the second floor of the Library, Jason realised they were making their way up the central dome. The more they went up, the more of Malion Jason could see. The city spread like a white blanket on top of the hills bordering the immense lake. They must have walked up at least ten flights of stairs, and at each floor, Jason stopped to admire the view. When they got high enough, Jason could even distinguish far ahead in the distance the immense wooden wall crossing Lake Malion, which marked the border between Erythya and Remara. Beyond it, the sky looked grey and dull, but in Erythya it remained blue and bright.

Baldor accompanied Jason, Gregor and Anyir to their rooms in the Lightbringer's quarters on one of the top floors of Rennhall's Library. The rooms were of modest size but not too luxurious, with a bed, a cupboard and a desk, and a porcelain basin to rinse their bodies and faces. Lightbringers were people of justice, wisdom and spirituality. There was no place for material possessions in the Order, except for their garments, books or weapons.

They dropped their belongings in their rooms before continuing up the final flight of stairs. Finally, they got to a heavy door at the end of the staircase, and Baldor halted. He extracted a large iron key from his pocket and inserted it into the lock. The door clicked and crackled as the pieces of the mechanism fell into place.

When Baldor pushed it open, Jason's jaw dropped. This was not because of the undeniable splendour of the Lightbringer's quarters, situated in the top floor of the central dome of the Library, but because Jason knew that place. It was the same place as in his dreams—the same place where he had seen the woman with the two infants, and where the Child Snatcher had kidnapped the babies. It was the same vast room with marble walls, blue columns, green carpets and lancet windows from which one could see the whole city spreading beneath. Jason recognised the grand marble table in the middle of the room, behind which the mother was cradling the new-borns. A map of Valkadia had been meticulously hand-carved on the table's surface; the details of each city, forest, mountain, and the famed Elora's Trench, were all engraved in the stone.

"We call this room the *Nädhirral*," Baldor explained. "This is where generations of Lightbringers before you have discussed, learnt and kept watch over all of Valkadia, long before the concept of separate realms clouded our world. Now, it serves as the headquarters for our surveillance program."

"Surveillance?" Anyir asked.

"Of course, where do you think the best spies get their training?" Baldor responded. "Here, we study old texts and use new information to learn more about our enemy."

"Where is everyone else, then?" Gregor inquired.

"The Library is big, and our trainees have much to learn and get busy with. We won't meet them today," Rhulani stated.

Jason's mind spiralled as he looked around. Why did he dream of that place before? Did he have to find the woman with the auburn hair and pendant? Did he have to save her children? Did he have to find the Child Snatcher?

"Jason," called Baldor. "Jason," he called again.

Anyir, seeing Jason uneasy, gave him an apprehensive look and nudged him with her elbow to snap him out of his thoughts.

"I beg your pardon, this place is just so… familiar," Jason said. "I think I dreamt of this place…"

"We must think of what we can do to help Valkadia with your newfound powers, Jason," Baldor interjected. "I realise you don't come from here, but as disturbing as it might be for you to be in our land, you will have to forget about your concerns."

"Right," Jason said, trying not to let himself be overwhelmed. "Alamor said you'd be able to help me get back home. I came here through an Elder Stone, but I don't know *how* or *why* I got here."

"What happened to you is highly irregular," Baldor mused. "There have been stories of animals managing to cross over—Aralays can do it, for instance—but never any other creature has been able to do so." Jason thought back at the books he studied at Grando's house, and the beautifully drawn picture of the Aralay appeared in his mind. With its candid antlers and long feathery tail, the winged stag was truly a creature of splendour.

"Perhaps somebody brought him here—somebody who can open a passage," Rhulani proposed.

"Did you feel anything strange before you entered Valkadia?" Baldor asked.

Jason thought back to the moment before he found the monolith. He was so exhausted, his mind in a dream-like state. Each time he was forced to recall that moment, he couldn't help but think of Clara. Jason thought hard about what he had told Alamor. "There was a sort of whisper, I guess," Jason told his newfound companions. "It was almost directing me towards the Elder Stone."

"Hm. You might be on the right track, Rhulani. Yet again, we would have heard of anybody strong enough to open a portal through an Elder Stone. Not even Lightbringers are that strong," Kiro said.

"The Elder Stones remain a mysterious Elven relic. There is not much information about them here in the Library, and we have studied everything we have. Elder Stones cannot be opened without the aid of the Steinndyrr, which is highly guarded by King Kavanagh's guards at the Ærindel and is protected with extremely powerful enchantments that only kings and Lightbringers can surmount. Perhaps it was activated for a brief moment, just to let you in, but the chances of that are exceedingly low."

Jason was disappointed. He had made it all the way to the Library to find information, but not even the Treasurers had answers. The path back home had just taken a sour turn. "Alamor said the only way I can go back is through an Elder Stone, but that before I do so, we must defeat Darkstrom," Jason said.

"That's right. Kavanagh will never activate the Steinndyrr unless Darkstrom's threat is gone," said Baldor. "It would be unwise to open any Elder Stone before the Red Raven has been defeated and his powers annihilated."

"Is there no way I can… skip that part? Can I like… give my Flare to someone else—one of you, perhaps?"

The Treasurers grew silent, and Jason felt like he asked the one question he should have never asked.

Baldor's tone became stentorian. "Your Flare is a blessing, Jason, and you should value it as such. It's your way back home, and the solution to the anguish that has afflicted Valkadia for too long."

Jason remained silent, awkwardly thinking of words to reply with.

"You will need the Eluir," Rhulani pointed out.

"Is… uhm… That's the dagger, right?" Jason observed reluctantly.

"The Astral Steel dagger that can kill Darkstrom, yes," Baldor replied.

"Alamor said you could help me find it," Jason said, succumbing to the inevitability of his quest.

"We have some ideas of where it could be, but you are asking some tough questions, lad!" Kiro commented endearingly, trying to cheer up the mood in the *Nädhirral*.

"Based on information from our spies in the Eiriksberg, there are three possible locations," Rhulani said. "One option is that Darkstrom put it deep within his private vaults in the Eiriksberg fortress. We think that might be too obvious, but it makes sense that he's kept it near him to protect it from spies or other interested parties. Also, those vaults are an impenetrable maze that only he knows how to navigate. The second option is that it lies in the most inhospitable place in Valkadia—around the blazing lands of Mount Rannor, if not inside the volcano itself. It is said that he keeps certain relics and artefacts most dear to him there, where he has a secret abode. The third option, which we see as most likely, is that the Eluir is in the Elven Ruins of Dorth. There is a rumour that it's hidden there, amongst the rubble. That place is a maze full of arcane secrets and makes a good hiding spot. Of course, we can't base our knowledge on rumours, and it could be somewhere else completely, but those are the options we've come up with so far."

"Hasn't Alamor been able to help?" Jason asked.

As he mentioned the Veheer, Rhulani let out an icy glare, while the Baldo and Kiro gritted their teeth in displeasure. Jason had already noted a certain frigidity towards his mentor, but now the trio's hostility was unmistakable. They looked at each other hesitantly, as if unsure how to reply. "Alamor has been... indisposed," said Baldor. "He hasn't been to the Library for years—since the fall of the Lightbringers. I had very occasional contact with him, but he's been silent for a long time."

"But... I thought you were all friends," Jason said.

The three Treasurers looked at the Lightbringer, anxiously. Kiro intervened, rubbing his neck with unease, "Just tell him, Rhulani. He deserves to know. He's not from here. I don't understand why we're hiding it from him. We must be truthful to the Lightbringer."

"He might not take it well, and we can't risk losing another Lightbringer," Rhulani argued.

"Alamor is the one who betrayed the Lightbringers, isn't he?" Jason bluntly stated.

There was silence in the Nädhirral for a long few seconds before Baldor finally spoke. "Alas, yes. The sword you are carrying is great, but also that of a traitor."

"Alamor betrayed the Lightbringers moments before they were about to defeat Emperor Darkstrom. He is the one we blame for the loss of the Lightbringers, for the struggles Erythya has been subjected to after the fall of the Lightbringers, and for the forfeit of the Eluir. Because of Alamor, many people have died," muttered Rhulani with a shaky voice, trying to control her anger.

"That's why he's spent so long at the Brotherhood of Thytelis..." Kiro revealed. "To repent his sins."

"Repent... not repent... it doesn't matter, people died..." Rhulani insisted.

"When one goes to the Brotherhood, all your sins become absolved, and King Kavanagh agrees not to divulge information about one's crime. Only very few people close to the criminals end up remembering their offences," Kiro explained.

"He's since reformed, but he is still not welcome in the Library," Baldor clarified.

"This doesn't take from the fact that he's tried to make things right ever since, and that he's brought you here to us," said Baldor. "But we, as servants of the Order, cannot fully forgive him. In Rhulani's case,

Alamor's stunt during the Battle of Tarvan Gher cost the life of her father and family."

"Rhulani's dad was a Lightbringer too," Kiro elucidated solemnly.

"He was?" Anyir asked, surprised.

Rhulani nodded. "Echo Trygve, Lightbringer for over one hundred years, terminated brutally by Emperor Darkstrom…"

"How come you are not a Lightbringer?" Gregor asked.

"The Flare usually passes from parent to child, but not always. I obviously wasn't blessed the same way my father was," Rhulani told, her face stern as she spoke with a tinge of resentment.

Once again, Jason was unsure what words to use. "I'm truly sorry, Rhulani," Jason replied earnestly. "Alamor has been a good mentor to Anyir and me. I can't expect any of you to forgive him, but I can only judge him based on how he's acted around us," said Jason, looking at Anyir endearingly as he remembered his mentor.

"I understand. You deserved to know," Baldor replied, his deep set eyes looking at Jason intensely. "The past is in the past, and it does not help to dwell on it for long… Let us continue your visit."

They headed down inside the Library's depths, descending through old stone tunnels that led to the profundities of the monumental building. The vaults protected secrets, rare and invaluable relics from before the time Valkadia was born. When they reached a heavy wooden door decorated with geometric patterns, Baldor placed his hand onto the brass handle and turned it slowly. The various locking mechanisms suddenly began moving and clanking, reverberating loudly within the vaults. The door opened, revealing a dark chamber with red bricks.

The room was empty and dark, but when Baldor hit the floor twice with his staff, the candles in the room lit up one after the other. What looked like a small chamber at first became a large hall entirely lit by candlelight from the brass chandeliers hanging from the ceiling. Like the exhibition room of a museum, artefacts were displayed proudly on altars and glass showcases, from sculptures to amulets, swords to staffs, armours to silk garments and cloaks. Meticulously woven tapestries made by the ancient curators of the Library hung onto the stone walls, each depicting a memorable battle the Lightbringers won.

"Welcome to the Lightbringer's Vault," Baldor announced. "This is where the relics of old Lightbringers are kept and where the almighty

Eluir dagger was forged. For now, this is where you'll get your armour and weapons, and anything else you might need during your feats."

Jason stepped inside the immense Vault and wandered around aimlessly, observing and admiring all the artefacts and items of insurmountable value that were kept within.

"Feel free to take anything you need, though only what you need. Lightbringers are creatures of mystic power, but they must be modest, or their magic can easily cloud their mind. You are one of them now, Jason, and you must learn how to act like one. That said, you are a warrior, and exceptional warriors like Lightbringers require the best weapons and armour available, made of the toughest, sharpest and lightest materials," explained Baldor.

"What about us?" asked Gregor eagerly, mesmerised by the fabled belongings of the ancient and mystical order of warriors.

"As companions of the Lightbringer, you will be allowed to take *one* item each, so choose carefully," replied the Half-Giant.

"Why *one*?" Gregor asked glumly.

"These are the rule of the Vault, and they have been so for thousands of years. They are enforced by mystical enchantments, and nobody knows what exactly would happen if one were to break them... although rumours suggest it would not be a pretty sight," Kiro teased as he moseyed around the chamber.

Every item reflected the orange light of the chandeliers, and though nobody seemed to have entered the Vault for decades, there was no layer of dust on the old relics—they were as polished as when they had just been placed there.

Jason passed his hand gently upon the smooth pauldrons and breastplates of a sleek leather armour hung on a wooden mannequin. There weren't many metal armours around, Jason realised. Alamor had once taught him that Lightbringers had to be quick and agile in the battlefield, and therefore a steel-plated armour was not the right protection. Like the old Veheer's leather items, the armour was embossed with intricate floral patterns, and the various pieces were kept together by buckles, leather straps and brass studs.

Next to it was the finest-looking helmet Jason had ever seen. It wasn't too complex—no intricate decorations of any kind or added visors of any sort, but it reminded Jason of the ones used by the ancient Spartan warriors. It was made of one solid piece of steel, with a long faceguard and a horizontal slit for the eyes. A thick steel crest of about two inches high ran from the top of the forehead to the back of the head.

Gregor had his eyes set on a simple leather scabbard enclosing a traditional Erythian kopís sword, engraved with runes spelling *Thomsor*—the 'Breaker'. It was the sword of Beatrice Lougar, one of the most ruthless yet wise Lightbringers of all time, who fought valiantly in the Battle of Dorth to protect the city from the Human's advance. The sword came with one magical ability, to reappear in its owner's scabbard if they ever got disarmed. Gregor would never be without a weapon, even in the most chaotic of battles. He took that sword for his own.

Anyir was content with the bow Grando had made for her, though she found a set of perfectly straight arrows made of lightweight steel with bright blue feathers. Rhulani explained to her that the arrows would fly through any weather, irrespective of wind or rain, so the target would always be hit. These were an invention of Rennhall's Library scholars and forged by the legendary archer and Lightbringer Cronin Olsar.

Gregor, who was still busy observing the precious artefacts kept in the Vault, suddenly called his companions. "Hey! Come have a look at this!"

"Ah, you've found something quite useful there, my friend," Baldor responded.

"I just found some old Jauls!" Gregor exclaimed, pointing at the contents of the large wooden chest he had just opened. Inside were eight of the spherical golden devices, though they were clearly old and rusty versions. "They're all broken though…"

"Ah, so *these* are the famous Jauls," Jason observed. "Alamor said he destroyed the ones kept at the Red Camp before we escaped. I fear I may sound silly, but what are they for, exactly?"

"They are communication devices," Rhulani elucidated. "They were invented by the Breegans a long time ago to communicate underground in the mountains where they dwell. They have a core of energy called the Green Aura, which is naturally attracted to itself like a magnet. By splitting the same mother material across different devices, it connects them and allows people to speak to each other even when separated by long distances."

"I bet you don't have *that* in the Otherside!" Kiro snickered.

Jason chuckled. "Not really like that, no. Our communication systems work slightly differently. See, we have a thing called *satellites*, which we send into *space* and keep our devices connected through *electromagnetic waves*," he attempted to explain. "The signal is sent from one device, bounces off the satellite, and is received from another device, no matter how distant."

"Hold on," interrupted Anyir, hers a face or utter bewilderment. The others stood aside, furrowing their eyebrows and scratching their heads. "What do you mean in *'space'*?"

"As in… beyond the atmosphere," Jason replied, assuming his companions knew anything about the intricacies of aerospace science. Seeing their muddled looks, Jason simplified by saying, "Between Earth and the Moon."

Gregor shook his head vigorously. "That can't be true. The moon is… the moon…"

"It's so far away!" Kiro exclaimed. "How do you send this bouncy technology up there? Don't your gods mind?"

To avoid getting himself into another theological debate and risk being called a heretic, Jason simply replied, "Erm… I don't think they mind… We send them up there with big flying metal machines called *rockets*."

Anyir's eyes brightened with delight. "Are they like those… what were they called… aryoplays?" she asked proudly as she remembered their previous conversation at Grando's house.

Jason laughed cheerfully, "You're close—they're called aeroplanes."

"The Otherside is a place of true wonders," Baldor pondered, looking up at the ceiling of the Vault as if it were the sky.

Hung on another mannequin was a tunic similar to the emerald green one that Alamor wore. This one was marigold yellow, with sleeves up to the forearms, brown lining and a thin lace keeping the collar closed. Along the neck, hem and wrists were embroidered with similar patterns to Alamor's. Jason thought it would be an excellent opportunity to replace his yellow trench coat.

"It's a *Væsnar* tunic," Rhulani explained. "The traditional garment of Lightbringers, designed for extreme durability, agility and protection. They have been woven over two solstices and blessed by the Head *Eredomyhm*, who dips them in the waters of Lake Medes in the Gartruth Forest."

"It also looks really cool," Kiro commented.

"Come on, try it on," Anyir encouraged.

Jason took his yellow trench coat off. The tunic fit Jason perfectly as if it was made just for him. He looked at himself in the mirror, new garments staring back at him, and for the first time could see more than just Jason McAnnon, a photographer from London. As he donned the embroidered tunic, he couldn't hide it any longer—he was a Lightbringer. Until that moment, he had just been floating along, trying to understand and adapt. Now, he felt part of this world and knew he could play a role in it. It didn't matter where his powers came from, or indeed where he came from, because he knew in his heart what he wanted, and he'd do anything to achieve it. Perhaps, it was time to give up the battered yellow trench coat for something more suited to his new life as a Lightbringer. Plus, as Kiro said, the tunic looked pretty cool.

Baldor approached Jason and put a large hand on his shoulder. "You're a true Lightbringer now," he said solemnly. Jason looked back at him with decisive yet somewhat anxious eyes.

As he walked up and down the vault, Jason felt that the tunic was heavier on one side, as if something was weighing it down. When he put his hand in the right pocket, he found a metallic device the size of a smartphone, with gears and cables sticking out and runes engraved on its casing.

"What is this?" Jason inquired.

"By Rotar's beard!" Baldor exclaimed, astonished. "We've been looking for that everywhere! Years ago, we found instructions in the personal records of Usnaar Bearol—a Breegan Lightbringer—about a tracker that he planned to build in case the Eluir ever went missing—a bit like a compass. We tried looking in the vaults, in the Lightbringer quarters—everywhere in the Library and in other places around Erythya, but we concluded that it was never built. Yet, you've found it."

"I think Alamor did mention something about it..." Jason observed. "How does it work?" he asked.

"If I remember correctly, there should be a small button somewhere to turn the device on. I'm not sure what happens afterwards," Rhulani explained.

Jason passed his fingers all around the device, but there seemed to be no button.

"Can I try?" Kiro interjected.

"Go for it," said Jason, handing the tracker to the Faun, yet not even he could find the button. "Baldor, you try."

When the Half-Giant took hold of it, something clicked. It was like a small round switch that needed turning, attached to the side of the tracker. Still, nothing happened.

"Is it broken?" Jason asked.

"Maybe you're doing it wrong," Gregor intervened.

"There are no other buttons," Baldor said. "This looks like the only manually movable part."

"Can't we ask the Breegans for help?" Gregor asked.

Baldor looked at him with trepidation. "Breegans are off the table. They don't want to know about anything to do with Erythya or Remara."

"Why is that?" Jason inquired. He thought all the creatures of Valkadia, except perhaps for Orcs and Omüms, would have wanted Darkstrom defeated.

"Well... during his rampage to expand the Empire, Darkstrom conquered the Breegan kingdom of Nalos to have control over their advanced technology. He turned all the Breegans into slaves and shaved their proud thick furs, and to this day, he forces them to obey his orders as if they were vermin. After the Battle of Tarvan Gher—when the Lightbringers were defeated—the Breegans secluded themselves in their mountain-fortress of Hegertan. For fear of being decimated by the Remaran army once more, they have since refused to fight alongside Erythya. Many Erythians, even king Kavanagh, have tried to convince them to join our fight in the past but nobody has been successful so far," Baldor explained

"A new Lightbringer might," Kiro proposed.

"We must try," Rhulani insisted. "Jason has arrived in Valkadia for a reason, and the Breegans must recognise that. If this device can really help us find the Eluir, we must try."

"I suppose we can go to Hegertan on the way to Niteria and try negotiating with them," contemplated Baldor.

"I... I know a Breegan..." Gregor interjected.

"What? How do you know a Breegan?" asked Baldor, caught by surprise. "Nobody just *knows a Breegan*."

"His name is Öken. I used to smuggle scraps for him. He had to get hold of some metals to finish one of his inventions and needed to avoid the suspicion of his fellow Breegans," Gregor told his companions. "He's the best chance we have to get the tracker to work. I just hope he remembers me."

"If you two trust this Öken, and you think he'll grant us safety in Hegertan, then that's what we'll do," Jason affirmed.

"We'll request council with the Breegan leader Uttol. He might not even let us into Hegertan, but if we manage to speak to him, we'll ask for Öken's assistance," said Rhulani.

The Lightbringer – Through the Elder Stone

"What makes you think they'll help us?" asked Kiro, his eyebrows pushed together. "We might not even be able to get close to Hegertan…"

"They would never refuse to welcome a Lightbringer and his companions," the Half-Giant responded, "though they might not like intrusion by us *non*-Lightbringers."

"If this Öken can help us with the tracker, then we need to take the risk," Rhulani replied.

"Well, I guess that's our plan then. We'll leave first thing tomorrow morning," said Baldor.

XXI

THE BRIDGE OF WHISPERS

"We're almost there, beastie," murmured Lok to the Ulkar as he patted its back. "Elora's Trench is not far now. Soon we'll be in Erythya."

As they rode from Orachlion to Sasken, Lok thought about the dream he had in the Necromancer's tent and was still unsure what to make of it. Was there a meaning behind what he saw? Or indeed had those events really happened and, if so, why did the Necromancer show them to him? Who were those babies and who was their mother? Why did the soldiers want the children? The Necromancer hadn't answered any of his questions and had only planted more doubts in his mind. The only useful thing that she told him was to go to Niteria to find Jason, and that's what he was going to do.

Lok kept riding with his gaze fixed into the distance; his thoughts circling each other.

"How long has it been since you've crossed over the Trench, my friend?" Lok asked the Ulkar, which replied with a growl and turned its head to face the rider.

"A while, huh? Is it true what they say in the stories—that you were a warrior, and that king Yohann transformed you into… this?"

The Ulkar growled again, nodding its enormous head and staring at Lok with its gigantic red eyes.

"I remember reading about you," Lok continued. "You tried to take some of the king's treasures and sell them to the nomads. You know what, king Yohann and the Elves are all dead, and you're still here. If you ask me, he did you a favour. Come to think of it, if Yohann hadn't cursed you back then, I wouldn't have met you, and I would have probably died in the Iron Wood. I guess in retrospect Yohann has helped both of us."

There was no reply from the Ulkar at first, which continued walking and kept looking ahead. When Lok was about to open his mouth again, the wolf shrugged brusquely in a sign of disdain to the rider's recent comments, making him fly off the beast's back and hit the hard ground. The Ulkar grumbled, though this grumble appeared to sound more like derisive laughter.

"Would you please stop doing that?" Lok complained. "I get it. I went too far. Sorry beastie. King Yohann was a coward, like all the other Elves of Old Valkadia."

The Ulkar nodded in agreement.

When they finally reached Sasken, Lok remembered how much of a sad little village it was. Scattered unevenly were battered stone huts and dry fields, peppered with sheep that grazed on the small amount of yellow grass which grew in sporadic patches here and there. In reality, Sasken was more of an outpost for the Remaran army due to its proximity to the Bridge of Whispers. It was a constant battlefield, as the Bridge represented one of the few ways to cross Elora's Trench, other than the gates at Lake Malion and the perilous path from the Dakkr to the Lumos Mountains. Alternatively, one could attempt climbing down one side of the enormous rift in the earth that descended more than one thousand feet, and up the other side, but that was a risky route that few dared to take. Lok had heard rumours about secret passageways and staircases used by Erythians that led all the way down and back up the Trench, but no one really knew where they were.

Lok kept his eyes open and constantly scanned his surroundings, ready for any eventuality as he led the Ulkar past the village. Carefully, they approached Elora's Trench, and as they got closer, the true enormity of the rift was revealed. *How do I cross it without my powers?* he pondered, anxious. The rift was about a thousand feet wide, and it ran all the way from one side of the horizon to the other like the trail of a gigantic snake.

Crossing over on his own and without powers seemed so much more difficult than he was used to. The previous times, his soldiers could bring along their enormous portable bridges and ladders. Now, Lok was left with only one option—the Bridge of Whispers, a sturdy and broad stone bridge that connected the two sides of the Trench. It was supported by an intricate system of archways and colonnades that went all the way down to the bottom of the pit and lost themselves in a layer of mist. Erythya laid on the opposite end, and one could see the sky change just above the Trench, transitioning from grey to blue. Lok had always been sickened by that sight, so pure and fabulous, but he knew it was all a façade. The *'Enchanted Realm'*, they called it, as if it was anything more than a land of monsters who hated Humans and refused to acknowledge their power.

All of a sudden, Lok realised the ground was shaking as if the gods had stepped foot on it. Though his powers were gone, he could still hear sharply the beating of hooves and the clangour of armour coming from miles away. Yet, this was not coming from the Enchanted Realm, but from the west—these were Remaran soldiers. Lok and the Ulkar turned around to face the army, ready to meet their fellow compatriots.

Led by general Tortugal and lieutenant Modùn, two of the most esteemed soldiers in the Empire, a troop of at least a hundred men advanced towards the Bridge. Lok found the battalion glorious and intimidating—all the soldiers rode black horses with red armour and brandished the dreaded Remaran emblem on large vertical banners. A truly remarkable sight. Amongst the men, Lok recognised two ghastly looking soldiers—one tall and slender, one short and stout—the Omüms.

"Ser Lok," Tortugal shouted from afar as they rode towards him. "I see you have made a new friend," Tortugal observed, motioning to the Ulkar. The horses neighed and halted, refusing to advance any further at the sight of the wolf.

"Come forth, general, the wolf won't harm. It is good to see you again," Lok greeted.

"What's the story with this… *beast?*" Tortugal asked.

"An unlikely but fortuitous encounter," responded Lok confrontationally, unhappy of how the general referred to his new companion. The Ulkar growled, making the general's horse retreat anxiously, its eyes like black pearls full of fear.

"Put a mouthguard on that thing, will you?" Tortugal snapped.

Lok ignored him and inquired, "What are you doing here?"

"We are looking for someone by the name of *Jason*. He is a Lightbringer, and Darkstrom has instructed me and my soldiers to find him and kill him."

Lok couldn't believe it. "Did you say *Jason?*"

"Aye," Tortugal affirmed. "Do you know him?"

"Something like that... I'm looking for him too. He took something from me." When Lok realised that piece of scum had taken his powers and used them to become a Lightbringer, he felt a wave of rage flow through his body.

Tortugal looked at Lok as the veins on his forehead bulged and his fists clenched, but before he could ask further questions, he heard a loud pulsating sound come from one of the satchels hung on his horse's back. The general pulled out a Jaul and flicked the small toggle on its side. With a crackle, a familiar voice emanated from the small device. "General Tortugal, you are late for your daily update." It was Darkstrom. Lok became anxious but relieved to hear that voice.

"Your Highness, what a pleasure to hear your voice."

"How is the search for Jason going?"

"We are at the Bridge of Whispers, about to enter Erythya. I have just encountered Lok, my Lord. Would you like to speak to him?"

"Lok? You are with him now?"

"Yes, my Lord, I am standing next to the General. It is a relief to hear your voice."

Tortugal handed the Jaul to Lok tentatively, trying to avoid making eye contact with the wolf. Lok was excited to speak to the Emperor, though terrified as well, as the mission was not going as planned. He turned the small toggle that established the connection with the partner Jaul.

"Lok, what is going on? I know about Karisa. Why did you do that? And why didn't you report to me when the mission was compromised? Has there been a problem with your Jaul?" Darkstrom asked with a serious demeanour.

"Sire, I must humbly apologise for what I am about to tell you," responded Lok in a hushed tone. "I... I..."

"Speak, son!"

"I lost my powers, my Lord." A long silence followed that statement, and anxiousness rose in Lok's heart. His chest felt tight, and his breathing was short and fast. If telling the Red Raven that piece of news wasn't humiliating enough, having Tortugal standing beside him listening to the whole conversation didn't help very much.

"What do you mean you have '*lost your powers*'?" Darkstrom repeated with a disturbingly monotonous tone.

"I was attacked by Alamor when I left Tarvan Gher, and he caught me by surprise. I found refuge in the Iron Wood, where I knew he wouldn't come looking for me, and it is there that I lost my powers to Jason. He took them, my Lord, I don't know how but he took them from me—the Necromancer said so. I think that is why he is a Lightbringer now, my Lord, but I can fix this."

There was a moment of silence as the Emperor pondered on what Lok had just told him. Then, Darkstrom spoke, slowly and clearly, his voice deep and metallic, "I put all my faith on you, Lok. Without your powers, you are no longer needed."

Each word hit Lok like a brick in the gut. The Emperor couldn't just dismiss him like that after everything Lok had gone through to be where he was—to be who he was. "I am going to get my powers back, my Lord. I promise. I will find Jason and I will kill him, and I shall be reborn," Lok implored.

"It's too late; the mission is over," the Emperor snapped, irritated by Lok's emotional plea. The stentorian tone of his voice had become apathetic and impassable. "You let a stranger take your powers, and he became a *Lightbringer*. Do you know how dangerous that is for the Empire? You have ruined my plans. We will have to attack Erythya without your help." There was a pause. Darkstrom's heavy breathing raised suspense in Lok's heart, which was already dropping through his guts. He could visualise the Red Raven's livid face as he spoke—he had seen it many times before—with ice-cold and glaring eyes, veins bulging, nostrils dilated. "General Tortugal," he said. "Change of plan: Jason must be apprehended alive. If he has Lok's powers, he can be useful to us."

"Certainly, Your Highness," the Orc replied. "That shouldn't be a problem. We have someone on the inside."

"Very well, I trust you, General, unlike Lok..." There was another unbearable pause. "You have disappointed me greatly, Lok. Never come to the Eiriksberg again," the Emperor said, the indignation in his voice palpable even through the Jaul.

With that, the conversation cut off abruptly and Lok was left speechless, without any closure, without any direction. "Sire? Are you there?" cried Lok desperately. There was no reply. "No, please, my Lord!" How could the Emperor toss him away like that? Lok was his best warrior, and he had done so much for Darkstrom over the years. He was his *son*. It was as if Lok had just received a blow in the stomach with a sledgehammer, and his heart got stuck in his throat. He almost couldn't breathe as he felt the weight of the world collapse onto his shoulders. Everything he had lived and worked for came tumbling down upon him. He squeezed the Jaul tightly in his fist and threw it on the ground before smashing it with his heavy boots. The device shattered, and the Green Aura faded away.

"I needed that, sir," Tortugal reprimanded, emphasizing the last word sarcastically, aware Lok had just been stripped of every title. *Sir.*

"Not anymore, you don't," Lok snarled, clinging onto his authority.

"How am I supposed to contact Darkstrom, m'lord?" Tortugal growled.

"The old fashion way, I guess. I can get you a pigeon if you wish," Lok taunted.

"Sarcasm won't end well, m'lord," the general said scornfully. Tortugal had finally risen above Lok's rank, and he wasn't going to let the Shadowcaster outshine him any longer.

"Yeah? For whom?" Lok kept challenging, raising his voice confrontationally.

The general placed his hand on the hilt of Rhazien, ready to unleash its dark blade on the once-Shadowcaster. "Clearly for you," he spouted.

"What do you think you'll do with that, huh? Even without my powers, I can rip you open!" he yelled wildly. Lok's eyes were wide open, deranged, his face turning red.

"Listen, you spoilt bast—"

Just as Tortugal started to unsheathe his sword, the ground began to shake once more. The general suddenly stopped talking and looked across the Trench with an unnerved expression in his eyes. He raised a fist in the air to silence his soldiers, who were murmuring among themselves in the background.

This time, the beating of the hooves came from the east. An Erythian troop was approaching from the other side of the Trench. The war horns resounded profoundly in the distance, their low braying frequency vibrating deeply inside Lok's chest. Every time he heard that noise, he felt a rush of adrenaline overwhelm his body, as he prepared for battle. This time, however, the rush was accompanied by underlying fear and anxiety that Lok couldn't shake. How would he fight without his powers? He grabbed a tuft of the Ulkar's hair with his left hand and grasped the hilt of Viggr with his right, ready to unsheathe it.

More than one hundred Erythian soldiers halted on the opposite side of the Bridge of Whispers, their bright blue banners and golden shields glimmering in the distance. A woman reached the edge of the Bridge on her white horse, leaving the rest of the troop behind herself. Her blonde hair reflected as much light as her golden armour. She waited there for a few moments. Both factions remained quiet, their hands tightly gripped onto their weapons. The silence filled the landscape with tension.

"Commander Sigrid, what a surprise," Tortugal finally said, trying to overcome the distance with his bellowing voice. "What do you want?"

"I have been sent here by king Kavanagh himself to apprehend ser Lok of the Eiriksberg. Surrender him to us, and there will be no bloodshed on this ground today," she demanded.

Lok glanced at Tortugal. He knew the Orc didn't like him, but he also knew he respected him for who he was, regardless of his powers. Lok was still a formidable warrior and was skilled with the sword. Tortugal could not ignore that. Yet, Lok had a terrible feeling about the whole situation. His fingers wrapped tightly around Viggr until his knuckles turned white.

"Why do you think we would give you Lok that easily?" Tortugal confronted.

"We have you outnumbered," Sigrid replied.

"That has never stopped us from slaying our adversaries," the Orc retorted.

"You will not win this if you decide to wield your weapons against us," Sigrid warned.

"We might not win, but we can kill the majority of you. If you wish death upon your soldiers, be my guest."

"Answer me this, general Tortugal, is Lok's freedom worth your life?"

The Orc thought for a moment before responding. "Lok is a respected nobleman of Remara and a great warrior. His life is certainly worth a lot more than many of our soldiers," Tortugal replied. "I'll tell you this… we must come into Erythya to apprehend a man called Jason. He caused quite a ruckus a couple of weeks back. Lord Darkstrom wants to 'talk' to him. We'll give you Lok if you offer us safe passage," Tortugal smirked and glanced at Lok as his sharp tongue stabbed him in the back.

As he heard those words, Lok realised he was now stuck between two enemies, and his inner instincts emerged. He drew his sword and wrapped both hands around it tightly, ready to pierce the armour of the men who had just betrayed him and those who wanted him bound to chains for the rest of his life.

"Beastie, this is not your fight. Leave now before it's too late."

But the Ulkar dug its claws into the earth and crouched backwards, ready to pounce, staring penetratingly into the eyes of its soon-to-be victims.

"No," Lok objected. "They'll kill you. Please go," he begged.

The only response he got was a growl.

"You're mad, beastie. If we don't make it, thank you for everything."

"I make no deals with Remarans," Sigrid replied to Tortugal from the other side of the Bridge. "Give us Lok, and we will spare your lives in return. That is my final offer. Are you sure this is what you desire for your men?"

"Men?" Tortugal asked. "These are not men…" His death stare gave way to a maniacal grin, and as he raised his arms before his troop, he shouted, "*Seynhar!*" Tortugal bellowed. *Transform.*

One after the other, the Remaran soldiers in the front line contorted and changed shape. Lok hadn't seen Fímegir in a long while, and his heart began beating fast. These monster-soldiers had pledged their soul to the Emperor, and the Remaran army used them like disposable weapons made of flesh. Their fierceness was unparalleled. As they transformed, the soldier's skin became grey and scaly. Their teeth turned into long menacing fangs and their fingers quickly transformed into razor-sharp claws. Spittle drooled from their jagged mouths and their eyes were black soulless pearls. Like a deformed mix between a reptile and a panther, the Fímegir prowled around Lok and the Ulkar with murderous intent.

The Erythian horn blew once more, and the Golden army charged as well, wielding shiny rectangular shields and the famed Erythian kopís swords. The Fímegir came flooding, running like a beastly, instinct-led horde thirsting for Erythian blood.

Lok and the Ulkar found themselves between the two factions when they collided. The Ulkar attempted to fight off the horrifying monsters, but they jumped onto him, biting and scratching like lions hunting an elephant. The Ulkar was stronger, but the Fímegir were too many. Their vicious claws ripped the muscles on the wolf's neck and back. A golden spear flew right past them, hitting a Fímegir, and the razor-sharp blades of the Erythian kopís came crashing into the chaos that surrounded them. The Ulkar growled and howled, and Lok did everything he could to help defend himself from the attackers on both sides. He swung his sword Viggr against the Fímegir to deflect the slashes of the monster's sharp claws, and he parried the incoming blows from the Erythian soldiers coming left and right.

The wolf was sturdy and powerful, but his blood now stained the ground. The shouting and yelling of the soldiers made Lok's ears ring. The disturbing snarling of the Fímegir was loud and threatening. He grew confused and irate, blood boiling in his veins.

One of the Erythian kopís cut Lok on his left bicep between the plates of his armour, loosening his grip on the Ulkar's hair. Lok and the Ulkar were getting weaker, but they fought back as much as they could.

The Erythian soldiers were skilled, yet the fangs and snarling of the beast made them tentative. The Fímegir, on the other hand, had no fear.

From the Erythian side, Lok heard commander Sigrid order, "Ready your bows!"

Lok knew precisely what that meant, and he realised there was no other choice. Behind them, the Fímegir were ready to attack again. In front of them, the menacing Erythian swords were prepared to slice their heads off. Below them, the one-thousand-foot drop was like a chasm ready to swallow them whole. If the Remarans got him, he was afraid Darkstrom would never forgive him; if he surrendered to the Erythians, they might spare his and the Ulkar's lives. They had one option: to cross the Bridge and join the Erythians before getting skewered by their rain of golden arrows.

"Nock!" Sigrid ordered. "Draw!"

Before the general could order the archers to shoot, Lok spurred the Ulkar to a mad race across the Bridge, trying to avoid the Fímegir and the Erythian infantry. Lok swung Viggr left and right, slicing the monsters' grey skin and stabbing the golden armour of Erythian soldiers. He paid no mind whether the flesh he cut was Fímegir, Veheers, Fauns, Minotaurs or Dryads.

"Loose!" Sigrid yelled.

Lok and the Ulkar were almost a quarter of the way across the bridge when the cloud of arrows covered the sky above and descended upon them like a deadly shower. They could only keep running—there wasn't much else they could do. The sibilant, high-pitched sound of arrows slicing the air instilled a fear in Lok that he never experienced before. For the first time in his life, he was afraid of death. He couldn't protect himself or attack like he used to when he had powers.

The Ulkar didn't budge and kept running even when two arrows hit its back, lodging themselves in his flesh and hitting the bone. Luckily, no arrow hit Lok, but there were more coming.

"Nock, draw, loose!" Sigrid yelled again, not even waiting between commands.

Another shower of razor-sharp arrows was released. There was still half of the Bridge to cross, and they were both getting weaker. The cut on Lok's left bicep was throbbing, and he was beginning to lose grip. As the arrows came crashing down on the stone floor of the Bridge, Lok thought how blessed he was nothing had hit him yet—but he thanked the gods too early.

"Nock, draw, loose!"

An arrow struck Lok violently on his left shoulder-blade. The impact felt as if it had just shattered his bone, though the adrenaline rush made him numb to the pain. He knew the wound was severe; he could feel the copious amount of blood trickling down his back, soaking the cloth beneath his armour. Other arrows hit the Ulkar on its back and neck, which growled and yelped, but it kept running. Even the beast knew that running was the only option to find safety, and it wanted to save Lok.

Alas, the last hundred meters were too much for either of the two companions. The Ulkar's legs gave way, and Lok lost his grip. As soon as the wolf hit the ground, Lok was jolted off its back and landed with a thud just a few feet away, his face on the cold stone of the Bridge of Whispers. The arrow snapped as he tumbled on the hard floor, fracturing his bone and tearing his wound even more. Lok's ears rang with a high pitch vibration, and all the surroundings became fuzzy. He looked back at the massive wolf. The Ulkar's eyes were closed. His body was motionless. A pool of blood began to spread on the white cobbles of the Bridge of Whispers. Lok wanted to shout, but words weren't coming out. His vision became hazy, and his surroundings blackened. Just before losing consciousness, Lok saw the blurry figure of a man in golden armour walking towards him.

The commander crouched down beside him and said with pride, "We got you now, *Shadowcaster*."

✷

XXII

EMERALD FIELDS

Anyir woke up sweating and confused, convinced she was still in her house in Karisa. When she found herself in an empty bed, it took her a moment to realise exactly where she was, but that was long enough to make her doubt everything she had decided so far.

A sudden sense of anxiety flooded her body, making her feel as if someone was compressing her chest more and more at every breath. Anyir felt aimless, her thoughts scattered as she tried to make sense of the road ahead. Was joining Jason on his quest the right way to deal with her husband's death, or her months of captivity in the Red Camp? Hastily, she got dressed, packed her bag, grabbed the bow and arrows that Alamor had given her, and quietly tried to sneak out of the room. She was going to travel back to Remara, back to Karisa. She didn't care how dangerous that would be for her. As she opened the door, she found Rhulani standing outside her room, startling Anyir.

"Rhulani! You scared me."

"I came to check if you were awake, we'll be leaving soon."

"Yes… erm… I'll be there shortly," she said, flustered.

"You're not going to come with us, are you?"

"Of course I'm coming. Why wouldn't I?"

"Anyir, stay. You won't find anything you're looking for outside the walls of the Library," the Dryad warned.

"How... how do you know I want to leave?"

"I can hear what your mind is telling you," she said with a composed smile.

"You can read minds?" Anyir asked sheepishly, her cheeks blushing.

"All Dryads can do it, some better than others. I like to think I'm one of the good ones, though it doesn't work with everyone. Some minds are more stubborn; some are simply deceiving."

"I need to go, Rhulani. I can't just stay here. I feel like I'm embarking on an adventure that I'm not suited for."

"This adventure is the best you can do to find your husband—if he's still alive. If he's not, it's the best thing you can do to honour him and his cause. Either way, he's gone right now, and you can do something great for all the people of Valkadia. Sometimes following your own path is the best way to find what you want. Call it trusting your destiny, if you will."

"What if this is not where I'm supposed to be?" Anyir questioned as she stroked the back of her hand, looking at her feet.

"If you weren't supposed to be here, you wouldn't be here. That's how life works. You are free to return to your old life, but I fear your road might be cut short and you would get lost in your own thoughts. If you stick with us, you have the chance to make a difference for everybody and not just yourself."

Anyir thought for a moment.

"I just feel like I'm not good enough for any of this. How am I supposed to fight the Remaran soldiers, the Fímegir, or the Emperor? None of you need me here... I'll just be a burden." Anyir's eyes grew sullen as she said this, remembering how helpless she had felt when Jason was drowning at the hands of the Omüms, or when the Goplen herd almost trampled them.

"Stop doubting yourself so much, Anyir," Rhulani said bluntly. "Whenever you think you're not made for this, think that Jason is not even from here."

"How... how do you do it, Rhulani? Staying so positive, I mean."

"I get scared sometimes, and I get stressed." As she spoke, Rhulani's eyes lost their usual sharpness, as if fondly gazing at distant memories. "The gods only know how worried I am about going to Hegertan and facing the Fímegir or the Emperor. When you live as long as a Dryad, there is a lot of time to dwell on one's past, but if I thought about that all the time, I would never be able to move forward. In life, we have no time to look back, Anyir."

"So, you think I should forget everything that happened to me? Karisa, Oblivan, the Red Camp?" Anyir asked, her emotions rising as the pains of the journey thus far rushed through her mind.

Rhulani observed the Remaran woman intensely. Anyir's painful memories reflected in her own consciousness, and the Dryad could sense each emotion, each moment of loss and difficulty. A tear rushed down Rhulani's freckled cheek. "Not at all. Those moments formed who you are. Use those hard times to push you, drive you forward. You are strong, Anyir, don't ever forget that."

Anyir noticed her tear-streaked cheek. She knew her friend was sharing those painful moments with her, and her heart felt a tonne lighter. "Thanks, Rhulani," she said, smiling endearingly. "Say, how did you end up here?" If Rhulani knew about her life story, Anyir now wanted to know hers.

"Why do you want to know?" the Dryad replied. Her tone was soft yet tentative.

Anyir felt awkward. She realised Rhulani was a very reserved person. "I'm... I'm just curious."

Rhulani smiled, clearly knowing everything that was passing through Anyir's mind, but she ignored it. "As you know, my father Echo was a Lightbringer and fought alongside Alamor and his leader Elgan Lannvard ..." She paused and looked outside the window. "When my father died, I decided that even if I couldn't be a Lightbringer, I could use my natural psychic powers and agility to do something good. So, I enrolled in the Golden Army to fight against Darkstrom and defend Erythya now that the Lightbringers were gone.

"Even though Alamor was the only one left, Darkstrom decided to decimate all the Lightbringer's families, paranoid more Lightbringers had survived. He feared their potential and believed they were hidden within Erythya, concealing their power until they could rise to face him once more. He sent spies and assassins to find my relatives and me, and he persecuted us until everyone was gone. I only survived because I hid in the masses, concealed by the golden armour of the Erythian army. That is when I met Baldor and Kiro. They had both fought alongside my father during the Battle of Tarvan Gher, and they decided to help me.

"We fought together against the Remaran army for years, but all three of us were convinced that fighting the Fímegir wasn't the right approach to defeat the Emperor. Baldor dreamt of becoming the curator of Rennhall's Library. He sought answers on how to defeat all the evils of Valkadia, including Darkstrom. So, we headed to Malion—at the time spoilt by warfare. Over time, Darkstrom's forces quietened down, and Malion returned to its old splendour. We spent the past decade at the Library learning the ways of the curators, studying anything we could put our hands on, reading the Lightbringer's old notes.

"Now we are here, and we are ready to finally do something about the tyrant that sits on his stone throne and spreads hate and death everywhere he walks."

Anyir remained silent for a while, unsure how to reply. "I never thought I'd be here," she said.

"Yet, you are. Embrace it. Come to the Nädhirral when you're ready," Rhulani said with a smile, before disappearing into the sumptuous corridors of the Library.

Anyir walked to the window of her room and observed the white city of Malion, which spread beneath her eyes like a candid, pulsating sea. Rhulani's words resounded in her mind. The Dryad was right. If she wanted to honour Oblivan's death, she had to stick with Jason and the others, and her heart finally filled with hope instead of anxiety and sorrow.

Anyir looked around the room and wondered whose it used to be. Many Lightbringers must have lived there, generation after generation. How powerful and wise they must have been, how ruthless yet kind-hearted they all were. Until that moment, her mind had been pulling her away from the reality, but now she could finally embrace it.

She took her belongings and headed upstairs to the Nädhirral without looking back.

Everyone was already waiting for her when she entered the room, but nobody seemed to suspect anything, or if they did, they were kind enough not to question her. She looked at Rhulani, who smiled back at her endearingly, glad she had made the right decision.

Baldor and Jason were already discussing what to do and where to go, sat behind the beautifully engraved marble table. That room, that table, the Library—they were all objects of legends, legends Anyir's mum had told her when she was younger and that she'd fall asleep to.

"We will depart soon after this meeting, and we will head to the Emerald Fields," announced Baldor to the rest of the group. "We'll travel along the Elven road from Malion to Lake Oren, and then we'll follow the Argal River until we get to Hegertan."

"Do you not think it's too much of an exposed route?" Rhulani asked.

"You're right—it's a risky road. Remaran spies will be watching our every move, but it's the quickest way to meet the Breegans. If we stick together, there should be no issues."

"What about Lok?" Jason asked with unease as if he was speaking about a ghost. The others suddenly looked at him with dread. Anyir remained silent, full of apprehension. She was sure Rhulani could feel everybody's fear as they spoke about the Shadowcaster.

"We've heard about Lok's travels towards Erythya. I doubt he'll make it over the border, and even if he does, he'll soon be apprehended by the Golden Army."

"Surely, if he's a Shadowcaster, he'll be looking for me," said Jason.

"If he's not found you in Remara, I doubt he will do in Erythya. It seems to me he has other orders from the Emperor," said Gregor.

"Gregor is right, Jason," said Rhulani. "And if he *is* looking for you, he'll be outnumbered."

"Apparently, he's riding the *Ulkar*..." Kiro observed.

"So I've heard..." Jason murmured. Anyir could sense her friend's anxiety across the room. Her skin chilled as she thought of ser Lok from the Eiriksberg riding the Ulkar. Stories of that beast were wild and distressing.

"I think Hegertan presents the biggest danger right now, in all honesty," Rhulani said. "We can deal with Remaran spies and shady assassins, but if the Breegans decide we're not welcome, we might have a few 'political' issues."

"If we act with the right ethos, and if Öken is as trusted as Gregor says, then we should be fine," Baldor replied. "Collect your belongings and your weapons. We depart shortly. Light shall protect us all."

From three companions, they were now six. Anyir was excited to start the adventure, though an impending sense of doom and sorrow still lurked in the back of her mind. She did everything she could to bury it and followed the group to the Library's stables, where they prepared their horses for the journey. It would be a long time before she'd see Karisa again, but if they were going to be successful, Valkadia would forever change for the better.

They jumped on their horses and swiftly headed north along the cobbled roads of Malion. Word of a new Lightbringer arriving in Erythya had travelled fast, and the magical inhabitants of the city were marvelled by the view of a Lightbringer, brightly dressed in his *Væsnar* tunic, leading his warriors towards their destiny.

The Elven Road, the road that led from Malion all the way through the Emerald Fields and the Gartruth Forest until reaching Niteria, was unlike anything Anyir had seen in the Empire. Most Remaran roads were ill-kept and dusty, they were always lurking with bandits, and one would go miles without there being a single tavern or watering hole for the horses. The Elven Road was just the opposite—it was a long, brick-covered path that brimmed with creatures from all over Erythya. Wagons whizzed past, full of supplies and sundries. People led mules transporting silks and cotton from the Ryhan Mountains in the north, while others carried spices coming all the way from the Flagos Islands.

Along the way, they came across a legion of the Golden Army. Anyir thought she would feel threatened by their presence as she always did when going past the Remaran soldiers, but she experienced nothing like that. The bright blue and golden banners parading the Aralay—Kavanagh's emblem—fluttered in the gentle breeze as the soldiers greeted Anyir, Jason and their companions with respect.

The bards were already singing songs about the Lightbringer and his companions, and the hope they had brought to Erythya, even before they had actually done anything. Of course, nobody knew where Jason really came from, but Jason's name resonated from within the streets and taverns of Erythya. They began calling him the 'Marigold Guardian', after the colour of his Væsnar tunic. Jason thought that sounded quite amusing, and happily took the nickname.

Anyir came to understand how important what they were doing really was for the people of Erythya. No more Empire would mean no more war, no more family members sent to the slaughter against the Remaran Army, no more unrest on the border. Defeating Darkstrom would save thousands of people from being turned into abominable monsters whenever a battle ensued, and it would forever stop Humans from harming Valkadia's people and nature. The Marigold Guardian was a symbol of hope and rebellion against tyranny. Anyir wasn't even sure if Jason knew how much he meant to the people of Erythya.

That night they camped in the middle of the Emerald Fields, just off the Elven Road. When it became dark, they realised why the great plains of Erythya were called 'emerald'. When the moonlight began to shine and the stars were out, the fresh green grass began to glimmer, and when anyone stroked it or stepped on it, the grass glowed even brighter. The hue of the fields was that of the most radiant emerald, and each breath of wind made the blades wave like an ocean, making it glow in pulses as if it was a live being. The breeze whooshing upon the plain sounded like the breathing of an enormous creature, gently sleeping.

But the peace didn't last for long. As they got together to eat, the Fields' quiet was suddenly disturbed by a rumble caused by what sounded like a hundred horses. A myriad of anxious thoughts whizzed through Anyir's mind as everyone jumped up and drew their weapons.

"Stick together!" Rhulani yelled, grasping her glaive. Gregor and Jason unsheathed their swords and Anyir her bow.

The rumble grew louder, and the tremor grew stronger. The sound of people's uproar made Anyir's breathing faster and her hands, usually so steady, began to shake. She gripped tight on her bow and readied herself to pull an arrow out of her quiver.

"Whatever happens, we've got each other's backs, don't forget that," Jason told her.

From afar, the troop really did look huge, and Anyir doubted that six of them could really defeat all those soldiers. Yet, as they got closer, everyone sighed in relief. *Centaurs.*

The tribe of magical creatures with half-human and half-horse bodies, galloped towards them yelling melodically. Anyir had heard a lot about Centaurs but had never seen one in real life. They were majestic, with their braided manes and muscular bodies. As they kicked their hooves on the ground leaving behind trails of glowing grass, they circled the six companions and galloped around them over and over.

One Centauress left the circle and approached Jason. She was tall, her hair dark and long and her coat a tawny colour. Her horse legs were muscular, and she wore a sleeveless leather vest and colourful beaded necklaces. A bow was strapped around her torso. "It's a pleasure to make your acquaintance, Jason McAnnon. Your name has resonated throughout Erythya. It is an honour to meet the Marigold Guardian. I am Isaine, chief of the Akani tribe," she said.

"The honour is mine, Isaine. Never in my life I imagined of meeting Centaurs. This is amazing," said Jason.

"We were hoping you'd be willing to join us for a feast," Isaine offered. "The Emerald Fields are part of our territory, and it is our tradition to honour our prized guests with our best food and wine."

Baldor quickly whispered to Jason, "Centaurs are touchy beings, accept their invitation."

"Of course, we'd love a feast!" Jason accepted.

"The Lightbringer said yes!" Isaine cheered, and an excited roar erupted from the rest of the tribe.

Suddenly, a group of Centaurs blew on their horns while others began playing large drums. The rhythmical beating and the thundering sound reverberated in Anyir's chest. The circle broke, and the Centaurs began to dance to the music. Some of them brought food while others carried barrels of wine—all as an offering to the Lightbringer.

Isaine grabbed a silver chalice from a fellow Centaur and filled it from one of the barrels. "It is our custom that the leaders of two clans drink the first glasses of wine of the night together, as equals!" she said as she offered it to Jason. Isaine then took another chalice, filled it, and clinked it against Jason's. "Let's drink, Marigold Guardian, let's drink!" With a wild smile on her face, Isaine guzzled the wine in a single gulp. When Jason finished all his wine as well, she proclaimed to his clan with his arms spread wide, "Let's feast!"

For three long hours, the six companions drunk and ate with the Centaurs, dancing to the constant rhythmic music they played and laughing with the mythical creatures. At one point in the night, the Centaurs decided it was time to indulge the Lightbringer and his companions with their traditional combat event—the *Dengah*. The rhythm of the music changed, and the singing became more like a baritone chant. The Centaurs beat their arms against their chest, while the Centauresses stomped their hooves on the ground, all in unison with the beating of the drums.

The Centaurs formed a circle once more, and forth came the first two contestants, each brandishing two wooden sticks. The aim of the combat was easy: try to hit each other in the back, and the first one who did would win. It was a contest of pure agility, accuracy and strength. Of course, with the Centaurs' long equine bodies, this was easier said than done, and the duels sometimes lasted as long as ten minutes, especially when skilled *Dengahneers* were in the ring. The duellists circled one another, trying to predict each other's attacks. Some of them used their front hooves to distance the opponent before striking. The concentration of each combatant was intense, and the flow at which they spun and hit with their traditional weapons was simply remarkable. The exciting show was aided by the spectacular scenery and emerald light shed by the glowing grass, which created mesmerising shadows as the Centaurs challenged each other in the art of the *Dengah*.

After most of the Centaurs had their go in showing off their skills, Isaine asked loudly, "Would the Marigold Guardian like to have a go?"

The other Centaurs cheerfully acclaimed the request.

"I think I drank too much," Jason slurred. He looked at Anyir, who stood beside him as they eagerly watched the Dengahneers. "Anyir… you should have a go! You'd be great!" Jason almost tripped over as he tried to hug her drunkenly.

Anyir found herself caught off-guard and she felt her face heating up as everybody looked at her. "Me? No way, I don't know the first thing of—"

"What a great idea!" Isaine interrupted before Anyir could finish declining the offer. "I gather you are quite the Sorcerer, so let's see how fierce the fire within you really is!" Isaine grabbed the two sticks from one of her friends and banged them together.

"No… I really don't," but before she could say anything else, Kiro began to chant, "Anyir! Anyir! Anyir!"

Soon, the whole audience was cheering for her to fight the Centauress.

"All right," Anyir then declared, pushing aside her fear and enjoying the sudden adrenaline rush. Isaine towered over Anyir's average height.

One of the other Centaurs handed two sticks to Anyir, and the fight began.

The Centauress was the first to attack, swinging decisively at Anyir's head with one stick before quickly striking again with her second stick, aiming at Anyir's ribs. Yet, the fire-sorceress was quick and nimble and promptly parried both blows. Anyir jumped and spun in the air, making it difficult for the Centaur to hit her. The sticks slammed against each other fast, but neither of the two combatants ever got close to hitting the other.

It was only when Isaine decided to rear on her hind legs to threaten her opponent that Anyir fell, but the fire-sorceress was quick to bounce back up and block the incoming attacks that came crashing one after the other like a mill.

"You're good, Anyir! It has been a while since I have seen one of your kind fight, and it is an honour to face you in combat. What you lack in experience you make up for in agility and determination. The question is—can you beat me?" Isaine.

"I can only try my best, Isaine, but you are a very skilled adversary," Anyir replied respectfully.

"Stop kissing her ass and kick it instead!" Jason shouted.

"The Lightbringer is right, my friend!" Isaine joked. "What are you waiting for?"

"Is that really what you want? For me to kick your ass?" Anyir confronted.

"That's right. Bring it on," the Centaur retorted.

The crowd was taken over by laughter, and they cheered for the duel to continue. The beating of the drums grew louder. Anyir and Isaine stared at one another intensely, carefully waiting for the other to attack.

Anyir's heart was thumping inside her chest, and her hair stuck to her sweaty forehead. She had completely stopped moving, waiting for Isaine to attack first. She had closed his eyes ad remained still, with the sticks held tightly in either hand but kept them low. She was relaxed. Though she didn't have the Flare, she had learned how important it was to clear her mind during a fight. She could hear the Centauress' hooves thumping on the ground, her mane fluttering in the wind. The drums repeatedly resonated in the background. It was when Isaine's muscular legs dug into the earth that Anyir knew just what she had to do, and how long she had to wait in order to achieve what she had in mind.

Just as Isaine whipped her stick back ready to strike, the air around Anyir grew colder. In an instant, she propelled herself with a blast of fire and jumped higher than Isaine's head. The burst of bright, hot flames made the spectators avert their eyes for a moment. Anyir flipped her body entirely upside down in the air. When she was over the Centauress, she swung her stick against the Centauress' back. Isaine was dumbfounded when she suddenly tripped and fell to the ground, landing forcefully on her side.

Isaine looked around, defeated. Behind her, Anyir stood victorious. The crowd erupted. Never had they seen such a duel of Dengah.

"You have bested me, Human Sorceress, and you fought valiantly. You have my utmost respect," said Isaine.

"Anyir's fire flows strongly within her!" Baldor commented.

"That's right," Isaine replied. "I am glad we have you here, Anyir. The Lightbringer should feel very lucky to have a companion like you. I shall tell all the chiefs of Erythya's clans that we are in good hands. We are at your service, whatever you need."

XXIII

ATONEMENT

Alamor had travelled for miles after the Goplens had caused turmoil in the Stonevale, allowing him to drive the Omüms away from Jason and Anyir. After a couple of hours, he had lost track of the two shapeshifters, and he had hoped to have bought his disciples enough time to flee to Erythya. Alamor had also left Isidir behind and prayed Jason had found the precious and fierce Elven sword. Even if he weren't there to help him, at least Jason would have a loyal companion by his side. He and Silvyr would soon head towards Niteria, but while he was still in Remara, he had to do something else first. After riding each day for as long as Silvyr could bear, Alamor arrived in Orachlion, where he had a long-overdue meeting.

"It's nice to see you again," said the Necromancer.

"It's great to see you too. It's been a while," Alamor responded, looking the woman in her white eyes. Her white tunic cascaded on her slim body. She had even more runes tattooed on her face than he remembered, the ink contrasting markedly against her pale skin.

"You've been quite busy lately, as I understand," she observed.

"I have been, indeed. We have come a long way, you and I," he stated.

"How have you been? The spirits tell me things, but you don't make it easy for them to find you."

"I've been well," Alamor replied. "I have travelled, seen places that many would not dare venture in. I have thought about all my wrongdoings as well as the beautiful days of my life." Alamor paused, and looked around the shaggy tent, shrouded with dark, dusty covers. "Have you lived in this decrepit hole all these years?" he asked.

"I don't need more material possessions," the Necromancer replied. "Since I found out about my gift, bones and herbs have been all I've needed. I'm old and not the fiery girl I used to be, so this is enough for me."

"I'm glad you're content. It feels like a lifetime ago since those days."

"It *has* been a lifetime ago, for many," she observed.

"I suppose so..." he responded, thinking of all the people he had met in his life; all those he had been forced to say goodbye to.

"The boy doesn't suspect anything, I hope?" the Necromancer asked.

"No, but I expect he will soon find out the truth."

"Good. He must find out on his own, or he won't accept neither his past nor his destiny."

"I still don't understand how you did it," Alamor said. "How did you get him through an Elder Stone without the Flare?"

"There are still some beings that can go through, whether the Steinndyrr keeps them opened or closed. The Stones are still doors, you know, and their locks can be picked by using the right tools."

"You won't tell me, huh? Secrets of the trade?"

"Something like that," she said, allowing a faint smile to come through her arcane-looking exterior. "Lok came to visit me a few days back."

"I thought he might have. What did you tell him?"

"I showed him something he had to see. He was looking for answers, as well as wanting to know where Jason had gone. I showed him to a memory that had certainly been suppressed by the Emperor."

"Are you talking about..."

"That day, yes. I've tried to show it to Jason as well, but he is too confused even to pick up anything other than distress from the vision," she replied.

"Maybe showing him in a dream was not the best way," Alamor observed pensively.

"They'll understand soon enough. We've waited until now, and the pieces are finally in place, but we must wait a little longer for *them* to put them together. We must be patient," the Necromancer said.

"Things are moving fast. We cannot wait any longer. Lok is not going to change any time soon on his own; he's made it clear. All he wants are his powers, and he can't see the bigger picture. He's onto Jason. If he finds him, he'll kill him, and then what's the point of all that we're trying to accomplish?"

"You can't interfere anymore, Alamor," reprimanded the Necromancer, her white eyes wider than ever. "If you do, they'll learn things they are not yet ready to know, and then all of this really will be for nothing."

"We can't let Lok get to Jason before he is reformed. This won't end well if I don't get to him first," Alamor responded.

"You've tried and failed so many times, Alamor. As you said, Lok is not changing anytime soon, so we must be patient. You can't force him to change—that has to come from within, or it won't be true change."

"So, you expect me to sit back and let things unfold like we've done all these years?"

"Please understand, Alamor. They must walk their own path and come to us when they are ready. Only then you can *tell* them the truth, and only then they will *listen* to the truth."

"I can't, I'm sorry. I've let you decide how to go forward for all these years, but now I must follow my instinct."

"Your instinct is wrong, Alamor."

"Maybe, but I need to do something. I'm tired of waiting. I need to make things right before it is too late."

Alamor looked into the once emerald eyes of his old friend and remembered of the first time he had seen her many years back, carrying books around the corridors of Rennhall's Library. Alamor kept looking at the Necromancer, who had changed so much since when he had last seen her. He knew she could tell what he was thinking, aided by the help of bygone souls, but in reality, he wanted her to know. He was tired of hiding himself, his feelings, his thoughts from the world. Too long he had lived in the shadows after what he had done, resenting himself for his betrayal.

"Alamor, those days are gone. Our lives have been what they have been. You have kept your word for all these years, even the spirits of those whom you've deceived have forgiven you. This represents a new beginning—a new hope. You mustn't repent anymore."

Alamor felt his throat tightening as he held back his sense of liberation. He had lived so many years in guilt and had tried to make things right ever since the day he had stabbed his brothers and sisters of the Order in the back. That was, until that moment. It was as if a thousand rocks that he had been carrying for years had just become feathers, and their weight was no more. Yet, he wasn't sure if that was real. He had been so used to dwelling about his past choices that this sense of relief was surreal.

"I'm sorry. Really, I am. But this is the right way. I need you to trust me," Alamor told the Necromancer. She looked at him sternly and nodded slowly. Then, with her skinny index, she painted Alamor's forehead with black ink. She whispered words in a language that not even he knew and blew a puff of ashes from her palm onto his face and shoulders.

"You must go now," she said. "You have a long journey ahead."

"I hope to see you again soon. Maybe Valkadia will finally be cured by its evil by then," he told her.

As he stood up to leave, the Necromancer grabbed Alamor's left hand and said, "Everything that you did, and everything that happened, was for a reason." She ran her thin fingers along the scar on Alamor's hand.

"Goodbye, my dearest," he said endearingly.

"Goodbye," she replied.

It was night by the time Alamor left the Necromancer's tent, and the air outside felt lighter—though the stench of manure and rotten food in the streets of Orachlion compelled Alamor to place his hand over his mouth. Silvyr was waiting quietly outside the tent, and she nudged Alamor on the shoulder as he walked by. He jumped up on the saddle and gently hit Silvyr's flank to begin their journey once more.

The reunion with his long-lost friend had given him much food for thought, but suddenly a strange feeling took over his psyche. The air around him felt gloomy and sad. Maybe it was the Necromancer attempting to contact him through the spirits as he left her tent. Or this could have been something else—something worse.

Droplets of rain started to fall from the dark heavens, hitting the dry Remaran ground and quickly turning it into mud that stuck to Silvyr's hooves.

Alamor pulled the hood of his green robe up and spurred his faithful companion along the dark alleys of Orachlion, advancing cautiously and trying to make the least noise possible. The city was swarming with soldiers and spies, and civilians ready to turn into Fímegir. Though he had extensive experience with all three types of threat, he did not wish to prolong his stay in that miserable grey place any longer.

Vigilantly, he ventured through a large muddy square by the outskirts of the city. He would soon leave Remara, where he had stayed for far too long, and he could return to Erythya and continue mentoring Jason. He hoped the boy had followed his instructions, and that he wasn't in too much trouble. More than anything, though, he wanted to meet Lok, and help him find himself again. Darkstrom had clouded his mind, and Alamor had to remind him who he really was. Only if Jason and Lok followed the right path, then the Emperor could be vanquished.

Suddenly, the figure of a man in a black cloak appeared in front of him. He was tall, and his cape fluttered like smoke even when the rain fell heavily. Only his iron crown glimmered in the weak moonlight.

Alamor urged Silvyr to halt, and he remained still, sat on his saddle, observing the man who obstructed his way.

"Only now you show up?" Alamor asked, knowing perfectly well who he was addressing.

The Emperor stood silent for a moment, then he responded with a deep, powerful voice. "Only now you have let your guard down, old friend."

"Aye, I suppose so," Alamor said, slowly moving his hand to the hilt of his iron sword. As much as he was glad Jason had Isidir, now he wished he hadn't left it behind. "Today, the past never seems to stop haunting me."

"If you hadn't gone back on your word so many times, the past would have let you live in peace," said Darkstrom. "Now, the time has come for you to become *part* of the past."

"Maybe. But what a story my life has been," Alamor replied.

The Emperor began to pace around the square. "You have many stories, Alamor. I'll give you that. But how many of them are entrenched with betrayal, lies and trickery? How many of them are filled with the blood of your own kind, and love for the kind you are *not*?" Darkstrom breathed heavily, the words coming out more and more like hisses.

"I did what I had to do, Ingvar. Anything I have ever regretted doing, I have atoned for. I have suffered because of my choices, but now I rejoice for the legacy I have left behind."

"What legacy? That new boy you have taken under your wing? He will never amount to much, and if he does, it will be because of *me*."

"Because of you? Look at what happened to your previous disciple," Alamor confronted. "Lok has *lost* his powers. And even if he still had them, do you think he would listen to your commands his whole life? He is not a fool, and he is not evil. He will change his ways, and when that day comes, it will mark the end of your despotic rule."

Alamor's hand grabbed the handle of his iron sword, and as he extracted it from the scabbard, he jumped off Silvyr's back. He whispered in her ears and then gave the horse a loud slap on her backside. She galloped away through the alleys that led outside Orachlion, like a white feather gently flying through the night sky. Alamor grounded his feet into the soil, and his body began to emanate a faint glow.

"You're making a mistake, old friend. My sorcery has grown stronger since our last encounter. Might I remind you—you've *helped* me grow this strong. It should come to no surprise to you that what you're doing now is going to mark the end of your journey."

"A glorious end to a glorious life," said Alamor.

He put his hands together, and between them, an orb of light formed. With a roar, a bright beam burst from the sphere, flooding the square and the Emperor. Alamor's magical stream was so powerful it tore down the wall of a butcher's shop in a stone building on the other side. Luckily, there was nobody in there, because the heat of the Veheer's Flare was so hot it could melt anything it encountered. Alas, when Alamor stopped summoning the power of the sun, the Emperor was still standing in the same spot.

"Is that the best you can do after all these years?" Darkstrom confronted.

"Unlike you, I don't have the souls of thousands of innocents to fuel my power."

"Shame. I gave you the chance to become stronger, but you turned it away. Now, your choices come with a price."

"If there is one thing I don't regret, it's choosing never to become a Shadowcaster," Alamor replied.

As Darkstrom stretched his arms to either side, he began calling to the spirits of the night. A purple mist swirled up from the ground and enveloped the Emperor, lifting him mid-air. The fog expanded, covering the entirety of the square, and Alamor felt lost. He looked around in search of his foe, but the mist was like a purple shroud over his eyes. Holding his sword ready to defend himself, Alamor started to advance into the thick cloud where Darkstrom was lurking.

"Now you're on your own, Lightbringer. Not even the light of the moon will come to your aid now," the Emperor's voice boomed from all directions.

"It's all right," Alamor said. "It's just a matter of time. I *will* find you, and I *will* put an end to this."

"And how will you find me? I'm everywhere… and nowhere."

The Emperor's voice echoed all around, its volume increasing and decreasing, become farther and nearer every second. Alamor lunged, thrusting his sword into the mist. Nothing.

"Ever played that silly game Pin the Tail as a kid? It doesn't seem like you were very good at it," Darkstrom taunted, his maniacal laugh resonating all around.

As Alamor slashed his sword to his left and his right, sharp pain to his bicep suddenly made him falter. The grim blade of Zarak, Darkstrom's two-handed Elven sword, had sliced Alamor's flesh like a hot knife through butter. Alamor shook his arm as if to send the pain away and passed his sword from one hand to the other as he adjusted to the discomfort. With the light from both sun and moon gone, he could only rely on the Flare stored up in his body. That meant he had to ration how much he used and directing it to quick wound healing was non-essential.

From behind the purple cloud, Alamor saw the incoming blade directed right to his chest, and he promptly deflected it with the agility and dexterity of a feline. Under each wallop violently inflicted by the Emperor, the old Veheer felt the cut on his arm quiver more and more.

Fuelled by pain, he focused and listened more carefully to the steps on the wet ground. When he was sure he had located his target, he used the wind to disperse the mist, exposing the Emperor's whereabouts. Promptly, Alamor drove the sword through his torso, but Darkstrom was one step ahead. What the sword hit was not the body of a man, but the hard wood of a tree by the edge of the square.

Alamor jolted as he felt his left calf being viciously slashed by the razor blade of the Emperor, who appeared behind him. This time the wound was deeper, and he felt all the heat building up as the blood throbbed from the gashed muscle.

With the mist now gone, Alamor turned around and finally saw where the Emperor was, leaning complacently against the wall of a house adjacent to the square. Then, Darkstrom appeared by the torn down butcher's shop and materialised again by a drinking trough not far away from where Alamor was standing. Soon a dozen copies of Darkstrom surrounded the old Veheer, who was starting to struggle keeping his body weight supported.

"If you are so powerful, why do you keep hiding, huh? Stop being a coward and face me with dignity," Alamor challenged. With a swift movement of his hand, Alamor launched a large stone from the broken wall against all the Emperor's copies, which one by one turned into smoke as the incoming ballistic piece of sandstone hit them.

Yet, when the rock approached the real Emperor, it exploded into a myriad of shards. Rather than let them fall to the ground, Darkstrom thought of a better use for them. As the sandstone shattered, the small fragments remained floating in the air surrounding the Emperor who, with a simple gesture, shot them forcefully at Alamor. The projectiles turned to dust as they smashed against a thick wall of protective air that the Lightbringer formed in front of himself.

"For someone of your age and nature, your powers honestly impress me. Such a shame you decided to waste them sitting in that decrepit temple on Mount Hargon. We could have made a good team, you know."

"I doubt it," Alamor retorted.

From the Veheer's hands, a torrent of molten magma emerged, rushing forcefully towards the Emperor. Pieces of the scolding, liquid rock fell on the ground leaving a trail of dry lava, but all the heat and power that Alamor summoned from deep beneath the Earth's crust were no match against Darkstrom's dark sorcery. Not only did the lava not seem to harm him, but he seemed to *enjoy* being immersed in it. Alamor was astounded. He grabbed hold of his sword and watched as the Emperor walked through the stream of glowing red sludge.

When Darkstrom got close enough to Alamor, he raised Zarak above his head, ready to pummel it down. The old Veheer lifted his sword to protect himself from the incoming blow, but the Emperor's energy was too powerful. Alamor's blade snapped in half, and Zarak proceeded its trajectory down to his clavicle. Alamor screamed as the blade of the Elven sword cut his flesh deep, and his green robe turned to red. Then, Darkstrom abruptly grabbed Alamor's head with his bony hand and pressed his thumb against his forehead. The old Lightbringer was catapulted back into the memories stored in his subconscious.

"Alamor! Alamor!" he heard calling from behind as he walked down the Elven Road in Niteria—the long, cobbled road that led from Malion to Niteria and passed under the Gate of Unity until reaching the majestic Ærindel. He knew that voice very well, and he turned around with delight.

"Maralen! Hello," Alamor said endearingly. She was the wife of Elgan Lannvard, the 'chosen' Lightbringer, whom Alamor found too arrogant and egocentric for his own good. Alamor felt like melting every time her rose lips pronounced his name, or she looked at him with her big green eyes. Her auburn hair fluttered in the gentle breeze. "How are you today?" the Veheer asked, enchanted.

"I'm absolutely great! I have some great news!" Then, she pronounced these words that always brought anger in his core, "Have you seen Elgan?"

"I haven't, sorry. I'm going to the Library to study with the others," he said. "You can come with me if you want, perhaps Elgan is there," Alamor offered. Those emerald eyes touched him deep in the heart. He shouldn't have taken her to the Library. Above all, Alamor felt like a fool to accompany Maralen back to Elgan, but that was the only way he could spend some time with her.

"It would be an honour," she replied and wrapped her arm under his.

"What's the news then?" he inquired eagerly.

"You'll have to wait. It's a surprise."

When they arrived at the Library, Maralen ran to her beloved Elgan and, after kissing him, she exclaimed, "I'm pregnant!" The other Lightbringers remained silent for a moment, then burst into powerful exultation.

Alamor, on the other hand, tried his best to hide his jealousy and hatred. He hated the child before it was even visible that Maralen was pregnant. They had decided to call their unborn child Zoaar—*enlightened*—as if to symbolise their power against the darkness of the Emperor. Alamor would have killed all the Lightbringers just so he could be alone with Maralen, and he wouldn't have hesitated even to kill the child.

Yet, he couldn't. He loved Maralen too much.

He had to stay in the Order of the Lightbringers and earn their trust no matter what. Their time would come, but he couldn't ruin a mission that took so long to prepare. He had to sacrifice his life as a simple Sorcerer of the Remaran Army in order to travel to Erythya and infiltrate the Order. Proving he was trustworthy when his morals were opposed to the Order's values was a difficult feat that took him years, but he did it for the Emperor.

Alamor's memory transported him to another moment of his life many months later, when the war against Tarvan Gher had commenced. He was running amongst flaming balls crashing into the ground, and around him, he saw the fierce faces of warriors screaming both for pain and fierce determination. To his left and right, he witnessed many of his comrades' deaths—people that he had learned to admire in his time living in Erythya, but also old acquaintances and friends from Remara. Many of the latter, however, didn't even look like his friends anymore. He watched as they turned into abominable grey beings, which were being slaughtered by the Lightbringers and the Erythian troops that advanced by Alamor's side towards the Eiriksberg. The worst part was, he had to kill them, too. He looked at his hands, covered with the black sludge of the *Fímegir*. Yet again, he had no choice, that was his mission—and it was soon about to end. He couldn't wait to be done with it.

"I knew I could count on you," Darkstrom told Alamor as he played with the Eluir dagger, sat on his imposing black throne. The Lightbringers were lying in front of the Emperor, inelegantly displaced on the floor of the Throne Hall of the Eiriksberg. Their dark blood spread like shiny tar on the black marble. "There is one more thing," he added. "That lady who Elgan impregnated—there is a chance her offspring might carry the Flare. I want you to go to Malion with the soldiers and kill her and her progeny."

Alamor felt as if a dagger had just been shoved through his chest. He took a moment and chose his words appropriately—that was always a good idea when addressing the Emperor. "Sire, with all due respect... I know Maralen, and she has never done anything wrong, and there is no guarantee her baby will possess the Flare."

"Any threat, even remote, must be eliminated. We have not come all this way to be challenged by a Lightbringer again."

"Have you thought about using the offspring's Flare to your advantage and turn them into a Shadowcaster? Perhaps you should spare the mother and the child."

"Nonsense! We must eliminate any new-born child with the Flare! I will be sending spies and soldiers to kill any infant, child, adult and elderly who I suspect possesses the Flare in Erythya *or* Remara!" Darkstrom pondered for a moment. "If this woman is indeed carrying Elgan's heir, their Flare might be very powerful."

"What should I do, my Lord?"

"All right, take the child and bring it to me... but you must kill the mother."

His memories launched him to a couple weeks later, after the siege at Malion. Suddenly, he found himself in an eerily familiar place where he hadn't set foot for decades. He was in front of Rennhall's Library, wearing his black cape and hood. The city of Malion laid before him in flames.

The Library's door was torn down, and a carpet of corpses covered the white marble floors. From the marks on the walls, it could be seen that the soldiers were not in their human form. On the curtains, on the wood, and wherever else he could look, there were scratches caused by the sharp claws and fangs of the Fímegir.

He ran up the Library's stairs, now on the verge of collapse, towards the Nädhirral. There, sat in a pool of blood on the marble floor, he found Maralen. She laid beside the large marble table in the middle of the room, cradling *two* small new-borns. The city below burst in turmoil as the Remarans took revenge on Erythya for the attack at Tarvan Gher, but Alamor decided he had done enough for Darkstrom. The woman he loved was dying on the cold floor of a lonely room that was about to collapse. She had just given birth on her own to a pair of twin boys.

"Shh," she murmured to her children. Her voice was soft and quiet. "Don't cry, my darlings. Everything will be all right. I love you both so much." She looked up with tired eyes. "Alamor?"

"My dearest," he said with tears in his eyes. "What happened?"

"My waters broke when the siege began… the soldiers came in… they killed everyone… I ran and hid here until…" She coughed, and blood spattered on her hand as she covered her mouth. "Until Zoaar… and Tyr… were born."

"Zoaar *and* Tyr," Alamor repeated. He looked at the two twins, their dark hair and hazel-coloured eyes. They were Maralen's sons.

"Take them, Alamor… save them… I'm dying…" she begged.

"Don't say that."

"Find somewhere safe for them… take them away from Valkadia. They won't be safe here. Take them far away, the farther, the better."

"Where should I take them?"

"Take them to the Otherside," she said.

"That's… impossible…"

"Elgan told me stories of Lightbringers that could do that… You're the only one left now; you must try."

Alamor looked into her emerald eyes, and then at the two innocent pink babies she was holding. There was no way they could be a threat if he took them to the Otherside. They would never come back. It was worth a try.

"I will honour your last wish, my dearest," he finally said, stroking her auburn hair. Alamor took the two twins, wrapped them in his cape and rushed out of the Nädhirral without looking back.

Alamor strapped the boys to his chest in a sling and jumped on Silvyr's back. They rode from Malion all the way to the ruins of Dorth, where he knew he would be able to find an Elder Stone. He knew attempting to open it and taking the twins to the Otherside would probably cost his life, but he had to grant Maralen's wish.

He crossed the Elven ruins, though he could hear the rumble of soldiers on horseback rushing towards him. Darkstrom wanted those babies. They were amongst the last to bear the Flare, and they were the heirs of Elgan Lannvard, the strongest Lightbringer of all time.

The Elder Stone stood before him, and its carvings depicting a large dragon looked down upon him and the twins like an ominous judge. He dismounted Silvyr and slowly approached the monolith. He placed his left hand on the stone, cradling the two babies wrapped up in the sling with his right arm. There was an intense flash as Alamor summoned the light and transferred it into the rock. The carvings on the Elder Stone lit up, and Alamor screamed as his hand burned with the scorching heat of the light.

Soldiers appeared behind him, brandishing swords and axes, followed by a gang of Fímegir. Alamor kept channelling all his Flare to his hand and through the Elder Stone. Suddenly, a breach opened in the monolith, like a bright blue void made of swirling water. He had done it.

Then, one of the soldiers grabbed hold of his shoulder, ripping the sling that was strapped around his back. Alamor managed to catch the two boys before they fell to the ground, but the soldiers pinned him down and took them from him. He fought against the soldiers with all his strength, attempting to keep the breach open. The only way he could save the twins was to jump through the Elder Stone once and for all, hoping the force of the enchanted door would help him.

He managed to push the soldier back forcefully, and before he knew it, he was in a tranquil forest. Rays of golden light shone radiantly through lush green trees. He was in the Otherside—he didn't know where, but he knew he had taken the twins to safety. Yet, when he looked down, he realised to his horror that he was only holding only one of the brothers. He had saved Zoaar, but the soldiers had managed to take Tyr. Alamor's heart sank. He had failed Maralen. The soldiers would either kill the other child or take him to the Emperor, who would use his powers to his advantage.

Alamor had to take Zoaar somewhere safe, but he also wanted to try crossing back to Valkadia and save Tyr from Darkstrom's evil grasp. He glanced behind himself and saw that the breach in the Elder Dorr was slowly closing. There was very little time left.

Like the sound of a bird singing after a battle, bringing angelic hope back into the world, Alamor heard the laughter of a woman travel from across the forest. A man accompanied her, and they spoke in a tongue he didn't know.

"*You always make me laugh, Robert! How do you do it?*" the woman said.

"*Ah, my darling Denise, you're the one that inspires me. I never thought I was funny until I met you,*" said the man.

"*I'm so happy around you—you know that, right?*" Denise said. "*Being in this forest with you makes me so calm, so serene.*"

"*I feel just the same—can you hear that?*" Robert said sternly.

"*Is that a baby?*" Denise asked apprehensively.

Indeed, Zoaar had begun crying, sensing that his life would change irreversibly from that moment on. By their jovial demeanour and cheerful tone, Alamor thought the couple sounded just perfect. He laid Zoaar on the soft ground, wrapped up in the blanket, and blessed him, "*Zo'or alegsiar eith*—light protects you". He kissed the infant's forehead, and swiftly jumped back into the Elder Stone, leaving Zoaar on the ground ready to be adopted.

Alamor was abruptly woken up from his dream by a sharp agonising pain that stopped him breathing. He found himself back in the square of Orachlion with his knees on the muddy ground, and the blade of Zarak lodged deep in his chest. He looked up as the blood began clogging his throat. Darkstrom's ice-blue eyes looked back at him with a confusing mixture of anger, regret and vengeance. "You've lived a long life, Alamor, but your Flare is weak now. Your time here is done," he said. Darkstrom pulled his sword out of Alamor's chest and let his body fall to the ground with a thud.

The old Lightbringer looked up to the moon, which shone exceptionally bright that evening.

"Zoaar is back," he murmured with his last breath.

✸

XXIV

THE CAVERN

The following day Jason woke up with the auburn-haired woman imprinted in his memory. He had dreamt about her and her children again. The dream was the same, though the Child Snatcher's face was still impossible to see. Jason's mouth was sticky, and the taste of wine stuck to his tongue. His whole body felt drained as if a balloon was inflating in his cranium. He couldn't remember how or when he fell asleep, but he found himself laying on a blanket, which was now damp from the dewy grass.

The Centaurs had gone. The only signs of their presence the previous night were the deep hoof prints on the ground, circling the large bonfire they had danced around, which was now a pile of ashes lifted by the morning breeze.

The sun had just risen over the Lumos range, and its warmth laid over Jason's groggy eyes. The air smelled fresh and reinvigorating, and the sound of birds and crickets enlivened the Emerald Fields. However, Jason felt too ill to appreciate any of it. Anything moving made him nauseous, and the high pitch sound of birds singing went through him.

His friends were scattered around the bonfire area, some awake, some fast asleep. Baldor and Rhulani were sat on two logs, boiling something in a pot over a small fire, the smell of which permeated the camp with its sweet and nutty aroma. Kiro, Gregor and Anyir were still dreaming.

Jason quietly wobbled towards his two awaken friends, trying to fight the nauseated feeling pushing through his stomach. He soon realised his shoes were missing; the grass was soft and poked gently between his toes like a thick carpet, so he kept walking without much bother.

"Good morning, Jason! I trust you had a good sleep... with all that wine!" mocked Baldor.

"Hi... Don't mention wine to me today, please..." Jason retorted. "I'm not getting near wine for a long while."

"Everybody says that, especially until they've tried the wine in Niteria. Once you sip what the kings of Erythya drink, you won't stop craving it."

"Please, stop," begged Jason, making Baldor laugh aloud.

"Would you care for some *Gurgum* instead?" Rhulani offered.

"No offence, but I'm afraid my stomach won't be accepting visitors for a while," Jason replied, who felt as if a nail had just been driven behind his eyes as he slowly stepped towards his companions.

"Ah, nonsense. *Gurgum* is the drink that cures everything," Rhulani responded. "It was invented by the Elves. Not many people know how to make it, so you're lucky I do. Please, try it. You'll thank me for it."

She poured some of the contents of the pot into a small ceramic cup and handed it to Jason, who picked it up reluctantly. The drink was a pale yellow and sludgy semi-liquid that didn't look inviting at all. It smelled vaguely like cinnamon, with a hint of turmeric and aniseed, and small bits of what looked like cereal floated on the surface. *All right. Let's give it a go*, he thought. The texture was that of a smoothie, though it was warm, and he could swear the cereal inside was rice. As he gulped the Gurgum, his headache faded, and he drank until there was nothing left in the cup.

"Wow," Jason exclaimed, feeling reborn. "The Elves really didn't mess around! Thank you, Rhulani."

"The Elves sure were an ingenious bunch. You're welcome."

Jason quietly observed the green expanse, waiting for his nausea to pass. In the space of a couple of minutes, Jason's mind cleared, and his mood abruptly changed. He felt euphoric and full of energy. "So, what's the plan now? Are we going to Hegertan? How long will that take us?" he said as he sprung up, rocking back and forth on his heels and toes. The young Londoner could feel his heart thumping fast, and his breaths were short and deep. His sense of awareness was through the roof, and his body shook involuntarily.

"Well, we should wake up those sleeping beauties there and have some more Gurgum," said Rhulani.

"More? Yes please!" Jason exclaimed, reaching towards the pot on the campfire, but he was soon cut short by the Dryad. She slapped the back of his hand as if swatting a fly.

"Nah ah! I think you already had enough!" she admonished. "You can wake the others up. We'll head to Hegertan soon." She then turned to Baldor. "We'll get there tomorrow afternoon, so we'll stop somewhere along the way for the night. When we get there, we'll have to be in our best shape and form, so it's best we take our time to travel and arrive well-rested."

"Come on then!" Jason exclaimed at the top of his voice. "Let's do this, folks! Wakey wakey!" he shouted, clapping his hands loudly.

Groans came from the other three companions who were still asleep. Kiro's horns popped out of the cover he had wrapped himself in and looked around, his eyes swollen with sleep.

"What is going on? Why are you yelling so much, Jason?"

"Time to get up, Kiro! Have some breakfast, get yourself ready. We're going to see the Breegans!"

"I've never heard of anyone who wants to see the Breegans as eagerly as you…" the Faun retorted.

"Get up, come on! You've all slept enough!" he incited. Anyir and Gregor sat up, confused by the racket Jason was making.

Kiro sniffed the air, and then asked Rhulani and Baldor, "Are you two making Gurgum?"

"We are," Baldor chuckled.

"Did you give it to the Lightbringer?" Kiro asked.

"We did," Rhulani replied.

"That explains a lot…" Kiro grumbled.

"What's all this racket?" Gregor grumbled from under the cover. He too wasn't feeling in his best shape.

"Gregor, Anyir! Come!" Jason called. "Try some of this; it tastes so good!"

"All right, all right. I'm coming," Anyir covered her shoulders with the blanket and groggily trudged across the camp where the Gurgum was being boiled.

"What is this slop that you're making?" Gregor asked.

"Try it!" Jason insisted. "You'll feel great in a matter of seconds! We have something similar where I come from. It's called coffee."

"*Coffee*?" Kiro ridiculed. "What a funny name! What does it taste like?"

"Well, it depends on the coffee, but usually it's quite earthy and nutty. Oh, and it's brown or black, not yellow like that!"

"Ew," Kiro responded. "A black drink that tastes like earth... no thanks."

"Ah, you'd like it! It's what most of us drink!"

"The more you tell us about where you come from, the weirder I think your world is," Gregor interjected.

"I'm sure you must feel the same about our world, Jason," Baldor commented.

"It's definitely super weird," Jason retorted with a cheeky grin, making the group chuckle.

Recovered from the eventful night after drinking more *Gurgum*, the six companions packed their belongings and strapped the saddles on their horses' backs. They travelled for hours, stopping regularly to let their horses rest, and Jason took the time to enjoy the view of the landscape. As they passed the lush grasslands of the Emerald Fields, they approached the hills at the foot of the Lumos Mountains, which rose and fell smoothly like a gentle sea, covered in bushes and trees. They rode along a path in one of the valleys between the hills and spotted an old derelict farmstead made of stone bricks at the bottom of a rockface, surrounded by trees and covered in moss and lichens. A river flowed by its side, trickling down one of the hills with a continuous metallic jingle. The building looked like it had been abandoned for aeons, with most of its eastern wall torn down and part of the roof collapsed.

"This looks ideal!" Baldor exclaimed.

"What? This old piece of junk? I'm not staying here," Gregor complained.

The sky clouded over, and it became darker. In the distance, coming from the Lumos Mountains, black clouds were approaching.

"You can sleep under the rain if you really want," Kiro said.

Gregor grumbled, but so did the thunders far away. "All right, then," he accepted glumly.

Water seeped through the cracks of the stone house, and wind blew from a hole in the roof, but at least they were less exposed to the elements.

The companions huddled close around the fire and cooked a mere portion of rice and beans, which disappeared in a matter of minutes.

Jason stared outside the window at the rain falling heavily onto the wet ground. He couldn't help but think back to the deck of the *Son of Odin* when the pitter-patter of the rain on the ship's windows turned into an indomitable storm. Jason knew something bigger was about to come his way.

"What is Lok like?" Jason asked his friends.

"Why do you want to know?" Baldor asked.

"I know he's on his way to Erythya, and that he's a Shadowcaster. That's all Alamor told me about him—otherwise, he seemed quite dismissive. If that's true, he's my biggest threat after Darkstrom, and if he's coming for me, I must know everything I can about him," Jason replied.

Baldor's face became stern, his tone dismal. "He was brought up by Darkstrom and his minions in the Eiriksberg. Trained from a young age to pursue the dark arts and learn the lessons of the Human's gods, Darkstrom used him to lead several missions on the other side of Elora's Trench, intent on colonising the land beyond. Every one of Lok's incursions was pushed back by the Golden army, but he has brought death and sorrow into Erythya, and his actions have weakened our reign. He is fearless and clever and lacks empathy and is known to have used the impaled bodies of Erythian farmers to mark his path across our land," the Half-Giant told.

"He's ruthless," Gregor interjected. "Cold as stone... he doesn't have any feelings or remorse."

"Have you met him?" Kiro enquired nervously.

"Only once, when he came to Karisa..." Gregor answered and looked at Anyir with sorrowful eyes. "He came into Karisa on the back of the Ulkar and demanded food and beer—"

"How the hell did he get his hands on the Ulkar?" Rhulani interjected, disturbed by the thought of the beastly wolf.

"Only Odin knows..." Gregor murmured with trepidation. "That thing is huge, just as terrifying as they say in the stories. Lok said he wanted food, so I took him to the Hammer and Anvil. When I asked him why he was there, he said he was looking for Jason. He wanted a new sword, so I introduced him to Oblivan..." he said in a deep voice, speaking slowly and looking at the wet ground. "The rest you already know..."

Anyir sat silently, immersed in her own thoughts and gazing into the campfire. The wood crackled amid its heat, and the flames danced and swirled with sinuous elegance under the sorcery of the Karisan woman.

"Lok was saying you took something from him. That's why he was looking for you," said Gregor.

"I… I've never met him…" Jason's mind was whizzing through his memories. When Grando told them about Lok, he said the Shadowcaster had disappeared into the Iron Wood three weeks before. That coincided when Jason had arrived in Valkadia. After he passed through the Elder Stone, the individual he met with black armour and long dark hair must have been him. His recollection of the man became clearer and clearer. "What does Lok look like?" he asked.

"Quite tall, very strong. He's got long hair; I think brown or black. His eyes are serious—the eyes of a man who has killed innocents all his life and has no regrets of it. He is quite an intimidating character. His looks alone made me nervous, but the death he carries on his shoulders like a cape is terrifying," Gregor explained.

"What colour armour does he have?" Jason asked.

"It's black if I remember correctly," Gregor answered.

"I was mistaken. I have met him… the day I arrived," Jason suddenly realised. He felt little droplets of sweat form on his forehead.

"Are you sure? You never told us about that day. What happened exactly?" Baldor enquired.

"I don't entirely want to…"

"You need to tell us, Jason. This might be crucial information that can help us understand what happened to you," Rhulani intervened.

"All right…" Jason told them everything about the shipwreck, Clara's death, and his arrival in Valkadia through the Elder Stone including his brief encounter with the shadowy figure of an armoured man in the middle of the Iron Wood.

"It sounds to me like you met Lok," Gregor stated.

"I just don't understand why he'd just leave you there and not kill you," Kiro questioned.

"Thanks, Kiro," Jason joked.

"No, I'm serious. He found someone strangely dressed wondering in the woods, why wouldn't he kill you if he is the ruthless monster we know him to be?" Kiro observed.

"I passed out, Kiro. I'm not sure how to answer that. Maybe he got scared?"

"Lok wouldn't get scared," Baldor commented. "Perhaps something else scared him, or perhaps something happened to him when he saw you. I think we're asking the wrong questions here. Rather, we should be asking why he's searching for you if all you did was pass out in his arms. What could you have taken from him?"

"Again, I passed out... I'm really not sure what he wants from me other than the fact that I'm a Lightbringer and he wants to kill me because he's a Shadowcaster," Jason replied.

Anyir, who had been silent throughout the whole conversation, suddenly murmured, "Why did you ever come here, Jason..."

"What do you mean?" Jason asked.

"Oblivan wouldn't be dead if it wasn't for you."

Suddenly, everyone around the fire went quiet and stared at Anyir uncomfortably.

"Anyir, why are you saying this?" Jason responded.

"If Lok weren't looking for you, he wouldn't have gone through Karisa. He wouldn't have wanted a better sword to fight a Lightbringer, and he wouldn't have gone to Oblivan to look for one," she said, her hands shaking and her face hard as stone.

"Anyir, Lok went to Karisa well before we went. He was just looking for me everywhere. He happened to go through Karisa first," Jason argued.

Gregor intervened, "Lok didn't have a sword at all when he came, that's why he went to Oblivan. He would've needed that sword regardless of his vendetta against Jason."

"I'm sure it wouldn't have mattered if Lok went through Karisa or any other town or village—he would have killed people there regardless. Maybe he was going to Erythya anyways, and then he lost his sword after meeting Jason. Perhaps he just needed to get to the first place he could find to get hold of a new sword, and Karisa is the first place you get to if you are travelling from the Iron Wood to Elora's Trench," Baldor added.

"You're wrong!" Anyir erupted. "It would have mattered! He could have gone to Sasken instead and not killed my husband! What if he wasn't going to Erythya at all, and he is only on his way here because of Jason? In that case, he's put us all in danger!" Anyir confronted with fear in her eyes. The campfire burnt wildly, roaring as the flames grew.

"If that's the case, he's come here alone, which poses less of a threat than he usually does," Rhulani countered.

"Don't you think it's your husband's underground operations providing weapons to Erythya that cost him his life?" Jason questioned exasperated. He hadn't asked to be catapulted into Valkadia, and his first few days were spent wandering behind Alamor, not conspiring to cause villagers' deaths. However, when he saw Anyir's face drop, he realised he had gone too far. "Anyir, I'm sorry…"

Anyir glared at him ragefully, the wood in the campfire crackling more intensely, and she stormed outside the house. Jason ran after her, regretting his words.

"Anyir! Anyir!" Jason called as he followed her out.

She didn't answer. She stood stock-still in the rain, looking up at the cloudy night sky.

"Anyir," he called again more gently as he approached her. "I didn't mean to—"

"I get it… you're right," she said as she turned around to look at the photographer, her eyes teary. "He was reckless, but he was doing it for the right reasons. At least he died knowing he fought for the right cause…"

"He'd be so proud to know what journey you've embarked on," he said sheepishly, his eyebrows pushed together with concern for his friend.

"I know… I just miss him. I was so close to seeing him, and he was taken away from me," her voice choked as she said those words. Jason could sense the mixture of anger, frustration, sorrow and regret in her voice.

"I get it, but when our loved ones go, we must cherish our memories of the times we spent with them, rather than be angry for all the time we could have spent with them before they were taken from us," Jason replied. His saddened frown turned into a hopeful smile when he recalled something Anyir had told him. "Like 'someone' said to me once, all we can do is remember our loved ones and bring them back to life in our mind. They never truly leave us if they stay in our memory."

Anyir looked at Jason deep into his hazel eyes. Her heart suddenly began to find rest as she heard those words being repeated back to her. She hugged him tightly. "Thank you, and sorry," she uttered.

"It's all right. I'm sorry too," Jason replied. "Let's go back inside and dry up."

Nobody slept well in the derelict farmstead that night, between the cold breeze and the sound of heavy raindrops bombarding the house. However, after drinking some Gurgum, they were ready to depart once again, aiming to arrive at Hegertan before the late afternoon.

As they travelled up the rising hills and slowly approached the Lumos range, a droning noise coming from the mountain tops enveloped the landscape. The braying bellow gradually developed into more of a melody. It was so constant and unique that Jason thought no normal being could produce that sound.

"Can you hear that?" Jason asked. "What is it?"

"That's the Breegans, my friend," said Baldor. "They're singing. They use it to communicate with each other from mountain to mountain. It's called *Ullarin*."

They crossed the wheat fields and farmlands outside the Breegan city, and as they got closer to Mount Dormund, the enormous mountain on which Hegertan sits, the throat singing grew even louder. Jason gazed above at the jagged peak of the mountain, which loomed before them and ascended so high it disappeared in the clouds like a fang biting into the white flesh of the heavens. Lush, green pines grew all over the surroundings, and snow was scattered here and there.

Jason was hypnotised by that droning song, which concealed any other noise. It was so intimidating, yet so captivating. It reminded Jason of the Mongolian *khöömii*, a type of throat singing that originates from southern Siberia and western Mongolia which involves producing more than one pitch simultaneously. The Breegan's singing travelled far, so far it reverberated in Jason's chest, miles down the mountain. It somehow made him scared of going any further, but also intrigued him about what he'd find travelling forward.

When they finally reached the enormous stone walls and iron doors of Hegertan, the singing stopped abruptly and gave way to an ominous silence. The six companions waited at the gates on their horses.

"What's happening?" Kiro asked anxiously.

"We'll find out. Stay calm," Rhulani replied.

Not five minutes later, Jason heard rustling and faint whispering rise from behind the wall. From atop the stone barrier crept what Jason thought looked like a mixture between Hobbits and Ewoks. The small creatures, perhaps half the size of him, were human-like, with large chests and large heads, but covered with the fur of a Yorkshire Terrier from head to toe. Their hair and beards were so cottony they looked like the manes of small lions.

The Breegans scattered along the top of the city wall, many of them with blue pigment smeared on their furs. Some Breegans brandished small spears and began to point them at the six warriors. They whispered and yelped, like fearful animals. "*Aruka!*" they kept saying. "*Aruka!*"

"What are they doing?" Gregor snapped, bothered by the shouting. "Can I give them anything to make them stop?"

"I don't think it's *things* that they *want*," said Kiro. "It's *us* that they *don't want* here."

"Well, they're bloody annoying," Gregor grumbled. "We'll leave soon!" he shouted back at the screeching creatures.

"*Aruka! Aruka!*" the Breegans continued yelling.

"What are they saying?" Jason asked

"I'm not sure you want to know…" Rhulani replied.

The singing began again, more vibrant and more portentous, rushing down from the mountain tops. The squealing became louder as more Breegans joined the havoc.

"Enough!" a voice boomed from behind the wall. The head of an old Breegan appeared on top of the large iron gates, his mane grey and his tunic green, lined with golden fabric. It was Uttol, accompanied by ten Breegan guards, each of them covered in sturdy iron armour and each holding a halberd.

"What have you come here for? Why are you disturbing our quiet, distressing our people?" Uttol asked.

Jason looked at his companions, who glanced back at him with concern, urging him to speak.

"We… erm… we came to speak to you, chief Uttol. I am Jason McAnnon. I'm a Lightbringer. These are my companions. We need your help."

"You are not welcome here, Lightbringer. My people are scared, can't you see? Leave, before it is too late."

"We mean no harm," Jason said, unsure what to tell the chief of a tribe who wished not to be contacted. "We only seek council with you, nothing more. We have gold and copper to offer you in exchange for your assistance."

"We have plenty of metal, we don't need yours," the old Breegan spouted.

"Chief Uttol, if I may," Baldor intervened. "We have come here to find a Breegan who goes by the name of Öken. We must get to him for the better of Valkadia."

"What makes you think we want to help you? My people wish to take no part in the conflict between Erythya and Remara," Uttol confronted.

"A Lightbringer has returned to help us, Your-Highness-Beneath-the-Rock. We must listen to the messages of the Gods. We're not asking for your people to fight alongside us," Rhulani replied.

"We only need Öken's help," continued Jason. "Once we have spoken to him, we'll leave and never bother you again."

"First you need my help, then it's Öken's help you look for. By the time you have left Hegertan, you'll have taken everything we own. Many have offered us deals in the past, and many have betrayed us. Valkadia has the habit of underestimating our people."

"We understand your concern, honourable Uttol, but this is of the utmost importance," Jason countered. "Öken is the only one who can help us find the Eluir, and we humbly ask for your permission to visit him. Without his aid, we stand no chance of defeating Darkstrom."

Upon hearing that name, all the Breegans standing on top of the wall gasped and shrieked. The chieftain looked at Jason right into his eyes and remained immobile for a minute or so, contemplating the options. "Drop your weapons on the floor," he demanded.

There was a clangour as they undid their belts and buckles to remove all the weapons they were carrying. Once all the swords, daggers, bows and glaives had been collected in a pile, the Breegan's chieftain looked at Jason once again and nodded slowly. Though Jason thought that was the end of it and the nod was a sign of approval, it wasn't.

"Guards! Open the gates! Take them to the Breegan Hall," Uttol ordered. He turned around and disappeared behind the wall.

Suddenly, the mechanism inside the wall began to creak and screech as the gear system pulled the large iron doors apart. As the gates opened, the majestic city of Hegertan was slowly revealed to them.

Houses made of stone were built around the large central square of the town. Many had been carved in the side of Mount Dormund, stacked on top of each other like a hive. The houses became fewer and fewer as one looked further towards the peak. Seemingly interminable staircases had been carved in the stone too, zigzagging like roads from one house to the other drawing lines on the mountain's rockface. Systems of gears and pulleys had been set up to pass goods between each level of the city.

As Jason and his companions jumped off their horses and ventured beyond the city walls, the inhabitants of Hegertan scattered, retreating into their hive of houses. Tentatively, the group proceeded along the large central square, where carvings filled with copper had been laid out all over the stone floor. On the opposite end of the square, there was a large, pompous bronze gate fit within a large rockface. It looked like a gate to the Underworld, into the deep guts of Mount Dormund. Geometric shapes were engraved on the metal doors, and a metal sculpture of a large elk's skull was placed on top of the keystone. Those were the doors to the Breegan Hall, where Uttol, chieftain of the Breegans, hosted his guests and held his feasts. It was also where he carried his ritualistic sacrifices and executions.

A group of guards marched towards the six companions and bound their hands behind their backs with manacles. While some of the guards escorted the companions to the Breegan Hall, others took their horses away somewhere in the depths of Hegertan.

When the enormous doors to the Breegan Hall opened with a dull, crunching sound, a cavern the size of a cathedral appeared before their eyes. It was inhabited by armies of stalagmites and stalactites accumulated over time, drip by drip, layer by layer. The gurgling sound of streams and channels rushing beneath the earth created a tingling sound that bounced off the wet rock walls and echoed throughout the empty spaces. The Hall was lit up by torches lined up evenly along the limestone walls. A slight haze and a strong smell of what Jason thought could be incense permeated the cavern.

As Jason's eyes wandered around the place, he realised that on each of the stalagmites were carved many faces, with long hair and long beards, their eyes closed as if they were sleeping. These entities were like a quiescent presence, ready to wake up at any moment if disturbed. The ceiling and the walls were carved too, with the runes of a language Jason did not recognise. It was most probably an ancient language from the old Breegan kingdom of Nalos.

Atop a small mound in the centre of the cavern, Uttol sat on his large throne carved in an immense speleothem, which would have taken thousands of years to form. The chieftain waited for them pompously, holding an elegant sceptre made of bronze and embedded with sapphires and yellow topaz. Around him were scattered the skulls and bones of deer and mountainous fauna—remains of both meals as well as sacrifices to the spirits of the underworld.

"Lightbringer," he called resolutely. "Come forth."

Jason walked unsteadily on the slippery ground of the Hall. When he got close enough to the throne, the two guards standing at either side of Uttol blocked his way by crossing their halberds. Though nervous to bits, Jason chuckled inside when this happened, as it reminded him of all the medieval movies he had watched in his childhood.

"You were not raised in Valkadia, am I right?" Uttol asked him.

"No. I come from beyond the Elder Stones, in the Otherside," he replied.

"Are you sure you weren't born here?" Uttol murmured back. "I see a familiar glare in your eyes. The spirits are confused by your origin, Marigold Guardian."

"I was born in a city by the name of London."

"How come you have powers?" the chief scrutinised.

"I don't know," he said frankly, looking into the Uttol's small eyes buried in his thick mane. "Nobody has been able to explain either how I got to Valkadia or how I acquired my powers. Many mysterious things have happened to me since I've been here, so I'm not surprised if even your spirits are confused."

"Your blood is akin to the people of Valkadia. The spirits sense it." Uttol paused as he made a sign to one of his subordinates, who handed him a pestle and mortar made of stone. As he began to grind a purple powder with some oily substance, he said to Jason, "You have been brought here against your will, as I understand, and you have been given powers you did not wish for. Am I right?"

"Yes, but I am honoured about this. My life in the Otherside has been upheaved, so this is my chance to make a difference," Jason answered honestly.

"Come closer," the chieftain invited. Jason cautiously advanced towards the chieftain, worriedly looking at the halberds of the two guards in case they came slicing down on him. His anxiety lessened past the guards, but his heart did not stop beating at double its average speed. "Us Breegans do not wish to partake in this silly conflict either. We have lost so much already, as I'm sure you have. I admire your strength and drive to attempting a quest you did not ask for, and I appreciate your respect for our wishes. I am honoured to help you."

Uttol dipped his thumb into the purple tincture inside a mortar and smeared it across Jason's forehead and nose. Then, he dipped all his fingers in and flicked the paint all over Jason's body. "You have my blessing, as well as that of the spirits of the mountain. You must now choose someone to come with you—only one other person can accompany you to Fyris Pass on top of Mount Dormund, where Öken resides."

"What about who stays behind? Can you promise no harm will be done to them?"

"You have until sundown tomorrow to be back and leave Hegertan with your companions. Afterwards, they shall be sacrificed to appease our ancestors," Uttol replied ominously.

Jason gulped and looked back at his friends. He knew who he had to pick, but the choice was nevertheless difficult. If things went wrong, he would have the life of whoever he left behind on his conscience. His companions looked at him apprehensively, but they too knew what the right decision would have to be.

"Make your choice, Lightbringer," said Uttol. "The longer you take, the less time you have to find Öken and save your friends."

"Can I at least take two people with me?" he attempted to ask.

"No. One other person only. Öken is not expecting any visitors, and he is not of the best temperament."

"All right… Gregor, you're the only one that knows him. He'll probably remember you, so I'll need you to introduce me." Gregor nodded and walked over to Jason. "We'll be back in time, I promise," Jason told his companions.

"It is decided then," Uttol declared. "You better go now—the time is ticking. Good luck."

As Jason and Gregor made their way outside, they heard the clanging sound of chains echoing in the Breegan Hall as Rhulani, Baldor, Kiro and Anyir were being imprisoned. The shouting of the Breegans as they restrained their companions made Jason's skin chill, but he couldn't look back. He had to find Öken first.

XXV

THE IMPERIAL BEETLE

They had him. Commander Sigrid was aware that what they had just done would infuriate Darkstrom and escalate the conflict more, but she also couldn't believe they had managed to actually imprison Lok. She thought catching a Shadowcaster would be near impossible, but Lok didn't seem to pose much threat. The Ulkar was possibly the most challenging part of the feat, but that didn't seem too difficult either. The body of the massive wolf, lying soulless in the middle of the Bridge of Whispers, was now a reminder that any Remaran trying to cross would encounter the wrath of the Erythian army.

The two cowards, general Tortugal and lieutenant Modùn, had promptly seen their defeat and had left along with many other men long before the battle was over. The Fímegir had been overwhelmed by the Erythian forces, and whoever had reverted to their Human form was running or riding back to Remara, trying to save their miserable lives.

When the Bridge of Whispers was quiet again, the only thing one could hear was the ominous sound of the wind blowing through the deep Elora's Trench. The soldiers grabbed Lok, still unconscious, and loaded him onto a caged wagon. The troop proceeded to march back to the Golden Camp, aptly named after the colour of the Erythian soldier's armours, located not far from Thorwyn's Forest.

The camp itself, even though its name stated otherwise, wasn't really that golden. Instead, the tents were cobalt blue, just like the House of Kavanagh's banners that fluttered proudly in the gentle Erythian breeze. The tents were positioned uniformly and neatly in six blocks of forty, each holding ten soldiers, with a total of two-thousand-four-hundred men.

The Golden camp was the largest of all the military camps spread around Erythya, and it had been tactically positioned. It was close to both Elora's Trench and the Bridge of Whispers, where most battles on the frontier between Erythya and Remara had been fought. Skirmishes had previously happened on the other side of the Trench, near the Lakes of Asghen and the Lumos Mountains, but the Remarans found it treacherous to cross the Marshes of Wrod in order to get there, so they preferred steering clear. Most historic battles had been fought either in the Stonevale, around the Bridge of Whispers, and sometimes all the way into the Emerald Fields if the Golden Camp had failed to protect it. That was why the Golden camp was so crucial, and why the men were disproportionately concentrated there. Many careful eyes would be watching the prisoner, and Lok would have no chance of escaping.

"Bring the Shadowcaster to my tent," the commander ordered. "I need twenty soldiers to follow me and guard the area. I want Lok to be under constant watch until we move him to Mount Hargon."

While Lok was still unconscious, the soldiers transferred him to Sigrid's private tent, tossing his unconscious body around roughly, trying to get it all done quickly. They were treating the Shadowcaster as if he was a drousy tiger ready to wake up and attack at any moment. They strapped Lok to a pillory, immobilising his head and arms between two wooden beams, and shackled his feet together.

Sigrid took her helmet off, her long golden hair flowing down her shoulders. She grabbed a chair and dragged in front of the Lok's pillory. For minutes upon minutes, she examined the prisoner's face. How strange being so close to a Shadowcaster, she thought. Such powerful and deadly beings. Not only they could control all the elements, but they could also control darkness—the one thing any being is afraid of. Unlike Lightbringers, a Shadowcaster could make their Flare work both in the bright of day as well as the dark of night, making them almost unstoppable. They could turn into shadows; they could conjure dark beings from the realm of the moon; they could cause deep psychological and physical pain on their victims by unleashing their worst nightmares. Sigrid was marvelled yet scared, and certainly was not going to give Lok the benefit of the doubt. There was a lot of magic in Valkadia that Sigrid admired, and although that of the Shadowcasters intrigued her, she thought it was artificial and unethical. It was Darkstrom's obscure sorcery that turned Lok from a Lightbringer to a Shadowcaster, and together, they had committed atrocities in both Erythya and Remara for years.

Yet, Sigrid thought that Lok's powers weren't as strong as she remembered. Why didn't the Shadowcaster use any magic on the Bridge of Whispers to save himself? Why was he relying so much on the Ulkar's help? Perhaps, that meant Lok wasn't strong enough to exercise his powers, or, maybe, his Flare had disappeared completely. She thought that was all highly unlikely. *The Flare can't just disappear*, she observed. Still, something made Sigrid suspicious—it had been a few hours since the fight on the Bridge of Whispers, and Lok's left arm was still wounded, showing no sign of magical recovery.

Nevertheless, the right precautions had been made, and Lok's powers weren't going to be an issue. If there was one thing that Shadowcasters hated, it was mistletoe. For some unknown reason, mistletoe had been an effective weapon against the worst Shadowcasters, and hence she had covered the pillory with this seemingly ordinary plant. With Lok's powers numbed, Sigrid could ask him anything she wanted without risking her life. She grabbed a bucket of water and threw it vehemently onto Lok's face, who gasped for air as he woke up.

"Where the hell am I?" Lok spouted.

"You're in the Golden Camp, ser Lok, under imprisonment for brutal acts against the realm of Erythya and the innocent people of Remara."

"The Emperor will have your head torn off."

"We're in Erythya now. The Emperor can't get to us," Sigrid replied. "You're in our hands, Lok, whether you like it or not."

"Why am I really here, *commander*? Don't tell me it's because of that shabby, treasonous village I burnt down."

"Partially, but not entirely. Why were you coming to Erythya, *Shadowcaster*? What has the Emperor ordered you to do this time, huh?"

"You are scared of me, aren't you?" Lok taunted.

"You have caused enough damage to Erythya as it is. We are trying to prevent any more sorrow," Sigrid replied. She *was* scared, though she was used to hiding her feelings after years of commanding the Erythian army. She couldn't afford to come across as scared.

"You know this flimsy plant won't suppress my powers for long, Sigrid," bluffed Lok. "Are these all the precautions you are taking?"

"Maybe it won't subdue you, but this mistletoe will buy us enough time to call for reinforcement. You are not a god, Lok. We can stop you."

"And which god are you talking about? Because if it's one of *your* gods, then *I* am certainly stronger."

"Don't make this about faith, Shadowcaster. Stop playing games and tell me where you were heading. What were you doing on your own travelling towards Erythya on the back of an Ulkar?" Sigrid interrogated.

"He and I are both creatures of the shadows, misunderstood warriors. We saved each other a lot of misery along the way. I owe him a lot."

"I don't care about that beast," Sigrid retorted. "Answer my questions."

"Use your brain, Sigrid. Where do you think I was going?"

"I have a couple of hypotheses, but I want you to tell me. Admit what you were scheming with the Emperor."

"What if I told you I came to kill you?"

"Doubt it. What difference would it make to Darkstrom if I died?"

"You have such little value for your life, commander. Why is that?" Lok kept provoking.

"*You* should have more value for *your* life, and you should start answering my questions, Lok."

"Oh, and why should I? Will you kill me?"

"You are worth nothing to us alive," said Sigrid, her blood boiling. She had only been in the same room as the Shadowcaster for a couple of minutes, and already she felt the frustration rising. She knew Lok was sharp with his tongue, but she didn't realise how difficult talking to him would be. Sigrid wasn't sure how she'd get any information out of Darkstrom's little pet. The commander had to make Lok feel like she had no use for him and instil some genuine fear into his subconscious. "You and Darkstrom are our worst threats, and though we might get some interesting information out of you, your death would be equally valuable."

"So why am I still alive?" Lok confronted. "You know I've been trained never to talk," he spouted.

"You're alive because we hope you can still be useful," said the commander, her heart tensing. There was a fine line between what she could and couldn't say to the Shadowcaster before losing his collaboration for good. "You see, Lok, we're merciful here in Erythya. If you consider selling out your Emperor, we'll consider letting you live."

Unfortunately, those were the wrong words. Lok spat in her face, and with a deranged grin, he yelled, "Kill me now, if you have the courage! I will never betray my Lord! Kill me!"

Sigrid found herself cornered. They *did* need him alive, and Lok *did* have information that Erythian spies would never find out. She just couldn't tell him that.

Lok let out a maniacal laughter. "You lie, commander. You'd never dare kill me, the things I know, your king would never forgive you if you lost such a valuable informant," Lok derided.

Frustrated and anxious, Sigrid pummelled Lok on the jaw with an armoured right fist. The golden steel slammed against Lok's face with a thud, and his head whipped back hitting the wooden pillory. Sigrid looked at the bloody mouth of her prisoner with a mix of anger and shame. "You are alive because I decided so," she retorted. Lok spat blood on the commander's shiny golden shoe and looked back at her with maniacal eyes, grinning.

Sigrid stood up and went to the back of the tent. When she returned, she held a heavy cast-iron box with a thick chain wrapped around it, held together by a large sturdy padlock.

"Have you ever heard of the Imperial beetle?" Sigrid asked. "It's a very aggressive species of beetle that is found in the Nebel Badlands. It burrows in granite boulders and uses its mandibles to create their nests by crushing the rock. You can imagine what kind of power is needed for an insect to gnaw through rock. This box is made of cast-iron for a reason—imagine what it can do to flesh." Lok kept smiling, staring at the commander with bloodshot eyes and a livid cheekbone. Sigrid placed the box on the chair in front of Lok. She slowly took a key out of her pocket and began unlocking the chains. As she did so, the box started to shake violently, and Sigrid was forced to hold it still with two hands. "I didn't want it to come to this, but I have managed to get the worse people to talk by showing them what the Imperial Beetle can do. I'm sure you won't be any different."

"That thing doesn't scare me," Lok said. "I've seen worse creatures."

"The Imperial Beetle is nothing like your Ulkar," Sigrid had unwrapped the chains by now. She looked at Lok and pointed at the small guillotine door on the side of the iron box. "Do you see this? If I strap this box against your chest and open this door, the Imperial beetle will feel trapped, and it will have only one way to escape. You know what I'm talking about, right?"

"No," Lok confronted. "Indulge me, commander."

"The beetle will gnaw its way through your thorax to escape. It will be a slow, painful and miserable way to die, especially for a warrior like you. Is that how you wish to die?"

"Do what you will, commander. I'm not afraid of death. I've tried to serve the Emperor, and I have failed him," Lok muttered.

"Will you tell me what I need to know?"

"Never. Do your worse."

"You've made your decision," Sigrid said as she nodded resolutely.

✳

Lok writhed and grunted as the commander shackled the cast-iron box to his chest. His shirt had been ripped, and the metal was cold against is bare skin. He could feel the Imperial Beetle wriggling inside. Lok closed his eyes. If he could tame the Ulkar, he could also tame this vicious insect. He wasn't going to allow a disgusting creepy-crawly to take him down, and he hoped his ability to speak to beasts wouldn't falter. *Hey, little beetle. Help me. I'm your friend,* he thought, hoping the Beetle would listen to him just like the giant wolf did.

"You'll talk now, Shadowcaster, or I *will* remove the guillotine," Sigrid insisted, her tone firm and resolute.

Lok, however, was too concentrated on communicating with the insect. *I can help you escape too. When they open that box, do what I say. I will free you once we're safe.*

Seeing she was being ignored, Sigrid raised her voice one final time. "You will speak, or you will die!" she shouted, the veins on her neck bulging.

Once again, Lok didn't respond. The commander opened the box.

The Beetle's jaws felt like a pair of scorching knives rapidly making their way through his skin. Lok gritted his teeth in agony, his blood trickling down his stomach. The Imperial Beetle was a lot stronger and a lot larger than Lok had expected, and his plan revealed to be a far more excruciating that he had envisaged.

As tears flowed from his eyes, he could see that even Sigrid was feeling extremely uneasy. *I bet she never expected it to come to this,* he observed. *I bet she doesn't know what's coming.*

As the Beetle gnawed through Lok's flesh, its potent mandibles dug a sideways tunnel making their way outside the box. The Shadowcaster's screams filled the Golden Camp. Blood oozed out, and the Beetle's emerald exoskeleton soon pushed through Lok's skin. *Good little insect.*

Like a tornado suddenly unleashed, the beetle flew against the commander, snapping its intimidatingly strong mandibles at her. Shocked, Sigrid's warrior instincts kicked into gear. She grabbed a helmet lying on the floor beside her and used it to smack the vicious insect forcefully, propelling it to the opposite side of the room. While defending herself, she lost her balance and tilted forward, edging towards the dark floor of the tent. The Shadowcaster saw the perfect window of opportunity and kicked Sigrid in the head with his shackled feet, making the commander drop unconscious to the ground.

Come here, little insect. Free me from this pillory.

The droning sound emanating from the Imperial Beetle's strong wings was eerie as it flew towards Lok. The beetle landed on the pillory with a thud. It was at least as big as Lok's hand, not counting the enormous mandibles that protruded out of its head. There was no doubt that if it wanted to, it could have killed Lok in no time. The Shadowcaster was amazed by the creature.

Quick, before a guard arrives. Lok heard the wood being sawed under the powerful jaws of the Imperial Beetle. There was a crash as the pillory fell to the ground, dismantled. *The shackles, too,* Lok ordered hastily. Just like the blade of an Elven sword, the Imperial Beetle sliced the iron chains on his feet swiftly. Finally, Lok was free. He stood over the body of the commander, which laid inert with her helmet still in her hand. He could still hear her breathing, and the temptation of killing her was abundant.

Before Lok could end Sigrid's life, two enormous Cyclops entered the tent, brandishing a pair of golden maces. "Is everything alright, commander?" When they saw the demolished pillory and Lok grinning ghoulishly beside it, they went for the attack.

Lok was too swift. He grabbed a handful of sand and launched it into the Cyclopes' eyes. As the soldiers screeched in distress, the Shadowcaster slipped out of the tent from the back.

✺

When Sigrid woke up, Lok was gone, and so was the Imperial Beetle.

The pillory had been destroyed. Splinters and shavings were scattered on the floor as if the wood had been sawed away.

Sigrid ran out of the tent with a pounding headache and unexpectedly stepped in a pool of blood that was draining out of a Cyclops's corpse. Her heart was beating so fast that it took a few moments to get words out of her mouth. "Where is he?!" she bellowed, but there were no soldiers around. She ran into the camp, trying to find someone, but only dead soldiers surrounded her—every single one with the same wound to the neck. What had happened was clear. The Imperial Beetle was under Lok's command, just like the Ulkar.

Sigrid was cold sweating, her mind spinning, her breathing tight. She felt as if she was in a nightmare. A bloodthirsty assassin was loose within the camp, or worse of all, he had made it out into Erythya. They had the Shadowcaster, and now they lost him. She had managed to minimise the losses of her troops during the skirmish at the Bridge of Whispers, but now she knew more of her soldiers would die.

Sigrid grabbed the war horn hanging from the side of her belt and blew into it ferociously. The deep, braying sound of the horn filled the air. The first blow was to get the soldier's attention. All those that had survived instantaneously stopped what they were doing and rushed out of their tents. When the horn blew once more, the message was clear: the camp was under attack.

She jumped on the back of her horse, ready to gallop out of the camp and chase after the fugitive. Dazed in a state of anger and focus, she looked around herself as dozens of other soldiers got hold of their weapons and mounted on armoured horses. "Lok has escaped, we must find him! I need two hundred men to come with me!" Sigrid spoke on top of her voice, straining her vocal cords.

The commander spurred her steed and exited the camp, followed by two of his troops. The rumble of hooves raised by the cavalry behind Sigrid was deafening, and if fuelled the commander's adrenaline. Even in this dire situation, the commander adored that sound, so intense and powerful.

Sigrid and her troop followed Lok's footprints on the damp ground, galloping through the fertile green grasslands around the Golden Camp. Sigrid knew where Lok was heading. Not far from the camp was Thorwyn's Forest—an ancient place, where many Elven warriors had come in the old times to be tested by the gods. It was also the perfect place to hide, and an even better place to ambush and take out entire armies.

The Erythian soldiers lined up at the edge of the forest and awaited the commander's order to proceed. The horses seemed tense, and the hounds were barking and growling towards the depths of the woods. Sigrid turned her horse around to face her troop and said, "Be careful, and good luck. Let's get that bastard of a Shadowcaster."

Slowly, the troop advanced one after the other into the thick green forest, keeping a tight hold of their horses' reins, looking around for anything lurking behind the trees. The soldiers had been in that forest many times before, and they weren't scared of the creatures living in its shadows—until now. It was as if the forest's peace had been disturbed, suddenly becoming ominously quiet. All the life had disappeared. Instead, the harmony had been replaced with a sense of gravity, heavily pressing onto each soldier. The forest smelled different too. If it once smelled like moss and earth, it now stunk of decay and blood, permeating the air with a suffocating miasma.

The mat of leaves on the forest ground crinkled as the horses' hooves trampled it, and the branches creaked and crackled as the soldiers moved them aside to make their way through the thicket. They proceeded carefully, keeping a scrutinous eye towards their surroundings where the trees closed in. Though the soldiers knew the forest well, at that moment, it looked all the same. It was a green tangled mass behind which death was hiding. The mere fluttering of the leaves by the hands of a gust of wind made everyone stop and reach for their hilts. Every time they paused, the silence became deafening; fear and anxiety were the chief emotions. Sigrid could feel every heartbeat quake her tense body, and the humid air seeped into her lungs as she breathed heavily.

Amongst the leaves and trunks, Lok was hiding somewhere. He didn't want to be found, and he wouldn't let himself be captured this time. The commander would fight with everything she had. She knew that forest like the back of her hand. Still, even without his powers, Lok was a formidable and terrifying warrior to be facing.

Suddenly, Sigrid's eyes flung to her left as she saw a shadow jumping from within the foliage and onto one of the horse riders, dragging him into the darkness so quickly that nobody could react. The Erythian soldiers grasped their swords, ready for a second attack, but they couldn't predict what was going to happen.

Another soldier fell from her horse without warning, her throat pierced by the powerful jaws of the Imperial Beetle, which whizzed straight past Sigrid, making the most harrowing noise with its wings.

"Cover your faces!" Sigrid ordered. "Do not keep any part of your body exposed!"

One after the other, Sigrid saw the soldiers around her fall prey to the beasts lurking behind the trees. Bodies dropped like bags of sand onto the brown leaves, never to see the light of day again. The terrifying screams of the soldiers echoed in the forest, and each shriek made the other Erythians tenser. Even the most formidable fighter was afraid. The Shadowcaster was swift and nimble and took down his adversaries systematically. Occasionally, the clangour of a steel blade clashing against another reverberated between the tree trunks, just to stop abruptly after a couple of hits. They should have never followed Lok into that deadly trap.

Sigrid dismounted her horse and lifted the kopís sword in front of herself. Carefully, the commander advanced, making sure not to tread on any of her soldiers' bodies lying amongst the leaves. Each sound and creak, even her own steps on the crispy ground, made Sigrid turn brusquely. Her eyes remained wide open, and her sword pointed towards the unknown as she ventured forward.

Then, a shadow appeared in front of the commander.

"Leave us," Lok demanded. He brandished a kopís and was wearing a golden Erythian armour which he had stolen from one of the soldiers he had just killed. A bloody handprint tainted the armour's chest plate.

Sigrid looked back at the Shadowcaster and tightened her hand around the hilt of her sword firmly. "I cannot allow that, Lok. You know that," Sigrid replied. She carefully advanced towards Lok, keeping her sword lifted and ready to strike. "Come with us. We will give you a much better life than the Emperor can offer, if you collaborate."

"And what life is that? The life of a prisoner?" Lok retorted.

"The life of a prisoner in Erythya is far superior to the life of a prisoner in Remara."

"Darkstrom wouldn't imprison me. He's not satisfied with my actions, but he will forgive me."

"Is that what you keep telling yourself, Lok? The Emperor has let you go. He doesn't care about you anymore. You might as well fight for the right cause. See the tyranny that Darkstrom imposes onto his people and his devotees. Realise the horror that the Fímegir are."

"The Emperor is fair. I shall not succumb to your idle words…"

"Are you really still willing to die for the Emperor after he abandoned you?"

Lok didn't respond. Instead, he opened his hands, revealing the Imperial Beetle. Sigrid looked into the Shadowcaster's eyes, who looked back at her with animalistic ferociousness. The commander remained still, keeping the sword up, her heart beating out of her chest. Against a creature like that, she knew she had no chance.

XXVI

ROCK AND SNOW

The sun had already begun to sink behind the horizon when Jason and Gregor left the Breegan Hall. That essentially gave them twenty-four hours to go up the mountain, convince Öken to help them, and get back down. If Jason had learnt one thing from his childhood hikes in the Swiss Alps, it was that it took hours to go up a hill, let alone a mountain. Of course, he didn't have any kind of magical ability back then, nor the strength of an adult man, but he knew what Uttol had asked them would be a trying exploit.

As they began their ascent through the city of Hegertan, heading up a long staircase carved out of the side of Mount Dormund, Jason curiously took a peek inside the houses of the Breegan folk. Inhabitants were preparing their meal at that time, and it smelled as if they were cooking lamb and potatoes with onions, garlic and other herbs. In one of the houses, Jason spotted a Breegan peeling potatoes and throwing them in a pan placed on a small table made of a black stone, with copper coils and pipes coming out of its side. It was a sort of pseudo-technological, Breegan kitchen arrangement, and Jason was mesmerised.

After less than twenty minutes of hiking up the stairs, the sun disappeared, leaving the sky free for the moon to take over. As it became dark, the houses and the staircases all over Hegertan suddenly lit up. Surprisingly, they were not lit by candlelight or oil lamps like in the rest of

Erythya but instead seemed to receive their illumination by a central power source. Small domes shining with orange light hung on the houses' outer walls, lighting the staircase, and inside the homes as well.

"Do you know where this light comes from?" Jason asked his Remaran friend.

"I think it's energy they get from under the mountains," Gregor replied. He was already panting despite his great shape.

"There must be a central generator or something that controls it. It lit up just like lamps do back home."

"We have nothing like this in Remara, that's for sure," Gregor commented as he looked around.

"I thought you were used to Breegan technology, since you already met Öken?"

"That was a couple of years back, and it's not like I came to Hegertan. This is miles off from anything I imagined."

"Did he not tell you what he was working on?" asked Jason, intrigued.

"No way. I gave him what he needed, he gave me money, and we parted ways." Gregor stopped for a moment, panting, and looked up at the staircase rising up the rockface. He took a deep breath. "By the might of all the gods, how many stairs do we have to climb?"

"I think Baldor said there are about twenty-two thousand steps. That's about double the longest staircase in the Otherside—the Mount Niesen staircase in Switzerland," Jason observed. "I remember my dad telling me all about it once," he mused.

"How many steps does that one have?" Gregor inquired, grabbing onto the iron rail that followed the staircase, and pulling himself forward.

"About twelve thousand, I think."

"And… how long does it take for people to climb up it?"

"There is a race every year for the fastest contender. It takes the best runner under an hour to complete. If we keep going at this pace, I think we can make it in about six hours," Jason explained.

"So, this one has twenty-four thousand steps? I hope you plan to take breaks."

"We'll take one break halfway, but no more. Drink while you walk. We'll take a proper break once we've arrived at Öken's house," Jason said resolutely.

"One break? Are you kidding me?!" Gregor moaned and huffed.

Jason snickered. "You sound like a child who has been denied playtime," he mocked. "We have a very limited amount of time, Gregor. Our friends need us back before sundown tomorrow. I didn't think you'd be so whiny!"

"I'm not whining," Gregor said with a frown. Then he turned around with a mischievous grin. "I'm complaining about your decision—there's a difference."

They followed the endless path that skirted the mountain's rockface and climbed higher and higher until they passed by the last Breegan's house. The staircase became thinner from then on, and there were no more rails to hold on to. So exposed and infrequently maintained, the steps were covered in a thick layer of dirt and were worn away by the wind. They carefully placed one foot in front of the other, leaning against the rocks and grabbing onto the weak roots that grew out of the stone. Jason did his best not to look down as pebbles occasionally precipitated off the path and into the abyss below. Slowly, they made their way forward, but it had already been a few hours, and the trail seemed only to get more difficult the further they went.

To placate Gregor's impatience, they took a quick break to drink and have something to eat for their dinner—just some cheese with bread and a couple of apples. They carefully sat with their backs against the rock, in the safety of a small niche in the rock where the path became slightly wider. Jason had kept his eyes on the road the whole way up, and only now did he allow himself to look away from the ground. As he gazed into the distance, he realised how much his vision had improved since acquiring the Flare.

Valkadia spread in front of him like a surrealist painting. With the bright moon and the stars shining in the clear skies, laying a blue hue over the landscape, all Jason could think of was Van Gogh's Starry Night—but this was not a mere oil on canvas. It was real, and it extended before the photographer's astonished eyes.

Spreading like waves in a black and white sea, the Lumos mountains curved up and down, occasionally spiking into the clouds. Below they could see the city of Hegertan, which glowed with golden light from the energy powered domes. Beyond the mountains, the Emerald Fields glowed with green, moving and shifting under the force of the wind. The lights of towns and cities surrounding the grasslands glimmered in the distance, adding to the absolute feeling of charm. Jason imagined all the different creatures that inhabited that land, from the cities of Eryndal and Aryon on the west coast, to the town of Herzal on the foothills of the Lumos Mountains in the south.

The chain of mountains looked immense even at night when the granite rock blended with the dark skies. Jason appreciated the millennia of geological processes which made the Lumos range into a real wonder, soaring resolutely with its snowy peaks towards the clouds.

To the north an interminable line of trees delimited the edge of the Gartruth Forest, covering almost half of Erythya like a blanket that followed the curves of the land. The trees' territory was only interrupted by silvery rivers cutting through the forest, and the tops of mountains poking through the canopy. Lake Malion and the neighbouring Lakes of Asghen lay far over the Emerald Fields, and the reflection of the stars in their water made it look like they had been sprinkled with shimmering dust.

Erythya was alive—a living being with its own conscience, breathing and changing in its own time, magically existing in its own enchantment.

Jason looked beyond Lake Malion, but he couldn't make much out of what laid further south. Though he could almost recognise Elora's Trench, which drew a long line in the distance from one side of Valkadia to the other, everything else was concealed by a dark mist. Heavy black clouds blocked the moonlight from shining through, almost as if even the skies themselves perceived the evil of Remara.

Despite Gregor's grunts, they resumed their climb. The staircase seemed increasingly unsteady and perilous as they went on. The steps grew narrower and steeper, and the moisture made the rock slippery. Only about half an hour later, Jason was suddenly forced to halt.

"There are no more steps," he announced, gulping with unease as he looked ahead.

"What do you mean?" Gregor asked anxiously. "Tell me what you see."

"I mean, there are no more steps. There is just a walkway made out of planks."

Gregor looked over Jason's shoulder, and to his dismay, the stairs had actually finished and had been replaced by a set of unsteady wooden planks bolted into the side of the mountain. He began sweating from his forehead as he tried to build up his courage.

"I don't really know how much I want to walk on that…" Gregor commented.

"We have to keep going I'm afraid," said Jason. "There is no time to spare, no matter how difficult the journey gets. Besides, we need Öken's help."

"All right… Give me a second before we begin, I just need to… erm… relieve myself," Gregor said.

"What? Now? This is not really the best place," Jason huffed. "Hmm... all right... but be quick about it, we don't have a lot of time."

"Hey, I don't choose what my body needs!" Gregor rejoined humorously. "I'll be quick, promise. You go ahead, I'll be right behind."

Gregor disappeared behind the curve of the path so that Jason couldn't see him anymore.

As he left his companion behind, Jason put his foot on the first wooden plank. There was no way to know how long this walkway would be, but if it was all as wobbly and creaky as the first plank, Jason thought he should have followed Gregor's example and gone to the toilet as well.

One carefully grounded foot after the other, Jason made his way onto the first plank, and onto the second, and so on for another five or six planks. Though he did not want to look behind and discover how little he had advanced, Jason kept an alert ear to listen to what Gregor was up to, in case he needed his help to climb the walkway. He didn't hear any creaks other than those below his feet, so he assumed Gregor only needed some more time to finish doing his business. The Lightbringer advanced a little further, but then stopped abruptly as Gregor's voice disturbed the mountain's ominous silence.

"Gregor? Are you all right back there?" Jason asked.

There was no reply, other than a faint mumbling coming from the behind the path's curve. He couldn't make much out of what Gregor was saying, but he distinctly heard the words *'Lightbringer'* and *'almost there'*. Jason thought that was odd, but he concluded it was only Gregor talking to himself.

"Gregor? Did you say something? Come on. We have to keep moving!"

"I'm coming, I'm coming! Can a man not even go to the toilet in peace?" Gregor emerged from behind the wall of stone and carefully advanced towards Jason. "I'm here, let's go," he said as he precariously put his left foot on the first plank. Jason felt Gregor's weight suddenly reverberating across the whole of the unsteady walkway.

"What were you saying back there?" Jason inquired.

"When?"

"Just then—I heard you talking."

"Oh! Don't worry about that, just talking to myself!" Gregor countered.

"I've never heard you do that..." Jason confronted.

"That happens from time to time when I'm anxious. I guess I'm more worried about this bridge than I seem."

Jason was perplexed, and the hazardousness of their new path was indeed making it challenging to think clearly. "Just don't look down," he said.

They carried on for what seemed like an eternity. The sun began rising over the horizon once more, making Jason increasingly time-conscious.

Step by step, plank by plank, they made their way forward, but the end was still out of reach. Only rocks ahead, and more planks, going upwards and upwards. Jason accidentally looked down, and a cold feeling crept up his spine. There was more rock below them than above. In a way, he was pleased, as it meant they would soon arrive at the Fyris Pass. On the other hand, nothing stopped them from falling hundreds of feet except a thin piece of wood lodged in the side of the mountain.

Suddenly, Jason heard a strange crumbling noise behind him. He quickly turned around. The plank Gregor was standing on was coming loose from the rock.

"Gregor... don't move."

The rock cracked, and the plank detached further. "What do I do?" Gregor said with his voice shaking. Before Jason could reply, he heard a loud snap, and Gregor's body suddenly dropped through the void.

"Gregor!" Jason yelled, his heart pumping fast. He launched himself across the narrow and unsteady walkway to save his friend. Somehow, Gregor had managed to grab the next plank, and he was holding himself up with his elbows as his legs dangled in the abyss.

"Grab my hand!" Jason shouted as he leaned over to help his companion, whose face had become the colour of a cadaver's. The void below could have swallowed them both if it wanted, and there wouldn't have been much they could do about it.

"Don't let go!" Gregor begged.

"I'll pull you up! Just hold tight!" Jason reassured him. He planted his feet on the wood and channelled the energy through his body, and he felt it rush through him faster than he had ever experienced.

Then, the Flare listened to him. The sun had risen high enough for his powers to fire up, and Jason called for the help of the wind. Eventually, Gregor's weight diminished as a gust of gentle breeze pushed his friend back onto the plank. Gregor and Jason took a sigh of relief as they sat on the hard wood looking down at the gap in the middle of the walkway.

Suddenly, before Jason could even thank Gregor for saving his life, another creak came from beneath them, and they sprung up immediately.

The rockface supporting the plank walkway was now compromised, and they looked at each other horrified as they watched the crack grow larger. "Run!" Gregor shouted.

Without further questions, they began scampering as fast as they could along the narrow slits of wood.

"Faster!" Gregor shouted as he saw the whole walkway collapse beneath his feet in slow motion.

Jason's perception of time was distorted at that moment, everything moving slowly, sounds elongating, and his body was moving faster than his surroundings. Before they knew it, there was no more plank left, but there was no need for it. They had made it to the top of Mount Dormund, and a white expanse lay before them. It felt good to have solid rock beneath their feet. Jason and Gregor fell onto the hard and cold ground covered in snow, their knees wobbling and their hands shaking. They looked at the steep rockface immediately behind them, and then glanced at each other. In a moment of euphoria aided by the adrenaline rush, they laughed out loudly, glad to be alive.

"Thank you," Gregor finally said.

"My pleasure," Jason responded between chuckles and heavy breaths.

They laid there for long minutes attempting to catch some air, looking at the tranquil blue sky above. The cold, gentle breeze on top of the mountain pierced Jason's skin like a handful of needles. This was a feeling he hadn't experienced since his trip on the *Son of Odin*, when he had looked into the mountains of Greenland's hinterland, so dark and ominous. For a while, he let himself be transported back to that moment, but he forced the thoughts away before the image of Clara drowning in the raging sea came haunting him again.

Jason took a deep breath and focused on the task at hand, the cold air seeping in his lungs. He hoped to get to Öken's house soon. Without a watch, Jason had no idea how long it had been since they had begun their ascent, but he was conscious that not much time was left to save his friends. With any luck, Öken knew another way down to the Breegan city, now that the walkway had collapsed into oblivion.

The rest of the way to the Fyris Pass was challenging but enchanting. Jason couldn't get over the enthralling landscape that spread before his eyes. Glaciers flowed from the top of the mountains like frozen serpents, crackling and snapping as the ice moved slowly down the valleys, melting into lakes and rivers of cobalt blue waters. All Jason could hear was a faint breeze, and all the rest was silent—except of course the crunching of fresh snow under his and Gregor's boots.

Then, the silhouette of a small creature covered in heavy clothing appeared from the top of the pass, accompanied by a huge mastiff. It was Öken. He wore a large pelt cloak that fluttered in the icy breeze of Mount Dormund, and a thick, dark mane framed his face. Only his eyes were visible, and he looked at the two visitors with inquisition.

Jason nudged Gregor to speak first, assuming Öken still remembered him. Gregor cleared his throat and said, "Nice to see you again, Öken! Remember me? It's Gregor! I sold you those metal scraps for your inventions…?"

Öken nodded and signalled to walk towards him, up the path that led to his house.

"Is he usually this quiet?" Jason asked Gregor.

His friend shrugged his shoulders. "I don't remember him talking much last time we met."

Jason began to address the Breegan. "Öken, it is a pleasure to finally make your acquaintance. My name is Jason McAnnon—I am a Lightbringer. We have come to seek your help," he announced, attempting to sound formal. "Would you be so kind as to take us to your house so we can talk?"

Again, Öken nodded silently and began walking up a small dirt path further uphill.

They followed the Breegan and finally made it to Öken's house, which was more like a large stone hut wedged between the rocks of Fyris Pass. The summit of Mount Dormund was not far from there—they could see its jagged white peak just above them, a few hundred meters further up, penetrating the orange and purple morning skies.

The house they walked into felt eerily quiet. Wolf and bear pelts were hung on the walls. The living room was lit by the Breegan domes placed on each of the house's four walls. There was a large wooden table in the middle of the living area, covered in papers full of scribbles and sketches, and bits of metal scraps, springs and bolts. Large boxes full of rejected devices and parts of discarded inventions were stacked behind the table. Two large armchairs were placed on the left side of the room next to a fireplace, which was burning eagerly. A metal-framed, uncomfortable-looking bed was situated opposite the fireplace, full of heavy ruffled covers.

How lonely that place felt, he thought, up high in the remoteness of the Fyris Pass. Outside the windows, one could only see white, and there was no noise other than the cold wind and the crackling of the wood in the fireplace. What convinced Öken to reside in such a place, even during the worst winter storms and cyclones, must have been drastic. He didn't expect convincing him to help would be easy.

"So… Öken… we are here because we have a very important device that we can't activate. The technology is Breegan, and Gregor here says you're one of the best inventors around. We were wondering if you could help in any way. We can pay, we have money and gems," Jason explained.

Öken looked at him, but instead of answering, he clicked his tongue, and his dog limped towards his owner. The Breegan started to pet it on the head.

"You're not a man of many words, are you?" Jason joked. He jumped back with shock as the mastiff suddenly barked at him and showed him its teeth, making him shudder and laugh nervously. He glanced at Gregor, who looked back at him with unease. "Gregor? Are you all right?"

The burly man scratched his neck compulsively and looked at the ground with a frown. "I'm… I'm sorry, Jason," said Gregor sheepishly, struggling to get the words out.

"What do you mean?"

A strange feeling began surmounting Jason's psyche. He looked more closely at the Breegan and the menacing dog. Under Oken's thick mane, Jason noticed that two long scars ran along his face. Looking at the limping mastiff, the young Londoner joined the dots.

"This is not Öken… and… I was asked to bring you here…" Gregor admitted in a hushed tone.

In an instant, the two shapeshifters changed appearance, becoming the dreadful Omüms, Etrel and Glod. Just moments later, a door opened on the other side of the living room, slamming roughly against the wall. A large man in Remaran armour appeared. His skin was green, and fangs were sticking out of his bottom lip. "Nice robe you've got there, dirt rat," thundered Tortugal.

Then, five more soldiers entered the house from the front door. Jason stood stock-still surrounded by the soldiers, in total disbelief. It was a trap. He glanced at his friend, who did everything to avoid eye contact.

Gregor, what have you done?

XXVII

SEYNHAR!

"How could you?!" the Lightbringer fumed, the feeling of rage rushing hot through his veins.

"I'm sorry, Jason," he whimpered, looking at the ground. A bead of sweat rolled down his forehead, even in the blistering cold of Mount Dormund. "I really am, but it was the only way…"

"I don't understand… why? The *only way* for what, exactly?" Jason asked, blood boiling and head spinning as he tried to figure out what he had missed.

"Darkstrom… he's… he's taken them. He's taken my parents. They… they left me no choice."

Jason was speechless for a moment. He tried to formulate an answer. His heart tightened under the feeling of deep betrayal and breach of trust. It was as if he had just been hit in the stomach with a brick. Why had Gregor never told them about his family?

"We were going to make things better together!" Jason paused, feeling lost, scrambling for words. "We could have helped you get your family back."

"I did what I had to do," Gregor muttered. "Time is running out for them, Jason. Back in Karisa, Tortugal promised me my parents' safety if I helped him find you," he admitted, tears now welling up around his eyes.

"They were going to start torturing villagers, Jason. This was the only way I could guarantee safety for all my friends and family."

"But I... I literally *just* saved your life! You wouldn't be here if it weren't for me! Did you tell them we were at the Thirsty Goblin as well?"

"I did..." Gregor revealed.

"You've been deceiving me since the start..." Jason realised, a hot needle pushing through his chest as he registered what his friend had really done.

"You've indeed been a very efficient collaborator, Gregor. Darkstrom will surely recognise your help when he knows the Lightbringer has been apprehended," Tortugal bellowed.

Jason looked at Gregor with a mix of resentment and disbelief, shaking his head slowly in disappointment. "I should have never trusted you..." he murmured. Recomposing himself, he addressed the general. "Is this even Öken's house?"

The general snapped his fingers, and a soldier emerged from the room behind him, holding a thick chain with both hands. Jason recognised that man too well. It was Modùn. The lieutenant yanked the chain a few times, and a small creature appeared shortly after, its long fuzzy hair filthy with blood and dirt. The Breegan stared at his shackled hands and didn't utter a word, shaking involuntarily.

"Is that...?" Jason was too afraid to ask.

"Yes, it's indeed Öken," Tortugal said. "If you hadn't come here, he'd still be fine."

Jason turned to Gregor, red with rage. "Why did you bring me here?"

"We needed... somewhere isolated..." Gregor muttered, his words marred with shame.

"And there is nowhere as isolated in all of Valkadia as Mount Dormund! Nobody would cross the Breegan's territory," Tortugal intervened gleefully.

Jason looked at the miserable Breegan with apprehension and rage from the other side of the room. "I'm so sorry, Öken. I only needed your help. I didn't mean for any of this to happen. I'll get you out of this."

"How do you plan on doing that? You're on your own, dirt rat," Tortugal mockingly snickered.

"That's not a problem," Jason replied sternly. "How did you get into Erythya?" he asked the general.

"Ah, you'll have to thank your friend Lok for that. He incited a skirmish at the Bridge of Whispers, and we used the distraction to sneak in," Tortugal said with a wry smile.

"He's not my friend," Jason barked.

"Oh, but you have much more in common than you think, dear dirt rat. He's looking for you too, you know. He wants his powers back."

As soon as Jason heard Tortugal say those words, suddenly everything fell into place. *He wants his powers back.* Their meeting at the Iron Wood, the sudden awakening of his powers shortly thereafter… it was all so clear. The Flare he had used to protect his friends as a Lightbringer, and the powers the Shadowcaster had used to bring terror to his foes, were one and the same. If that was indeed true, that meant he would have to do everything to keep the powers for himself and away from Darkstrom's reach. Surviving this trap suddenly became more than a life-or-death situation. He was carrying the fate of Valkadia on his shoulders.

"The powers you have are Lok's, and he is eager to get them back by any means possible. He's no use to the Emperor anymore, but you can be. If you really want to do something good with those powers, you'll let us bring you to Darkstrom. He can help you keep them," said Tortugal.

"And become a Shadowcaster? Never," Jason replied resolutely. "Unlike you, I won't follow a *tyrant*, no matter how powerful I could become. I never even wanted these powers anyway."

"Too bad… I thought you'd be smarter. If you really think you can get away and escape Darkstrom's wishes, then you are a fool. Your powers will die with you."

"I'd rather die and take my Flare to the grave than succumb to your '*lord*'," Jason confronted. He reached towards the hilt of Isidir, but he realised he had left it at Hegertan. A feeling of trepidation crept up his spine as he found himself without his faithful weapon.

"You stand no chance against the Red Raven, dirt rat. You're the only Lightbringer left. Not even your dear friend Alamor can help you anymore."

Jason stopped breathing for a moment. "What did you say?" He didn't want to believe Tortugal's words.

"Haven't you heard? That traitor of a sewer rat is dead."

Jason's world slowed down. *This can't be true,* he thought. *He's trying to manipulate me.* "Why… why should I believe you?" he confronted.

"A week ago, by the hands of the almighty Emperor. Alamor died alone in the streets of Orachlion with his face in the mud. He stood no chance against Darkstrom, and neither do you."

The world around him became an empty space with no sound. Everything halted. Jason could only look at his old friend for support, but Gregor reciprocated by staring at the ground. Jason felt utterly alone. He had already lost too much: his girlfriend, his home, his friends, his job. Alamor had given him hope and had made him feel at home in a land so strange and far away from his own. Jason had always been confident he would see his mentor again. Now, Alamor was forever departed.

For an instant, the friendly face of the old Veheer flashed through his mind. He could still see the white-haired, pointy-eared mentor who had taught him so much in the short amount of time they had known each other. Now, he had no one to guide him anymore.

The young Londoner realised he was the last Lightbringer. As he felt the weight of the world crushing down on him, a familiar itchy feeling beneath his skin made his adrenaline skyrocket. His Flare grew stronger with his wrath.

Then, with a rumble that reverberated in Jason's head, Tortugal ordered, "*Seynhar!*"

One by one, the Remaran soldiers surrounding Jason contorted, their bones moving beneath their flesh, their skin becoming grey and full of scales. *Fímegir,* Jason realised—the soulless soldiers of Darkstrom's army, which could be transformed into blood-thirsty beasts with a single command. Their teeth were sharp and long, and their claws, protruding out of their thin and bony fingers, were razor-sharp. The monsters drooled as they looked at Jason with their soulless beady eyes, prowling around him on all fours like panthers about to ambush prey. Their bodies were slender and their ribs visible, but their snake-like heads were oddly large, disproportionate. Only Tortugal and Modùn weren't transformed, and they stood at the back of the room eagerly waiting for the imminent fight like spectators at a gladiator show in the Roman times.

Fuelled by rage and grief, the Lightbringer took a deep breath and channelled his Flare.

The Fímegir beasts leapt at Jason with their hook-like claws and their rapier teeth.

A blast of ice suddenly emanated from Jason's hands. Frozen shards cut their scaly skin and drew their thick dark blood. One of the sharp claws slashed Jason's bicep, a stinging pain pulsating from the wound. The

Lightbringer paid no mind and kept blasting the monsters with his glacial sorcery, but his attacks came short of lethal damage. The Fímegir were too quick, too ferocious, and there were simply too many. Jason fell, and one of the bony monstrosities jumped on top of him, snapping its reptilian jaws exceedingly close to the Lightbringer's throat.

Jason tried to concentrate on his Flare, but at that moment avoiding the threat of the beast's razor teeth was more vital.

Suddenly, a blazing arrow shot through the window of Öken's house, striking one of the beasts in the eye. The ghastly creature screeched and fell with a thud beside Jason, its grimy black blood flooding the floor. The Fímegir turned around and looked outside, beyond the Lightbringer. Before they could do anything, another flaming dart ripped through the scaly flesh of a monster.

The door burst open with a blazing bang.

"Anyir!" Jason exclaimed with a mix of confusion and delight. His companions had come for him. "How did you... What..."

"Thank me later!" she shouted. "Get up and use your Flare!"

"Come get me you vile beasts!" Rhulani yelled at the Fímegir as she ran through the door, brandishing her glaive and effortlessly decapitating a Fímegir. With her feline moves, she jumped across the room and slashed the arm of another monster. Baldor and Kiro joined in, summoning the elements of earth and wind to attack the beasts that pounced at them ferociously. With his magical staff, Baldor controlled the rocks and the boulders of the mountain, crushing the scaly creatures. Kiro, brandishing his two curved daggers, called for mighty gusts of air that swept the Fímegir out of the house and over the edge of Mount Dormund.

"By the way, this is yours," said Baldor as he tossed Jason a hefty bundle of rags.

Jason immediately realised what was hidden inside. *Isidir.* He looked at the Half-Giant with disbelief and proceeded to hastily unwrap the Elven sword. When he unsheathed it from its leather scabbard, its shiny blade rang sharply. The Lightbringer lifted his weapon, just in time for another monster to launch itself his way. The creature shrieked loudly when Isidir's blade drove through its flesh.

"Thank you!" he cheered, but Baldor had already gone to slay more grey beasts.

Though reunited with his faithful companion, there was no trace of Jason's Flare. He couldn't concentrate enough to calm his mind, so instead he slashed his way Fímegir after Fímegir, releasing his anger against the monsters. The thought of Alamor's death clouded his consciousness.

Undefined body parts of the Fímegir were now scattered in a sticky, bloody pool on the ground. The battle had now moved on the snow-covered peak of Mount Dormund, where his companions were busy fighting the soulless inhuman soldiers. In the house, the scorched marks on the walls were evidence of Anyir's powerful, newfound sorcery. Outside, one of the beasts was leaving a trail of black sludge as it dragged itself slowly back to the hut. A sudden sense of nausea rose up Jason's stomach, but he held it in. The Lightbringer scanned the house to search for the vicious Omüms. He wanted them dead; they had caused too much havoc in his life. Yet, they were nowhere to be seen.

There was no sign of Gregor either. He had left as soon as the pandemonium unleashed by the Fímegir began. *I really wanted to help him*, Jason thought. As he tried to swallow the betrayal, he examined the house in search for Öken. Although he couldn't see the Breegan, he could sense his presence.

Suddenly, an eerie voice bellow behind him.

"Nicely done, dirt rat," Tortugal said, standing over him imposingly.

"What have you done with Öken," Jason growled.

"He is safe with Modùn. Why worry about that Breegan when you should be concerned about your life?" Tortugal snarled back.

"Where is he?" Jason insisted. "I can sense him. You either tell me, or I'll make you." His heart was beating as fast as a thousand horses.

"Oh! Wow! I knew you were a bit of a feisty one, dirt rat, but threats are never the way to begin a fair fight!" the Orc taunted.

Jason launched himself towards the general, and the blades of Isidir and Rhazien collided with a loud metallic clangour. Tortugal responded with a violent kick at Jason's diaphragm, propelling the Lightbringer against one of the wooden walls, which smashed into pieces under the brutal force. Jason found himself outside in the open, covered in snow.

As he regained his footing, Tortugal charged at him, brandishing his wicked sword Rhazien.

Just before Tortugal's black blade could slice his flesh, Jason felt a familiar tingle rushing through his veins. The Flare was finally under his control, blazing through his body once again. With one single swift gesture, Jason summoned the earth. A boulder emerged from the ground, levitated up in the air, and propelled against the Orc, smashing him to the ground.

"I see your skills have improved," said the general as he wiped the blood from his mouth. "Your rage is powerful, Jason... it reminds me of ser Lok's. You'd make a great Shadowcaster."

The thought of joining the dreadful soldiers who followed Darkstrom and turned innocent civilians into monstrous undefined creatures made Jason's stomach churn.

"Join us, Jason. Darkstrom needs a new apprentice," continued the general, his voice deep and furious.

"Never," the Lightbringer barked back. Fire build up in his arm and enveloped Isidir. *This is new*, Jason thought, looking at the flaming sword with wide eyes. He swung the burning blade of Isidir at the Orc, who staggered backwards but readily responded with a decisive parry. The heat coming off Jason's weapon was fierce, and the flames reflected in the general's beady eyes. The Orc looked like a harrowing demon risen from the Underworld.

The carcass of a Fímegir suddenly flew across the snowy Fyris Pass, hurtling heavily onto Tortugal and taking the general down with it. The Orc roared as he tried to get the dead monster off himself. Jason looked over, and saw Kiro's beaming smile, as powerful wind magic warped the air around him.

"Kiro!" Jason greeted gladly. "We need to get Öken!"

"Jason! Yes—give me a sec!" The Faun leapt with his goat-legs towards another Fímegir nearby and swiftly slashed it with his daggers. Black sludge sprayed onto the white snow. "All right, I'm ready now," he chortled nonchalantly as if slaying beasts was his every-day pastime.

The Lightbringer and the Faun ran back into the house. There was no sign of Öken, but Jason could sense the Breegan; he could hear his muffled cries. "I can feel his presence, but I can't tell where he is," Jason said.

"Isn't there another—quick, behind you!" Kiro yelped as a beast came crashing through a window, its claws ready to tear Jason to shreds.

Like an involuntary muscle reflex that took even Jason by surprise, a light beam shot out of the photographer's hand. The Fímegir was sliced in half like butter. He had done it—somewhat unintentionally, but he had done it. "Did you see that?" Jason gasped.

"Woah!" the Faun exclaimed, his eyes widened in awe. "Hadn't seen something like that in a while!" he cheered with the largest grin on his face. His alert ears flickered as a Fímegir's shriek filled the Fyris Pass. "Where is Gregor, by the way?"

Jason sighed, the weight of the betrayal heavy on his chest. "I'll tell you later," he dismissed. "We need to focus on Öken now."

Kiro nodded. His eyes scanned the room and his ears flickered. "He's in the attic," he declared decisively.

Jason was stunned by the speed with which the Faun had deduced that. "How can you tell?"

Kiro pointed up. "There's a hatch."

"That makes sense."

Jason and Kiro pulled the handle of the hatch, and a wooden ladder slid down. They rushed up the creaky, unsteady rungs. As they peered into the dark attic, their eyes struggling to adjust, a terrifying scene appeared before them. Öken's slumped, bruised body, was being forcefully held captive by Lieutenant Modùn, who pressed a shiny blade knife to the Breegan's neck. As they advanced carefully into the shadows, however, it became clear the lieutenant was shaking.

"D- don't come any closer, Lightbringer. I'll... I'll slit his throat."

Jason lit Isidir on fire, casting a raging red light into the darkness. "Move, or I'll make you," he threatened.

The lieutenant's face turned white. He anxiously moved aside and pressed against the slanted roof of the attic, allowing Jason to cut the Breegan's shackles and set him free. Clearly, Modùn was defenceless unless he was backed up by Tortugal's menace.

"We need to get out of here. Can you run?" the Lightbringer asked. Öken looked at Jason and Kiro in awe, too disturbed by the recent events to reciprocate verbally. He nodded his head.

They ran to the hatch, leaving the lieutenant in the shadows at the back of the attic. They hastily made their way down the ladder, helping the weakened Breegan find his footing. When they reached the bottom, a looming presence suddenly appeared in the house. Tortugal slammed the entrance door behind him, which was now pointless as most of the walls had been torn down. He waited for them with a perverse grin, the black blade of Rhazien glimmering in the shadows.

Jason stretched his hand forward, intent on blasting him with another light beam, but this time the Flare faltered. "Not now!" he groaned.

"Your powers acting up, dirt rat? Such a disgrace..." he growled, shaking his head. "Alamor's rotting corpse must be turning in its grave."

Tortugal's grinning face turned from green to white as he felt a deep rumble shake the ground beneath the house. Jason tried to plant his feet and looked around as the mountain shook, struggling to determine the cause of the quake. The general raised Rhazien, determined to inflict his vicious blade upon Jason once more, but a violent shock flung everyone to the floor.

"Run! I've got this!" Jason told his friends, attempting to calm his mind and control his Flare.

Kiro grabbed Öken and leapt out of the house as the floor began to crack.

Tortugal staggered back up, visible concern now painted across his face. Another shock brought the Orc down, his right tusk hitting the ground hard as he fell, breaking upon the impact. Panicked, the general clenched his fist and stared at Jason, fear now tinting his eyes. "Jason, please don't do this," Tortugal begged.

"I'm... I'm not doing anything..." Jason muttered as the floor of the Breegan's house cracked, dull crunches reverberating through the mountain.

"Please, I shouldn't have doubted your powers," continued the general.

As Mount Dormund shook, the Lightbringer was dazed, overwhelmed by the amount of energy running through him. The Flare was not only working—it was bursting out of him. His mind was muddled with anger and grief, and he had lost control. He stared at Tortugal with vapid eyes as a deep gorge opened up between them. The general grabbed onto a wooden beam, his square face struck by terror.

"Jason!" Baldor shouted from outside. "Get out of there!"

Then, the side of the mountain broke off. Massive boulders came hurtling down from the peak with a deafening rumble. Öken's home was engulfed by the gigantic landslide and was crushed like a tin-can trodden by a heavy boot. Tonnes of rock crashed raucously in the valley below, echoing across the land. Jason's Flare, burning brightly until now, slowly faded into nothingness. Then, everything went quiet.

XXVIII

WHITE HORSE

The Fyris Pass was once again a desolate, cold and quiet place. Now, where once stood Öken's house, there was a pile of boulders. Everything beneath it had been crushed.

"Jason! No!" Anyir screamed. Baldor, Kiro and Rhulani stood by her silent amidst the snow, unable to fathom what had just transpired. A multitude of Fímegir cadavers laid around them mutilated. Öken looked at his crushed home, speechless, and fell on his knees. Anyir was the first to run ahead, carelessly ignoring the unstable ground and the deep cracks that had developed.

"What are you doing, Anyir?!" Rhulani called. "It's not safe!"

"I don't care!" she yelled back. "I've lost enough! I'm not losing Jason too…"

Rhulani and the others looked at each other, and without further contemplation, they rushed to Jason's aid too and began using their supernatural strength and powers to move the boulders. Even Öken rushed to the Lightbringer's rescue, a sign of devotion after Jason had saved his life from the vile Remaran soldiers. As they lifted stone after stone, nothing was left of anybody still in the house at the time of the rockfall.

"This can't be…" Kiro muttered, rubbing his cheeks compulsively.

"K- Kiro…?"

Everybody turned around with utter surprise upon hearing that voice, which emerged from a few feet away under the rocks.

"Jason! By Rotar's beard! You're alive!" Baldor exclaimed, anxiously trying to locate where the Lightbringer's voice had come from. "Where are you?!"

"I'm here…" the photographer's feeble voice called.

The companions hastily scrambled on the mound of unsteady rocks. "We're coming, Jason!" Anyir cried. Once again they all cleared the boulders away, and soon after they spotted Jason's face peeking through a gap between the stones. He was covered in dirt, wet from the snow, scratched and bruised. They carefully removed his contused, weak body from the aftermath of the rockfall and helped him out onto the steadier ground of the Fyris Pass. Jason groaned as they helped him walk.

Anyir embraced her friend. Jason smiled, gritting his teeth as she squeezed his ribs. "I'm so glad you're alive!" she said as she sighed in relief. "I was afraid you had been crushed…"

"It's OK… I was lucky…" Jason murmured between heavy breaths. The cuts and bruises healed almost instantaneously.

"What happened back there, anyway?" Kiro cut in, anxious and curious. "You know—the whole earthquake thing."

Jason looked at his friends, who all waited for an answer. He knew what had happened, but he felt ashamed to admit it, especially after what his powers had done to the Breegan's house. "I don't know…" he muttered. "I guess I was so focused on defeating Tortugal that I lost control… How did you guys get here? Didn't Uttol imprison you?" the Lightbringer asked, quickly changing the subject.

"A message arrived about Remaran soldiers roaming the Lumos Mountains, so he let us go. He would rather have us dealing with them than his own people," Rhulani explained.

"Still, how did you get here so fast?" Jason enquired.

"Tunnels," Kiro answered. "A lot of dark and grimy tunnels."

The photographer's glance then landed on the very Breegan they had gone to the Fyris Pass for, who stood silently looking back at his crushed home. "Öken. I can't express how sorry I am for what happened," he said with a heartfelt tone.

The Breegan looked up at him. His dark eyes, hidden by his mane of rough and dirty fur, were sad and yet filled with determination. "I owe you my life, Lightbringer." His voice was deep and solemn. "I heard your proposal, and I accept it gladly."

"You do?" Jason was surprised, after the aftermath of the Remaran attack. "But… your house…"

"I was only up there because I don't like living in Hegertan, and I never had a good reason to leave my hut. Nothing is keeping me here any longer."

"Well, I think there might be a job opening now that Gregor is gone!" Jason replied, trying to make light of the situation, but yet the words came out choked.

Baldor looked at him, raising his eyebrow. "What do you mean?"

"He betrayed us," Jason said bluntly. "He was in contact with Tortugal and the Omüms the whole time. That's why they attacked us at Ocran. Gregor must have made a deal with the general to keep them updated about our whereabouts. They arranged a trap at Öken's house because it was the most isolated place they could think of in Erythya."

"Gregor… this makes no sense at all," Anyir said, shaking her head, looking down. "It's my fault—I should have never asked him to come with us."

"It's not your fault, Anyir. I decided to bring him along too."

"But why would he do that?" Anyir probed, her eyebrows furrowed, her nose crinkling.

"He said Darkstrom had taken his parents, and that this deal would grant their protection. Anyways, the important thing is that you are all safe, especially Öken." Upon saying that, he couldn't avoid thinking of Alamor. His heart tightened, and he tried his best to force his emotions down.

"Is everything all right, Jason?" Rhulani asked, sensing his unease.

"Not really… Tortugal gave me some news." Jason looked at Anyir. He took a deep breath. What he was about to say would only make it more real. "Alamor… he's dead. Darkstrom killed him." Hearing those words, the whole company went silent for a moment. Anyir remained quiet too before hugging Jason tightly. Anyir, just like Jason, had lost just about as many people as she could bear. Her tears fell onto Jason's Væsnar tunic.

"I'm so sorry," Baldor said mournfully. "He must have died with honour."

"He might have *fought* with honour, but he *died* alone in the mud. I wish I had gone back to find him when he left Anyir and me in the Stonevale."

"If you had, Darkstrom would have found you before you were ready and you might be dead by now," Rhulani said.

"Perhaps, but if we went back for Alamor, Darkstrom would have had to fight two Lightbringers instead of one. Alamor didn't even have his sword… he left it to me…" He looked at Isidir, the emerald leaf reflecting the light bouncing off the snow.

"Then you wouldn't have met Gregor, which means your path would have been very different. Who knows if you'd have reached Erythya, or found the tracker? Most importantly, without Gregor—traitor or not traitor—we wouldn't have met Öken," Rhulani retorted. "We now have a chance to find the Eluir and defeat the Red Raven for good."

"If I can learn to use my powers properly, that is… Tortugal said that the powers aren't even mine—they're Lok's. He must have accidentally transferred them onto me when I met him in the Iron Wood. That's why he's looking for me."

"This means… Lok is powerless," Baldor realised.

"One less Shadowcaster to worry about!" Kiro observed.

"Yeah, but Darkstrom is after me for my powers," Jason replied.

"That was always going to happen, Jason. You're a Lightbringer—his worst nightmare. He'll try hunting you down with much deadlier means than Tortugal and his shapeshifter friends," Baldor pointed out.

"At least Lok's Flare is in your hands and not someone worse than him," said Rhulani. "Kiro is right. Lok poses less of a threat. He's still a ruthless killer, but he is no more dangerous than any of us."

Jason looked at the mound of boulders that laid precariously before them. He had been lucky to survive, and he hoped to be able to control his powers if he ever met Lok.

Before they could make their way to the Niteria, the new six companions—with Öken the inventor instead of Gregor—had to retrieve their horses at Hegertan. This meant travelling back through a series of tunnels to face Chief Uttol after the catastrophic turn of events at the Fyris Pass.

Jason didn't look back as they rushed down a long series of tunnels that cut through the mountain and led directly to the Breegan Hall. These tight passages had been excavated by ancient Breegans more than two thousand years before and stretched like a network along the entirety of the Lumos Mountains, serving as highways of commerce as well as providing safe travel. However, as a result of the enslavement brought about by Darkstrom, Breegans preferred to remain hidden away from the rest of Valkadia in their highly fortified city of Hegertan. The tunnels had been abandoned, their long dark passageways completely devoid of life. Only certain parts of the network closest to Hegertan were still operational, but these were highly guarded against the threat of intruders. If anyone did choose to attack the Breegans by venturing into their underground tunnel system, they would likely get lost and perish. Besides, the tunnels were pitch black. The extreme darkness was something Jason had never experienced, and he couldn't imagine trying to find his way alone.

Luckily, Öken knew every turn to take and shaft to crawl through.

"How far are we from Hegertan? I'm struggling to keep track of where we are under here," Jason asked.

"I'm not surprised. It has taken thousands of years of passing down knowledge from our ancestors to learn the ways of these passages. As a Breegan, the map is entrenched in our blood. Plus, we can see in the dark, which helps," Öken explained. "Anyways, it'll probably be another couple hours until we get to the Breegan Hall."

Indeed, after about two hours of Jason trying to keep up with the Breegan and his friends, crawling and hunkering through the tunnels as fast as they could, they reached an open vestibule with a myriad of passages to choose from. Öken didn't even stop twice to think or look back and rushed through one of the tunnels. Jason was impressed by the Öken's memorisation of such a puzzling place. Still, he was also apprehensive about whether the Breegan had just made the right choice.

Thankfully, they were soon greeted by the faint haze of natural light from the outside, seeping into the tunnel system. The voices of people became louder and louder, and before they knew it, two Breegan guards halted them. They were shocked at the sight of Öken, whom they hadn't seen for decades.

"Let us through," Öken said resolutely. "We must get to Uttol immediately."

"Öken? Is that really you?" one of the guards asked.

"Yeah, it's me. Now move aside, please," he replied, barging through the armoured Breegans and their steel axes. Jason and his friends followed the hairy inventor through the tunnel, and they shortly found themselves in the Breegan Hall, where Uttol was sitting pompously on his throne.

The chieftain sprung up from his regal seat when he saw the company walk in, dirty and covered in Fímegir blood. When he saw Öken, Uttol gave him a wholehearted embrace. "It's nice to see you," he greeted, "although I can't say the same about everybody else… What the hell happened up there? We could feel the Mountain shaking!"

"You must thank Jason for saving my life. General Tortugal would have killed me if it weren't for him."

Uttol's face lost all its colour at once. "Tortugal?!" Jason wasn't sure if he was afraid or angry. "I knew about the Remaran soldiers, but I didn't think an Orc would trample our sacred ground! I knew I should never have let you in!" he hollered at the Lightbringer.

"Chief Uttol, please understand…" said Jason as he tried to dampen Uttol's anger.

"Understand? I think I've been understanding enough! I even let all your companions loose! How more *understanding* should I be?!"

"He's dead," Öken interrupted. "Tortugal, the soldiers. They're all dead. Jason and his friends killed them all. As for the Orc, Jason crushed him."

Uttol looked at Öken, dirty and bloody, and then glanced back at Jason, who was full of mud from crawling in the cave system of Mount Dormund. "Where is your other friend? He is unaccounted for."

"Gregor was… found to be unfit for his role," Jason said. "Tortugal and his soldiers trapped Öken and attacked me. I shouldn't have trusted him. Thankfully, Öken has agreed to join us in his place."

Uttol nodded slowly. "I'm glad you're safe, Öken; Jason—thank you for getting rid of that vermin of Tortugal and his minions. However, this wouldn't have happened if you hadn't arrived, *Marigold Guardian*. I was wrong to let you into our home."

"I meant no harm, chief Uttol," Jason said. "We seek to make Valkadia better."

"You have noble aims, but you have a target on your back, from the Red Raven no less. Your powers, your goals, they will inevitably bring harm to all who harbour you. When my people learn what happened up there, they will not want you and your friends here anymore. The thought of the Remaran army taking their loved ones, it makes the strongest among us weep. The wounds we suffered at their hands are far from healed, and our children must never experience such horrors. Hegerthan must remain a safe heaven. As soon as your friends are brought back, you must leave swiftly."

"Of course," Jason said. "Thank you, chief Uttol. We owe you a lot."

"Just promise you'll defeat that tyrant."

"I'll do my best," Jason responded solemnly.

"Wait. One last thing before we go," Öken interrupted. From his pocket, Öken extracted a Jaul and put it in Uttol's hands. "I expect there will be some difficult times ahead. If you ever need me, just call."

Before they left, the two Breegans embraced a final time. Then, the companions jumped on their horses, leaving the mysterious underground city of Hegertan behind. Jason glanced up to the peak of Mount Dormund and couldn't believe what happened up there. He was exhausted, his legs were weak and his head pounding. He tried to ride as long as he could, but his eyes struggled to focus. Every time the horse's hooves hit the ground, he felt as if a knife was being lodged through his lungs. Not long after their quick getaway from Hegertan, Jason's fatigue caught up to him, and like a sack of potatoes, he fell off the horse.

Jason woke up the next morning to find himself laying on a blanket. The smell of campfire permeated the air, and all around him was a blur of green. His companions had travelled through the night, and they transported him to the edge of the Gartruth Forest, where they had set up a small camp.

Niteria was close now.

Jason drunk a cup of Gurgum to regain his energy, and quietly admired the magical forest. The immense line of trees stretched east to west, seemingly never-ending. It reminded the photographer of pictures of the Amazon rainforest that he had seen back at World Cloud. Tall trunks overtaken by crawling plants and vines, umbrella-like tree crowns merging to form various layers of canopy, lianas drooping from branches. Even the horses felt compelled to stop to admire the beauty of such an enormous stretch of greenery. A great solemnity was emanating from the forest.

When they resumed their journey and crossed the borderline of trees, Jason felt a sudden punch in the stomach. It was akin to standing next to a large speaker, the bass sounds and drums vibrating his body.

"You felt it, didn't you?" Baldor asked.

"What was that?" replied Jason mesmerised.

"It's the power of this sacred forest. It's impressive," Rhulani added.

"You'll get used to it after a while," Kiro said.

The sensory overload of the forest's mysticism, coupled with the continuous noise of insects, birds and other myriad of animals, was disorienting yet wonderful.

As they led their steeds through, the path was slowly enveloped by the unimaginably broad tree-trunks, leaves as big as horses, and a canopy so tall it blended with the sky.

"Make sure you follow the Elven Road," Rhulani told Jason and Anyir. "It's easy to get lost in there when everything starts to look the same. Dryads and Elves created this road thousands of years ago, to avoid the ancient dangers that lie in the forest's thicket. Just stick to the path and you'll be fine," she said, pointing at the long road that cut through the forest.

"Jason," Öken called as he rode the horse behind him. "I know what's wrong with the tracker."

"What? Do you? How did you even get it?"

"Well, we didn't have much to do last night as you slept, so Öken had a look at it."

"The core of the tracker is missing. That's why it's not working. It's not getting the energy it needs to function from anywhere," Öken explained.

"So, it's basically missing its batteries," Jason commented.

"What's *'batteries'*?" Baldor asked.

"Never mind, please go on," Jason dismissed.

"There's just one problem—the core must be made of Astral Steel," Rhulani pointed out.

"Astral Steel? But that's…"

"Really, really, really rare? Yes, that's right," Kiro responded.

"How do we find it?" Jason asked.

"Kavanagh might be able to help us with that, I hope," Baldor answered. "The Ærindel is full of riches. We only need a small piece of Astral Steel to make the tracker work, isn't that right, Öken?"

"That's correct. Once we have the piece, we just have to open the casing of the tracker and lodge the piece in a little slot. When we turn the knob on the side of the tracker, then it should work."

"Definitely missing its batteries then," Jason concluded.

"What is it with you and these *'batteries'*?" Anyir asked.

Jason was glad Öken had figured it out so quickly, although he really hoped Kavanagh would have some Astral Steel lying around, and that he'd be willing to share it with them. Even with the tracker working, there was no guarantee they'd find the Eluir.

Immersed in his thoughts about the tracker, Jason gazed up into the canopy. The vegetation was so dense that it absorbed every other sound. Occasional screeches of birds and deep roars of monkey-like creatures filled the forest. A troop of iridescent blue monkeys jumped above their heads from one tree to another, trying to find fruit to eat. When they were done eating the strange purple fruits growing in the highest branches, they threw the pits on the ground, almost hitting Jason on the head.

Everywhere armies of tiny green and blue ants rushed along the ground. Spiders hung in webs between the branches. Millipedes crawled on fallen tree-trunks, and small understorey birds came whizzing past or perching within the dense vegetation. Jason remembered reading about creatures that lived in the Gartruth Forest in *The Harmony of Creatures: Life in the Olde Forests and the New* by Rogor Dreymos. He recognised a Kuaru perching on a branch high up in the canopy, showing off its yellow feathers to potential mates. He also managed to spot an Emerald swallow rustling with leaves in the understorey, probably busy finding twigs to build its nest with.

Trees that were standing just days before were now resting on the ground, opening up space for new colonisers. The dark and decomposing soil continuously replenished the forest with nutrients, which in turn fed dead leaves and wood back into the ground. The smell of this life cycle was everywhere. The air was sweet yet musty from the damp earth, the wet wood of fallen trees, the stagnant water, the decaying leaf litter.

From within, the forest was very dark and shaded, but the sun still managed to find a way through the canopy, shining between the branches like beams and hitting the forest floor with the warmest and most welcoming light. It took Jason a while to fully embrace the immensity and overwhelming beauty of it all, and he began to understand how alive the Gartruth Forest was. The forest was a truly hectic place, and Jason could feel it under his own feet. He could *really* feel it—the vibration of the earth; the movement of the leaves; the beating hearts of the creatures around him; the water rushing beneath the ground. He realised his Flare had connected him to the life growing among the forest in a way he had previously never experienced.

Before he knew it, Jason found himself lost. Overwhelmed by the connection he felt with the forest, he had somehow taken a completely different path to his companions, and now he was alone. He realised he wasn't even riding his horse anymore. Suddenly, all the beauty of the forest disappeared and was replaced by fear. He didn't know where he was, or where he was going. He looked left and right. Green blended with more green. While a minute ago he had forgotten about all his mishappenings and daunting responsibilities, now all he could think of was how to get back. People were relying on him, and he had gone through too much to die alone in the middle of a forest.

"Hey!" he shouted. "Is anybody there? Baldor! Anyir!"

For a while, nobody responded. Then, a figure appeared from behind the thicket. His heart skipped a beat when he realised who it was. Overwhelmed, he fell to his feet.

"Clara?" he muttered. "Is that you?" She was wearing the same light blue coat as the day he last saw her, and she was wrapping herself with the same thick tartan blanket. Her fair, silky hair draped over her shoulders, and her eyes were the bluest he'd ever seen them. Yet, her rosy cheeks were now pale, and the look in her eyes was vapid.

She giggled, and reached a hand towards him, with the palm facing upwards. "Come," she said with the most delicate voice. Jason felt a chill run down his spine. He hadn't heard her speak for so long that he had almost forgotten what she sounded like. His heart was full again.

Jason was attracted to her like a magnet. When he grabbed hold of her hand, her skin felt soft and smooth just like he remembered. He couldn't believe he had found her again. "I thought you were dead," he said. "What happened? I saw you drown…"

Clara looked deep into his eyes and smiled lovingly. "That is not important now," she said. "Come with me; I'll show you the way back home."

"You know how to get back?" Jason asked, both shocked and relieved. "But… the Elder Stones… how…"

Clara placed her index finger on his lips to stop him from talking. "I'll show you. Don't you trust me?"

"Of course I trust you, my sweet dove. I just can't believe you're actually alive."

Clara giggled again and began pulling his hand just like she had done on the *Son of Odin* to convince him to go back inside the lounge of the ship. They started to walk through the forest together, and the beauty of the raw nature surrounding them returned to overwhelm him. Now more than ever, he felt free. He wanted to tell her everything he had been through and know everything about her since the day he lost her.

"I'm so sorry I lost hold of your hand. I promised I wouldn't. I thought I had lost you."

"I'm here now," she said. "And we'll go home together. I'll take you there, and we can be happy again."

"I'd like that," Jason said, but as he kept following Clara, his peripheral vision became darker. The trees around him turned into a green tunnel, and the only thing he could focus on was Clara herself. She was so beautiful, and her laugh guided him through the tunnel.

Then, before Jason could comprehend the order of events, chaos ensued.

There was a flash of white, and for a minute all Jason could see was smoke. The sound of birds and animals had disappeared, replaced by a screeching sound. When Jason's vision went back to normal, he realised he had been lied to. There was no Clara. Instead, in front of him was a horrifying creature with human traits over a ghostly smoke. A white stallion had charged into the spectral being, breaking its form. As Jason broke free from the trance, he recognised the true identity of his saviour.

"Silvyr?!" Jason exclaimed.

The white horse thrust its front legs at the creature of smoke, which shrieked as Silvyr shattered its enchantment. Every so often, the shadow would become Clara again, returning quickly back to its natural form. Soon after, anything that resembled Clara had vanished entirely. Jason was dazed. The love of his life was gone—again. The smoky creature had dissipated into the forest, and now only the horse and the Lightbringer were left.

"Silvyr, what are you doing here? What was that? Clara…" Jason babbled. He stood immobile, in shock after being tricked into seeing his dead beloved. The horse approached him slowly, its hooves stepping silently on the forest floor. Silvyr moved gently as if walking on a cloud, its white coat glimmering under the rays of sun that shone through the trees.

"She wasn't real…" Jason muttered, words getting stuck, his eyebrows pushed together in disbelief. "But… you are, right?" he asked the steed, scared to get too close to it in case it vanished into smoke too.

Silvyr lowered her head and snorted, gently nudging Jason's arm. As he stroked the horse's soft nose, Jason's mind struggled to perceive reality. The bristly hair was real, and the warmth coming out of Silvyr's nostrils felt real. Yet, also Clara's hand felt concrete when it wasn't.

Seeing Jason in such an altered state of mind, Silvyr forcefully stamped her hard hoof on the photographer's foot. The sheer pain that overtook Jason immediately jolted him out of his spiralling thoughts. "What was that for?!" he jerked. Silvyr replied by neighing and bopping her head up and down. It was only then that Jason fully realised Silvyr was actually standing in front of him.

"Silvyr! I can't believe you're here! How did you find me?" Jason's spurt of excitement was soon taken over by grief once more. Tortugal's words suddenly reverberated in his head: *Alamor died alone in the streets of Orachlion with his face in the mud.* Jason looked up to the white horse, and with an exhausted voice he asked, "Is Alamor really dead?"

Silvyr remained still for a moment upon hearing those words and then lowered her head solemnly. Jason knew what that meant. The image of Alamor's cheery face, with his pointy ears and golden eyes, flashed for a moment before Jason's eyes. His mentor, his friend, his provider of many soups... he was gone.

"I'm so sorry," he said, slowly stroking Silvyr's candid mane. "I'll never forget what he did for me."

Silvyr raised her head, placed it gently over Jason's shoulder and hugged him as much as a horse could hug. Jason tried to hold the tears down, but they flushed out involuntarily. He grabbed onto the horse's neck, and together they cried for their dear friend.

"I need to get back to the others," said Jason, sniffling. "They'll be looking for me."

Silvyr nodded, and she slowly began to walk through the thicket of the Gartruth Forest, and Jason followed. They wandered back through the scrub for what felt at least like an hour, and Jason made sure never to lose sight of Alamor's horse. Soon later, Jason could finally hear his friends' voices, who apparently were still looking for him.

"Jason!" they called repeatedly. "Where are you?"

"I'm here!" Jason shouted back. Nobody seemed to hear him, so he shouted again. "I'm here! Look who I've found!"

Suddenly, Anyir's face popped up from behind a bush not far away from him. "Hey! Where have you been? We've been looking everywhere for you!" she asked, almost annoyed. When she realised Silvyr was standing beside him, her slight frustration suddenly turned into an uncontainable smile. "Silvyr!" she cheered and flung her arms around the horse's neck. Anyir looked at the mare with droopy eyes. "I heard what happened. I'm so sorry. I know you and Alamor have gone through a lot together." Silvyr's eyes were wise and tired. She nudged Anyir quietly.

The other companions rushed towards them, excited to have found Jason and eager to listen to his recent adventure in the jungle.

"There you are! What were you doing, wandering off the path?" Kiro jeered. "I see you've found a friend though," he said smiling as he stroked Silvyr's back. "Nice to meet you!"

"You won't believe what happened to me back in the forest," Jason told her. "I was attacked by a smoke demon or something like that, but Silvyr arrived and saved me."

"That *smoke demon* is a Riuku," Rhulani elucidated. "They're spirits, trapped in this plane of reality. They're mischievous and like to lure people deep within the forest where they get lost and cannot escape. Often, they feed off people's energy, so it is likely that this particular Riuku sensed your Flare and considered you a tasty treat. You are lucky this horse came to helped you, or the Riuku would have taken you further through the forest until it found another victim to feed on."

"I thought Erythya was only full of nice little creatures," Jason said jokingly.

"Riukus are not bad, but they can be dangerous. Erythya is still a raw and wild place."

"Come on," said Baldor. "We have to keep going. Now that Jason is back with us, we must proceed. Niteria is not far, and King Kavanagh is waiting for us."

XXIX

THE ARALAY

The gloom of the night had laid over Orachlion like a black shroud. Darkstrom was gone, and Alamor's motionless body rested on the muddy ground, exposed and unattended. What had happened there moments before permeated the streets with a deep melancholy. Soon, the moon would give way to the murky Remaran daylight. The inhabitants would flood out of their houses to take care of their daily tasks, only to find the remains of the old Veheer and, most certainly, dispose of his corpse in the quickest way possible. Veheers were a bad omen, and nobody wanted the unnecessary attention of the Emperor's soldiers.

While the people were still fast asleep, a creature came gliding gracefully through the clouds. Its golden feathers glistened under the moonlight. The wide, strong wings slammed downward and came back up with force as it circled the city. With the protection of the nightly shadows, it quietly landed in the square where the epic battle had occurred not long before. It tucked its wings by the sides of its body, and its hooves stepped silently on the wet ground as it approached Alamor. The winged stag moved gently, as if walking on a cloud, and a long, feathery tail trailed behind it, flowing fluidly in the air. Its branch-like antlers shimmered even in the shadows.

The legends of the Aralays were many, each granting the rare beast a myriad of otherworldly powers. Some of them spoke about its wish-granting antlers; others of its silver-turning feathers. The stories were plentiful, but in the long history of Valkadia, few had ever come close to meeting one. They didn't respond to the mere requests of mortals and mostly acted under their own ephemeral will. They remained mysterious to even the most knowledgeable scholars, their behaviours and habitats still unknown. Nevertheless, their allegiance was clear. They were on the side of life.

The winged stag stood beside the old Lightbringer's inert body and lowered its head, sniffing Alamor's garments and hair. The wounds on his clavicle and chest were deep, and the Veheer's thick blood had pooled beneath him, mixing with the wet dirt. Alamor's face was pale and cold, and his resting eyes were marked with two swollen, purplish dark circles. The old Lightbringer had accepted his end, though the Aralay knew his journey wasn't quite finished yet.

As the Aralay's large, gleaming eyes watered up, a single silvery tear rolled down its bristly cheek. The tear fell through the air, hitting Alamor's deep chest wound where Darkstrom had lodged Rhazien. Almost instantly, Alamor's body regained colour, and the wounds began to heal. With a harrowing gasp, the Lightbringer's eyes opened wide, and he sat up as if being lifted by a ghostly essence.

Alamor had been brought back from the Eredom, though he had not met any soul or god during his brief trip. Now, he found himself soiled with blood and dirt. He slowly regained memory of what happened, and he could still feel the vicious blade of Rhazien piercing his flesh. Frantically, he unbuttoned his tunic and ran his fingers on his bloodied chest and shoulder. The slashes inflicted by Darkstrom's sword had only partially healed, with strands of muscle and skin loosely connected to each other. It hurt to move, but he wasn't bleeding. He breathed deeply, attempting to summon his Flare and complete the restorative process, but he was too weak. His powers weren't responding any longer.

The Lightbringer looked up at the fantastical beast that stood before him, which shimmered with gold in the darkness or Remara. It was a creature of true wonder. "Thank you," he said solemnly. Speaking felt like pushing a thousand needles in his lungs. The Aralay nudged its head towards Alamor, who stroked it gently, in total awe.

He tried to get up, but as soon as he put his weight on his shoulders and ribcage, he fell back down to the ground, squeezing his eyes shut and gritting his teeth in pain. When he opened his eyes again, the Aralay had vanished.

In the meantime, the sun had begun to rise over the horizon, and the citizens of Orachlion were starting to wake up. Alamor heard the sound of a door being unlocked nearby and realised the streets would soon be swarming with Remarans. He grunted as he dragged himself behind the rubble of the torn down butcher's shop, which had taken the brunt of his and Darkstrom's fight. He waited there, hoping that the sluggishly awakening Orachlioners would be too distracted by their daily chores to notice him. When the shop owners and stone merchants entered the square to start their day and saw the damage to the buildings surrounding it, they gasped and murmured.

The stabbing pain from Alamor's half-healed wounds made him whimper involuntarily, but he put a hand on his mouth to refrain himself. All he had to do was remain quiet and hidden until he was strong enough to walk. Then, he could leave that godforsaken place.

Alas, the pain was too much, and everything suddenly turned to black once more.

When Alamor woke up, he found himself laying on a heap of hay. He was moving, and he wasn't in Orachlion anymore. He heard the sound of hooves clapping on the soft ground and wheels squeaking at every turn, and realised he was being transported on a wagon. The old Lightbringer raised his head to see where he was, but his chest and ribcage shot rivers of pain as he moved. The light was bright, and the grass was green. He was in Erythya.

The thick scent of cigar smoke rose in plumes. When he realised who was driving the wagon, Alamor sprung up, ignoring the pain that flooded his sore body. "Grando!?" he exclaimed in total disbelief.

The bearded man turned around, briefly taking his eyes off the road. The grin on his face was wide and cheery. "Hello, old friend! I'm glad you finally woke up!"

Alamor was astounded, his eyes wide as he looked at the alchemist. "How did you find me?"

"You underestimate the power of my little birds! My network reaches far and wide, and I came as soon as I heard what happened to you. I knew you got separated from Jason and Anyir. I am happy to let you know they are safe—"

"They are?" Alamor sighed with relief, his voice shaky. "We need to get to them. They must already be in Niteria or at least on their way there—"

"Easy there, old fella. You need to rest," Grando admonished. "They've met Baldor and the others, so they'll be ok without you for a little longer."

Alamor slumped back onto the hay-stack on the back of the wagon. "How long was I gone for?" he asked.

"Three days or so," he responded. The bearded man puffed on his cigar. "Those wounds look bad, Alamor. Can you not heal?"

"I think I'm too weak..." the old Lightbringer admitted. "My Flare isn't working. It's a miracle I'm alive."

"What happened back there? The stories are wild... everybody is saying you're dead." Grando's joyful voice suddenly turned sombre. "Did you really face Darkstrom all on your own?"

"He caught me by surprise," said Alamor, replaying the events of that night in his head. "There wasn't much else I could do. I thought my time had come, but an Aralay brought me back."

"An Aralay?" Grando squawked. "But that's...."

"Impossible? Aye, I thought so too—just stuff of legends—but I was wrong. Darkstrom killed me, and everything was black. Next thing I know, I am awake and an Aralay is standing right in front of me. You should've seen how magnificent it was," Alamor mused. "Then, it vanished into thin air."

"You're a lucky old git, you know that, right?" Grando teased.

"I know, my friend, I know."

Grando and Alamor sat quietly as the wagon journeyed along, and they looked ahead into the Erythian landscape.

They travelled for six days and six nights along the quiet roads of the West, steering away from busy areas. Though Alamor was a Lightbringer, and though many Erythians had now forgotten about him, some still held grudges. Alamor was in no condition for confrontation. Of his Flare there was no trace, and he couldn't even conjure the simplest gust of air to help feed the campfires. Though the wounds were healing, it was happening nowhere near as fast as he'd hoped, and that made the Veheer's temper short-lived and explosive. He could soon stand up and walk, but running or sword fighting were out of the question.

One evening, as they hid between trees on a shore of Lake Oren and they sat around the fire, Alamor's face grew unusually grave. "There is something I must tell you, Grando," Alamor said, his eyes fixed onto the flames.

The bearded alchemist drew on his cigar and looked at his old friend intensely. "What is it?"

"There is something not many people know, and I fear that this secret will be buried with me once I die for good."

"Does it concern Jason's powers?" Grando guessed with anticipation, though his words were marked by a touch of concern.

"Yes and no, dear Grando. It's about the real origin of Jason and Lok…" The Veheer's eyes glowed with the colour of ember, "…or should I say, Zoaar and Tyr."

The alchemist's eyes anchored onto Alamor's with devoted attention. He remained silent, waiting for the Veheer to tell him more.

✹

XXX

ENTER THE ÆRINDEL

The gigantic trees that populated the Gartruth Forest began to shrink and grow sparser, leaving room for dirt paths and paved roads that ran through the understorey. As they approached the capital of Erythya, small cottages made of wood and enveloped in flowering plants began appearing. People working hard, either ploughing the ground and tending to their crops in the managed allotments under the forest's canopy, raised their heads away from their work in astonishment as they saw the Marigold Guardian and his warrior companions.

No walls were surrounding Niteria—the forest was enough of an impenetrable defence to protect its inhabitants from Remaran enemies and intruders. They proceeded to walk along a wide paved road at the end of which was a large marble arch that demarcated the entrance to the capital. The Gate of Unity, as it was called, was covered in green ivy and purple wisteria, and the pedestal it stood on was dense with joyfully colourful flower patches. The façades of the arch were decorated with reliefs depicting important moments of Valkadian history and Eredomyhm belief, such as the birth of the gods from the petals of the Primordial Orchid and the creation of the Elder Stones by the ancient Elves. In the middle dominated the royal emblem of the Kavanagh family—the Aralay.

Opposite the Gate of Unity and far down the other side of the Elven Road, which meandered gently through Niteria, Jason caught a glimpse of the sumptuous Ærindel, the Palace of Kings. Its two golden domes dominated the inhabitants' wooden houses, and its taupe sandstone walls were peppered with immense oval windows of irregular shapes and sizes. The undulating roofs, topped with a golden mosaic and an array of chimneys that spiralled upwards to the sky, reminded Jason of Antoni Gaudí's 'Casa Batlló' in Barcelona.

The warm colour of rosewood and the lush green of the trees dominated the grandiose city. Sporadically, the bright blue and golden banners flaunting Kavanagh's emblem appeared, adding hints of the most brilliant and beautiful hue to the streets of Niteria.

Long wooden porticos ran along the bottom of beautifully built and intricately decorated houses with arching doorways and lush balconies. Large oaks and beeches sprung out of the ground in every corner of the city, making it still feel like they were in the middle of the forest. Inside the trunks of some of the largest trees, people had even built houses, with spiralling staircases that went up into the canopy so they could have a complete view of Niteria. From above, Jason imagined one could admire red-tiled rooftops and quaint collection of beautifully carved wooden bridges that crossed the many ponds and streams scattered around the capital.

The allure of the metropolis was evidenced by both the quantity and elegance of its inhabitants. Just like in Malion and everywhere else in Erythya, creatures of all shapes and sizes hustled along the streets of the capital, carrying their goods, riding their horses, driving their carts and working hard in their shops. The ancient origins of the city—which had stood in the middle of Gartruth Forest since the time of the Elves—had led to a plethora of cultures and a rich variety of trades that coexisted merrily, creating a pulsating and vibrant atmosphere.

Jason would have loved to have his camera with him and take what could have been the best photos of his life. He imagined what Arthur O'Donney would have thought if he saw pictures of this place. Most likely, he would have considered them cleverly Photoshopped pictures. He took a mental picture instead and promised himself to immortalise the stunning view and fascinating culture in his sketchbook as soon as he found the time.

When the residents of Niteria realised who had just stepped into their city, they fell to their knees in awe. "It's Jason!" they whispered to each other as they watched the six companions ride towards the Ærindel. "The Lightbringers are back!" someone cheered. One by one people flooded from the shops and houses onto the street to witness Jason's arrival. The excitement was palpable, yet everyone remained composed, thus creating a wholesome atmosphere.

The sacredness of that moment was suddenly interrupted by a small girl with long pointy ears sticking out of her fair hair. She pattered with her bare feet onto the cobbled road and approached Jason.

"Nice tails," Jason said to the girl as he saw the fancy red coat she was wearing. "What is your name, little girl?"

"Vicken, sir," she replied confidently. "I'm sixty years old, by the way…"

Jason laughed, embarrassed. "Oh! Beg my pardon! I didn't realise you were so big!"

"You are the Marigold Guardian, right?"

"I am, Vicken."

"I like your tunic," she said.

"Thank you very much! Do you know what it's called?"

"No…"

"It's called a Væsnar tunic," he explained. "It's been the traditional garment of Lightbringers for centuries. It's designed for extreme durability, agility and protection." Jason looked back at Rhulani, who had told him those same words when he found the tunic in the Lightbringer's Vault.

"Do you think I could wear it one day?" Vicken asked.

"It's a tunic that is only meant to be worn by Lightbringers. Who knows, perhaps someday you'll be the next Marigold Guardian. Would you like that?"

"Very much, sir. I'd like that very very much."

"Well, I'll tell you what—why don't you hold onto my tunic until you're old enough to wear it?" As he said that, he took off his tunic and reached down over his horse to pass it to the little child. The crowd watched in amazement, and his companions looked at each other in bewilderment as Jason gave away his precious garment.

"Jason, do you think that's a good—" Baldor began, but Jason quickly interrupted him.

"It's fine; I can get another one. We must spread hope to future generations," Jason said.

"But *you* are the last Lightbringer," Kiro pointed out.

"Am I?" Jason countered. "Here you go, Vicken," he said as he handed the tunic down to the little girl.

"Really? For me?" Vicken asked, shook, as she held the draping tunic in his small arms.

"That's right."

"I will tell all my friends! Thank you, Jason—I mean, sir!"

"You can call me Jason," he replied. "Try it on."

Vicken's smile was the widest Jason had ever seen on any child's face. The tunic was obviously too big, with baggy sleeves and the hem trailing onto the floor. Over the red tailcoat, the combination of colours reminded Jason of a circus clown, but that didn't seem to bother the small kid. She flapped his loose sleeves and looked up at Jason in delight.

"Vicken! Where is your mother? She'll be worried sick. Go now, stop bothering our guests," said a deep guttural voice coming from the top of the Elven Road. It was a Minotaur, wearing a long sapphire blue cloak lined with golden silk. He seemed to be of some importance within Niteria, as he evoked an aura of power and the citizens slightly bowed as he passed by them. He wore his long white horns more like a crown than a pair of deadly weapons. "Jason McAnnon, it is a pleasure to finally make your acquaintance, it has been my dream for a long time to see a Lightbringer return. My name is Dorean Amble. I am the king's chamberlain. I have been instructed to lead you to the Ærindel."

Jason observed Vicken as she scattered away and disappeared into the crowd with the marigold Væsnar tunic trailing behind her.

"It's a pleasure to meet you too…" Jason finally said, but his distracted mind impeded him from remembering the chamberlain's name.

"Dorean Amble…" the Minotaur dressed in blue repeated, his voice monotone and his face serious.

"Yes, of course—Dorean," Jason repeated.

"The king has been expecting you for quite some time. He thought you'd make your way to the Ærindel much quicker. Have there been problems?"

"A few," Jason replied. "The journey hasn't been easy."

"I understand… and I can see you have a couple more travel companions than we expected," Amble observed, his eyes scanning the riders surrounding Jason.

"Nice to see you again, Amble," Baldor interjected.

"Baldor. What a surprise—and Rhulani and Kiro are here too, how great," Dorean Amble rejoiced. "It's been a while."

"It has indeed," Rhulani replied. "I'm sorry about how our last meeting ended…"

"Not to worry," Dorean said as he snorted through his large nostrils. "It's all in the past."

Jason was confused. As Dorean spoke to Baldor, he leaned over to Kiro and whispered, "What happened?"

Kiro chuckled quietly. "The last time we came here, Dorean advised the king not to give the Library any more funding because *apparently* there were more important and less expensive investments to be made. Rhulani called him a 'parsimonious prick'. Dorean didn't take it well."

Jason laughed along with the Faun but then realised that this might not play in his favour. "How long ago was this?"

"About five years ago, but Dorean is a politician—he clings on to the past with his teeth and claws."

Dorean's voice suddenly became louder as he addressed Jason once more. "I cannot see Alamor. Where is he? The invitation was extended to him as well."

"He's… dead… Darkstrom killed him…" When Jason uttered those words, everyone who heard him gasped. He could hear the crowd whispering to each other around him.

Dorean Amble remained impassable, his bovine face severe and unmoved. "My condolences," he finally murmured. "Still, I am glad you and your companions made it. The king will be extremely pleased you have made it. He and queen Emiliya have been preparing a feast for your arrival for a few weeks already. They're very excited to meet the new Lightbringer."

"We have come a long way. We would be delighted to meet the king and queen," Jason gratefully replied.

"Shall we?" said Dorean, leading the way along the final stretch of the Elven Road, towards the doors of the Ærindel.

As they approached the luxurious limestone palace in the middle of the forested city of Niteria, Jason felt all the responsibility fall heavily on his back. When before he was distracted by the beauty of Erythya, or busy trying to survive the clutches of Tortugal and his goons, now he realised that he was there for a purpose. A purpose that others before him had died for, nonetheless. Jason's anxiety rose, and his stomach began to burn. He couldn't back out, especially not now, though he only really wanted to be back home.

With a bang, the large golden doors of the Palace swung open, and a pompous man appeared. It was king Kavanagh, dressed in a sumptuous purple silk tunic embroidered with gold thread and a large fur coat draped over his shoulders. On his head, shining under the golden light of the Erythian sun was a large golden crown with intricate carvings, embedded with sapphires. Under his well-groomed yet bushy beard, King Kavanagh had an expression that evoked trust and respect. His dark eyes were soulful and cheerful, and at the same time solemn and stern.

"My friends!" the king bellowed. "Welcome to Niteria! How great to finally meet you."

"Your Highness, I present to you Jason McAnnon and his travel companions," Dorean Amble introduced.

Jason climbed down his horse, and so did his friends. They bowed solemnly in front of the ruler of Erythya—whom Jason had been waiting to meet since leaving the Leynahüs. "It is an honour to meet you, Your Highness," Jason said. "We have travelled far to come to see you. Much has happened since you sent your invitation. Unfortunately, Alamor couldn't make it. I also realise you haven't planned for this many guests…"

"Nonsense, Jason. Your companions are very welcome to stay and feast with us! I already know a few of them—Baldor, Rhulani, Kiro," he welcomed with a quick nod of the head. Then, he extended his hand towards Anyir and smiled. "And you are…?"

"Anyir Sköld, Your Majesty. It's an honour to meet you," she said as she curtsied, dipping her body downward slightly and bending her knees.

"The pleasure is mine. I also see we have a Breegan among us. Did chief Uttol finally decide to help our cause?"

"Not really, sire. My name is Öken. I decided to leave Hegertan and help Jason myself. Uttol merely allowed me to leave—I was an outcast anyway."

"Well, we are so thrilled that you have all made it all this way. We have much to talk about. Follow me," Kavanagh invited and led Jason and his companions through the immense golden doors of the palace.

The inside of the Ærindel was an astounding mixture of architectural styles and functionality, ranging, by what Jason could understand, from gothic to more modernist mid 20th Century aesthetics resembling art nouveau. The Entrance Hall on its own was a work of art, recalling the shapes and uneven curves of nature. An imposing staircase with alabaster steps and carved wooden bannisters that whirled up to the upper floors of the palace was the first element one encountered upon entering the regal building. Scattered along the network of long corridors that snaked through the ground floor were huge oak doors, hand-decorated with the most organic and curvy shapes. Large stained-glass windows, of varying shapes and sizes, illuminated the enormous spaces with ample natural light. The only objects interrupting the sun's rays to hit the wooden floor were the tall swirling columns of limestone. All in all, walking through the Ærindel felt like roaming inside the living body of an ancient beast.

One of the things that stroke Jason the most was the number of guards around the palace. There were two in every room—and there was a lot of rooms.

The Palace of Kings had been designed by the ancestral Elves of Valkadia thousands of years ago and was one of the only remaining buildings that stood the test of time and conflict. It was a testament of times gone by, and of a civilisation that venerated beauty as well as knowledge. To Jason, it felt like the Ærindel had a Flare of its own rushing through its walls. He could almost hear the palace breathing.

"Tell me, Jason," the king said as they walked through the hall, surrounded by sinuous walls and spiralling columns. "What happened to Alamor? I would have very much liked to speak to him. He was a controversial character, but he has helped us in a significant way by finding you and helping you get here," said the king.

"He's not with us anymore. Anyir and I were crossing the Stonevale when a pair of Omüms attacked us. Alamor led them away from us, and we haven't seen him since. Only recently, when I went to seek Öken's help on the top of Mount Dormund and met Tortugal and the Omüms again, I found out about Alamor's fate. Darkstrom killed him on the streets of Orachlion. I think he was about to cross over to Erythya, but the Emperor got him before he made it to Sasken."

Upon hearing the news, Kavanagh stopped and lowered his head in grief. "I am very sorry to hear that, Jason. My deepest condolences. Although Alamor and I—or Alamor and many other Erythians, for that matter—didn't have the best of relationships, I realise you and he had become very close. He was, after all, your mentor. I have no doubt Alamor fought valiantly, and I am sure that dying while battling our greatest enemy secured him a well-deserved spot in the Eredom. We will have a wake in his honour."

"Thank you for your kind words," Jason replied.

"It's no problem at all, Jason. Now, however, we must celebrate your arrival and speak about what is ahead of us. You represent a priceless opportunity, Jason, to do what Alamor couldn't. If the Erythian Crown and the Order of Lightbringers can work together once again, then we stand a chance against the Emperor."

They proceeded along the corridors towards the Throne Room. When they reached an immense wooden double door, Kavanagh put a hand on it and pushed, revealing a cavernous white room with a large alabaster throne sat on the opposite side beneath a tall stained-glass window. Their steps echoed as they walked into the room. The grand catenary arches, the cream white walls and the soaring ceilings gave the room an airy and fresh atmosphere, and the wide windows with wooden frames meant one could enjoy the beautiful view of the capital in all its glory from within the palace walls. Around the throne, long tables made of cedar wood were arranged in a U-shape and set with the finest china and silverware in all of Erythya.

Right by the alabaster throne, there was a pillar made of amethyst. Sitting in a small pocket carved inside the deep purple stone was a pyramidal object the size of a Rubik's cube made of bronze and gold, with carvings and precious stones all over it. Jason couldn't believe it.

"Is that what I think it is?" Jason dared to ask.

"It is indeed—the Steinndyrr," Kavanagh replied. "Valkadia's most precious possession, as well as its most dangerous object."

Jason was in awe. It was such a precious-looking device, so small and yet so powerful. It glowed with an aura of green and blue, like the colour of the Northern Lights. The Steinndyrr was mystical, and it was Jason's way back home. He was so close to the one device that could bring him back to the Otherside, back to his family, back to where he could mourn Clara in peace. He wished he could just take it and activate it and disappear. Yet he knew he couldn't. He was a Lightbringer now, and he had come all that way to resolve something much greater than his own life.

"It wouldn't be dangerous if it weren't for Darkstrom," Baldor commented.

"That's true, although I fear that if Darkstrom weren't after the Steinndyrr, there would be someone else in his place. It is an object as old as Valkadia itself, and older than the Otherside too, holding together the balance between our two worlds. Since its creation, many have tried to put their hands on it," Kavanagh told.

"What stops people from getting to it?" Anyir asked.

"For a long time, it was the Lightbringers that protected it. Now, it's a lot of enchantments. Only those with a strong enough Flare or a rightful king can get past the defences that keep it safe," Rhulani replied.

"And only the king of Erythya can activate it, although Darkstrom believes otherwise," Baldor explained.

"So Darkstrom couldn't get to it even if he made it to Niteria?" Jason asked.

"That's right. But that's why Lok is so important to him—or was before he lost his powers. His powerful Flare was the key to get past the enchantments, but that key has been passed onto you now, Jason McAnnon," said king Kavanagh.

"You know about that—the origin of my powers?" Jason enquired.

"Of course, Jason. I'm the king of Erythya."

Waiting patiently by the entrance to the Throne Room, were an elegant woman and an impatient teenager, both dressed in noble attire. It was clear the girl had been waiting eagerly for the arrival of the Lightbringer and the beginning of the feast, as she rocked back and forth on her heels and toes uncontrollably.

"Jason—and friends—I present to you my fierce and beautiful partner in life, queen Emiliya, and our daughter, princess Thurin, heiress to the throne," introduced the king, motioning towards his family.

Queen Emiliya was indeed beautiful, with long and curly dark hair and penetrating green eyes. A dainty silver tiara rested on her head, and the green emerald embedded in the middle matched perfectly the colour of her green velvet dress, decorated with silver thread. She stood elegantly upright with her chest pushed forward, the sign of many years of being accustomed to the manners of a royal lifestyle. In contrast, Thurin looked like a typical teenager forced to wear elegant clothes at a family gathering—uncomfortable and eager to rebel. With a thin crown that lay precariously upon her short dark hair and eyes the colour of fire, Thurin looked like she wanted to be Dolores O'Riordan, the lead singer of the Cranberries.

"It's a pleasure, ser Jason," said Thurin, awkwardly approaching the Lightbringer with her hand extended rigidly to Jason.

Jason shook his hand firmly, but he was confused by the way he had just been addressed, "The pleasure is mine, Your Highness. I am unsure whether I would class as a *ser*, however…"

"A Lightbringer is automatically recognised as a knight, my friend," the king replied. "You are a protector of our land, and your abilities make you a far more valiant warrior than any nobleman that inherited a rusty sword from their father."

"Is it true you can kill people by shooting light rays out of your eyes?" the princess asked excitedly.

Jason laughed loudly, caught off guard. "I've not tried that yet," he answered. "If I ever manage to do that, I'll make sure you'll be the first one to know!"

"What a great honour it is to meet a real Lightbringer," the queen interjected, her dark curly hair waving as she curtsied.

"I feel fortunate to be here," Jason replied, holding her hand and kissing the back of it gently, just like he had seen done on many medieval-themed movies.

The queen smiled at Jason and blushed, and then raised her eyebrows in surprise when she saw who was accompanying the Lightbringer. "Rhulani, I can't believe you're here too!"

The two women embraced and remained in each other's arms for a few seconds.

"It's so great to see you, dear old friend," Emiliya said. "And it's great to have you all here," she told everyone.

The king clapped his hands and rubbed them together, looking at Jason with anticipation. "Well, now that we all know each other, let the feast begin!"

XXXI

A GHOST IN NITERIA

When Grando and Alamor finally arrived at the edge of Niteria, delimited by crop allotments and farmer's houses beneath the forest canopy, they could hear music and cheers from afar. It was clear Jason had arrived. The city was filled with fervour and joy.

"Not the time for celebrations", Alamor muttered sternly. "Lok is here, I can sense it."

Grando led the wagon through the Gate of Unity, but they were soon stopped by the sea of creatures that had come from all over Erythya to see the new Lightbringer. Before Grando could protest, Alamor jumped off the wagon, his jaw clenching as he landed.

"What do you think you're doing, old git? You're not strong enough yet!" the bearded man protested.

"Stay here," Alamor told the alchemist, his eyes already inspecting the crowd.

"What do you mean 'stay here'? You'll get killed for real this time!" he yelled, but the Veheer had already darted into the crowd, limping on his left leg. In just a few seconds, he had disappeared into the buzzing streets of Erythya's capital.

Crouching behind the bushes and the trees to hide from the Erythian guards, Alamor made his way into the alleys of the city. His wounds ached as he ran, but the adrenaline rushing through his veins compelled him to ignore the pain.

As he made his way along the streets, the crowds feasting and rejoicing for the return of the Lightbringer were dense, jam-packed with people playing music, serving food and dancing in the streets. Stubbornly, the Veheer squeezed through various groups of Niterian folk, occasionally shouldering people to get past. Finally, up ahead in the distance and poking in the space between two buildings, Alamor spotted one of the golden domes of the Ærindel. The palace looked less than ten minutes away, but with the crowd flooding against him, it would take him hours to arrive. He felt like a salmon trying to swim upstream of a mighty river.

Then, Alamor stopped. The ghost that had tormented his consciousness for all those years suddenly appeared before him.

Lok.

He was dressed in full-clad Erythian armour, golden and cobalt. Even disguised, Alamor was sure it was him. Lok too was slithering through the crowd, hiding in the shadows of the colonnades and the houses. Like a jaguar that had spotted its prey, Lok silently prowled towards the Ærindel.

Alamor sped up, limping and clutching his wounded shoulder, not caring anymore about being seen by the soldiers who scouted the capital. Alamor hurried along the cobbled road and pushed people aside carelessly, fearing he might never reach the Ærindel before Lok did. He had to stop Lok and take him to the Ærindel himself. He didn't know how, but he expected that, without his powers, Lok wouldn't pose too much of a challenge.

However, before he knew it, Lok had managed to make his way up the crowd a lot faster than Alamor did. "Lok!" he shouted, but the Shadowcaster didn't hear him. "Lok!" The second time Lok turned around, but not being able to find who had called his name, he only worried and accelerated. Swiftly, he took the first turn left into a smaller alley with fewer people.

Alamor ran after him, his head low as to not be spotted, gritting his teeth at every step he made. Hearing the rapidly approaching steps of his pursuer, Lok turned, bitterly glaring at the old Veheer. For a brief moment, they locked eyes. Then, with the lethal dexterity of a wild cat, Lok sped up, stealthily leaping from shadow to shadow. Alamor followed fast, sweating and out of breath. Lok might have lost his powers, but he still retained a warrior's instinct and strength. Alamor's lungs burned, but he ignored the pain. This wouldn't be the time his body gave up on him.

Frustrated, Lok aimed at a pile of wooden boxes, stacked tall, idly resting by a fruit stall. The crates crashed helplessly to the ground, inadvertently obstructing Alamor's pursuit. Apples and oranges fell onto the cold ground, but these weren't enough to stop the old Lightbringer. Alamor jumped over the obstacle and hurtled his way down the street, his weakened leg almost buckling under the weight.

Bystanders looked at each other with indignation, surprised anybody would disrupt the city's peacefulness—especially at a time of celebration. Though Niterians would often get inebriated on mead, nobody ever became quarrelsome, and certainly nobody had ever seen a Veheer chasing an Erythian soldier.

Lok swerved into a different street, this time to the right. Alamor dashed in the same direction, but by the time he arrived, Lok had vanished. He looked around, and to his dismay, he saw a pair of Erythian guards walking towards his direction.

Alamor ran into the nearest dark alley and pressed against the wall of a house to hide from the soldiers. Once he was sure they had walked past him, he took a moment to breathe before recommencing his pursuit. Suddenly, a hard fist crashed against Alamor's back, shooting spiteful needles along his spine. The invisible enemy grabbed the old Lightbringer by his tattered green tunic, and forcefully launched him to the ground. When Alamor looked up, he saw Lok's deathly eyes looming over him.

Without waiting, Alamor grabbed Lok's legs with both his hands and pulled forcefully, making the Shadowcaster violently hit the floor. Lok waited for no one and launched his body on top of Alamor's, hammering his fists into the Veheer's face.

"You? Again? What do you want?" Lok barked as his knuckles hit Alamor's cheekbone, splitting his skin.

Alamor grabbed one of Lok's arms and flung him to the side. "You can't kill Jason!" he shouted.

"Why not?" Lok growled.

"Have you ever wondered why Jason took your powers?" Alamor punched Lok in the ribs, making him cough. "He's your brother!" he shouted, feeling an unsurmountable amount of relief when those words finally left his lips. "You *share* the Flare! You cannot kill him!"

Lok's expression went from deadly to deranged. "What did you say?!"

"You and Jason. You two are bro—" but Alamor couldn't finish his sentence as Lok kicked him with both legs in the stomach, making him fly against the wall on the opposite side of the alley. The Veheer slowly rose, holding his aching ribs, blood trickling from his mouth. He breathed in and looked into the Shadowcaster's blazing eyes, doing his best to stand upright. "You are brothers!" he declared from the top of his voice.

Lok said nothing for a moment. Instead, he pulled the kopís out of its scabbard and pointed it at Alamor's throat. "You're lying," he croaked. "Jason is nothing but a thief and a coward. We are *not* brothers."

"Stop being so blind, Lok. Why do you think he was able to take your Flare? You share blood as much as your powers. You two are both sons of Elgan Lannvard." Alamor muttered.

"You're lying!" Lok screeched.

The Shadowcaster tightened his grip on the kopís, eyes ablaze, fully intent on gutting his rival's throat. As his arm moved to strike, a soldier's voice pierced through the alley.

"Hey! What's going on here?!" the man in golden armour shouted.

Lok glanced at him and then turned back to Alamor. "Consider yourself lucky," he said before hurriedly rushing into the shadows.

Two hefty soldiers charged towards Alamor and landed on him, binding his arms behind his back. "Stay still!" they shouted. "Who are you?!"

"Let me go!" Alamor yelled back, with his face pressed against the hard cobbles. "You don't know what you're doing, let me go!"

"You assaulted a soldier!" they stated. "You'll have to come with us!"

The hefty weight of the soldiers on his back began to compress Alamor's lungs, who struggled to breathe. "Get off me! You *need* to let me go! That wasn't a soldier. That was Lok!" he said, his voice impaired.

The soldiers finally eased their weight off him, but still kept his hands bound. "What did you just say?"

"That's not a soldier! It was Lok. He is heading towards the Ærindel. I was trying to stop him, and I would have caught him if you didn't capture me. Now the king and the new Lightbringer are in danger..."

The two soldiers looked at each other, panicked. "How do you know all that, old man?"

"I am Alamor Eklund—the *old* Lightbringer."

"How do we know you're not lying?"

"By Rotar's beard... do you really think I'd make this all up? We have no time to waste, Lok must be apprehended before he gets to the Ærindel!"

The guards knitted their eyebrows and looked at each other smugly as they silently made their decision. Alamor thought he had convinced them when one of them grinned, but they instead grabbed a pair of steel manacles and swiftly bound the Veheer's hands. Obstinately, they pulled him off the floor from under his arms and ordered, "You're coming with us."

"You pair of fools! You're making a huge mistake!"

"What are you going to do about it?" the soldier threatened.

Alamor looked at him fiercely, then forcefully bashed his forehead against the soldier's, who fell to the floor, confused. Before the other guard could get anywhere near Alamor, the old Lightbringer closed his fists tightly, electric bolts sizzling between his fingers. A bolt of scorching lightning fell from the sky and, like butter, the manacles melted under the voltage of Alamor's sorcery. He was free again. Alamor's pointy ears perked up at the clangour of armour down the street—more soldiers were approaching, making their way through the crowd. Before they could see him, the Veheer brought forth another thundering bolt of lightning, landing it squarely at the soldiers' feet.

Alamor darted back into the crowd. Lok couldn't have gone far.

There is still time, he thought, as he fretfully ran towards the Ærindel.

XXXII

HYMN OF THE SUMMER ROSE

The doors at the back of the Throne Room burst open, and a quartet of flute, violin, drums and a singer entered the room, playing a melody that Jason recognised well, as it was one of Grando's favourites. It was the Hymn of the Summer Rose.

Through the dark shall light pierce unrelenting.
Over stones shall the roots of oaks thrive.
After years will the fire come bursting
from the mountains long thought not alive...

As they all enjoyed the folky sounds of the famous Erythian song, which filled the air with joyful notes, a caravan of maids entered the room. They smiled and swanned to the rhythm of the music, carrying large silver platters overflowing with food. Soon after, they were followed by footmen serving jugs filled with mead and pots full of aromatic Oreka tea. The servers were dressed in bright colours, and they danced energetically as they brought fragrant food of all sorts, reminding Jason of scenes from the Disney movie *Fantasia*.

"Take your seats, my friends! It's time to celebrate!" announced king Kavanagh.

"I can't wait, I'm starving!" said Kiro.

With eager anticipation, the guests sat down at the elegantly laid out table. There were more gold-rimmed porcelain plates and crystal glasses than Jason had ever seen, and at least ten different pieces of silverware had been set for each person. Everything was sparkling clean, and the napkins were made of luxurious white linen. The servers daintily filled the table with plates brimming with roasted vegetables, mounds of cheeses, brightly coloured and juicy fruit, buttery baked goods. Jason looked over to Anyir, who smiled at him with twinkling eyes and a gleeful grin.

Then, a thunderous crash echoed through the Throne Room, sending the waiters and dancers into a frenzy. The guests gasped and yelped as the largest window in the throne room exploded, spraying tinted shards of glass all over the feasting table, ruining the lavish foods.

Bursting through the glass, a golden figure descended upon the diners, cracking the cedar wood surface as it landed. Jason knew who it was in an instant, his blood chilling. Like a demon from the underworld, Lok's black hair flowed ominously over golden armour, his Erythian kopís emitting a deathly shimmer.

Instinctively, the group extracted their weapons. Isidir's blade rung sharply as Jason gripped it tightly in his hands. All the maids and footmen rushed out of the room, clamouring in fear. Jason's mind was racing, and his blood was pumping fast. He had finally come face to face with his dreaded adversary.

"Lok," Jason murmured, looking intently into the eyes of the man standing in front of him, who gazed back menacingly at him. The time of their encounter had finally come.

Kavanagh turned to Dorean Amble, who cowardly hid behind a wall. "Ser Amble, take the queen and the prince somewhere safe!" he shouted commandingly. Tentatively, Dorean moved Emiliya and Thurin away from the Throne Room and hurried them back through the corridors of the Ærindel.

"You!? You killed my husband, you bastard!" Anyir erupted. With unbelievable speed, she pulled an arrow out of her quiver and placed it on her bow, ready to shoot.

Jason quickly reacted by lowering his friend's weapon. "Not yet," he said.

"He killed him, Jason! He killed Oblivan!"

"Oh, was that your husband? So sad. I feel so unbelievably guilty,"

Lok derided. Then, he turned to Jason. "Give me my powers back, you fraud," he growled.

"I'm the fraud? You had powers that could change the world, and you used them for evil, passing yourself as the bloodstained paladin of Remara. You don't deserve these powers."

"And what are you? The newfound hero of Erythya? You're a nobody, Jason. If you need these powers to be somebody, then you're a joke."

"I don't need your approval, Lok. I'm just someone who arrived at the right time, to take the Flare away from you and stop you from causing irreversible damage to both Valkadia and the Otherside. Why do you even want to help Darkstrom open the Elder Stones? What's in it for you?"

"What's in it for me?" Lok repeated ironically. He composed himself, growing stern. "Glory beyond belief", he then replied. "Erythya has obstructed the progress of Valkadia for hundreds of years, and they continue to refute the inevitable triumph of the Empire. King Rennhall cursed us Humans by locking us in this god-forsaken land, and Darkstrom and I will be treated like gods when we finally free our people."

"A god? You? There is no way you'll be treated like a god when all you know is how to kill."

"My people will fear me like a god of war and death, and they will respect me. They will do as I say, and we will bring order to this messy, rebellious world. No unruly magical creatures will ever stop our progress again."

"Is that your goal? To be an obedient dog to the dictator of a barren land? Because that's all you'll be. Besides, without your powers, you're worthless to him. You are nobody to the Emperor, but you could be somebody if you help me defeat him. We can create a better Valkadia for everyone, where the land is fertile, and people are treated fairly."

"Listen to me, you free-spirited scum. I will never join you. What I *will* do, however, is get my powers back." What he said next gave Jason chills under his skin. "*Seynhar!*" he ordered.

For a moment, there was a silence, and everyone stood stock-still, unable to fathom what horrors the infamous command would unleash. Then, like a wave growing by the second, a flood of screams arose from the people crowding in the streets of Niteria. Lok, Darkstrom's trusted servant, had the power to transform anybody who pledged their soul to the Emperor into Fímegir. Though Niteria seemed peaceful, it had been infiltrated by Remaran spies who were now transforming into blood-thirsty monsters.

"What have you done…" Jason murmured, as the sound of war horns filled the capital. "Baldor, Rhulani! Help protect the entrance to the Ærindel!" he shouted.

His two Erythian companions nodded and swiftly rushed back through the palace to join the soldiers in the front lines.

"Anyir, Kiro, I need you to watch my back. Öken, please follow the king somewhere safe and stay with him—we need you alive to help us make the tracker work."

"Screw that," king Kavanagh said, clutching the hilt of his very own Elven sword, *Dolear*. "The Ærindel has never fallen, and I'm not letting it happen on my watch."

"I'm not going anywhere either, Jason," Öken replied. "If I'm the only one alive after this, what's the point of fixing the tracker?" As he said this, the Breegan pulled a regular-looking stick from his boot, but when he pressed a button on the side, it unfolded mechanically into a sturdy steel double-headed axe.

Jason looked at the axe as it transformed, dumbfounded. "Where'd you get that? What—did you have that all along?"

The Breegan smiled, a cunning glint in his eye. "A Breegan always has something resourceful up their sleeve, Lightbringer. We're not to be underestimated." He lifted the weapon, casting into a fighting stance. This time, he was ready for battle.

A pair of Fímegir entered the Throne Room from the window, moving like vicious predators and showing their gnarly teeth. They threw themselves at Anyir and Kiro, who combined their powers to create a flaming tornado and used it to propel the beasts across the hall. Kavanagh and Öken ran to their aid as more monsters flooded in, leaving Jason to face the Shadowcaster.

Lok stood on the opposite side of the Throne Room with glass scattered around his feet. He scowled at Jason, veins bulging on his neck and temples. "What a nice little group of friends you've got there, *fraud*," Lok snarled. "Powers, friends… You probably grew up in a nice little family too. You had everything, and you took all that was mine. Now, you'll die for your wrongdoings." Lok launched himself against Jason, spinning his sword around maniacally.

The clangour of metal resonated in the hall as the blades of Isidir and the kopís collided. The force of Lok's blow was greater than Jason expected. His adversary was strong, but Jason's Flare was stronger. Without wasting a second, Jason blasted Lok against the opposite wall with a violent gust of wind, so potent the limestone of the wall cracked where the Shadowcaster had landed.

Lok stood up and dusted himself off, stupefied but outraged. "Not bad, Lightbringer. I see how your mind works. However, it's nothing I've not trained for." He grinned perversely and rammed against Jason. The Lightbringer held his sword low and readied for the incoming series of slashes coming in his direction. Jason parried the first hit, but Lok was too skilled and quick and managed to drive his blade along Jason's right side, severing his skin. Warm blood began dripping from the open gash, but Jason had no time to stop and inspect the damage.

Jason swung Isidir and hit Lok's kopís twice before getting kicked hard in the gut by the Shadowcaster's armoured foot. Lok grabbed hold of Jason's head with his hands and slammed it against his kneecap ferociously. There was a sharp crack as Jason's nose broke under the force of the impact. Crimson blood trickled from both his nostrils, and he felt a mixed sense of dizziness and numbness. Then, Lok drew his fist back, and ploughed it into Jason's stomach.

Furious, Jason summoned fire with his Flare and a river of flames burst out of his hands, heating Lok's armour until it became scolding. With a screech, Lok let go of Jason's head and jumped back, allowing Jason to attack.

Before Jason even managed to lower his Isidir's blade, Lok used Jason's momentum to grab his legs and throw him off balance. The Lightbringer fell with his back against the cracked banquet table, breaking it in half. Stunned yet focused, Jason sprung back up and, with a swift movement of his wrist, made the shards of wood and glass levitate in the air. A rain of sharp fragments flew at bullet speed against Lok, but the Erythian armour he stole was too thick for the ballistics to dent. Only a small fragment of glass managed to scrape Lok's cheek, and a small trickle of blood rolled down his face.

"What are you waiting for? Is this all you can do with my powers?" Lok confronted. "Where is the famous light you're meant to harness? Aren't you a Lightbringer?!"

Lok was right, thought Jason. All the other elements were listening to him, but the light wasn't. It was as if the Flare refused to fully operate at that moment.

Jason looked over to his companions, who had already slaughtered the two Fímegir but were already waiting for more incoming beasts from the corridors and windows of the palace. Outside, the agonised screams of mauled soldiers and dying civilians filled the air.

Lok leapt and kicked Jason in the shin before slicing him again, this time in the arm. Jason found himself struggling to predict Lok's attacks. The Shadowcaster was too skilled and too precise, the result of a lifetime of training. If Jason were to win, he would have to use his powers and manage to succeed summoning the power of light.

Exasperated, Jason concentrated on the large slab of wood from the broken table and hurled it at Lok, catapulting him out of the window and onto the hard, cobbled ground of the Elven Road.

※

Anyir picked up arrow after arrow and shot her flaming darts at the ferocious monsters that leapt at her and her companions. There were far more Fímegir than they had faced at the Fyris Pass, and this time they were backed by the many Remaran spies who fought with wicked sorcery. Niteria crawled with enemies, and they had all been unleashed at once.

As a Fímegir jumped at Kiro, a Remaran soldier propelled a jet of ice at Anyir, blocking her incoming arrow. Readily, Anyir shot a stream of fire out of her hand, melting the ice and engulfing her enemy. Her fire had grown strong. The spy's garments caught fire, and dropped to the floor, rolling to extinguish the flames as he screamed. The violence of her act and the smell of burning flesh gave her a sudden sense of nausea.

Beside her, Kiro, Öken and Kavanagh fought valiantly, but her skin chilled at the sight of Jason facing Lok. Deep in her heart, a fire of revenge brewed as she stared down the man who had killed her husband. She raised her bow and aimed a blazing arrow at the Shadowcaster. She thought she could hit him without striking Jason, but the two men kept changing position as they fought. There just wasn't a way to kill Lok without harming Jason. Anyir's attempt was cut short by another attack from a Fímegir, forcing her to use the flaming dart on the scaly monster, which dropped dead at her feet with a thud.

"Anyir! There are more outside! We must go help Rhulani and Baldor," said Kiro.

She looked back at Lok once more, hoping Jason would survive the Shadowcaster's wrath. Then, she followed the Faun, the king and the Breegan outside of the Ærindel. When they saw what laid out of the palace's doors, Anyir froze. An immense battle had broken out in the streets of Niteria. Grey monsters and soldiers in gold battled to the death everywhere she glanced. The deafening clangour of swords and the dying cries of warriors filled the city. Anyir looked at the king, who stood petrified as he looked at the butchery that had unfurled outside his palace. His eyes were wide open, unable to blink.

Not far from the Ærindel, Rhulani and Baldor were fighting side by side. As the Dryad decapitated the monsters with her glaive, the Half-Giant crushed his challengers by summoning the earth. Seeing his friends in danger, Kiro was the first one to act. Brandishing his daggers, he threw himself into the fighting masses. Öken and Kavanagh followed, but Anyir was unable to move. Her bow rested in her trembling hand, and she couldn't take her gaze off the burning city, the dying soldiers, the torn down buildings. Nothing could have ever prepared her for that.

A war horn suddenly brayed, and a legion of Erythian soldiers swarmed into the city streets. Leading them was a valiant woman, skilfully slashing her way through the army of beasts with her kopís. Her hair was long and fair, and one of her arms was missing, bandaged haphazardly with torn rags tainted in ruby blood. Anyir had heard of her. Commander Sigrid Gudmund—a legend, known for surviving the worst situations and facing the most formidable enemies.

The reinforcements provided by Sigrid's legion were immense, brushing the monsters aside like insects. Sigrid shouted encouragement to her troops and ordered them to push forward. Her leadership gave each soldier heart and hope, and the Remarans suddenly found themselves dreadfully outnumbered and out skilled. The legion split into two factions, rampaging through the disordered yet ferocious Remaran mob. The Fímegir screeched and wriggled in pain as the soldiers crushed their attack. The Erythian soldiers rode through the monsters' corpses and pulled the spears and swords out of the bodies to throw them back at the other beasts that assaulted them.

Anyir grasped her bow tightly as she watched the battle unfold in front of her. When a Fímegir suddenly jumped on Sigrid's horse and pulled the commander off her saddle, Anyir readily lifted her bow and knocked an arrow on the string. The burning dart flew across the Elven Road and struck the beast, saving Sigrid from its razor-sharp fangs. The commander stood up incredulous and looked over at Anyir. She smiled and nodded thankfully, and then swung her kopís around as another Fímegir attacked, readily decapitating it. Then, she disappeared amid the fighting masses. Anyir lifted her bow and knocked another arrow, ready to strike the monsters that threatened her friends.

✳

Lok was crawling on the ground of the Elven Road, dragging himself towards a collapsed wall.

"You're not bad, Jason," the Shadowcaster groaned, "but you're a waste of time if you can't summon light. You're such a disappointing adversary."

To Jason's surprise, Lok still had enough energy to pounce at him. The Shadowcaster tackled the Lightbringer to the ground, pinning him down with his muscular weight. Before Jason could fight back, Lok began bashing his armoured fists into his face.

"Give me back my powers!" Lok barked. "I'll kill you if I have to!"

The brute force of Lok's punches sent Jason's head bashing against the cobbled street. Though he could heal quickly, the damage inflicted by the Shadowcaster was too fast and too strong to recover in time. He felt drowsy; his Flare wasn't listening. He felt helpless, air struggling to seep into his lungs. His vision grew darker as his adversary kept walloping him, trying to squeeze his powers out of him.

Suddenly, a blinding beam of incandescent light flashed before Jason's eyes, hitting Lok in the chest. The ray's brightness was more intense than a star, and the Shadowcaster was catapulted to the ground, unconscious, freeing the photographer from his wrath.

When Jason looked up through his swollen eyes to make sense of what happened, he saw a familiar face standing a few feet away.

"Alamor?!" Jason gasped with his mouth full of blood. "Alamor? Is that really you? I thought you were dead!"

"Jason!" the Veheer exclaimed. "I'm… I'm very much alive, son." Before he could walk up to Jason, Alamor's knees buckled, and he fell to the ground. He had used the very last remnants of his Flare.

"Alamor!" Jason yelled, rushing to his mentor's aid. He lifted the old Veheer and quickly realised how severely wounded he was. His left clavicle had been snapped and his tunic was tattered with blood around his chest. "Alamor, stay with me!" he cried, his eyes tearing up. The noises surrounding them became muffled. At that moment, there were only him and Alamor.

The Veheer's droopy eyes opened slightly, and he mustered the last strands of energy to talk to his apprentice. "Listen, Jason... there is something I need to tell you," Alamor began. "It's about you and Lok..." With great effort, the old Veheer tried to get the words out, but his voice grew quieter, until there was only a whisper. "He's your... he's your br... he's..."

"He's what, Alamor? What are you saying?" Jason cried. The old Lightbringer was dying before his eyes, and he felt hopeless. Memories of his mentor flashed through Jason's mind, from the very first time he had seen the Veheer in the Iron Wood to the day he disappeared in the dust of the Stonevale. "Alamor!" the young Londoner insisted, shaking his friend's depleted body. The Veheer's wrinkled eyes looked at Jason endearingly.

Before Alamor could finish his last words, a looming shadow appeared in front of them. With bloodshot and deranged eyes, Lok drove the kopís into Alamor's stomach, silencing him forever. The blade pierced through his torso, sending dark blood splattering all over Jason. Alamor gave his successor a last look before his eyes went vacant and he took his true last breath.

"Alamor?" Jason called. "No!" He cried, his voice breaking. "You bastard!" Jason was about to get up and launch himself at the Shadowcaster when a deafening explosion drove both him and Lok violently into the wall of a house nearby. For a while, everything went black.

When Jason regained consciousness, he found himself amid rubble and smoke. For a moment, Jason forgot where he was. He slowly stood up and looked around, the wound on his arm throbbing and his head ringing. Lok was lying a few meters away, covered in rubble and blood, unconscious. Corpses of Fímegir and Erythian soldiers were scattered all around.

"We need to bring him to the Ærindel, quickly," a muffled voice was shouting.

Jason's vision was blurry, but he could make out the shape of a familiar man with a bushy beard lifting the Veheer's body and carrying him through the remains of buildings. The Elven Road now looked closer to a derelict war site rather than the prestigious street of the pristine Erythian capital. *Grando?*

Then, two people rushed to Jason's aid and lifted the Lightbringer from under his arms.

"Jason!" they called. "Are you ok?" Kiro and Anyir kept asking.

He wasn't. He felt as if he couldn't breathe. Throughout his whole time in Valkadia, nobody he had actually been close to had died. Sure, he had experienced death, and he had even crushed Tortugal and his soldiers at the Fyris Pass, but nobody had been executed like that in front of him. He felt a nauseous sensation pushing through his stomach. The vision of Lok's blade piercing through Alamor's abdomen and blood spurting out replayed in Jason's mind over and over and over again. His ears rang, and his knees buckled as his two companions dragged him to the Ærindel. How unfair and gruesome the world was, he thought. Just when he had reunited with his mentor, he had been taken away from him.

The eerie voice of a murderer echoing in the warzone quickly snapped the Lightbringer out of his grieving thoughts.

"Give me the Steinndyrr, or the king dies."

To Jason's horror, the Shadowcaster held Kavanagh hostage and pressed the king's own sword, Dolear, against his throat. Distracted by Alamor's death, Jason had lost track of Lok for a moment. "I'm sure you realise this sword cuts necks like butter," Lok said as he grinned, his mouth full of blood.

"I thought it was your powers you wanted," Jason responded.

"It doesn't matter anymore. Darkstrom will only take me back if I bring him the Steinndyrr. I don't need my powers if I can let *you* do the work."

"We can come to an agreement, Lok," Jason implored. "I will give you my powers back if you let him go, but I cannot let you take the Steinndyrr."

"Don't give him your powers, Jason!" Kavanagh bellowed. "You're the only one who can defeat the Emperor. It doesn't matter if I die."

Lok smirked. "Don't be stupid, Jason. You know that's not a deal I'm willing to accept. It was great to have powers, but I'm here now. This is the end of my mission, and my mission was to get the Steinndyrr. If killing the king is what it takes, I *will* kill the king. I've got nothing more left to lose."

Jason looked at his companions, who watched apprehensively as the scene unfolded. None of them knew what to do. The stakes were too high.

The young Londoner felt as if he had just drunk five espressos in a row—his heart was pounding, and his mind was racing.

"All right," Jason sighed. "I'll give you the Steinndyrr, but on one condition: you can't come back looking for your powers. From this moment on, you surrender your powers to me. If you want the Steinndyrr that badly, that's the price you must pay."

Lok remained silent for a moment, piercing into Jason's eyes as he considered the options. "Your friends stay here," he growled.

"That's not the deal," Jason rebutted, but Lok simply pushed the blade closer to Kavanagh's neck, drawing a drop of blood. "Fine," Jason said resolutely. "You guys stay here. If we're not back in ten minutes, come rescue us." His companions nodded, respecting Jason's choice and placing full trust upon him. The time for Jason's duty as Lightbringer and protector of Valkadia had come, and now he was on his own.

Jason walked in front of Lok and Kavanagh, leading the way to the Throne room. Every so often, he'd look back to see if the king was safe, and continued walking.

When they finally entered the Throne Room, a gruesome battlefield sprawled before them. The corpses of Erythian soldiers and *Fimegir* carpeted the marble ground. The large alabaster throne had streaks of red blood sprayed on it, but the amethyst column in the middle of the room had been left untouched, and the Steinndyrr dwelled safely inside it.

Jason walked across the room, and as he got closer and closer to the pillar, he felt his energy depleting. The ancient magic keeping the Steinndyrr safe was strong. Every step he took a new enchantment assaulted him, syphoning his power, weighing him down, stinging his body from the inside out. Without the Flare, his soul would have been drained of all its energy, and his body consumed to the bone. When he reached the pillar and moved to grab the mystical pyramidal object, a burning sensation assailed him, as if he had just put his hand inside a scorching fire. Yet, he didn't get burnt or injured, though the pain was excruciating. Groaning, he tried to overcome the agony and quickly removed the Steinndyrr from its place in the amethyst pillar. Before even his Flare would succumb to the enchantments, Jason rushed away.

Jason turned to Lok, "What now?"

"Give the Steinndyrr to me, and I'll let the king go."

Jason found himself utterly undecided. Even after Lok got what he wanted, there was no guarantee he would let the king free. However, the photographer knew exactly how much Darkstrom's devoted follower wanted the Steinndyrr.

In an instant, he hurled the magical key to the Elder Stones across the room towards Lok. "Think fast!" Jason yelled. Immediately, Lok let go of the king and threw himself in the direction of the incoming golden object. As he grabbed it, Jason focused the into a devastating a ray of light, which shot brutally through his foe. Blood splattered on the limestone walls as Lok's left hand was severed from his arm. The Steinndyrr hit the ground with a clunk, toppling across to the other side of the Throne Room.

Lok fell to the floor in anguish, holding his crimson stump. He looked at Jason with bloodshot eyes and veins throbbing at the side of his head, his dark hair dangling over his forehead. As if spawned from a nightmare, Lok crawled towards the Steinndyrr lying on the marble floor just a few feet away, leaving a streak of blood behind him.

Jason limped across the room and grabbed the Steinndyrr from the ground. "Was all this really worth it?" the Lightbringer asked the Remaran warrior, who glared back at him abhorrently, his mouth twisted into a snarl of angst and hate. Jason's skin crawled as he stared into the Shadowcaster's eyes. Never had he seen someone so unyielding. Then, overwhelmed by the blood loss, Lok fell unconscious with his face pressed against the cold marble.

A unit of soldiers entered the Throne Room. Moments earlier, the king had pressed a button hidden by the side of his throne, alerting the palace's guards. "Your Highness, are you safe?" asked one of the soldiers. Jason's companions followed soon after, hearing the commotion.

"Take him away to the dungeons," Kavanagh replied bitterly. "His time here is done."

Baldor, seeing Jason holding the Steinndyrr in his hands and looking at Lok with a shaken expression, walked up to him and said, "Jason, it's over now."

As if awakening from a bad dream, Jason jolted, and glanced back at Baldor and the rest of his friends surrounding him with a blank face. "What are they going to do with him?"

"They won't kill him, if that's what you're thinking," Rhulani interjected. "There will be a trial, but they'll either keep him in the dungeons or take him to the Brotherhood of Thytelis on Mount Hargon."

Jason looked at the object he was holding tightly and realised what it was. "I need to put this back in its place."

Jason smiled at his companions and proceeded to enter the perimeter of the enchanted pillar. He quickly placed the Steinndyrr back in the pocket carved inside the amethyst and promptly stepped out again. He watched as the soldiers chained Lok up and brought him away from the Throne Room, and into the dungeons beneath the Ærindel. He turned to the king and asked, "What's going to happen to Lok?"

"There will be a trial to decide his fate. You need not worry about it—that's *my* job to do. You've done yours, and I am eternally grateful. The Steinndyrr and I are safe... for now."

"I wish I could have done more. We lost many people today," Jason said.

"That was inevitable," Rhulani interjected. "We did everything we could."

"We'll have a funeral in honour of your friend... Alamor didn't deserve the end that he encountered," Kavanagh said.

"Thank you," Jason murmured.

Just as Niteria returned to its tranquil state after the harrowing battle, a soldier ran into the Throne Room holding a Jaul.

"Sire, sire!" he shouted. "Something terrible happened!"

"What's wrong now?" Kavanagh asked, tired of so many bad news for one day.

"It's... it regards the queen Emiliya and the princess..."

"Yes, what about them?"

"They... They've been kidnapped."

"What did you just say?" the king stuttered, stunned.

"Ser Amble gave me this Jaul, he said you and Jason need to listen," he explained said as he handed the gadget to the king. When Kavanagh flicked the small toggle to initiate the connection, a deep voice resonated from the Jaul.

"Hello, Noes. Hello Jason," the man on the other side croaked. When Kavanagh realised who it was, he froze. "We have the queen and the princess," Darkstrom snarled. "If you want them back and alive, bring me the Steinndyrr in a fortnight. Gather your troops and march them to the Bridge of Whispers. We'll swap our goods there. If you're lucky, there won't be the need for any more bloodshed. Oh, and Jason—I hear Lok met your wrath. I look forward to seeing what Alamor taught you. I hope you'll be a more satisfying adversary than he was." Just like that, the call cut off, leaving the people present in the room dumbfounded.

Kavanagh was the first to break the silence. "If Darkstrom wants a full-on war, then that's what we'll give him. We are ready." He turned to Jason. "We need your help. You're the only one who can defeat the Emperor. Help me get my family back, and let's end this once and for all."

Jason looked at the king, and then at his companions. He drew Isidir once more, and with a resolute tone he declared, "We'll give it everything we've got."

XXXIII

SMOKE ON THE WATER

The sun cast an orange haze in the Erythian sky, reflecting in the ripples of Lake Medes. Jason sat on a bench overlooking the water and flicked through the various sketches in his small leather-bound booklet. He ran his fingers on Clara's portrait, the first drawing he had made at the Leynahüs, and thought of all the events that brought him to that particular bench. Since the day he left his small apartment in London, he never thought he would end up here, as a Lightbringer. Though Clara was gone, Jason thought she would be proud of what he had achieved. Still, he missed her dearly. He turned the next page, and Alamor's face appeared. In the sketch, his mentor was sitting under a tree while Jason was practising his swordsmanship. How he would have survived without Alamor's help, Jason did not know.

"Jason," a tender voice called, followed by the rhythmic clapping of a horse's hooves against the soft ground. It was Anyir, accompanied by Silvyr. Silvyr looked whiter than ever, and Anyir was dressed in the most beautifully embroidered emerald tunic. Her hair fluttered in the gentle breeze, and her dress trailed behind her on the grass. She carried her alabaster bow with her—the one Alamor had gifted her. "It's time," she said.

"I'll be right there!" He rushed through the pages of his sketchbook to another drawing he wanted to see before leaving that quiet, idyllic place, and join his friends. It was a sketch of all his companions together the night they met Isaine and the Centaurs. Gregor sat next to Kiro, and the burly man laughed as they all drank mead by the fire. To Jason, it didn't matter what Gregor had done, or how much the Erythians hated Alamor. Valkadia was a testing place, and both men had fought valiantly by his side despite their personal issues. For a moment, he wondered; what had Alamor tried to tell him before Lok killed him? Jason doubted he'd ever find out.

Jason stood up and adjusted his tunic. It was Marigold, just like his old one, but this one had been freshly made for the occasion. Over the heart, using red thread, he had asked the tailor to embroider a simple symbol that Alamor had taught him about during one of their first discussions—Rotar's sun. To Jason, it wasn't just the god of light's symbol, but also an emblem of hope, as it was the first thing he had seen on the Elder Stone after he was washed on the shore of Greenland.

He walked over to his friends and companions, including king Kavanagh and his trusted chamberlain Dorean Amble. They were there to commemorate the bravery and dedication of a fallen warrior. Floating on the water about fifty feet away from the shore was a small boat, on top of which Alamor's body was resting covered by a white linen blanket.

Lady Lera, the amphibian Head Priestess of the Eredomyhm faith, commenced the function by singing in Hæmir with an angelic voice. It was a prayer, but she made it sound like opera, with prolonged, high-pitched vocalisations. It was fascinating yet saddening, a true ode to the sacrifice Alamor had made for Valkadia. When she was done singing, she looked at Jason and nodded.

The photographer's heart was beating fast. He walked on the pier where Lady Lera stood, in front of the whole audience. He had never spoken to so many people, and definitely none as influential as those standing before him that day. Jason cleared his throat, trying to ignore the sweat beginning to form on his forehead.

"Dear friends," he began. "We are gathered here today to commemorate the loss of a true hero, the Lightbringer Alamor Eklund, son of Sehr the Bold. I only knew Alamor for a short while, but he quickly became one of the most important people in my life. It is difficult for me to stand before you and attempt to honour Alamor Eklund—a Veheer, a Lightbringer, a mentor. Alamor took me under his wing when I was clueless and helpless and has made me into someone I am proud to be. His mission has been passed onto me, and I couldn't feel more honoured to bring the Order of the Lightbringers forward. Seeing Alamor fight until his very last breath has given me the drive to continue my journey, and I vow to his soul that I will do whatever is in my power to complete it. I will never forget his teachings, his kind words, his whimsical personality.

"I know some of you might stand here today and still not be able to forgive him for his actions, but from what I learnt in my time here in your world, Alamor was, above all, a Valkadian. He fought for what he thought was right for the future of Valkadia and did what he could to make this land a better place. He indeed made mistakes along the way, but that only makes his last acts more genuine. He was never looking for redemption; he was never looking for acceptance. Alamor only tried to make things right irrespective of what people told him. Now, Alamor's soul will be watching us from the Eredom, reunited with Rotar. Now, the light protects him."

"Light protects him," the audience repeated solemnly in unison.

Farewell, dear friend.

Jason glanced at Anyir, who stood beside her, and nodded, signalling that it was the time to use her bow. She took one of the ceremonial arrows from her quiver and placed the tip over the burning fire by Lady Lera's side, setting it alight. She gracefully put the nock on the bowstring, and with a deep breath, she straightened her back and pulled the arrow resolutely towards her ear. As she let go of the string and the dart hit the boat, there was a roaring blaze as the fire enveloped Alamor's body. Soon, all that was left of the old Lightbringer was smoke dancing on the surface of the water.

Among the crowd of guests, there was somebody that Jason didn't recognise. It was an elderly woman dressed in black, with grey hair and one candid white lock draping down the side of her face. She had symbols and patterns tattooed on her cheeks and forehead, and her eyes were completely white. Yet, those weren't the things to strike Jason the most. It was what was hanging around her neck that caught his attention—the same silver necklace that he had seen in his dreams, with a metal pendant the shape of a droplet.

Before he could tell anybody what he had just seen, the woman vanished. He walked through the crowd to the spot where he had just seen her. In her place, lying on the grass and reflecting the sunset's orange light, was the silver necklace. Speechless, Jason kneeled and picked the necklace off the ground. He was soon joined by his companions, who had spotted his erratic behaviour.

"What is it?" Baldor asked.

"It's the necklace. The one from my dreams."

"The dream with the woman and the two infants, and the Child Snatcher?" Anyir inquired further.

"That's right. I think I just saw her, though she was old. Her eyes were white instead of green, and her hair was grey instead of red, but I'm pretty sure it was her."

"Why would she leave the necklace?" Kiro wondered.

Öken squeezed next to Jason and inspected the necklace. "Whether it has a mystical meaning or not, this necklace is certainly a blessing."

"What makes you say that?" Jason asked.

"Because it's made of Astral Steel," the Breegan replied solemnly. "You know what this means, right?" Öken prodded.

"We can get the tracker to work again," Jason realised. Excitedly, Jason extracted the device from his pocket and handed it to Öken. "Try it."

"Here? Now?"

"Yes. Here and now," Jason responded, his hazel eyes glowing.

"Good thing I always take my tools everywhere," Öken said.

The Breegan took the tracker and opened the back of it using a retractable toolkit. He slid the pendant off the chain and placed the droplet of Astral Metal inside the dedicated slot. When the metal touched the inside of the tracker, the device lit up with a bright green glow and began beeping.

Jason looked at his companions, a bright smile on his face. "Let's go find the Eluir."

A CONDENSED VERSION OF *THE HARMONY OF CREATURES: LIFE IN THE OLDE FORESTS AND THE NEW* BY ROGOR DREYMOS (FOR THE PURPOSES OF THIS BOOK)

ARALAY: A mysterious creature, the Aralay transcends our understanding of nature. It has the body of a stag, with tawny-gold fur and large branch-like antlers. Unlike regular deer, this creature has a pair of strong wings similar to those of an eagle's. A long feathery tail trails behind its sinuous body, helping it move gracefully through the air. The Aralay's habitat and specific behaviour are yet to be fully understood, as few have been able to observe this magnificent beast. From existing accounts and the many fables, it appears that Aralays are benevolent beings. Their antlers are said to grant wishes, its tears can bring back life, and their feathers turn to silver when they shed. The reason they appear and help creatures in distress is unknown, but they do not seem to obey any master, acting upon their own will.

AZUR: The Azurs are water-dwelling people that have evolved to assume almost amphibian characteristics. They inhabit the Lakes of Asghen, between lake Malion and the Lumos Mountains. Azurs typically have blue or blue-green hair, and they display gill-like membranes which protrude from the sides of their face and help them carry out their underwater chores. Their homes float upon the surface of the lakes, and they use an intricate system of buoyant paths to travel from one house to another. Azurs believe in the Eredom, although their traditions are intertwined with those of their hydrophilic ancestors and often have rituals to celebrate their prophet Asgu.

BOLEAR: The Bolear is a large fish, abundant in the waters of Erythian lakes. They have elongated bodies covered in purple iridescent scales, with a bulky head and lengthy tail. They feed upon a variety of insects, flies in particular, which they sense by poking their snout over the water's surface.

They are large, weighing over one-thousand pounds and measuring up to six feet in length.

BREEGAN: Mountain-dwelling folk, Breegans are highly skilled in crafting and engineering. They are short and stocky, covered in a thick black and brown fur, with a bushy mane framing their faces. Breegans have an innate ability to see in the dark. Their society is entirely dependent on resources from the mountains of Valkadia, which they use to power their cities and underground systems. The energy they harness seems to derive from the guts of the earth, and their technology is still unmatched. They do not follow the Eredomyhm belief, as they pray to their ancestors within the mountain. Breegan rituals and traditions seem in complete dichotomy with their advanced machinery. Alas, Breegan people are not as welcoming as before, so studying their society has become problematic. Their kingdom was attacked by Emperor Darkstrom and their people decimated by the Remaran army. Breegans are now secluded to the city of Hegertan, and they refuse to cooperate even with Erythians. Many Breegans have been enslaved over the years by the Remarans, who shave their proud manes to humiliate them.

CENTAUR: These ancient creatures possess the head, torso and arms of a human, but the body and legs of a horse. They roam Erythya in herds, inhabiting mainly the Emerald Fields and the surrounding lands. Centaur society is based on strong social bonds and a strictly matriarchal system. They live in small tribes of forty to fifty individuals, constantly changing allegiances to other groups. Warfare is not uncommon between Centaur tribes, though they are kept in check by the Golden Army, and the conflicts are rarely fatal. They adore drinking wine, feasting, and practising the art of Dengah—in which combatants must fight using two sticks and attempt hitting each other on their equine backs. Centaurs are also known to be irascible and hold grudges.

CYCLOPS: Cyclops are peculiar beings. Much like Half-Giants, they can measure up to fifteen feet in height, but they are more clumsy and less clever. The single eye in the middle limits their peripheral vision, and their large bodies impair their movement. They are native to the Islands of Flagos, where they lead a reserved and highly fish-based life. Cyclops, despite their low acumen, are skilled fishmongers and hard-working Erythians, devoted to the king and to the Eredomyhm faith.

DRYAD: These ancient dwellers of Valkadia, also known as Forest Nymphs, now inhabit the most densely wooded areas of Erythya. Their name derives from an arcane language and is said to signify "protector of the oak tree". Their connection with nature is so strong that they have the ability to communicate with other creatures telepathically. Dryads tend to have tall, elongated bodies with lengthy arms and legs. Their skin is usually green, ranging from pale to dark, with freckles often spotted on their nose and cheeks. Their eyes are uniquely large and of a deep purple, like the colour of amethyst, and their hair is thick and bristly, as if made from roots or lianas. Dryads are skilled warriors and agile beings, although they prefer to live in peace. They worship the gods of the Eredom, and have a particular affection for Tresha, the goddess of fertility, animals and plants.

ELF: *Extinct*. The ancient rulers of Valkadia, tall and slender, with slightly androgenous characteristics. There was little difference in physical appearance between males and females, except of course for their reproductive organs. Elves, much like their descendants—the Veheers—had pointed ears and golden eyes. Their vision and hearing were excellent, about the same acuity as a hawk's, enabling them to spot danger from afar. Their hair, which ranged from a light blue tinge to a dark midnight blue, was usually kept long. Elves were light of foot and agile, making them deadly adversaries. They were highly skilled with the kopís, a traditional weapon that has now been passed down to the Erythian army. The Elves were Children of the Eredom, first to inhabit Valkadia and establish themselves as an intellectually elevated society. Their cities, with their capital Dorth located in the Suraan Hills, were advanced and mostly powered by their transcendent magic. To this day, only Lightbringers come close to equating their superior level of sorcery. Elven culture is still highly present in Valkadian society, with their language, Hæmir, being widely used in sorcery.

EMERALD SWALLOW: Though it looks like a regular swallow, the only apparent physical difference being its green plumage, the Emerald swallow is a rather special magical bird. Native to the Gartruth Forest, this species is about three to six inches long and weighs around two ounces.

They are often seen in flights of around two-hundred individuals, and they have adapted to aerial hunting, feeding mostly on insects. Their bodies are streamlines and their wings pointed, and their tails are forked to allow them greater manoeuvrability in the air. Their iridescent green feathers are deceptively thick and tough, like the exoskeleton of a beetle, which makes them impervious to knives and arrows. In the spring solstice, between sunset and dusk, flights of up to one-million individuals can be seen forming peculiar vortexes and shapes in the sky.

FAUN: These Elf-goat hybrids are a particularly jovial folk. With ram's horns, hairy goat-like legs and hooves, and the pointy ears of an Elf, Fauns are faithful creatures. Their sympathetic, youthful faces are framed with woolly curls, and their cheery smiles make them irresistible to befriend. However, do not let their naïve demeanour deceive you. They are highly intelligent and deadly combatants. Agile and fast, they prefer close range fighting and often brandish weapons such as daggers, clubs and sickles. Most Fauns are woodland dwellers, and many have made their homes in the giant mushrooms of Rodan. They like to live a simple, family oriented life.

FÍMEGIR: These beings are not natural—they have been created by the dark sorcery of Emperor Darkstrom, who takes the souls of Humans in exchange for money, influence, land, food and safety from the Remaran army. After absorbing their soul to increase the power of his dark sorcery, Darkstrom traps his victims in blood-binding contracts, which compel them to transform into the dreaded Fímegir. Thousands upon thousands of people have been subjugated by his spell. Upon hearing the command '*Seynhar*' (transform) the cursed humans, which are often enrolled in the army, shapeshift into abominable creatures. Fímegir resemble a deformed panther cross-bred with a reptile. Their skin is scaly and grey, their claws are long and sickle-shaped, and their fangs are as razor-sharp as steel daggers.

GIANT: *Extinct*. Arriving shortly after the Elves, Giants were among the primordial creatures of Valkadia. Little is known about these mysterious creatures, and most of what we know derives from ancient texts. This monumental, humanoid folk is said to have reached over thirty feet in height, their bodies bulky and muscular, adapted to a highly quarrelsome life. Giants spoke a rudimentary tongue which has never been deciphered, and they followed a particularly gruesome ritualistic religion which involved blood magic. The arrival of Humans, along with disease and internal conflicts, caused the demise of Giants in Valkadia.

GNOME: Gnomes, also known as tiny-folk, are small humanoid beings. They are usually an average height of forty inches, with bodies resembling those of a Human toddler. Their skin is blue and their hair white irrespective of age. Many of them grow long beards and wear tall pointy hats. Their ears are particularly pointy and extremely elongated, an evolutionary feature that allows them to sense predators and gives them time to hide in the Gnome-burrows. They prefer living among hilly areas and feed mostly on potatoes.

GOPLEN: Native to the Stonevale, these mastodontic beasts are the largest terrestrial animal of Valkadia. They have thick, grey skin made of plant matter, and they grow lush gardens on their fertile backs. Their heads are large and square, with yellow beaks very similar to those of a turtle's. As a defence mechanism, they curl up and camouflage into the landscape to appear like small hills. As they need plenty of nutrients to feed their plants, they are often seen by lakes or rivers, bathe and drink, store water within their bodies, and slowly release it as they roam the land. An adult specimen can weigh up to twenty tons and measure more than twenty feet in height. Sadly, many Goplen herds have begun to fall sick ever since Darkstrom's mining campaigns. As metals and other ores are extracted from the ground, the Stonevale became infertile. The pachyderms cannot get enough nutrients, so they resort to drinking contaminated water. The plants growing on their backs are deformed, and the Goplen themselves are deranged, frantically looking for clean sources of water. If that wasn't enough, the Remaran army captures them and uses them as towing animals.

HALF-GIANT: Half-Giants are sizeable humanoid folk with bulky and muscular bodies. They can measure up to ten feet in height. Contrary to most people's belief, Half-Giants are not hybrids between Humans and Giants. Rather, they are the result of a natural selection process which has allowed the smaller individuals to fit in with Valkadian society better than their full-sized counterparts. Less quarrelsome and more intelligent,

Half-Giants have been able to live along Elves and Humans and establish a more tolerant relationship. For long, they retained their rudimentary language and animistic beliefs, but in more recent times they have assimilated with Erythian—in particular Veheer—culture.

MINOTAUR: Although their benevolence has been often questioned, Minotaurs possess a strong heart and a gift for strategy. They are tall peoples, averaging seven feet tall, with the body of a human and the head of a bull. Their skin is covered in thick bovine fur of a variety of colours and patterns. Minotaurs are native to Keri Island, beyond the Strait of Merya, where they live in a highly sociable society and venerate Grimmon, the god of thunders and life. Their houses are typically wooden and circular, with terracotta tiled roofs. Minotaurs raise their children in a collective way, with multiple families dwelling in the same abode. They are lovers of mead and music.

MOLTER: This species of 'flying' fish is most commonly found in the waters of Lake Malion. They have long, thin bodies that resemble those of a moray, with black and blue stripes. Their large orange fins enable it to propel itself out of the water and glide in the air, using their sizeable dorsal fin and tail to adjust their trajectory. Molters can reach up to one foot in length, although larger specimens have been found. They mostly swim in schools of hundreds of individuals, and they can often be seen leaping out of the water together and gliding for five or six meters before diving back in.

OMÜM: Another ghastly creation of Emperor Darkstrom, though this spell is reserved to few soldiers of the Remaran army who must give up all their titles and possessions in order to gain inhuman powers. After pledging their soul to the Emperor, these soldiers become shapeshifting creatures that can turn into any animal at will. Their powers are limited to transforming into one creature at a time, so they *cannot* become hybrids such as Aralays, Minotaurs or Centaurs. At the same time, they *can* turn into Fímegir. If they experience physical damage, they will retain those features even in their altered form.

ORC: Devoted supporters of Emperor Darkstrom, Orcs have established themselves as an elite minority in Remara. They are tall and bulky, with bodies built for battle. Their skin is green and scaly, their heads usually bald and they often display two fangs that protrude from their bottom lip. They are not known for their acumen, although they are good at following orders and will not stop at anything to achieve their goal. Orc culture is deeply engrained in war, and they have their own animistic religion which celebrates passage into adulthood by sending their children into battle.

RIUKU: In Erythya, the Riuku is seen both as a benevolent spirit and as a mischievous demon, who guards the nature of the rainforest against intruders. This creature is said to transform into either a loved one or a friend and drive the unsuspecting victim down a false path and leave them deep in the forest, lost and disoriented. Riukus are hungry for energy, and they will hunt down the strongest members of a party that dares enter their territory. These spirits are found everywhere in Valkadia, but they have been mostly reported in the Gartruth Forest.

ULKAR: This creature is the result of an eternal curse inflicted by the Elven ruler king Yohann. Once an ancient warrior, the Ulkar has been damned to live the rest of time in the form of a gigantic wolf which hides in the Iron Wood. It is said that the man was cursed after trying to steal the treasures of king Yohann and was caught red-handed. Now, anybody who accidentally ventures in the Iron Wood risks becoming the victim of this immense predator. From the accounts of survivors, we know that the lone wolf is larger than an adult bull. Its fur is black and bristly, and its mouth crowded with razor-sharp teeth. It is clear that the Ulkar has retained its human intelligence, but it has also learnt how to behave like a true predator, stealthily pursuing its victims and devouring them without remorse.

UNAHM: Native to the Gartruth Forest, this wildcat species can be distinguished from house cats in a number of ways. Their most striking feature is the long, bushy tail that resembles that of a fox, and a pair of sabre-long teeth that protrude from their top lip. Their fur is brown with a purplish/red hue, and a white streak on their back that begins from the tip of their nose and ends at the tip of their tail. Unahms have one special ability—to glow in the dark in order to attract preys such as mice and small birds. This magical wildcat is highly intelligent, and kittens are able to hunt in a matter of weeks after birth. Weighing between eight and eleven pounds, their legs are strong, and they can jump as far as ten feet in length.

VEHEER: These folks are a result of crossbreeding between Elves and Humans and retain capabilities of both peoples. Tall and slender, but with athletic muscular bodies, they are the most common group in Erythya and the closest relatives of the Elves. Their eyes are an amber-gold colour, which brightens in the sun, and their ears are pointed just like their Elven ancestors. A Veheer's hair can range from fair to dark, as well as their complexion. Veheers are highly intelligent and very skilled warriors; they are also more prone to magic than any other folk. Most Lightbringers and some of the strongest Sorcerers—since the extinction of the Elves—have been Veheers. After the death of the last Elven ruler, king Rennhall, the Veheer Amos Arganthal took power over Erythya, allowing more of his people to rise to influential positions. Veheers society has thus become prevalent in Erythya, spreading prosperity across the land and improving upon the Elven infrastructures. They are devoted followers of the Eredomyhm belief, and their religion is engrained in most of their everyday activities, allowing them to remain connected to nature and grounded to their morals.

LIST OF CHARACTERS

ALAMOR EKLUND – son of Sehr the Bold. A Veheer, and the last member left from the Order of the Lightbringers. Spent much of his later years at the Brotherhood of Thytelis. Brandishes an Elven sword called Isidir.

AMOS ARGANTHAL – Veheer, king of Erythya, successor of the Elven king Rennhall and predecessor of king Kavanagh.

ANYIR SKÖLD – daughter of Rongvald and Galeena Soward. Lived in Karisa with her husband Oblivan Sköld, but was apprehended by general Tortugal and brought to the Red Camp.

ARTHUR O'DONNEY – director of World Cloud.

BALDOR HARAL – Half-Giant, curator of Rennhall's Library. He is wise and knowledgeable and uses a magical staff to summon the power of the earth.

BEATRICE LOUGAR – legendary Lightbringer who fought at the Battle of Dorth. She brandished the magical sword Thomsor, which reappears in its scabbard if it is ever lost.

CHIEF UTTOL – ruler of the Breegans and chieftain of the city of Hegertan.

CLARA – biologist aboard the *Son of Odin*, romantically involved with Jason McAnnon.

COMMANDER SIGRID GUDMUND – Veheer, valiant leader of the Golden Camp's army.

DANNY PORTERMAN – photographer at World Cloud.

DOREAN AMBLE – Minotaur, king Kavanagh's chamberlain.

ECHO TRYGVE – Dryad, member of the Order of the Lightbringers together with Alamor Eklund and Elgan Lannvard.

ELGAN LANNVARD – Veheer, leader of the Order of the Lightbringers at the time of Darkstrom's rise to power. Married to Maralen.

EMILIYA KAVANAGH – Veheer, queen of Erythya.

EMPEROR DARKSTROM (INGVAR MADDOCK) – son of Jahrto Maddock. Also known as the Red Raven, he is the tyrant ruler of Remara. He dabbles in dark sorcery and can manipulate souls.

Blood-thirsty, power-hungry, all-round malevolent. Brandishes an Elven sword called Zarak. Seeks to conquer all of Valkadia and open the Elder Stones.

ERIK THE RED – Human, viking ruler from the Otherside (10-11th Century) and famous explorer. First Human to discover Valkadia.

ERIKA – publican of the 'Hammer and Anvil' in Karisa.

ESTRID ØLLNIR – Human, Head of Secrecy of Erythya.

ETREL – Omüm, a shapeshifter Remaran soldier from the Red Camp. Has two long scars on his face.

FITSUK – publican of the 'Hammer and Anvil' in Karisa.

FREYDAR IVOR – son of Pytar. Dryad, assistant at the docks of Malion.

GENERAL TORTUGAL – Orc, leader of the Red Camp. Brandishes a sword called Rhazien.

GLOD – Omüm, a shapeshifter Remaran soldier from the Red Camp. His left leg is missing.

GRANDO BERGFALK – son of Tod. Alchemist, first and foremost. Works as an informant for king Kavanagh in Remara. Lives in the invisible house that his son Yron made him in the middle of the Stonevale, known as the Leynahüs. Loves cigars.

GREGOR SVENN – son of Bron. Human, and chief of Karisa. He can control storms and lightning with his powerful sorcery.

HIGH GOTHI – Human, head of the Gothis, a sect of priests that preach the teachings of the Æsir (the Norse gods).

HILDA JONES – marine mammal biologist and leader of the *Son of Odin*'s expedition.

HOD – Elf, was forced to let the Humans into Valkadia.

ISAINE – Centauress, chief of the Akani tribe.

JAHRTO MADDOCK – Human, former ruler of Remara preceding Darkstrom. Killed and deposed by his son, Ingvar Maddock, later known as Darkstrom or the Red Raven.

JASON MCANNON – son of Robert and Denise McAnnon. Human, photographer from London in the Otherside. Worked at the World Cloud printing lab, but now his job has changed. Loves Clara dearly.

KIRO HUSTAD – son of Tov. Faun, Treasurer at Rennhall's Library. Skilled with the daggers and powerful wind sorcerer.

LADY LERA – Azur, Head Priestess of the Eredomyhms.

LIEUTENANT MODÙN – Human, spineless follower of general Tortugal.

LOK – Human, lethal Shadowcaster. Darkstrom manipulated his soul so Lok could use his Flare to conjure dark sorcery. Trained by the Emperor since the age of four, he is now the most feared warrior of Valkadia. Wields a sword by the name of Myrkyr, but is forced to replace it with Viggr. Hates Gothis, Breegans, Veheers, Lightbringers… will do anything for his master.

LORAS RENNHALL – Elf, the last Elven ruler of Valkadia, successor of king Yohann and predecessor of king Arganthal.

MARALEN – Elgan Lannvard's wife, and Alamor's dear friend.

MUNIN YOHAN – Elf, one of the ancient rulers of the Valkadia, predecessor of king Rennhall.

NOES KAVANAGH – Veheer, king of Erythya. The successor of king Arganthal. Wields an Elven sword called Dolear.

OBLIVAN SKÖLD – son of Vidar. Human, the best blacksmith in Karisa. Anyir's husband.

ÖKEN – Breegan, hermit who lives on top of Mount Dormund. Skilled inventor. Wielder of mechanical axes.

OLAG – Gnome, driver of a steam-powered carriage and quirky Cicerone.

RAY HUGHES – unconventional ichthyologist aboard the *Son of Odin*.

RHULANI TRYGVE – Dryad, Treasurer at Rennhall's Library. Brandishes a glaive and is a talented psychic.

ROGOR DREYMOS – Veheer, author of '*The Harmony of Creatures: Life in the Olde Forests and the New*'.

ROLLO WALDYR – Veheer, Chief of Justice of Erythya.

SILVYR – Alamor Eklund's faithful steed.

SYRIO FROY – Dryad, Master of Treasury of Erythya.

TAMALI RAJAN – zoologist aboard the *Son of Odin*.

THE NECROMANCER – mysterious woman who can communicate with the souls of the dead. Lives in a tent in Orachlion. Arcane tattoos mark her face.

THE ULKAR – formerly an Elven warrior, now a gigantic wolf that inhabits the Iron Wood.

THURIN KAVANAGH – Veheer, princess of Erythya. Looks like Dolores O'Riordan from the Cranberries.

USNAAR BEAROL – Breegan, member of the Order of the Lightbringers together with Alamor Eklund and Elgan Lannvard. Inventor of the Eluir-tracker.

VICKEN – Veheer, king Kavanagh's tiny messenger.

ACKNOWLEDGMENTS

Writing this book has been one of my most significant personal projects so far, and seeing it come to fruition fills me with joy. I would like to thank all my friends and family for supporting me throughout the whole process. Thank you to my parents for always encouraging me to complete this novel and pursue my creative endeavours as well as my academic career. In particular, a huge thank you to my devoted dad Joseph for always listening to my new ideas, no matter how absurd or confusing, and for reading every new draft of the Lightbringer—both in Italian and in English. I am also profoundly grateful to my dearest friend Jonathan Cuonzo for all the feedback he has offered throughout the years and the immense help editing the final version. The book has truly taken a mature form thanks to his dedication. Finally, my appreciation goes to the staff at Author House for making this publication possible.

ABOUT THE AUTHOR

Dael Sassoon was born in Milan, Italy, in 1995, and he has lived in the UK since 2014 to undertake his studies at The University of Manchester. During his spare time, Dael is a writer, artist, photographer, bass-slapper and world-traveller, exploring diverse environments, from the depths of the Amazon rainforest to the frozen terrains of Iceland. Initially, he came up with the idea for The Lightbringer when he was only fifteen years old. Since then, the story has evolved from various short versions into a fully-fledged novel, with his encouraging father Joseph by his side the whole way. Much of what Dael writes is inspired by nature and travel, due to his background in geography and conservation, but he's also drawn to the myths and legends of ancient cultures. Through his words, Dael evokes a sense of enchantment and escapism as he invites the reader to travel with him to mysterious lands full of unexpected challenges, inhabited by eccentric people and at the persistent threat of powerful enemies.